DRAGON QUEEN'S RECKONING

Descendants of Twilight: Book 3

BY

C. M. SUROWIEC JR.

Dragon Queen's Reckoning is a work of fiction. Names, characters, places, and incidents either are the product of the author's imagination or are used fictitiously. Any resemblance to actual persons, living or dead, events, or locales is entirely coincidental.

10 9 8 7 6 5 4 3 2 1

To request permissions, contact the owner at

Breeze@CMSurowiecJr.com

Hardcover: 979-8-9859622-8-4

eBook: ASIN: B0DPCXJ4KG

Paperback: 979-8-9859622-9-1

Dev / Copy Line Editor: Marthese Fenech

Cover Art Design: C.M. Surowiec Jr.

Cover Art Illustration: Brian Flores

Map Enhancement: Khayyam Akhtar

CMSurowiecJr.com

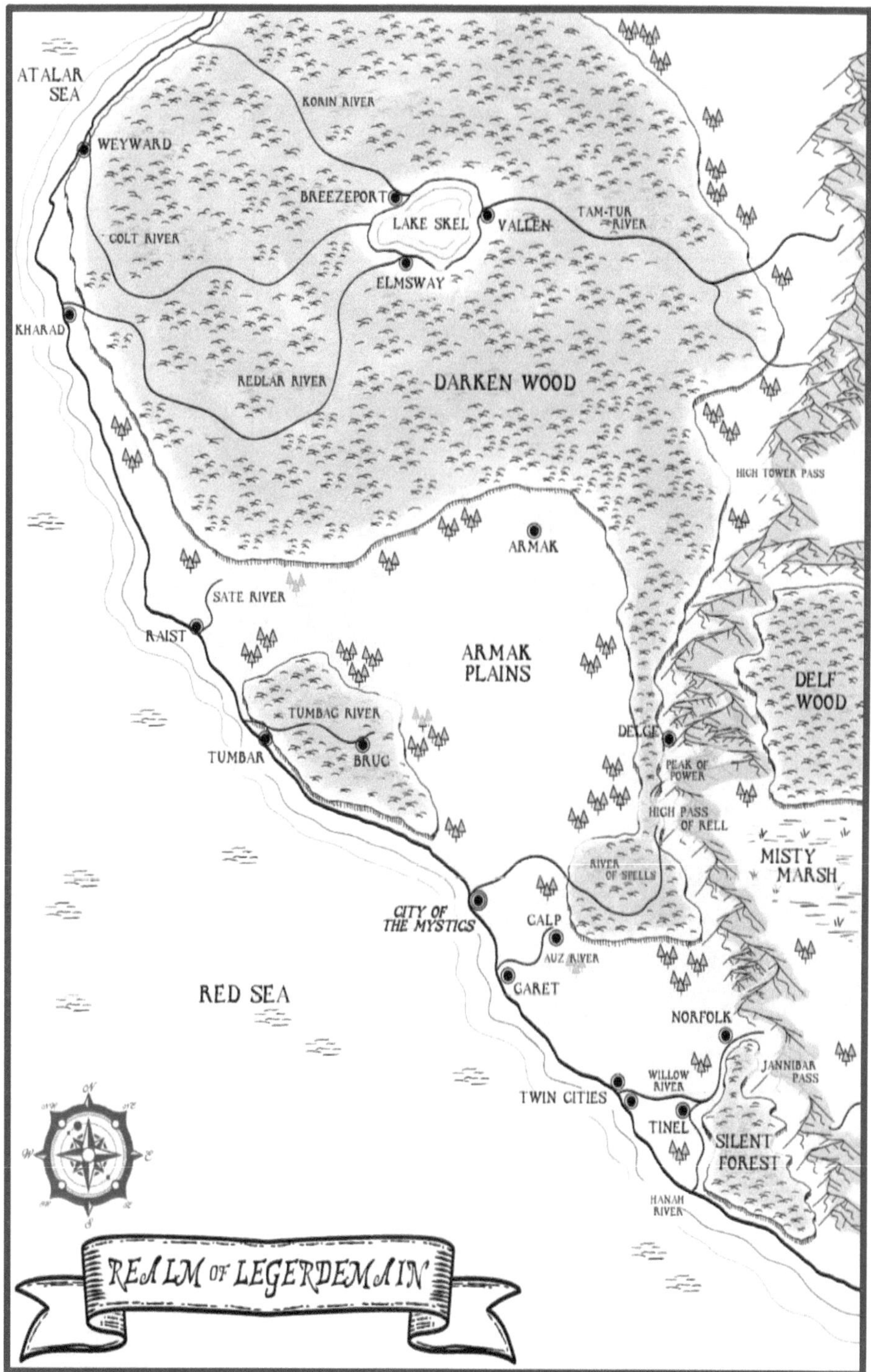
ATALAR SEA
WEYWARD
KORIN RIVER
BREEZEPORT
LAKE SKEL
VALLEN
TAM-TUR RIVER
COLT RIVER
ELMSWAY
KHARAD
REDLAR RIVER
DARKEN WOOD
HIGH TOWER PASS
ARMAK
SATE RIVER
RAIST
ARMAK PLAINS
DELF WOOD
TUMBAG RIVER
TUMBAR
BRUG
DELGE
PEAK OF POWER
HIGH PASS OF RELL
MISTY MARSH
RIVER OF SPELLS
CITY OF THE MYSTICS
CALP
AUZ RIVER
GARET
RED SEA
NORFOLK
WILLOW RIVER
JANNIBAR PASS
TWIN CITIES
TINEL
SILENT FOREST
HANAH RIVER
REALM OF LEGERDEMAIN

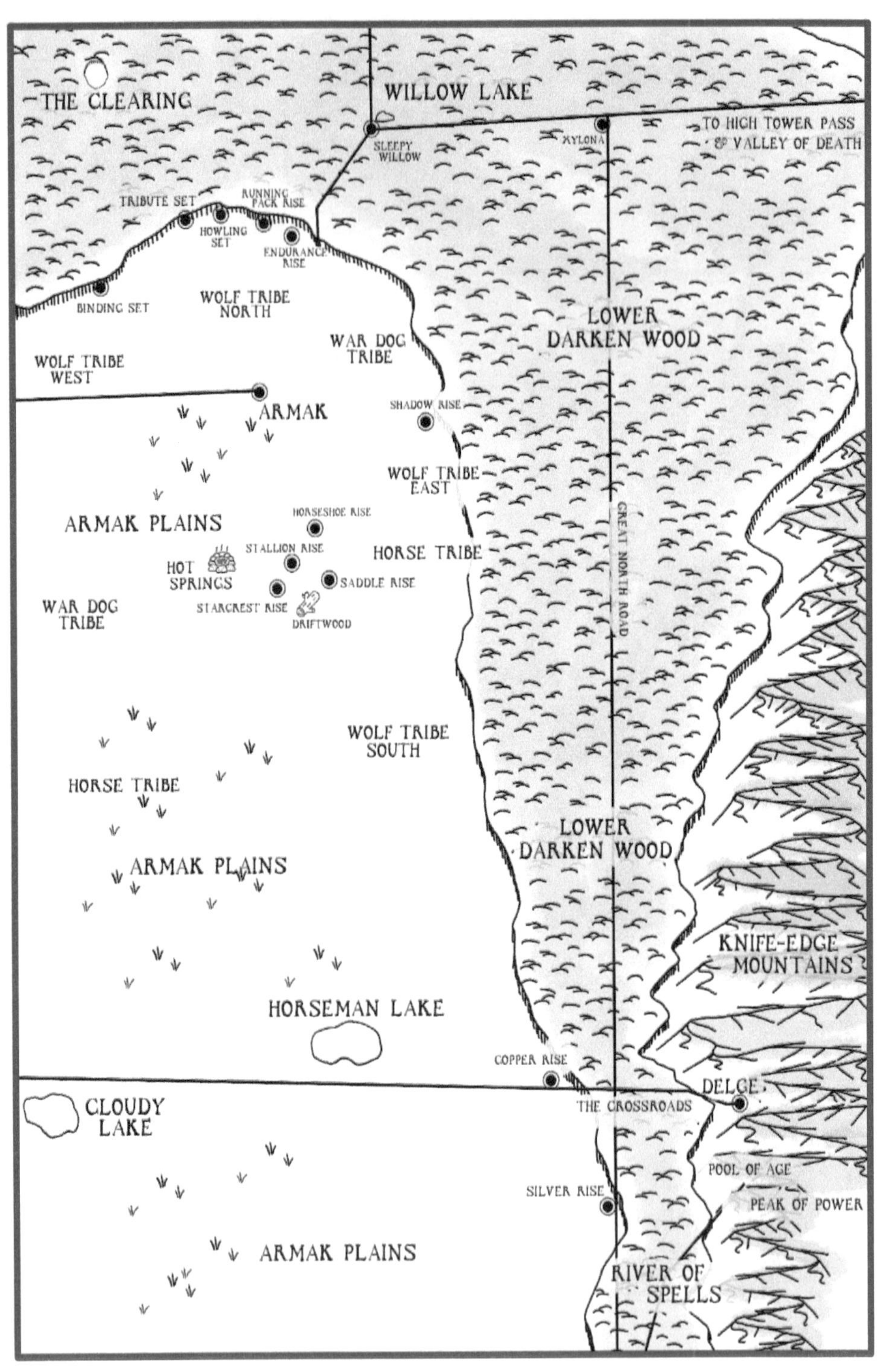
THE CLEARING
WILLOW LAKE
SLEEPY WILLOW
XYLONA
TO HIGH TOWER PASS & VALLEY OF DEATH
TRIBUTE SET
RUNNING PACK RISE
HOWLING SET
ENDURANCE RISE
BINDING SET
WOLF TRIBE NORTH
WAR DOG TRIBE
WOLF TRIBE WEST
LOWER DARKEN WOOD
ARMAK
SHADOW RISE
WOLF TRIBE EAST
HORSESHOE RISE
ARMAK PLAINS
STALLION RISE
HORSE TRIBE
HOT SPRINGS
SADDLE RISE
STARCREST RISE
DRIFTWOOD
WAR DOG TRIBE
GREAT NORTH ROAD
WOLF TRIBE SOUTH
HORSE TRIBE
LOWER DARKEN WOOD
ARMAK PLAINS
KNIFE-EDGE MOUNTAINS
HORSEMAN LAKE
COPPER RISE
DELGE
THE CROSSROADS
CLOUDY LAKE
POOL OF AGE
SILVER RISE
PEAK OF POWER
ARMAK PLAINS
RIVER OF SPELLS

For:

My Parents,

who taught me right from wrong and always encouraged me to reach for the stars.

Erogothian Calendar

1. First Twilight 1/24 - Terazhan's Twilight	2. Progression	3. Breeze
4. The Initiate 4/4 - Terazhan's Twilight	5. Harvest	6. Rhomerian 6/14 - Terazhan's Twilight
7. Anuberis	8. Oderian 8/24 - Terazhan's Twilight	9. The Holy One
10. Gathering	11. Sendarian 11/4 - Terazhan's Twilight	12. Final Harvest
13. Last Twilight 13/14 - Terazhan's Twilight		14. Festival

PANTHEON OF DEITIES

	Plane of Power	Color of Phylactery	Deity's Home Plane	Ethical / Moral Compass
7 Planes of Heaven	Dreams	Cobalt Blue	Melandri	Conforms to Order and Good
	Light	White	None	
	Mists	Amber	Terazhan	Law/Order and Good
	Nature	Hunter Green	Schaleah	Law/Order and Good
	Tides	Turquoise	Feldarius	Conforms to Order and Good
	Time	Cinnamon	Vallerielle	Conforms to Order and Good
	Wind	Canary Yellow	Dilantro	Law/Order and Good
9 Planes of Hell	Ashes	Deep Hickory	Ledaedra	Chaotic and Evil
	Darkness	Black	None	
	Delights	Tangerine	Jakarrak	Chaotic and Good
	Fear	Indigo	Marekai	Chaotic and Evil
	Ice	Ice Blue	Harendread	Chaotic and Evil
	Lava	Molten Lava	Hymnoch	Chaotic and Evil
	Shadows	Violet	Malekai	Chaotic and Evil
	Spirits	Crimson	Azreala	Chaotic and Good
	Storms	Dark Silver	Bardonril	Conforms to Order and Evil

DM  Breeze

Dragon Queen's Reckoning

Prologue

"It is a tricky thing to be thought of as a god, especially when one knows they are not. Longevity does not make one a god, nor does possessing a phylactery, even though it encapsulates one's soul.

A god is timeless, boundless, and immortal; however, I am not. So, I continue this ruse as a demi-god because I enjoy being worshipped by others. The devotion of another is quite invigorating, and nothing compares to the power one receives when worshipped by a throng… It is—intoxicating.

I will miss the rush, the tingling feeling that results when my name is said aloud. It is with much trepidation that I leave this life and wonder what lies ahead. With my final breath, I curse Ledaedra with one thousand deaths."

- Phindazar

1

A Surprise Encounter

Cymm

A bead of sweat hung from the tip of Cymm's nose, while dark, massive shapes materialized to either side of him. The mist hung thick on the night's air, and the wind hid from unseen horrors that hunted in the gloom. His pulse quickened. Tree trunks lurched through the fog, but his dread lingered, as if the forest itself were holding its breath. His friend, Brogan, had told him a story about the walking trees they had encountered in Lower Darken Wood.

The sharp *snap* of a branch reported from ahead.

Cymm froze in his tracks.

The mist swirled and darkened. A being emerged with a grin and a snarl. It would have appeared human if not for the thrashing tail, the cloven hooves, and its almost eight-foot-tall stature. However, its eyes were the most striking feature. They blazed a fiery-red and reminded him of Azreala's.

Cymm's forehead creased as he mulled the possibilities. "Feldarius?"

The creature fixed Cymm with a wry smile. "Is it that obvious?"

Cymm cleared his throat. "She has mentioned her brother to me many times."

"Her *twin* brother?" Feldarius folded his arms over his chest and smiled approvingly.

Cymm's eyebrows arched. "She has more than one?"

"A few," the deity answered nonchalantly. "Azreala needs your help."

"My help? What can I do that you couldn't do without me?"

Feldarius came closer, his pupils still vibrant and glowing. "Thanks to my *brother*, Bardonril, I am banished from the Material Plane for one hundred and eighty more years. Azreala remains a prisoner in *your* world, and you will help her."

Cymm did not appreciate his tone. He had no right to demand anything from him. Especially since he had helped Azreala defeat Bardonril and exact revenge or justice for Feldarius. As Cymm's anger rose, he paused, something did not feel right.

"You claim friendship, yet you hesitate. Is your loyalty so brittle, human?" Feldarius shuffled his feet, clearly irritated.

"How are you here? How am I here?" Smoldering in Cymm's mind's eye were the lanterns in Delge's streets, the last thing he could recall.

Feldarius glanced at the ring lying against Cymm's chest, Bria's necklace. "Are you going to help my sister or not?"

A pang of guilt shot through Cymm. Feldarius and Azreala had orchestrated the parade of souls from Stallion Rise for his benefit, including a final farewell from his mother and father. They had also imbued the ogre ring, his prized possession, with a final message from his sister Bria, and given it to him freely. "Of course, I will, but how did I get here? If you are not allowed in my world, where are we?"

Feldarius wrinkled his nose, then bared his teeth as he scanned the foggy sky. "Do you forget that I am the Spirit Master? I am only here in spirit, inside your mind." A feral growl escaped his lips as he glanced over his shoulder.

A shimmering golden ball hovered in the distance, winding its way through the scraggly trees. The mist dissipated with proximity and did not return.

Cymm's original fear upon entering the murky forest had disappeared, replaced now by a profound foreboding.

Feldarius's eyes widened. "I must go. Tell no one of this meeting. Head back to Delge immediately before they take her body."

"Wait!" Cymm's hand involuntarily reached out toward the demi-god, but his essence had already turned ethereal.

The absent wind returned with vengeance and scattered Feldarius and the remaining haze.

Cymm stood transfixed.

The amber ball of light morphed into a humanoid figure as it drew closer and seemed to be searching for something. It was…Lykinnia.

An intense pain grew in the pit of his stomach. *What is she doing?* He approached slowly. "Lykinnia?"

No response came. She continued to the next tree.

Cymm's pulse hammered as he followed her from one tree to the next, twelve all told.

She paused and knelt, then glanced over both shoulders. Near the base of the tree, among the roots, she dug furiously for several moments. In the hole she deposited an amber ball the size of her thumb, shifted its position twice before covering it up. Lykinnia rose and placed her hands on her hips, admiring her work.

Her smile faded with her body, leaving Cymm alone with his thoughts.

2

Dragon Siege

BrimStrakenstone

BrimStrakenstone surveyed his army from the head of the first phalanx. Ledaedra, the Dragon Queen, had given her chief advisor and first general specific orders, and he insisted on taking no chances. The big red dragon had assembled three full squads of warriors for this mission. He shook his head fiercely and his ears whipped against the side of his face. *Failure is not an option—not for the queen, not for dragonkind, and least of all for me. We need to secure our place in this new world.*

The previous attack on the City of Bruc had almost become a catastrophe. He had lost two captains, one of whom could have made general within a decade or two, and they had almost returned without the prince. The Prince of Bruc, called Leighton by the humans, was a Descendant of Twilight and the prime objective of that mission. Brim's army had enjoyed devastating the city and killing the humans, but they had almost killed their target. The dragons had whisked the prince away in an unconscious state to Fire Island. They had treated his wounds, and he had finally recovered before they magically bound him with the others in the Transference Chamber, near the Chamber of Acceleration.

BrimStrakenstone focused his attention on the imminent attack. He had rehearsed this siege a hundred times in his mind, tweaking each scenario until it ended in victory with a successful capture. No one would ever accuse him of being spontaneous or a risk-taker. From a wyrmling until now, Brim had never fought a battle unless guaranteed to win. He had become lieutenant and captain in the Queen's Army quickly, but he had bided his time for general. To become a general, he must defeat a current general, usually a battle to the death.

No other dragon alive could rival his size, not even DetonKonraber, ZaphMordakai's uncle. When Brim stepped into the general's circle a decade ago, he accomplished something unheard of among dragonkind in their four centuries on Erogoth. All seven generals had backed out of the circle and two had fled in terror. He had become a general and their leader without any bloodshed.

The dragon phalanxes continued to close on the city of Norfolk. Its walls glittered on the horizon, small and fragile.

The air itself trembled from the power of their wings. Each pulse brought them closer. The enormous red dragon breathed in deep and imagined the mixed scent of molten rock and human fear to come.

Brim ground his fangs. ZaphMordakai—one of the queen's biggest disappointments—had failed his mission, requiring this attack. She removed him from a short list of potential candidates for future generals and scheduled him for termination, an ending Brim would happily enforce sooner if any warriors were lost in this imminent conflict.

These humans were hard to reason with, especially when it came to their offspring. The Princess Jenaleya had already been secured and held prisoner in a secluded cave while they built the Transference Chamber, but ZaphMordakai had abandoned his post against the

Queen's orders. Allowing a human to slay the young lieutenant, BelCharius, and return the princess to her father.

Brim had developed a plan to avoid a long, drawn-out siege. After he captured the princess, she would be immediately remanded to Fire Island with the other three descendants: Prince Leighton from Bruc, Haskins the half-orc, an easy capture while living alone in the wilds, and Ronks the ogre-magi, who studied at the City of Mystics. The latter would have been a much more difficult task if the ogre priestesses of Hymnoch had not turned on him, cast a sleep spell, and delivered him up to Ledaedra's disciples.

The first part of Brim's plan required a show of force to set the stage for the second phase. The leader nodded to each side and the three phalanxes formed distinct groups. They flew low over the plains on their final approach, trying to hide their presence and number. All fifteen dragons tightened their individual formations, even the maverick captain ZaphMordakai fell in line behind him.

Trumpets cut the air and horns blared as the front city gate came into view.

BrimStrakenstone's eyelids became mere slits. "You will know the meaning of fear, humans."

3

Awaken

Azreala

Azreala's wrists throbbed from the tight manacles that sapped her energy. Her arms were held out to each side and backward. Her torso leaned forward, her head lolling to one side. The magical restraints wound around her neck and ankles too, suspending her above the stone floor and creating intense pressure points on her body. However, the pain did not keep her lucid; she wavered in and out of consciousness the past few days.

"What do you want from me?" Azreala shouted into the dark recesses.

The other three prisoners, bound similarly, did not move, their catatonic state undisturbed.

A foggy memory came back to Azreala. The tentacles of a two-headed ebony creature emerged from a dark recess and clobbered her. The thing had lain in wait as she searched the dungeons of Delge for Cymm and his friends. The demon's fingers had elongated into tentacles and bored into her head, stealing memories, and causing excruciating pain before she lost consciousness. She groaned. How long have I been here?

"Where am I?"

Still no answer.

She could feel her magical power returning, but her energy lagged. The demi-god blinked several times and fought the urge to sleep. All the spells in her repertoire required a gesture component. A spell flickered at the edge of her mind. She wiggled her fingers, and they responded sluggishly, but even if they were functioning properly, her pockets containing the bone dust and bat fur were out of reach. Azreala growled with clenched teeth. The manacles seared her flesh again as she fought against them, trying to reach the hidden secret pockets once more.

Her tail swished and wrapped around her body. "Hello, beautiful," she cooed with a gleam in her eyes.

"Wait!" A cloaked figure stepped out of the shadows on the far side of the room. "Before you do something you will regret with that tail—"

"How long have you been standing there?" Azreala demanded.

"The queen wishes to speak with you."

A hot flash of power surged within the cloven-hoofed goddess, and she railed against her bindings. "I have no queen!"

"Nevertheless. The Queen of Dragons awaits." The black cloaked creature waved its scaly hands, and she began to move toward the exit of the circular room.

Azreala traveled around the corner to the right and down the corridor. Slowly at first, then with increasing speed, she raced across the floor and into the portal at the end of the hall. The magical bindings released inside the gateway, and she zipped out of the connecting portal.

She hit the ground hard but deftly rolled and bounced to her feet. The sulfuric fumes and the taste of ash on her tongue indicated she had entered the Plane of Ashes. She scooped a handful of ash and sifted it through her fingers. A wave of nostalgia hit her, remembering when her father brought her here to meet the former master of this plane, Phindazar. She sensed a presence. A ball of crimson energy coalesced in the palm of her right hand.

A towering figure cackled in delight. "You would attack me on my own plane and in front of my altar?"

Azreala delayed her action and scanned her surroundings for an escape route. Underneath a bruised sky of orange and gray, ten-foot-tall stone posts erupted from the ground to either side of an immense stone altar like bookends, one with a prisoner chained to it. No other structures or defensible positions existed nearby. She glanced up at the looming figure and locked eyes with her adversary—Ledaedra.

"How dare you take me prisoner like some commoner."

The Dragon Queen cocked her head. "Compared to me, you are."

Azreala's jaw clenched, and a spark of crimson flickered in her eyes, but she remained silent. She had built up a certain tolerance to being treated as inferior by another deity.

"Why did you join my enemy? You have reason to hate them as much as I do. I assumed your support in this war." Ledaedra crossed her arms, waiting for a response.

"I didn't pick a side—"

"Liar! I have captured your co conspirator, and he had much to say." Ledaedra glanced toward the prisoner, drawing the young demi-god's attention.

Azreala's head moved slowly side to side. "No." The word escaped her lips hesitantly as she tried to ascertain the likelihood of this information being true. "Feldarius?"

The prisoner had long, unkept hair that framed his bowed head. Thick robes hid most of the body's physique.

The Dragon Queen waved her hand toward the prisoner with a flourish and stepped back.

Azreala approached with caution, never shifting her eyes from Ledaedra. She sidled up next to the captive, keeping the pole between her and the Dragon Queen. Her heart beat a frantic, uneven rhythm. *Not Feldarius. Please, not my brother.* She reached out, fingers trembling, and swiped the coarse hair on the side of the face behind the ear. A man, but too small to be her brother. She lifted his pale chin, turning it toward her.

She gasped. "How…how can this be? Cymm?"

4

Good Graces

ZaphMordakai

The easterly breeze coming off the Knife-Edge Mountains fluttered the tucked membranes of ZaphMordakai's lower ears. An enormous air stream created by BrimStrakenstone's immense body allowed Zaph to draft and glide into position. His heart raced with exhilaration from his inclusion in his first city raid.

A week ago, the queen had summoned him, and he had almost refused to answer. He contrived a simple plan, flee to his uncle's lair and submit himself to the *training* if the queen exhibited any form of irritation. Uncle DetonKonraber would never allow him to be taken without a battle.

His fear of the queen killing him may have overwhelmed his senses, but he did not detect any awareness on her part of his betrayal. He had even convinced her to allow him to take part in the raid on Norfolk. Zaph lacked the deceptiveness of a green dragon, but he congratulated himself on his own cunning and how he handled the exchange.

ZaphMordakai scanned ahead. The hindquarters of other dragons blocked most of his view, but the deep, sharp inhalation could only be BrimStrakenstone's. His roar and exhalation came fast enough to flutter the eardrums of those nearby. Impressive. Even Zaph could not handle the heat from the recoil and peeled off to the right.

The black dragon released his own breath weapon, pushing beyond his normal limit. Zaph had something to prove. They would regret not including him in past raids and would always include him in the future. The parapet atop the corner wall's turret shuttered, then cracked, before sliding diagonally down its ruined stone column base. It crashed to the ground in a pile of rubble and dust. He banked around to reform the phalanxes as instructed by the general.

BrimStrakenstone accepted the report from each squad leader.

The first wave of the attack had devastated their outer defenses. The red-hot barbican dripped molten lava upon the mangled front gates. Several large breaches in the front wall rendered it useless from a defensive standpoint, however; against dragons, it had never been useful in the first place.

Zaph listened intently from high above the city, but his heavy breathing drowned out the nearby conversations. He found himself glancing around. His cohorts wore the same malevolent grin upon their faces.

"Listen to me!" the big red demanded.

ZaphMordakai's head snapped back to the front. "I am."

"Now it is your turn…"

Wings arched, and Zaph prepared to dive.

"Wait! You don't know your assignment yet." Steam billowed from Brim's nostrils.

Zaph rolled his eyes. "Seems pretty obvious. Lightning—Death—Destruction—"

"No. You will land outside the gates, then enter and request a parley."

"A parley? Are you trying to get me killed?"

"You asked to join the raid. We cannot risk killing the princess. You better hope your negotiating skills are strong enough to save both your lives."

I should have known there was a catch to my coming. Zaph sighed and bowed his head. *You can do this.* After gathering himself for several seconds, the seeds of anger germinated in his core, and he shot Brim a menacing glare.

The enormous red dragon's grin evaporated as he drifted back a dozen yards. "Now, ZaphMordakai!"

Zaph's wings tucked slightly, and he rocketed forward, then plummeted like a rock before the army's general. Strong emotions continued to churn in his belly, but he would not allow his discomfort to give the other captains any satisfaction. He swooped away from the ground to slow his descent, then landed with a double-wing buffet.

His feet struck the shattered stone pavers, and he instantly began his transformation. Scales dissolved, bone twisted, and muscle tightened, then with a shudder flesh and sinew reshaped itself into his dark elf form. He cracked his neck to both sides and rolled out his right shoulder, all while walking toward the front wall. For a heartbeat, the oppressive heat caught him off guard. He avoided the dripping globs of lava at the entrance by weaving through a breach and the scattered wall fragments back to the main roadway.

Ahead lay an interior wall with another gate. The drow slowed his pace, then came to a halt before he entered bow range—or so he hoped. "I wish to speak with your king."

An arrow *thwacked* into the ground a few feet in front of him.

He stepped back. "We will continue the assault then, frightened human."

"I fear you not, Agent of Evil!" came a clear response from behind the wall. "I can't imagine anything we have to talk about."

Zaph's voice rang out like a clarion. "What about the lives of your citizens? If we resume the attack, we will not stop until everyone is dead."

A clang of metal, followed by several more, led to a groan as the gates opened wide enough to emit a score of horsemen.

Lavender lightning coursed out of Zaph's fingertips, and he produced three large columns of energy, evenly spaced before him. He had no intention of letting the cavalry ride him down.

All but three riders halted thirty yards away. Two wore full plate armor including a helm with the visor pulled down. The knights' gauntlets creaked as they tightened their grips on their lances. An ornate set of chainmail and a red cape adorned the third. His gray hair and beard fluttered in the wind as he approached, his horse sidestepping and flaring its nostrils.

"You have my attention. What is your offer?"

From the wall above, a dozen archers peered down, arrows notched but not yet drawn.

"In exchange for Princess Jena—"

"Absolutely not. No. What is your obsession with my daughter?" demanded one of the two knights in full plate armor.

The man dressed in regal attire gawked at the boisterous man, his red cape fluttering in the wind.

The knight did not abate. "Well, what is your intent with my daughter? Why do you want to kill her?"

ZaphMordakai recovered from his initial identity confusion. "So, you're the actual king then. Know this, if we wanted to kill the princess, she would be dead already. I protected her for months and treated her fairly as a prisoner in the cave. Now, the queen wishes to speak with her."

"She is not involved in matters of state. She knows nothing!"

"That is for the queen to decide. You have two hours. If anyone quits the city before she is delivered, they will be killed." Zaph forced a smirk before turning to leave, ignoring the cold bead of sweat that crept down his neck.

"Dragon!" the King of Norfolk called. "If my Jenaleya is harmed, you will have to deal with Cymm Reich!"

ZaphMordakai's jaw quivered, and he slowly turned back around. Many retorts rushed through his mind. *Cymm has already been dealt with*, and *Cymm has his own problems to deal with right now.* His nostrils flared. *However, if he believes Cymm can help, maybe he will give his daughter up more willingly?* He sighed. "He is a mighty warrior. You have two hours."

5

Departure

Lykinnia

Sunlight spilled over the valley near the Peak of Power, glinting off mithril armor, weapons, and dew-soaked grass. The air was sharp, tinged with pine, and the waterfalls, cascading down the mountain, roared gently in the background.

Lykinnia rushed back inside.

Terazhan paced before her abode, casting shadows on her door in the early morning light. "You will not let her out of your sight!"

Solar gave a half bow. "Of course, my Lord."

"Father! Leave him alone," Lykinnia cried from inside, frantically inventorying her packed spell components.

"It is time to leave, Unie," Solar called from outside. "We can always teleport back if you forgot something."

Lykinnia could imagine the smug look on his face right now. "No! My first trip will not be marred by any magical means of movement." Nothing could taint her good mood right now, even though she had told him this a dozen times.

"Very well, but if we do not leave soon, Cymm will have already left Delge by the time we arrive."

This final statement caught her attention. Lykinnia emerged from her house, a leather satchel slung over her back and a mithril mace in her hand. The weapon would have required two hands for most people, but not for the deceptively strong daughter of a demi-god. She wore a skirt similar in design to the one Solar favored, except constructed with plates of mithril. The shingled pattern hung to the top of her knees. She wore fashionable pauldrons interwoven with an equally beautiful bodice. Underneath lay hidden her true armor, a mithril corset.

Terazhan's feet followed his eyes when he caught sight of her. "Keep this mace with you at all times. It is imbued with—"

"I know." Lykinnia rolled her eyes.

Her father scowled. "And it will—"

"I know. Father, hug me and wish me safe travels." She lifted her arms toward him.

They embraced for several seconds with her head tucked into the nook of his sternum.

Lykinnia broke away first. "Besides, what could possibly go wrong with three chaperones?"

"Three?" Terazhan glanced at Solar who shrugged.

A *pop* resounded through the area, and Uncle Jakarrak appeared through a portal next to her father. "I am far too busy to be galivanting through the countryside."

The ground rumbled in consecutive bursts. Kamac and Camak strutted past the winged man, intentionally flicking their tails in his face.

"Yeah, three!" came the baritone growl of Kamac.

Camak added his own roar. "Do you think we would let her travel alone?"

Solar's wings bristled. "Alone?" After a brief pause, he added, "I am glad you are joining us. When we tire of walking, we will have beasts of burden to ride."

The sphinx brothers trembled with rage and bounced off each other trying to confront the winged man.

Solar effortlessly launched himself into the air.

"How dare you!" Kamac leaped and missed.

"If this continues, I will leave the three of you in the middle of the night." Lykinnia winked at her father.

Uncle Jakarrak lifted his arms out wide.

Lykinnia rushed forward and embraced him.

"Enjoy your freedom, but be careful," said her uncle.

Lykinnia stepped back with a twirl. "I will. Yesterday I was very busy, but when I return in a couple of weeks, we will speak more about the spell book and the ring."

Uncle Jakarrak's face went ashen, and he glanced at his brother—her father—then gave a barely perceptible nod.

The young girl's eyes narrowed. *What was that about?* She made a note to ask later.

"Are you sure you want to go?" Terazhan whispered.

Lykinnia rolled her eyes and replied telepathically, *"I am sure you will be watching me, and we can speak any time you would like to. I have asked the Tavii to keep watch for trespassers."*

She took several long and prancing strides, heading for the path down. The nervous lump in her throat caught as she tried to swallow, but it did nothing to taper her excitement.

"Solar, you are failing your mission already," said Terazhan.

Lykinnia's three chaperones quickly fell in line as she had assumed they would.

6

Victory

ZaphMordakai

ZaphMordakai pulled Princess Jenaleya along with a thin silk rope tied around her wrists. She did not resist, so his tugs were gentle. Her father, the king, had been waiting for him at the two-hour mark as instructed.

The princess cleared her throat. "I knew you were a dragon."

The dark elf scoffed.

"No. I really did. The ground trembled right before you entered the cave on several occasions."

"Enough. You need to put your blindfold down. The aura of fear that emanates from us will be lessened if you can't see."

"The green dragon didn't scare—"

"BelCharius didn't scare anyone. Blindfold—down—now." ZaphMordakai kept the rope taut to guide her.

Jenaleya's boot caught on a rock. She lurched forward but caught herself. "How did you know our wizards had traveled to the City of Mystics for the Celebration of the Initiates?"

"It was—well—it was quite obvious," replied the drow.

The princess sighed. "You didn't know. We were defeated by dumb luck."

Zaph hissed. "No more talking. They approach." He continued to walk until the ground trembled around him.

"Why is she blindfolded?" BrimStrakenstone roared.

The dark elf shook his head in disapproval. "Even you would suffer the queen's wrath if we returned the princess as a babbling idiot."

The other dragons snickered.

Steam billowed from the red dragon's nostrils.

Zaph had pushed him too far.

Brim drew closer to the princess. "Why did your father turn you over without a fight?"

"His first duty is to his people. Even if I die, he'll have saved thousands of lives," she answered with her shoulders thrown back.

BrimStrakenstone chortled with gleaming eyes. "What gave him that idea?" His neck craned back over his shoulder. "Prepare to attack!"

"No! You can't. It will make my father look foolish and weak!" Princess Jenaleya exclaimed.

"Silence!" Brim stomped his foot in her direction, then turned to leave.

Zaph cleared his throat. "I would attack from the mountains to the east to avoid as many of the arriving wizards as possible. Most should be gathering in or around the tower in the south-west corner."

The festive mood amongst the other dragons changed immediately.

BrimStrakenstone's head came back around with his fangs bared. "What…wizards?"

Zaph dropped the rope and took several steps away from the princess. He drew a deep breath to calm himself. "The ones arriving from the other cities for the Celebration of the Initiates. I'm quite familiar with the surrounding area. I'll transform back and show you the best approach to use. I can even lead the assault if you wish. We'll hit fast and fly before—"

Brim lunged.

Zaph recoiled with a short breath before an avalanche of red scales pinned him to the ground. He twisted and surged, then finally poked his head out above the webbing between two talons.

Brim pushed his snout in close—each word a furnace blast. "If there are so many wizards in the city, why are you alive and the princess here?"

The dark elf transformed into a black dragon instantly, shrugging the leader's arm off his back with a groan. "Her father believes Cymm Reich will protect his daughter and rescue her if needed."

The two combatants locked gazes for several seconds, then both began to laugh. There were not many things they agreed upon, but both believed dragons were superior to all the humanoid races on this planet.

"General!" A black dragon lumbered up close to him and whispered, "He approaches."

Both stared at Zaph accusatorily then stared into the sky away from the city.

The bright, cloudless sky washed out Phoenix, the dull red moon. However, following their gaze, Zaph discovered a black object amongst the red backdrop and growing as it approached.

Brim addressed his warriors. "Our mission is accomplished. Return to Fire Island." His neck snapped around toward Zaph. Under his breath he muttered, "I should let him take you."

ZaphMordakai's eyelids constricted to mere slits, then shot open wide. The massive black stain in the sky could be only one thing. "How did he find us?"

BrimStrakenstone chanted in a low monotonous tone, and he ceased when the ebony form of Ledaedra appeared.

The Dragon Queen dark silhouette absorbed light and returned none. "Report!"

Brim cleared his throat. "We have the princess and suffered no losses. However, DetonKonraber is approaching, and we need an extraction for the prisoner."

Zaph spun in a circle. Panic seized his chest. *Where is she?*

Ledaedra waved her arms and with an audible *pop*, a portal big enough for a human appeared ten dragon lengths away.

With a panicked surge of energy, Zaph launched himself into the air. His surveillance lasted only a few moments before he dropped back to the ground, transforming as he fell. He ran in drow form to the crumpled figure mostly hidden by scrub grass and brush.

The princess lay unconscious or dead, probably swept away by a tail whip during his scuffle with Brim. A large cut on her forehead and the tears in her clothing were very concerning. Zaph did not hesitate. He scooped her up and threw her over his shoulder.

He had expected to see the cowardly Brim in full flight toward the mountains as he sprinted for the portal. Quite the contrary, the red dragon general charged his uncle using one of his innate abilities. Brim had excelled from an early age at replicating himself. A prodigy, his father had claimed, when he produced his second replication at a very young age. Zaph found it quite annoying back then when tormented by Brim. Now he could produce seven, all of which raced ahead to engage his uncle, DetonKonraber the Devastation.

ZaphMordakai stood before the portal, transfixed by the imminent battle.

Before the initial collision, Deton tucked his wings, then blasted through two colossal red dragons, causing them to plummet, unmoving, to the ground. Five others attacked his flanks, while a solitary figure raced for the mountains.

If his uncle cared, he would have seen the real dragon fleeing like a coward.

So engrossed in the battle, Zaph had not realized Ledaedra's specter remained present and watching. He took one last glance at his uncle, who now had his eyes locked on him, and stepped through the portal.

Two cloaked figures rushed over to lower the unconscious princess to the stone floor.

One addressed him, "We will tend her wounds. The queen wishes to speak with you."

"With me?" Zaph asked.

"Yes. Through the portal around the corner," replied the robed acolyte.

The dark elf scanned his surroundings, in no rush to comply. He stood in the middle of a prison or torture chamber with four captives and four vacant holding devices.

An auburn-haired, giant woman glared at him, her crimson eyes flaring. "What in the nine hells are you looking at?"

Lavender lightning crackled in the palm of ZaphMordakai's left hand. With a sneer, he released a miniature bolt at the metallic structure holding her.

The woman convulsed for several seconds, unable to resist the effects of the energy surge. When her eyes opened, she hissed, "I will kill you, and your soul will be mine!"

With a chuckle, Zaph walked in the indicated direction and stepped through the next portal to the Plane of Ashes.

Ledaedra immediately loomed before him. "ZaphMordakai, your uncle continues to interfere with my plans and resist my efforts to recruit him."

Zaph shuffled his feet. "He has always been stubborn. Would you prefer me in my dragon form?"

"No. Your current form better suits the reunion," she replied.

"Reunion?"

Ledaedra stepped to the side and turned with a flourish, indicating a prisoner chained to a post next to her altar. It was a female, a drow female, her black skin glistening with sweat.

The captive glanced up at him, almost too weak to lift her head.

Zaph's breath caught in his throat. His gaze shifted to Ledaedra, seeking answers, but none were forthcoming.

The Queen of Dragons stared back, unmoving, a predatory grin upon her face.

"How?" His voice raw and pleading.

Still, no response came.

Zaph stepped forward, trembling arms poised to embrace her. "Mother?"

7

Spelunking

Cymm

Cymm Reich and Grendella Ironcore approached the City of Delge cautiously, not knowing what to expect. His horse and her pony nickered and side-trotted, clearly sensing their uneasiness.

The cramping in Cymm's neck muscles reminded him of how drastically wrong this could go. He had insisted on leaving the Peak of Power immediately after receiving the message from Feldarius, a day after Lykinnia's lifeday. She had stood there with her hands on her hips, furious with his decision, but had eventually promised to meet him in Delge.

Light traffic in and out of the city caused him to pull the brim of his hood down lower to cover more of his face.

Several guards blocked their path, bringing them to a halt.

One grumbled, "State your business."

Grendella, also wrapped in a cloak, replied, "Do you make a habit of asking dwarves why they enter their own city?"

Cymm blanched as the guard's gaze passed over him.

"Not him—me—I'm the dwarf, you rock head!" Grendella fumed.

Old Man Semper couldn't have said it better. Cymm almost smiled to himself.

"You!" A captain exited the door from the right most gate tower, pointing at Cymm. "Remove your hood." He continued to close the distance.

Cymm and Grendella exchanged a panicked glance.

She shook her head and allowed her hand to drift toward the haft of the warhammer strapped to her back.

"No," Cymm whispered to Grendella, before addressing the captain, "I will leave." He turned his horse and prepared to mount.

The captain shouted, "Everyone back to your duties!"

Cymm finished securing DragonSin, his sword, to the side of his saddle, and came around the front of his horse.

The captain stood there blocking his path. "I know who you are, Cymm Reich. I recognize your horse."

Cymm sputtered, then croaked, "Who?"

With a hammer in hand, the guard replied, "Half of the city wants to kill you, while the others would parade you through the streets with a hero's welcome and a feast befitting a king. Be glad I am one of the latter and not interested in hunting you down like a cave rat. Insanity, foolishness, or desperation brought you back to Delge. Which is it?"

Cymm waved off Grendella as she started his way. "Desperate. I left something in the dungeons of—"

"You're mad!" The captain glanced over his shoulder apprehensively, then resumed in hushed tones, "I will not help you break into the dungeons of Delge."

"Help me? But…but—you're—Who are you?" Cymm sputtered.

He puffed his chest. "Captain Stormaxe." With glittering eyes, he stared at Cymm.

"What?" asked the First Paladin of Terazhan.

"I saw you fight in the colosseum. You both are survivors of the greatest arena battle ever, which makes you heroes," replied the captain.

Cymm pushed through the awkwardness. "Can you help me get into the city?"

Captain Stormaxe pointed extravagantly away from the city. "Go!" In a confidential tone, he added, "Go to the stables and come back in an hour after the change of the guard."

8

Freedom

Lykinnia

Lykinnia could not contain her giddiness. She had seen many of these sights before, but the green leaves on the trees seemed more vibrant, the singing of the songbirds made her dance, and the smell of the forest, intoxicating. She charmed a dozen birds, and they currently circled her and each other in intricate patterns, providing enchanting entertainment.

They were well into their second day of travel when Solar groaned when Lykinnia alternated from walking to jogging again.

"What?" asked Lykinnia.

"I have never walked this far in my life!" Solar's wings erupted from his back, and he flexed them.

Lykinnia pointed at him with pursed lips. "No! You promised."

"This is not magic. These are *real* wings." Solar's face expressed false astonishment as he lifted off the ground.

She folded her arms and stomped her foot. "I should have expected this from someone who lost the two-day challenge when I turned five hundred."

"I was winning until you cheated! I had six more loops than you on day one," he responded.

"I did not cheat. *You* decided to go to sleep, and I kept running. If I recall correctly, I beat *you* by three loops." Lykinnia smirked, remembering the expression on Solar's face the following morning when he arrived at the starting line, lagging by thirty-three laps. The first day he performed lackadaisically and even called her names like "stumpy legs", "sprinting turtle", and "rolling rock" as he did just enough to stay ahead.

The names he called her on the second day were much worse, especially in the last few hours as he sprinted around the edge of the Peak of Power trying to catch her. Eventually, he could not speak, as the labor took its toll, and the sweat glistened on his body, dripping off his elbows, earlobes, and nose. To antagonize him, she had danced her final lap around the course.

A grand idea sprang to mind. "Hey, I will race you to those giant boulders ahead."

"You will lose," Solar proclaimed, dropping back to the ground.

"No wings!" Lykinnia leaned in, prepared to launch forward.

Kamac landed on the ground before them. "Quiet! Get off the road!"

Camak joined his brother. "Quickly!"

The first two days of Lykinnia's golden adventure teemed with promise, but with the thundering of footsteps, the spell shattered. She pressed up tight against a mossy trunk, gripping her mace tight enough to turn her knuckles white.

Ogres and orcs surged past them, in the same direction they were heading. The forest trembled from the weight of the horde, and a pungent musk drifted through the immediate area.

An enormous, violet-skinned horror led the column of creatures. Hair as black as night framed its face, while tufts of shorter hair covered its body in patches. Short horns topped its head, and pointy spikes protruded from its elbows. It ran hunched over, arms extending to the ground like an ape, with massive biceps bulging. Two more violet monstrosities brought up the rear.

"This is not good," Solar muttered, wings half-spread. "Those colorful beings were calendri, agents of Malekai…demons."

"I thought they were banished from this world," said Lykinnia.

"They are…." Solar scratched the side of his head. "…or were. Lykinnia—"

"No…we are going to Delge," she demanded.

Solar pointed at the disappearing enemy force. "*They* are going to Delge. *We* are going home, or Lord Terazhan will be furious."

Tears ran unbidden down the young woman's face. "Fine. We can teleport to the city."

Solar nodded once to Kamac, and the brothers were gone.

Lykinnia's neck craned side to side, scanning for the sphinxes. "Since when do they listen to you?"

Solar disregarded her question. "Now that Bardonril is banished from this plane, Malekai moves swiftly to claim Delge for himself. We cannot proceed."

"We need to warn the dwarves."

"You mean, we need to warn Cymm," countered Solar.

Her eyes pooled with tears again. "Is that a bad thing?"

"No Unie, it is a good thing, and we will if—"

Kamac crashed through the tree boughs, landing with a groan. "They have changed direction and are heading back."

Solar tapped his pursed lips with an index finger. "Really?"

"They slowed, then came to a stop. The lead calendri sniffed the air as if tracking something."

Kamac and Solar stared at Lykinnia.

Concern flooded the priestess's face. "Where is Camak?"

Solar wound his arm in a circle with an apprehensive glance at her. "You need to leave."

"Now, Lykinnia! I will find Camak," growled Kamac. He wheeled around and took a defensive position between her and a thrashing in the underbrush, amplifying as it approached.

Lykinnia hesitated before the portal, gazing into the bushes. She gasped and rushed forward. "Camak?"

The missing sphinx stumbled into the mini-clearing and collapsed. He resembled a porcupine with numerous arrow shafts for quills. "They…are coming…"

Lykinnia fell to the ground by his head and stroked his mane. "We know. Kamac told us."

Camak fidgeted and groaned. "No. There is a second group… from the south…led by an indigo creature…black horns, barbed tail."

"A devikin? Terazhan help us. Come on!" Solar waved them hurriedly toward the portal.

Camak attempted to rise but faltered.

Kamac rushed forward to support him.

Lykinnia reacted quicker. "Tybor maekesha velit vasha." With the circle of one hand and a lift with the other, Camak never hit the ground.

The injured sphinx hovered at waist level, then floated toward the portal.

Blue lightning crackled through Solar's wings, drawing everyone's attention. A gigantic bolt released with a thunderclap and raced toward the lead calendri to their right. It hit with tremendous force and ripped the demon in half while scattering a score of ogres and orcs.

Kamac roared and advanced to Solar's side.

The rest of the horde continued to charge.

Lykinnia's concentration never wavered as she moved Camak to safety. Her next spell would have to wait until after the completion of this one.

From the south, the trees split with a *crack*, and a new horror—indigo and horned—strode into the open.

Camak's depiction of the devikin had failed to register an image in her mind. He had also left out a key descriptor; its body had the smokey composition of a shadow dragon.

Solar backed toward the portal. "That is definitely a devikin, a devil *immune* to lightning."

"Demons and devils working together? They slaughtered each other in the Age of Fire," said Kamac.

"The Planes of Shadows and Fear are both against us. It would appear Malekai and Marekai are setting aside their differences to join with Ledaedra," replied Solar.

Lykinnia barely heard them as she sent Camak through the portal and continued to gape at the devil. She had seen this creature when gazing into the future with her father. The twisted skeins of fate that had made her heart clench.

This is the creature that will kill Cymm Reich.

9

Runs Deep

Cymm

Brogan entered the silversmith shop to find Cymm and Grendella resting comfortably in the customer chairs. The sign on the door still read "Stoneheart Silver" in honor of his late friend Karaz.

The big man closed the door slowly, then turned. "What in the nine hells are you doing here?"

"Hello to you too," Cymm replied. "Ibor let us in. I see he has taken over the business for his cousin."

"Why are you here, Cymm, in Delge?" Brogan demanded.

The young paladin shrugged his shoulders. "I need to retrieve something from the dungeons."

"Have you lost your mind? I have come close to dying only twice in my entire life, and you were involved on both occasions."

"If you had listened to me, Grendella and I wouldn't have had to save you in the arena. As far as the gnoll cages, you were already captured when I saved your life." Cymm pondered his next comment, then blurted, "And I forced Azreala to bring you with us as we escaped the dungeons. So, actually you almost died three times."

Brogan shook his head. "That doesn't help your case. What are you doing here?"

Cymm rose and opened his cloak, revealing a large, black-metal mace strapped to his side.

"Dego's mace," said Brogan.

Cymm's face quirked. "No, this is Azreala's mace. She is trapped somewhere in the dungeons and needs our help."

"And why would I help her? She wanted to let me die. You said so yourself." A tremor rippled through Brogan's immense chest.

The paladin patted the big man on the back. "Because you are better than her. Brogan, we help those in need."

"Not everyone is like you, Cymm. I don't fight every crusade and search for injustice in every corner." Brogan flopped down in one of the chairs, rubbing his temples.

Grendella rose. "We didn't come to recruit you. Nor do we need you. Ibor takes us in tomorrow morning." She headed for rooms deeper, beyond the shop.

Brogan's face displayed his hurt. He glanced quickly at Cymm, then stormed out the front door.

"Brogan…wait." Cymm watched the door swing shut. Compiled guilt—from the arena, the battle with Bardonril, and everyone who paid the price for being his friend—momentarily overwhelmed him. He turned and scowled at Grendella, who had paused at the interior doorway.

"Why?" Cymm asked with his palms raised.

"He needed a reason not to go. How many of his friends died in the last grand adventure? Let him enjoy his newfound peace and leave me alone."

Cymm returned to the storefront and sat there alone for a while ruminating on the day's events. Draining his stout, he settled back into the soft chair. The day's fatigue pressed him deeper into the pillow, and he sank slowly at first, then rapidly. The world around him narrowed to the thrum of his own heartbeat.

A sudden chill raced through Cymm's body. Bubbles escaped his mouth, tickling his cheek. In a panic, he clamped his hand over his lips in the dark, wet environment. The slimy skin of a creature brushed against the back of his leg. He lurched forward. His lungs were constricting. In every direction he scanned and found complete darkness. With a closed mouth he screamed; fear had taken hold.

"How do you think my sister feels?" came a voice from behind him.

Cymm froze, processing.

"Answer me!"

The water evaporated instantly.

"Feldarius? I came as quickly as I could," replied Cymm.

A turquoise starburst blinded him, then reshaped itself into a shadowy figure. "Not quick enough. They took her this morning."

At least your sister is alive, Cymm thought but held his tongue. "Instead of berating me, shouldn't you be looking for her?"

"There are others to blame for your sister's death, not me. You need to focus your energy on saving Azreala, not the ghosts of the past."

Cymm shook his head, a heavy burden settling on his shoulders. "I don't understand. Why me? You must have hundreds of devout followers to do this task."

Feldarius hissed unintelligibly. "Thousands, but none want me to join their army, or would you prefer I join Ledaedra's side?"

Cymm shifted uncomfortably. "Not my army…Terazhan's army."

"One and the same. Are you going to help me or not?"

"And in return, you will help eradicate the dragons?" asked Cymm. He had not relinquished his desire to rid the world of the menace that had murdered his entire family.

"I will help defeat Ledaedra, and in the process kill many dragons. I believe this to be *Terazhan's* actual crusade." Feldarius's face became more life-like, and with a cocked head he raised his eyebrows.

"Of course. That's what I meant," replied Cymm, his face blazed with heat.

"Of course. Then it is settled."

Cymm's head bobbed in affirmation. "How do we find her?"

"My sister is on Fire Island in the dragon stronghold. The question is how you get in and out quickly, and how can I help even though I can't be there?" Feldarius became substantial as he paced back and forth.

"We could—"

Feldarius tsked. "I'm not sure how this worked with my sister, but *I'm* the brains and *you're* the brawn." He considered his statement and mumbled to himself, "She probably thinks she's the brawn. She's definitely not the brains." He cackled wildly in a short burst.

Cymm's eyes flitted side to side. *Is he talking to me?*

"My home, the Plane of Tides," Feldarius began, fixing his eyes on Cymm, "is connected to every other plane of existence, just like the Material Plane. You will come here, then I will create a portal for you to Fire Island. Once you locate and free Azreala, you will return here."

"That is a terrible plan. I can't go stumbling around searching room to room hoping to find her." Cymm's body shook violently, and he almost fell.

"Someone is trying to wake you. I must prepare. Be ready tomorrow night." Feldarius faded away.

Cymm's index finger remained in the air, his mouth agape, when he began to fade as well.

10

Arrangement

ZaphMordakai

ZaphMordakai continued to fawn over his mother, combing her matted hair with his fingers. "You seem so weak. Are you hungry or thirsty?"

She did not reply.

"Why are you a drow? You hate this form."

His mind drifted back to one of his earliest childhood memories, before they had come to this world. While resting in their home a friend of his father's had warned his family The Chamber would arrive shortly. The cult of dragon-hunting assassins had finally located their lair.

He recalled his father, Sire, rushing back into their home in his dark elf form. "We are already surrounded. If we fly out of here, our son will die. You must transform!"

Tears streamed down his mother's face. "Zaphling is too small to take the drow form."

"He can still fit through the tunnel, but we must leave now!"

His mother reluctantly took on the dreaded shape of a dark elf.

Zaph had never understood why she so hated it. Father had told him not to ask.

They slipped into the tunnel, his mother already falling behind.

"ZaphMorlak, where are we going?" his mother asked.

"Erogoth. The Dragon Queen has promised us safety." Sire beckoned them forward.

"How do you know we can trust this Queen of Dragons? Maybe she is part of The Chamber, and this is a trap."

Father hissed for silence.

Mother persisted in a whisper, as she prodded Zaph along. "Maybe all the previous families are dead. We've not heard from any of them."

"What choice do we have?" he whispered back.

The light at the end of the tunnel became blinding as it grew quickly up ahead. It suddenly wavered as a massive trellbac lumbered into the mouth of the tunnel, squatting on all six legs.

Before its eyes could adjust and its mouth could open, twin lightning bolts sailed off his parents' hands. The creature danced and jiggled, jerked and flailed, but finally its head lolled to the side, and it crashed to the ground.

ZaphMordakai whimpered. His first recollected time of feeling afraid stuck with him after all these years.

"Zaphling, do you wish to get us all killed?" It was his father's harshness, but his mother's voice.

He shook his head, too frightened to speak.

"Then utter not another sound and stay close. Sound will carry much farther outside this tunnel." Mother stepped shoulder to shoulder with her husband. "Ready?"

Father swallowed hard and stepped out into the late afternoon sun.

ZaphMordakai moved into the middle position after a rough push from his father, then crawled over the segmented body of their dead enemy. Suddenly they were off and running. His wyrmling footfalls and breathing were heavy on his own ears, but he could still hear the caterwaul calls of nearby trellbac. He quickly scanned up and down the mountainside, but none were in sight.

The foot of the mountain came quickly, and his father directed them toward a depression in the rock.

The sidewalls raced up and over Zaph's head, creating a deep ravine.

Sire called a halt.

Between gasps for air, Mother asked, "Do you know how to get there?"

"The crossover gate is in the Sand Basin—"

She groaned.

"It's not that far—"

Pebbles and sand fell all around them.

A quick motion from Sire sent them all scurrying for the shadows against the wall.

Another curtain of dirt and dust rained down upon them.

Zaph scanned the faces of his parents and fear assaulted him yet again.

Two caterwauls proceeded a grunt, and moments later the dense body of a trellbac pounded the ground before them.

Lightning crackled between the fingers of his parents' hands like a spiderweb, but the trellbac reacted quicker.

Concentric circles of visible sound waves pummeled his father, driving him into the craggy rock wall. The loose skin of his face pulled tight, the excess gathering by his ears. A bellow of agony echoed through the ravine.

ZaphMordakai attempted to hide behind Mother's altered, diminutive body, as she zipped off two lightning bolts.

An enormous terror fell from the sky, and she stumbled back into him. The ebony monstrosity crashed into the trellbac and efficiently separated its head from its body with one swipe of its razor-sharp claws. Its gaze fell upon Zaph and his mother.

Mother sighed. "DetonKonraber, I thought you were…"

"Uncle Deton?" Zaph gaped.

His uncle transformed instantly into a drow and hoisted Father onto his shoulder. When he turned around his face contorted in rage directed at Mother. "You should have left the whelp and fled!"

"Never!" his mother retorted.

"If my brother dies, you'll wish you had." He fixed a baleful glare on Zaph. "If you can't keep up, we *will* leave you." Uncle Deton took off running down the ravine at a fast clip, even carrying his father.

Half an hour later they broke out of the widening canyon into a forest of mushrooms. Most were taller than a dragon, but the ancient ones were immense and had soft glowing indigo fins under their caps, illuminating the forest floor below.

Uncle Deton called a halt and set Father down, resting him against a mushroom stalk. "Brother." He shook him vigorously. "Zaph!" Another shake.

Sire moaned.

Mother hugged ZaphMordakai's neck tightly.

Tremors ran through Uncle Deton's cheeks and when his fist struck the ground an electrical discharge scorched the moss. "Let's go! Maybe the Dragon Queen can help him."

ZaphMordakai thought the pace quick before the break, but he had been wrong. Twice he considered giving up, but Mother kept prodding him along. Not once did Uncle Deton look back to see if they were still there, and he knew what would happen if he stopped.

Now, a shiver went down ZaphMordakai's spine as he snapped out of his reverie. His gaze drifted to the chains around Mother's wrists, then immediately to Ledaedra. "Release her at once!"

"No. Not until you deliver on your promise."

"What promise?"

Ledaedra's right arm shot forward, then her left, and two colossal dragons—green and black—appeared behind him. "The one you're about to make."

Zaph scoffed nervously. "Why does everyone think they can torture me?"

"You?" Ledaedra chuckled into a sigh.

ZaphMordakai's brow furrowed excessively, then released. "No. Leave her alone!"

"Zaphling, what's the matter?" His mother's weak gaze fell upon him.

He had watched his mother die once before, or so he believed, and he could not bear the thought of losing her again. With lavender lightning crackling across his teeth, he glared at Ledaedra. "What do you want?"

"Lykinnia."

11

Decision

Cymm

Grendella gripped Cymm's wrist firmly in front of the portal. "You're not going alone!"

He turned to face her but failed to free himself. "Feldarius was quite clear about this being a solo mission."

"Oh, he was, was he? So, he said 'and leave that dwarven cleric home to bake you berry bread for when you return'." Grendella did her best to generate a deep baritone.

Cymm could not help smiling and licking his upper lip. "No, not exactly."

Ibor and Brogan stood in the doorway to the room, drawn by the commotion.

"I—am—going. I don't report to the Master of Souls, and last time I checked—neither do you." She released her grip and walked into the gateway.

Cymm glanced at the two spectators, rolled his eyes, then quickly followed. A great river of magma rippled and bubbled as it flowed past him and hit him in the face with stifling heat. "We've been tricked."

"And you wanted to come alone." Grendella scoffed and reached for her warhammer.

"*Scan the vicinity for evil.*" DragonSin slid slowly from its scabbard, while the paladin turned a cautious circle. "Where in the nine hells are we? The Plane of Tides is clear skies and blue water, a beautiful place."

"This…" Grendella waved her hand in a circle "…is a beautiful place."

"*I detect nothing,*" replied the sword.

Feldarius appeared before them. "This is the Plane of Tides, except you are seeing it from a dwarven perspective. Whether you call it River of Tides, River of Binding, River of Souls, or one of twelve other names it is known by, it is right there. You should see it from a vampire's point of view. Now, put away your weapons, and follow me."

The two visitors had to quicken their pace to keep up with the lanky strides of the demi-god.

Feldarius came to a halt several hundred yards from where they met. "I was able to obtain a cloak similar to what the acolytes wear inside the mountain. Keep to the shadows, and don't let anyone see your face, especially the dragons."

Grendella cleared her throat. "And what am I to wear?"

"You will be waiting here with me for Cymm to return with my sister." Feldarius brushed her aside and delivered the cloak to Cymm.

"There are no short creatures, dwarves, kobolds, or other, that serve this Dragon Queen?" asked Grendella.

"For anyone with a discerning eye, Cymm will appear short compared to the other acolytes. Your presence would destroy any chance of success for the mission." The Master of Souls signified the end of the conversation with a wave of his hand.

Grendella moved into position behind Cymm. “Fine. I will hide under his cloak.”

“A fat acolyte with four feet? Maybe you could wear a cow bell around your neck, too. If this mission fails, I will torment the souls of your entire family!” he said to Grendella, then turned to Cymm. “Azreala is in a huge chamber with one entrance, large enough for a dragon to come and go. When you enter, if you see two golden vessels, leave immediately. She will not be in there, and your chances of detection will be great.”

Cymm swallowed hard. “That’s it? You have no other words of wisdom?”

The demi-god stroked his chin. “Well, there are five main levels and two lower ones. The lowest chambers are where the servants and acolytes sleep, I would also avoid those as well. If you are looking for a map, or for me to portal you into the same room with her, neither is going to happen.”

“And why not?” asked Grendella with one hand raised in the air.

Feldarius’s upper lip curled, and he snarled. “The upper levels inside the mountain are blocked from scrying and other magical means of manipulation. Stealth is our only option.”

“We don’t have to do this. The chance of this mission succeeding is low.” Grendella waved for Cymm to follow as she walked toward the original gateway, back to Delge.

Cymm took several steps in a neutral direction and leaned into a craggy outcropping. Rivulets of sweat ran down the side of his face and the middle of his back.

The dwarven cleric paused and stared at him.

Agitated, the demi-god stood poised for action, silent words on the tip of his tongue, but to his credit, he gave Cymm the precious moments he needed to think.

The Paladin of Terazhan rose with his shoulders proudly thrown back. "No. Azreala would try to help me. She saved us in the dungeons of Delge from Bardonril and certain death. I'm going."

A broad grin on Feldarius's face and a new portal materialized at the same time. "You have less than eight hours until sunrise. At which time, the halls inside the dragon keep will be bustling with movement."

Gawking at Grendella, Cymm motioned toward the gateway with his head.

Without hesitation, the dwarven cleric ran straight for it.

Feldarius lunged to grab her with a fading smile and missed.

"Keep this open!" Cymm stepped through.

The sweltering heat dissipated abruptly, replaced by cool, dank air. The darkness enveloped Cymm as he breathed in deep. He waited for his eyes to adjust while the dripping of water kept time in the distance, but his vision never changed.

"What are you waiting for?" whispered Grendella.

"I can't see. It's too dark," he replied.

She grabbed his hand and led him forward, grumbling, "He can't see in the dark. We're going to die. Of course, he can't, he's human. Feldarius, if you're listening, you're an idiot."

"I can cast a light spell." Cymm's boot scuffed against the roughhewn floor, and he stumbled.

"That's a bad idea, but we might not have a choice. Come in here." She pulled him forcefully to the right.

Cymm heard the creak of a rusty hinge and again as the door closed behind them.

"Don't move." The volume of Grendella's footfalls receded as she moved away.

Cymm partially removed the acolyte robe he wore and unsheathed DragonSin. The eerie green light from the blade and gemstone barely penetrated the inky blackness. The radius of the small sphere of light did not reveal the boundaries of the room nor the dwarf.

He took two slow steps to his left, and linen shelves appeared at the hazy edge of his vision.

Neatly stacked robes lined the shelves along with sashes and crude sandals.

Cymm rotated to his right and jumped as Grendella emerged from the darkness.

She held up a robe in front of her. "This is the shortest I could find. Will your sword cut through it?"

"Yes," Cymm answered as he sliced at the indicated spot. He sawed back and forth carefully cutting the fibers and not her fingers in a circle around the garment. "You are as stubborn as Semper. You just had to have your own robe."

Grendella fixed him with a menacing glare. "Couldn't stay by the door, could you?"

Cymm ignored the comment and moved farther from the entrance down a row on shelves. "Hey, we could use this." Cymm placed his hand on a large wooden cart filled with crumpled linens.

"What for?" she asked.

"You can hide inside it, under the robes." Cymm rocked it back and forth with a metallic groan.

Even in the viridescent light, the redness of anger flooded her face. "I will not hide like a nursemaid or a child."

"You were going to hide under my robe. What is more important, your pride or the successful completion of this mission?" The young man rolled the cart toward her.

It groaned and squeaked again.

"No, I wasn't. Half of the inhabitants in this mountain will hear us coming." Grendella finished pulling the shortened robe over her head.

"DragonSin, levitate the cart high enough to slide my foot underneath it." He pushed it silently toward her with a grin. "Any more excuses?"

The dwarven cleric folded her arms over her chest.

The playful energy flooding Cymm's mind tempered. "How do you think the conversation with Terazhan will go when you tell him both Azreala and Feldarius have joined forces with Ledaedra?"

"Listen up, farm-boy—"

The rattling of the door handle preceded the familiar creak of the rusty hinge.

Cymm's heart beat a fast rhythm, and he exchanged wide-eyed glances with the dwarf.

Grendella rolled over the side and fell into the cart.

After quickly pulling two clean robes off the shelf to cover her, Cymm sheathed DragonSin, plunging them back into darkness. He had adjusted his bandolier-style scabbard long ago so one side of the cross guard would rest comfortably against the back of his neck.

Footsteps beat a steady rhythm in his direction.

Cymm turned to face the shelves and busied himself with blind sorting and shuffling.

A gasp indicated the stranger had discovered him.

A guttural, raspy voice called out in an unfamiliar tongue.

His mind raced, unsure what to do. He ignored the newcomer until he felt a firm grip on his shoulder.

12

Inquiry

Lykinnia

Terazhan stroked his unseen chin hidden in the shadows of his cowl, while everyone else gathered, awaited his response.

Lykinnia leaned forward, observing his unusually rigid frame, then finally erupted. "Father?"

"This does not change anything. We continue with our plan," he replied, an edge to his tone.

"But Father, you saw the vision, too. It is the creature that killed Cymm!" she replied.

"The creature is not a singularity. There are hundreds of them. We focus on the dragons, and kill as many as possible, weakening Ledaedra in the process. Each of you has your assignment," said Terazhan.

Solar folded his arms and leaned against a large boulder.

Kamac and Camak glared at each other with chest-rumbling growls.

Uncle Jakarrak fidgeted, and his gaze flitted around the group. "There are many dragons that do not support her, and a few we could convince to renounce her."

"We would not hunt the Silver Dragon Order, the gold dragons, or the others we call friends and allies," said Lykinnia.

"Of course not, but there are still others: the Cabal of Copper Dragons, the sea dragons, and even DetonKonraber. I think we should choose our wording more carefully." Uncle Jakarrak peered at his brother.

Terazhan harrumphed, then turned and headed toward his abode.

Everyone else took his lead and began to disburse.

"Uncle Jakarrak, I would have that conversation now, if you please." Lykinnia performed a stag leap to catch up to him.

He rolled his eyes, and his shoulders slumped. "We shall converse tomorrow."

She stepped in front of him. "No. You said that last time."

"Very well. What do you want to know?"

"I have not been able to puzzle through your ring story. You played matchmaker, they were married, then what? How did it benefit you?"

"That was the benefit. *I* selected my older brother's bride." A huge genuine smile blossomed on his face, revealing his teeth.

Lykinnia's face quirked. "I do not think so. What was your endgame?"

"You are on a fool's errand, Princess. Your father knew about this *treachery* long ago and came to grips with it. He loved your mother." Uncle Jakarrak turned to leave.

"Not so fast."

He froze mid-step.

What is he hiding? She absently tapped her finger on the side of her cheek. "Did you know there are maneuvers in altagee called long plays, which extend the game and can significantly increase your chances of winning?"

He rounded on her with a sneer. "Of course, I do. I invented the game as well as most of the tactics."

"Uncle, how would a long play have worked in real life on my mother?"

He scowled.

"Easy, Unie. Your uncle is not used to being challenged intellectually." Solar projected into her mind.

Lykinnia gave a cursory glance around but could not locate him. "*Not my problem.*" Aloud, she said, "How long ago did you make a deal with Ledaedra?"

"Many years ago. Why?" Uncle Jakarrak's face screwed up in suspicion.

"A grandmaster thief should not find any enjoyment in picking the pocket of a bumpkin."

She almost giggled but caught herself. "How many years ago?"

Her uncle's eyes flared white. "So many, I do not recall. Are we done here?"

"Instead of the spellbook, what should you have received?" Lykinnia's mind buzzed and churned with the roar of an avalanche.

Uncle Jakarrak hesitated, his mask slipping a fraction. "Young lady, this is feeling more like an interrogation and less like a discussion."

While gazing at the clouds, it hit her—the checkmate maneuver. "I am sorry uncle. I have no more questions."

"Good. Safe travels to Delge and the City of Mystics when you resume." His shoulders dropped several inches.

"Thank you. A favor, if you please? Since the spellbook you *stole* is my mother's, I would like to have it. Please bring it to me this evening."

The smirk vanished, and he blanched. He recovered immediately and summoned a portal while clearing his throat. "Of course, my dear."

The portal imploded, taking her uncle with it.

Solar pantomimed the opening of a door, and he appeared in front of her. "What game are you playing? You already have the book."

"*We* know that, but *he* does not. How will he explain its disappearance? More importantly, consider this, how did the green dragon obtain it? The same green dragon that slaughtered Cymm's village. It appears to be less of a coincidence than originally thought."

Solar gasped with wide eyes. "Your audience with the mages in Delge and the City of Mystics will have to wait. We need to play this out."

"Oh, I intend to."

13

Encounter

Cymm

Cymm cringed under the weight of a clawed, meaty hand. The guttural unknown language rang out again, but halfway through, his head jerked up.

"…anyone. Will you?" asked the acolyte.

Before he could stop himself, Cymm responded. "What?"

"Please don't tell anyone," the stranger answered, apparently not noticing he spoke in the common tongue.

Or had he. While Cymm contemplated this strange conversation, he adjusted the cloaks covering Grendella.

"Please!"

"*He is waiting for a reply,*" said DragonSin.

"If you leave now, I will not mention you were here." Cymm remained with his back turned.

"Thank you, Great One." The acolyte scurried to comply.

Great One?

"He saw the green aura when he entered and assumed you were about to steal his soul," said the sentient sword.

Steal his soul? Why not blast him with a fireball or lightning bolt? thought Cymm.

The door creaked open.

"Wait," said Cymm.

A deep sigh accompanied a shuffle.

"Is the prisoner safe?" asked Cymm.

"Yes. All of them." The door latched with a *clunk*.

All of them? Cymm withdrew the bastard sword again, bringing sweet relief to his eyes.

Grendella popped up like a jack-in-the-box. "You need to study the spells available to you more thoroughly."

Cymm returned a confused stare.

"I cast a language spell on you. Did you think you learned a new language instantly, orc-brain?" The cleric of Terazhan hoisted her leg over the edge of the cart.

After blocking her exit, Cymm pushed her back inside. "We're leaving. I have an idea. What if I cast a light spell on the bottom of the cart. Anyone looking will assume it is a levitation spell, without a second glance."

Grendella raised an eyebrow but grumbled, "It might work."

Two minutes later they were on the move and the door creaked closed behind them.

Cymm impressed himself. The recessed bottom of the wagon accommodated the height of the wheels, and the channeled light radiating onto the floor resulted in a magical appearance.

Following Feldarius's vague directions, they turned right and climbed the sloped tunnel.

"How long will that language spell last?" Cymm whispered to his partially buried friend.

With her nose resting above the edge of the cart, she replied, "Two hours."

A short time later they came to the first intersection, interspersed with three doors. Cymm recalled the description of Azreala's prison—one entrance big enough for a dragon—and ruled out all three man-sized doors. The flat tunnel to the right ran straight, farther than his source of light, however, the passage to the left doubled back immediately and climbed aggressively.

"This way," Cymm said, primarily to himself, pushing the floating cart up the incline to the left.

The grade made him grunt a few times but leveled off after one hundred feet. Dressed in his acolyte robe, Cymm popped out into a large cavern, of which he could not see the sides. Straight in front of him, a much larger tunnel loomed, big enough to accommodate a dragon.

Cymm paused, listening.

"What's the matter?" asked Grendella.

"I thought I heard something. Can you see anything to the left, or right?"

"Cavern walls but no exits. Keep going straight." The dwarf tucked back into the makeshift wagon with a huff.

Cymm continued ahead. "*DragonSin, do you sense any evil?*"

"*No.*"

"*Keep vigilant.*" Cymm entered the passageway with a glance back.

Two more empty chambers came and went, as well as a third. In this cavern were two exits, one of which sloped up.

Cymm hesitated. "This level seems to be unused. I think we should skip the rest and go up a level."

"Agreed. I didn't expect it to be this big. We better pick up—"

A scrape echoed behind them, and they both froze.

"Can you see anything?" Cymm whispered.

"Nothing," Grendella answered while trying to peer around him.

Cymm grunted as he shoved the cart toward and up the inclined passage. As he climbed, he noticed the damp air became musty with a sour tinge. The wooden handle became slick with sweat after only a dozen steps. The laborious effort continued for several hundred feet of roughhewn floor, then abruptly opened into the first cavern on the next level.

The dwarven cleric sunk below the rim of the cart.

Cymm could not see anything.

"Three evil sources directly ahead," came DragonSin's warning.

"I can't see any exits. What direction should I go?" Cymm whispered to Grendella.

"By Bardonril's Furnace, how should I know!" the dwarf hissed, still crouching low.

"They are headed this way," said DragonSin.

The cart drifted to a stop a moment before the first acolyte entered his sphere of light. "What are you doing up here? You should be in the lower levels."

Cymm's relief over Grendella's active language spell lasted only an instant. *What am I doing here?* He swallowed hard. "Ahh..."

"This level is restricted at night. What are you doing up here?" asked a second acolyte.

The young man pointed toward the linen cart. "I am—collecting dirty laundry." He braced himself. *"DragonSin, get ready to take them down."*

"With pleasure." The sentient sword was practically singing already.

A sneer appeared on the guard's face.

Cymm felt his heart pounding as the acolyte's palm filled with red energy.

A scrape on the stone drew everyone's attention.

A fourth acolyte appeared. "Great One, I am sorry for my tardiness." He turned to the other three and said, "By dirty laundry, he means dead bodies, and unless you want to end up in the cart, you'd best return to your duty."

The original guard scoffed, a ball of energy appearing in his hand.

"Take them down!" Cymm commanded DragonSin.

Metal slammed on stone as the cart hit the floor.

The red balls of energy dissipated before the guards grabbed their heads in agony.

The fourth acolyte stepped forward. "Great One, I think they have learned their lesson. We will not have room for three more bodies."

"DragonSin, hold up for a minute. Let's see how this goes." Cymm lowered his arm, trying to time the relief and create a dramatic effect.

The guards continued to writhe on the floor.

"DragonSin!"

Cymm only waited a few more seconds before pushing his shoulder blades out and breaking physical contact between his bare neck and the sword.

Instantly, the flailing stopped, and the acolytes moaned.

"On your feet and out of my way!" Reluctantly, Cymm reengaged with the sword. *"We will not kill until after we have found Azreala, then we will rain down death on our way out. Levitate the cart, we need to go."*

DragonSin did not comply.

The guards wobbled on their knees.

"We should leave, Great One." The friendly acolyte indicated a new direction with his clawed hand.

"Trust me!" Cymm grabbed the wooden edge of the cart.

The guards staggered to their feet.

Pressure pushed against Cymm's hands as the cart rose. He pulled hard to rotate it and followed the acolyte to a side passageway.

A dozen strides down the tunnel their guide came to a halt. "Why are you here?"

"Why are you whispering?" Cymm asked, avoiding the question.

"Do you want the guards to know you are not a Great One?"

Cymm bristled. "How dare—"

"The game is over. This one knows the truth," said DragonSin.

"Take him down. Quick!"

"No. This one is not evil. Let's hear him out."

"If you yell, I will kill you," said Cymm.

The acolyte fully turned to face him. "Why are you here?"

Cymm contemplated his answer, scanning the lizard-like face for any signs of deception.

"Or, should I ask the one in the cart?"

14

The Gate

ZaphMordakai

ZaphMordakai's imprisonment at Ledaedra's hands began yesterday. He awaited the opening of the portal so Lykinnia could contact the queen. He had hoped to be friends with the young woman, but the choice between her and his mother was a simple one.

Zaph sat next to his mother, rubbing her back. "I'll get you out of here. Don't worry. It'll be soon."

She moaned and shifted, rattling the chains that tethered her to one of the stone columns near the altar—where Ledaedra stood.

The Dragon Queen surveyed three scrying windows hovering before her. In the center one, his Uncle DetonKonraber ravaged a dark blue dragon, ripping his head off halfway down his neck. She roared in anger and exploded into six dragons. Each of her dismembered arms and legs bloating into a behemoth dragon of corresponding color, as well as the red and shadow heads attached to her body.

In the background, Zaph could clearly see the volcanic peak on Fire Island, which reminded him once again of the day his family fled their home world.

At a blistering pace, Uncle Deton had led them to the Sand Basin where they crouched at the lip. At the bottom of the sixty-foot-deep bowl, three trellbac guarded a gateway. The oval shaped doorway resided in the middle of the bowl and shimmered a hickory brown with a crimson-red outline. An equal number of dragon lengths behind it, the depression's far side wall climbed back up to a steep edge.

Zaph had never seen a trellbac before that day and remembered the serpent-like way their bodies reticulated as they moved. Their heads were similar to a dragon's, but the similarities stopped there. A supple golden skin covered their rippling muscles and feathers adorned their pate. They did not have tails, and their seventh and eighth appendages, or arms, were also segmented and could bend in any direction. Most of them preferred to carry spears or staves.

His uncle scanned the horizon in all directions. Finally, he bent low and said, "I will lead them away, and you will take my brother through the portal."

"Me?" his mother asked. "I cannot—"

"Transform if you must, but you will carry him through!" DetonKonraber hissed.

She sputtered, then acquiesced with a nod.

Zaph rubbed his snout against her shoulder. "We can do this."

Deton shot him a death stare. "If you get in the way…" He backed away from the rim several dragon-tail lengths and resumed his natural form. Two leaps and a bound took him airborne but heading in the wrong direction. He climbed between two large mushrooms and vanished.

An ear-piercing whistle sundered the silence from above, a moment before a massive bolt of lightning struck the centermost trellbac. Its body exploded upon impact and arms and legs flew in every direction.

DetonKonraber pulled up with a swoop and barely missed the rim on the opposite side of the bowl. Two sound blasts chased after him. One ripped through the lip of rock, but both sailed over the top of him as he disappeared from view.

ZaphMordakai almost laughed when he saw the enemy give chase. Although they were extremely fast, their legs individually twirled in a circle, propelling them forward.

Mother hoisted father's drow body onto Zaph's back in front of his wings. "Get ready—let's go."

Up over the lip and down into the depression they went. Slowly at first, but they unintentionally gained speed. The excessive weight pushed against his neck and threatened to topple him over with every step, but with every step, freedom drew closer.

Finally, the descent leveled out but carrying Father became more arduous. Zaph's legs began to tremble with every step, and he had to stop after reaching the midpoint.

"It's ok, Zaphling," Mother cooed. She slid Father to the ground, then draped his arm around her neck, hoisting him to his feet.

After a dozen steps, she began to struggle, but fortunately ZaphMordakai had recovered some of his strength. He hooked the spike of his wing in Father's armpit and lifted, then shared a broad smile with his mother. When their gazes reverted to the front, their happiness instantly disappeared.

A trellbac had returned unseen from chasing his uncle, using the portal to mask its approach. It passed through the doorway, unphased, its serpent tongue flicking excitedly. An obscene grimace appeared on its face, and it opened its maw slowly, enjoying the moment before the kill.

In a panic, Mother tried to defend them with a lightning bolt, but her right arm remained entangled with her mate's body. "I love you, Zaphling."

The trellbac exploded in a shower of blood and guts. A massive chunk of flesh hit ZaphMordakai in the face and an arm hit his wing.

DetonKonraber roared past them. "The other one returns with a dozen friends!" He banked and made a second pass. "Quickly!" He disappeared into the portal.

Only five more steps. Zaph dared to glance up to the rim.

The first trellbac crested the edge and emitted a shrill caterwaul. Two by two they quickly joined him down the descent.

Three steps left and Mother screamed in frustration.

The stampeding footfalls resonated in the bowl like roaring thunder as they reached the bottom.

The final step and Mother pushed him and Father into the portal.

DetonKonraber, already a drow, immediately took possession of his unconscious brother and carried him several dragon leaps away before lying him on the ground.

ZaphMordakai stared at the portal, his heart in his throat, remembering the ice-cold needles that had prickled his hide as he passed through the gateway. "Mother?"

She finally burst through to join him. She clung to his neck with tears in her eyes. "Zaphling!"

"What took you so long?" Zaph demanded.

She proceeded to inspect him snout to tail. "We are safe now. They cannot pass through the portal. The magic prevents it."

Zaph sighed in relief.

Voices rose behind them.

"You will!" Uncle Deton screamed into the face of a younger Ledaedra.

The queen's shorter stature back then and lack of confidence caused her to retreat a step from his fury. "I will not. His insides have already begun to sublimate."

"I have seen you heal this injury before. You *will* heal him, or you will regret it," he snarled.

Zaph and his mother drifted over toward the argument and stood there quietly.

With a wave of a talon, Ledaedra summoned a new portal behind her and disappeared without another word.

Uncle Deton fell to his knees beside his brother, turned his face skyward, and screamed at the star filled sky. His balled fist rose, and he turned as if to strike Zaph.

The slap of skin on skin resounded. "No!" Father had Uncle Deton's wrist in his hand.

Everyone spoke at once.

"ZaphMorlak!" Mother moved quickly to be by his side.

"Father!" ZaphMordakai also pushed up.

"Zaph?" A tiny glimmer of hope had crept into Uncle Deton's voice. "Why? Why didn't you fly out of there?"

In fits and starts, Father replied, "You know—why, and…you would—have—done the same. Protect them." ZaphMorlak's body shuddered, and he groaned.

Mother laid her head on Father's chest, sobbing, as he took his last breath.

DetonKonraber stormed away transforming with every step. He took wing on his sixth step and never looked back.

Zaph shook his head to clear the memory and scoffed at his uncle's boldness. The bad blood between him and the Dragon Queen continued to mount.

Another synchronized roar from the six dragons comprising Ledaedra's body prompted Zaph to head for the portal to the prisoner's cave. He did not want to become a pawn in the middle of their conflict.

DetonKonraber never wavered from his plan to make her pay—as he had promised—even centuries later.

Now, Zaph would wait for Lykinnia to make contact.

15

Rescue

Cymm

Grendella popped up in the middle of the cart, palms glowing. "Step back."

The stranger took two steps back, hands in the air. "The robes do not block the heat coming off your body. If the guards approached any closer, they would have seen it too, just like I did when we first met."

"Stop talking!" Cymm hissed with a look over his shoulder.

Grendella also glanced back and locked eyes. "This one knows too much—"

"Wait! You haven't heard my offer yet." The acolyte held both arms straight in front of him as if to shield himself.

Grendella hefted her warhammer. "Make it quick."

"I will guide you to the prisoner chamber if you promise to take me with you when you leave."

Cymm's mouth fell open. "What makes you think—"

"You said to make it quick. Do we have a deal or not?" asked the acolyte.

Cymm shot a glance at Grendella, who stared back mutely.

"DragonSin, your thoughts?"

"This creature has a complex mind and is very old. He could even be part dragon—green dragon. Even though some of his ideals are questionable, his history of deeds leans towards good," replied the weapon.

"Deal. How long until this place gets busy?" asked Cymm.

The acolyte shook its head. "No business before names. I am Rakai." His forked tongue extended the first letter into a long trill.

They introduced themselves while Cymm started the cart moving again.

Rakai led them through two more caverns then paused at the bottom of a sloped tunnel. "There will be guards when we reach the top."

Cymm peered up the passageway. "How much farther?"

"It is the first room after the guards."

"We should try to avoid the fight if possible." Cymm glanced at Rakai for support and received none.

"There isn't going to be a fight." The female cleric did not expound upon her bold statement.

"Care to share, so I can help?" Cymm did not plan to move without more information.

Grendella hopped out of the cart and patted her warhammer. "I'm going to put them to sleep."

Cymm grabbed the edge of the cart, and it levitated—he still needed it to see. "All right, let's go."

As they crested the top of the rise, the guards stirred and spoke in an unfamiliar language.

A slight breeze buffeted Cymm's elbow as the cleric rushed past. She smacked her weapon against the metal, corner brackets of the cart and directed the head forward.

All four guards fell to the ground.

Cymm glanced around. "Where's Rakai?"

The draconian acolyte had vanished.

After stowing the magical warhammer upon her shoulder, the dwarf glanced about. "By Ledaedra's chaos! I knew it."

"Keep moving. I'm right here. And don't say her name again."

Cymm spun, searching for the source, but the voice projected out of the darkness accompanied by the familiar scrape on the stone floor.

"I'm invisible." Rakai materialized right in front of him for the briefest moment, then faded out of sight again.

"If you can turn invisible, why do you need us to help you escape?" Grendella asked suspiciously.

"We are on an island in the middle of the sea. What good is invisibility?" Rakai asked.

The dwarf growled. "That way you can drown, and I won't have to see you!"

"Quiet!" Cymm commanded.

The passageway took a sharp turn to the right and moonlight poured in from a large opening on the left.

The cart settled to the ground, while Cymm freed DragonSin from the scabbard. "*Do you sense any evil in the area?*"

"Yes. There are many sources ahead."

Grendella peeked around the corner.

Cymm caught up. "See anything?"

She nodded with wide eyes.

He pushed up to the edge and found no door, only a cavernous chamber with a smooth stone floor and eight holding devices. Six were already occupied. One of the prisoners brought a smile to his face.

Azreala's head lulled to the front, arrested by the iron bracket around her neck, then popped back up. She blinked twice and dozed off again, only to repeat the pattern ten heartbeats later.

All the prisoners were in some state of repose, three on the nearby wall around to the right and three on the far wall. They varied in shape, size, race, and gender. The largest captive—an ogre, or at least a half-ogre—was taller and four times Azreala's girth, who occupied the metal rack next to him. On the other side, a dark-skinned human with a muscular build dozed fitfully. Across the room in the middle of three racks slept a lithe female. Her head hung forward and her long blonde tresses blocked every detail of her face. A half-breed boy slumbered to her right, a cross between an orc and a human. The final captive, a pudgy young man approximately Cymm's age, still wore his court finery. There were only two empty restraining devices remaining.

The bright light of Primordian overpowered the crimson rays of Phoenix to chase away most of the shadows, revealing no guards or acolytes. However, the deepest corners of a recess between the prisoners refused to reveal their secrets.

Cymm tiptoed to stand directly in front of his friend, The Mistress, and pulled back his hood.

Her head bobbed again, and their eyes met briefly, then flared open moments later, recognition apparent upon her face. "What trickery is this?"

"Good morning to you too, sunshine," Cymm said brightly.

"Return to your master, lackey, and bother me no more." She closed her eyes.

Grendella stood next to him. "Are you coming with us, or not?"

The prisoner to the left began to stir.

Azreala's eyes remained closed.

The dwarf poked her in the belly with the butt of her warhammer.

Azreala's eyelids flew open, revealing blazing red orbs of fury. "Do you want me to drain your soul, toadstool?"

Cymm forced himself between them, as Grendella reversed her weapon and gripped the shaft proper. "Azreala, you asked me to trust you once. Now, I am asking you to trust me. We need to leave. Feldarius awaits, and we are all in great peril."

A glance at his sword caught her attention, and she grinned.

"No, leave. They tricking you," said the ogrish prisoner next to her.

"Shut up, Ronks!" Azreala barked. She squinted at Cymm. "How did you escape?"

He pulled up his cowl. "Escape?"

"Story time later!" Grendella fumbled with the shackles around her ankles. "How do we free you?"

The device holding the demi-god had no latches or locks, and the restraints were too small to be slipped off. The brackets secured her neck, both wrists, both ankles, and her tail. They felt cold to the touch, like metal.

Cymm slipped his finger under the manacle. "Oww!" Pain shot up his arm. He rapidly withdrew a blackened, sizzling finger, and shook it.

Ronks released a baritone hoot.

"Keep it down." Grendella hissed, chasing his hand through the air.

"It zapped me!" Cymm grunted.

"We have company," came a whisper in Cymm's ear.

Grendella grabbed his wrist. "Terazhan, heal this servant of yours."

Yellow energy coursed through his hand.

A gust of wind caught Cymm's shoulder and spun him in a circle, while Grendella flew into the wall behind them with a resounding *smack*. She crumpled to the ground.

With his finger fully healed, he gripped the pommel of his sword and charged the draconian mage. Three magical missiles struck him from the rear. His back arched in pain, and he lurched toward his target.

With a *poof*, the wizard disappeared.

Cymm spun to find two new acolytes waving their claws and chanting. Four more balls of energy sped toward him. He raised DragonSin. "Dispel magic!" Three of them hit the emerald in the hilt with a shower of dazzling sparks, but the fourth ricocheted off course, careening into Cymm's neck.

Pain exploded in his mind, replaced immediately by fear. He could not breathe. His hands raced for his throat to heal himself, but he could not speak. "*DragonSin! Can you help me?*"

No answer came.

In his panic, he had dropped his sword. A dizzy, light-headed sensation took over. His gaze lifted to meet Azreala's eager return, and he understood her intent. He blinked slowly and nodded.

A crimson dart of energy hurtled from her body, forking at the bridge of Cymm's nose and slamming into both eyes. His hands and forearms contorted, he grew half a foot, and long, blood-red talons sprouted from his fingertips. He struggled to see through the pooling red haze in his eyes, his body no longer his to control.

Fire shot out of the hands of two more acolytes, but it struck an invisible barrier in front of him before fragmenting into particles.

Crimson mist swirled around the avatar as Azreala commanded him to rise. Yammering skulls coalesced. They hovered for only a moment before rocketing forward with tendrils trailing. They crashed into all five mages, each in the middle of casting their next spell.

The skulls disappeared, but the wisps of necromancy remained, throbbing and pulsing with a life of their own.

With horror-stricken faces, the acolytes froze amid a shriek of agony. With each pulsation the wisps grew, and with each throb came strength and knowledge. He had not noticed it the first time, but he could sense the wizards' thoughts, or more precisely, their fears.

Cymm's back ached and his throat burned, but he could breathe now. More power coursed back through the vines, feeding the beast within him. A prowling, impatient essence, waiting to come out. Cymm did not sense evil, nor good, just raw power. A juggernaut of—the avatar screamed in ecstasy.

Another quick glimpse of his surroundings filtered through the curtain of blood in his eyes. The dried husk of an acolyte hovered in the air before him. Blackened shingles of flesh cascaded from its body with each pulse, like the release of spores from a mushroom, then turned to ash. A ring of cinders formed below each victim.

A final *crunch* signified the collapse of the draconian bodies and the evaporation of the crimson wisps.

"Cymm?" called a sleepy, apprehensive voice.

Azreala directed her avatar over to her motionless, shrunken body, ignoring the call. Given the smaller size from her transformation, the manacles slid off her ankles, wrists, and tail effortlessly, but not her neck.

With control of his body, she repeated Cymm's error from before and slipped both hands inside the remaining manacle. Smoke rose from the avatar's fingers, but the collected power from the acolytes surged within him. He ripped the shackle into two pieces, then caught the body of the demi-god as it collapsed, hoisting the lifeless form onto his shoulder.

"Let's free the others," said Cymm.

"These are adamantine restraints," replied Azreala.

"So?"

"So, I used all of the drained energy to break the one on my neck," Azreala snapped.

"Fine. Drain the ogre, and—"

"No!" replied Azreala and DragonSin simultaneously within the avatar's mind.

"The ogre is not evil," said the sentient sword.

Cymm grumbled in disbelief. *"Grab Grendella and let's go."*

"Grab the what?" asked Azreala.

"The dwarf on the floor. Don't leave her."

Azreala bent low and grabbed the scruff of the dwarf's neck, then dragged her toward the exit.

Grendella began to struggle. "Let go!" She swung her arm wildly over her head to emphasize her point. Sitting up, she prayed, "Lord Terazhan, heal this faithful servant." A golden light bloomed inside of her. The dwarf's eyes went wide with fear. "We must leave! Terazhan says dragons are coming!"

"Lead the way," instructed Azreala.

Grendella scooped up her hammer and the bastard sword lying on the floor. "Cymm, here's your—whoa—what in the nine hells happened to you?"

"Are we in a hurry, or not?" asked Azreala.

Grendella ran for the exit.

"Cymm, I knew you would come for me!" exclaimed the same female voice from before, presumably one of the captives.

The young man could not wrinkle his brow or scan the room. *Who is calling my name?*

An acolyte materialized next to them, running.

The sharp intake of breath from the dwarf let Cymm know she had seen him, too.

Rakai glanced over.

"Thanks for the help!" screamed Grendella.

"I never said I would help, only lead you to the chamber." He pointed toward the platform, the open sky, and the dozens of approaching dragons and added, "Although, it looks like you could use a little now."

"We will travel faster in our own bodies." Azreala did not wait for a response and instantly began to transfer.

Who called my name? The voice sounded familiar to Cymm, but he could not place it.

Rakai spread his scaly talons and braced himself. "Trevli ooka Magoo." Tangerine filaments shot forth, spanning ceiling to floor and wall to wall. It shimmered in orange perfection before becoming translucent, then invisible.

Azreala, now in her own body, approached the barrier slowly, rubbing her wrists and neck.

Searing pain exploded in Cymm's neck, his pre-existing injury the source. He staggered in multiple directions before Grendella assisted him to the ground.

The dwarven cleric called out to Terazhan for healing yet again.

Golden light accompanied a warming sensation in his body, and he sighed in relief.

Grendella jumped to her feet, her warhammer gripped in two hands before her. "What are we waiting for?"

Cymm sat up.

Azreala growled at the barrier.

"He can't get through. Let's go!" yelled Rakai.

A dark figure stood at the invisible barrier, gripping the elbow of another.

Cymm shot to his feet. "ZaphMordakai, what are you doing here?"

"Your days are numbered, Cymm Reich, as are hers." The dark elf thrust the young lady forward with a grin upon his face.

Cymm blanched, he knew the prisoner—Jenaleya, the princess from Norfolk.

Dazed and confused, Cymm stumbled along being pulled down the tunnel by Grendella with ZaphMordakai's screams chasing them.

16

Same Old Story

Talo

Talo continued to brush his faithful warhorse, while it nickered and whinnied. Their friendship began over seven years ago, and Talo could not imagine life without him. The young man scanned the barnyard, and his brow furrowed. He emitted a long burst whistle which culminated with an abrupt finish.

Several of the horses in the vicinity stomped a rear hoof or shook their head in irritation.

Jalko raced around the corner of the nearest building with a jackrat in his mouth, its head barely attached. These fearless vermin grew as long as a horse's tail and came with a voracious appetite. The farm dogs usually ran from them, unless there were puppies involved. In the past four months, the dire wolf had decimated the population of jackrats, and the other households were ecstatic. Jalko received regular rewards in the form of food and had become the village hero.

Cymm had made it clear not to harm the livestock, but the jackrats and the occasional prowling wolves received no dispensation.

"Jalko! You just ate." Talo shook his head, not in disgust—he had grown accustomed to it now—but in disappointment. "I planned to roast the antelope Dirk Darkmane dropped off this morning."

The dire wolf had already found a comfortable spot and made short work of his snack.

Talo smacked the warhorse on the rump, and it trotted away. After packing up his grooming supplies, he headed for his barn, formerly Otec's.

Jalko's body rubbed up against his arm. When the dire wolf took a proud stance, the fine beast could look Talo in the eyes.

Standing somewhat shorter than Cymm and much lighter, Talo had always wondered if he could ride Jalko should an urgent need arise. He tousled the wolf's ear, trying to avoid the sticky red fur. "Cymm's been gone over two weeks, and we were left at home again. What happened to our deal?"

Jalko's head cocked, and he whimpered.

"I'm sorry, friend. I know you miss him." Talo tried not to mention his cousin's name around the wolf, because he would usually mope around for the next couple of hours. "I have good news. We are going to accompany Vena to Starcrest Rise tomorrow so she can visit with her mother, and you can hunt jackrats."

The last word made Jalko hop like a rabbit, causing Talo to laugh.

Talo skinned the antelope while it hung from the barn rafters—a simple task—but as he neared completion, a shadow darkened the entryway.

Jalko let out a low grumble but did not rise.

Talo glanced up. "Dirk, what brings you by?"

"Did your father tell you I stopped over this morning?"

"Yes, and thank you." Talo indicated the hanging meat.

Dirk scuffed his boot into the dirt. "Do you know when Cymm is expected to return?"

Jalko whimpered.

Talo turned to face him and gripped the skinning knife tight. "Well, that's a strange question to ask. Have you any business with him?"

"No, but I need to talk to him about a personal matter." Dirk's head jerked to the side.

"As soon as he returns, I'll let him know."

"Alright, thanks, Talo." Dirk turned to leave, then paused.

"Something else?"

"Do you think Jalko could track him down if he needed to?"

Talo's eyes rolled up into the top of his eyelids. *I never thought about that. I bet he could.* "I doubt it. He is very happy here. Thanks again for the antelope."

Dirk left without another word.

Talo exchanged a glance with Jalko, then slid his hidden dirk dagger back into its sheath.

17

The Chase

ZaphMordakai

The barrier shimmered each time a black fist struck it. ZaphMordakai no longer held Jenaleya's arm, and in a rage, he beat upon the barrier with alternating hands. Hyperventilating, he withdrew a few steps, his upper lip quivering.

Jenaleya mumbled to herself, "He didn't even look at me."

"Shut up, you whining wretch." Zaph paced along the edge of the barrier, his quarry already two minutes gone.

The princess pulled and twisted a strand of blonde hair. "Why didn't he look at me? Maybe he couldn't…his eyes were bleeding." She wrung her hands. "And The Mistress left me, too."

"When I'm finished with him, his bloodshot eyes will be the least of his problems." The dark elf waved his hand, and Jenaleya levitated once more. He hurried into the chamber and forcefully returned her to the ceremonial restraints.

"Oww! Why are you being so mean?" Jenaleya adjusted her back with a painful expression. "I can't believe I liked you."

This last statement, although a reoccurring sentiment by others, made him pause a moment. He shrugged and exited the chamber. Zaph had awaited Lykinnia's contact for only two days, but it felt like a month. He sighed, knowing what he must do, and stepped through the portal at the end of the hall. The inky blackness shifted to a red spectrum and a sweltering heat followed.

Ledaedra had her talons upon the surface of the onyx altar. Her droning chant ended abruptly, and her malevolent gaze fell upon him.

"I did not summon you. Leave!" Ledaedra fumed.

Zaph came to a halt and glanced over his shoulder at his escape route. "I'm sorry to disturb you, but one of the prisoners is escaping. If you come quickly, we should be able to recover her."

"Fool, she is not a Descendant of Twilight. Her escape is irrelevant." The Dragon Queen's attention returned to the altar.

"Forgive me, My Queen, but she is escaping with the help of Cymm Reich."

"The peasant? What are they up to now?" She paused for several moments in deep thought. "Feldarius must be involved—he would not allow his sister to be a prisoner for long—which means I know where they are going."

"Do you mind if I join the fun?" asked the dark elf.

Ledaedra's talon zipped through the air, and a much larger portal appeared next to the existing one. "I insist, and this is the one plane where I don't have to ask for permission."

Her statement made ZaphMordakai's skin crawl, and he glanced at the escape portal again.

Ledaedra corralled him with her green arm and forced him through the larger portal ahead of her.

It took a few moments, but the dark elf's vision cleared enough for him to witness the grand reunion of his enemies on the bank of a crystal-clear river. A tall man hugged the former prisoner joyfully, surrounded by Cymm, the dwarf, and the draconian traitor.

Zaph and his liege lord went unnoticed, and he marveled at their ignorance. *I could kill them all right now. One forked, lightning bolt would end their celebration. Although, one at a time would be more fun. My first target would be you, dragonslayer. No…you do not deserve a quick death. My lightning bolts will be used on the others, and I will slowly rend your body limb by limb.*

While he awaited Ledaedra's command to attack, he racked his brain, trying to identify any of Cymm's cohorts. *None of the people were with him before. How does he have so many friends?*

The dwarf's eyes suddenly went wide; she had discovered the intruders.

An uneasy speechlessness fell over the reunion, and they all turned to gape.

The largest man spoke first, "You dare attack me on my own plane in front of my altar."

Zaph sneered and stepped forward. "Let the killing begin," he whispered.

A clawed talon grasped his shoulder. "Feldarius, no one has attacked anyone. We wanted to validate your sister's safe return."

With an exaggerated sidestep, he indicated his sister. "She has, so now you can leave."

Feldarius? Zaph's gaze shifted to the former prisoner. *Sister? Drag me through the seven heavens. I electrocuted Azreala.*

The goddess of death stared at him with hatred.

ZaphMordakai waggled his fingers at her.

A crimson skull raced toward the dark elf, wailing.

The dark elf stumbled backward into Ledaedra's leg, trying to escape its path. The skull slammed into his chest with significant force, but no pain. Then again, he never really experienced much more than discomfort. His eyes focused on the thin strand of smoke exiting his body. It slithered and undulated in the air as it made its way back to its origin.

Azreala waggled her fingers back at him, then clenched her fist.

Searing pain shot through his body and mind, so intense he barely remembered to breathe. He emitted a bellowing roar of agony as he watched the smokey tendril become a thing of substance. He clawed at his own skin, desperate to escape. His body stretched; he could not control the transition back to his natural form. *So, this is pain. No wonder torture works on most people.*

The crimson strand enflamed, and the pain intensified. His spine arched. A ripping, tearing sensation occurred within his body—the removal of his very soul.

A bubble enveloped him, and the crimson strand evaporated with a *pop*.

ZaphMordakai glowered at Cymm, then smiled.

Cymm stood transfixed, mouth wide enough to catch a bog fly.

She never told him. Hmm. What does that say about your relationship, Cymm Reich?

The bubble condensed to the size of a man as Zaph transformed back into his drow form and floated slightly to the right of Ledaedra.

"Cymm, be a good messenger, and tell your friend Lykinnia that I am holding her consort prisoner."

The godling twins stood shoulder to shoulder whispering to one another.

Cymm stewed.

Zaph could not contain his glee. After a few exalting seconds passed, her choice of the word *prisoner* finally registered. He quickly scanned his liege's countenance.

By the sinister gleam in her eye, Ledaedra had achieved exactly what she wanted, which could mean anything for ZaphMordakai.

The trespassers withdrew back into the portal and materialized on the sweltering Plane of Ashes. They immediately turned into the next gateway and returned to the massive cave with the prisoners.

Jenaleya began to wail at the sight of the Dragon Queen—her aura of fear more intense than a red dragon's—waking the rest of the Descendants.

ZaphMordakai rubbed his temples. Although the princess irritated him, he felt bad for her. His back slammed against a metal beam and a manacle closed around his neck. He could not resist; his wrists and ankles had also been seized. He had become a prisoner, held by the same restraint that had recently bound Azreala.

18

Awakening

BrimStrakenstone

BrimStrakenstone shifted his bulk while standing behind Ledaedra and staring into an immense crystal geode. He ignored the other, departing generals, dismissed by the queen. The hollow rock rested behind the dark obsidian ledge she enjoyed lounging on, and it rose ten feet above the ground in a cathedral shape. The inside teemed with extravagant shades of orange gems. The darkest formed the outside edge, while many on the inner rim seemed to dance with a radiant fire. Gems occupied most of the interior, except for the small pocket of air in the middle.

For the past hour, Ledaedra scrutinized the actions of a powerful female dark elf. A true dark elf—not dragonborn—although Brim could not explain the difference. Lorelei, the daughter of Marekai, remained one of three Descendants of Twilight to be captured, but they did not have a good plan in place—or any plan.

Lorelei, a devout priestess of Marekai and his one weakness, would be difficult to take. His pride and fondness for his daughter stretched back centuries.

Brim's claws tightened, digging deeper into the ground. Every second in Ledaedra's presence stretched his nerves taut—he should be breathing gouts of fire, not treading on thin ice. "Are you certain she is worth the risk? The god of fear made it very clear he will leave and take his army of devils if we touch his daughter." His voice, softer than intended, came with a tremor, which the queen noticed.

"We will take Lorelei last, and I will deal with her father. Myra will be next, followed by Lykinnia…" Ledaedra's voice faded as another red general approached. "Did I summon you?"

"Apologies, My Queen. I have urgent news," said the general.

"It had better be. Your life depends on it."

The general glanced at BrimStrakenstone for reassurance, then spoke to the queen, "A cloaked figure advances on the tomb. What are your orders?"

"Is it him?" she asked.

"Perhaps. It was impossible to tell without revealing ourselves."

Ledaedra tapped her claw slowly on the obsidian ledge, then fixed the newcomer with a glare. "Leave and wait for my instructions."

She waved her green talon and Lorelei faded away. In her place appeared a huge mausoleum, resting atop a magnificent plateau on the coast of the Red Sea between the human cities of Tumbar and Raist. At its base grew a young forest of evergreens. Ledaedra panned in and out and wove a pattern through the trees. Her search ended on a figure.

A cloaked figure, shrouded in shadows, observed the monolith from a distance, tucked in tight against the trunk of a rough-barked tree. It could have been a statue, for nothing stirred except a small lock of hair driven by a light coastal breeze.

Brim still could not discern the identity, no matter what angle the Dragon Queen shifted their view to. The sun dropped low over the water, casting even longer shadows, and the figure disappeared.

Both Brim and Ledaedra grumbled at the same time.

"It's him. He's in the burial crypt. Get your team in position," commanded Ledaedra.

The big red dragon sent a messenger with his instructions, then glanced at his liege to confirm he had completed the task.

The image in the geode shifted again, and they were inside the mausoleum. The fading sun on the horizon lit the main chamber dimly, and the multiple recesses were not illuminated at all. To provide a spectacular overlook, the wall facing the sea was missing, but massive pillars held the roof in place.

With the vestiges of light, the mysterious figure centered themself on the raised platform with the sarcophagus resting on it. With outstretched hands, he collected the waning sunrays in a sphere above the coffin.

They danced, and their illumination grew until they chased the shadows away that hid the face inside the cowl.

Terazhan's eyes twinkled.

The grind of stone on stone reverberated off the back and side walls, and the lid slid the length of the structure before coming to rest gently at the foot and cocked at an angle.

The demi-god waited, then retreated a step and cast a light spell at the ceiling. The entire chamber became visible, and he crept forward to peer over the edge. Dust and tattered cloth covered the remains of the ancient hero. He leaned his hips against the sarcophagus and placed his hands before his face in a circle. Low chanting resulted in a ball of amber energy blossoming in the void.

A skeletal visage thrust up and forward—inches from his face—screaming.

Terazhan gasped and fell backward down the steps, diffusing his spell.

The skull floated above the edge of the coffin, followed by its shoulders, ribs, and hips. Strands of cloth and dust fell from the bones, as well as the calcified remnants of beetle carapaces, knocking thythmically against the ribcage on their descent. A bony hand raised, pointing a solitary finger. "Why have you disturbed my rest?"

Terazhan shook his head to clear his foggy gaze.

The skeleton leaped into the air wielding a mighty warhammer. Hefting it high above his head, he brought it down on the demi-god as he landed.

A golden shield appeared with a reverberating *pop*, and magical energy arced in every direction.

The death knight pulled back for a second swing. "How dare you return here!"

Terazhan flicked his wrist to the side. "You cannot use my own weapon against me, fool!"

The warhammer sailed into the far wall, dragging the death knight with it, his grip still firmly in place.

Terazhan rose and dusted himself off. "What madness is this Melcorac? I came to wake you. It is time for you to return to the world."

The risen warrior also regained its feet, lifted the warhammer and charged.

Another wave of amber energy appeared between the combatants, but this time it wrapped itself around the death knight.

The warrior flailed and resisted. "I will have my revenge! Three and a half centuries I have lain here awake, while the beetles ate my flesh, and the rats gnawed my bones!"

"Melcorac, the Holy One, my greatest disciple. You must regain your sanity. Why would I do this to you?" Terazhan stepped toward him with his hands held up between them.

The magically encased skeleton moved an equal distance, stride by stride, toward the far wall. Melcorac's cavernous eye sockets blazed to life. "Then you lied! You said you were the only one that could break the enchantment."

"I…" Terazhan sputtered. He pulled his cowl down around his shoulders, then hung his head in shame. "I—will fix this."

BrimStrakenstone chortled. "This was your work?"

"I woke him hundreds of years ago, hoping this day would come," cooed Ledaedra.

"I'm an abomination!" Melcorac dropped to his knees, lamenting, crying bone-dust tears. "How can I walk among the people looking like this?"

"Calm down! Maybe I can reverse the effects." Terazhan pushed him against the wall to emphasize his point.

After a final explosive flail, the death knight's movement subsided, and his head slumped.

Terazhan unwrapped the magical restraint from his former disciple slowly at first, then with increasing speed. He remained at a safe distance, hands at the ready.

Brim held his breath in anticipation, but nothing happened.

Terazhan rolled his shoulders out, then closed his eyes. He took a deep breath, then his eyes popped open, as if expecting an attack. Golden beams shot forth, hitting Melcorac about the head and shoulders.

Flesh instantly wove a pattern across the skull and multiplied rapidly. Tendons formed around the mandibular joint, and corded muscle twisted down and around his spine, forming his neck. When skin and hair appeared, the Lord of Healing refocused the golden shafts of light on the skeleton's chest. The heart and lungs were small at first but swelled instantly to full size.

A smile tugged at the corners of Melcorac's mouth as large arteries snaked out of the heart toward his arms, legs, and torso.

The amber light winked off and back on several times, sputtering.

Terazhan inspected his hands in disbelief; his expression revealing his thoughts of betrayal.

Ledaedra cackled in delight. “Watch.”

The new flesh blackened on the edges and ulcers erupted on his skin. Melcorac staggered, staring in horror and dismay. “No! Not again.” His knees buckled. He clawed at his own face as the leprosy worked its way up his neck.

In that moment, Brim saw the true cost of immortality. This madness in the guise of devotion unnerved him, and fortunately the queen fixed her penetrating stare elsewhere. “Wicked.”

“Very.” Ledaedra beamed.

Attempting to speak several times, Terazhan finally said, “I can fix this—not here—I need the help of a new disciple.”

“Send in the dragons,” Ledaedra instructed.

BrimStrakenstone’s brow furrowed. “My Queen?”

“You heard me.”

“They do not stand a chance against Terazhan and Melcorac. They will be slaughtered,” counseled Brim.

“Maybe, but they will attack nevertheless.”

19

Altagee

Lykinnia

Several days passed since Uncle Jakarrak departed the Peak of Power, and he never returned, with or without the book.

Terazhan returned earlier this morning from his mission to Melcorac's tomb on the Plateau of the Magnificent Sunset, and he called a council meeting for noon at the altar, which would start imminently.

Lykinnia arrived first, hoping to chastise her uncle.

Aunt Sehaleah appeared, tall and regal, the embodiment of grace. Her long blonde hair woven around her pointy ears, and the rest of her tresses cascading down her back. Her emerald eyes glinted in recognition and salutation.

Lykinnia blushed and nodded. She had never been included in a council meeting, evident in her aunt's facial expression.

Solar unzipped a seam in the fabric between planes and peeked his head through, then the rest of his body followed. He stood next to his ward with only a glance.

A raging vortex of wind deposited her Uncle Dilantro on the opposite side of the circular gathering. He was a stoic giant, a full head above even her father, with a canary yellow cape that apexed at the side of his shoulders and flared with a five-inch collar.

"Where is everybody?" Lykinnia whispered to Solar.

The winged man shrugged. "Obviously Bardonril and Feldarius are banished and will not be here."

"Father is never late," she said softly. "And what about Uncle Jakarrak, Aunt Melandri, and…"

A golden portal appeared at the edge of the stone platform. Terazhan and Uncle Jakarrak stepped out. Her father seemed…taller. He had grown a couple of inches.

Solar shot her a taciturn glare. "Wipe that scowl off your face before someone sees it. You can deal with your uncle later."

Father wore the Mantle of the Gods. The usekh collar was large enough to be a full set of pauldrons. It hung over the edge of both shoulders and drooped from lack of support, and the seven layers, one for each plane of heaven, swooped down past his sternum. A fist-sized, amber cat's eye rested comfortably as the centerpiece, while gems, beads, and polished ingots adorned the remainder. Along the bottom fringe dangled teardrop gems—deep hunter-green emeralds interlaced with dark cobalt sapphires. A daffodil-yellow topaz rode high above the collarbone and the upper edge of the mantle to complete the representation of all seven planes.

The mantle shimmered.

How beautiful. Lykinnia stood transfixed. She fought the urge to reach out, to wear it. A hunger built deep inside her. She imagined it draped around her neck. The mantle pulsed. A beckoning call that drew her in deeper, even though she had no desire for power. Through her mind stormed a vision. A cold world devoid of life—her world. Some catastrophe had befallen it and the fires raged until they burned themselves out—but what had caused it?

A pyromancer! One wielding great power brought hellfire down upon this world and no one survived. Her body tingled with a cold sensation—a warning.

She had overheard Solar and her father discussing the power of the mantle. It exacted a toll from each head of the council, a small part of the wearer's lifeforce and power. The artifact housed this energy in one of the vessels attached to it and grew in strength with each succession. The current wearer could call upon any or all encapsulated power as they saw fit.

Solar elbowed her.

Lykinnia blinked several times. Her obsession with the mantle ended with a shiver.

Aunt Melandri had joined the gathering at some point and smiled warmly to her. Azreala nor Vallerielle had made their appearance yet, neither of whom she could call aunt due to their age and the fact she had never met them before.

"...recent banishment, I would not expect him to join us." Father's gaze lingered on her for a moment as he glanced around the circle.

"Why is Azreala not here?" asked Uncle Dilantro.

Her father shifted uncomfortably. "I am reasonably certain she is with us, and therefore her brother, but hard feelings persist."

Uncle Jakarrak avoided her gaze. "Our young friend, Cymm, has been very instrumental in securing their commitment."

"What about Vallerielle? Has she contacted anyone?" Aunt Melandri scanned the group.

No one responded.

"I will try to contact her again," Terazhan finally said. "Now, for the main purpose of this meeting. I intended to awaken Melcorac yesterday, but when I arrived, he was already awake."

A collective gasp escaped everyone's lips, including reticent Aunt Schaleah.

"How is that possible? Only you should have had the power," said Solar.

Uncle Dilantro frowned. "Azreala or Feldarius?"

"No. I do not believe so. Nor do I believe the dragons that attacked us, a coincidence. Ledaedra remains a step ahead of us. Melcorac has changed significantly, not just in appearance but in demeanor. Actually, every aspect of his personality." Terazhan paused, struggling with something. "He—attacked me."

The quorum erupted in chaos.

Lykinnia fought to understand the now unintelligible speech. The words slowed, then instantly sped up, and her aunt's face became stretched and distorted. Everyone seemed to be moving sporadically.

Solar placed a hand on her shoulder and smiled reassuringly.

"That is preposterous!" Uncle Dilantro seethed.

A tall female materialized in the middle of the circle.

Lykinnia retreated a step.

Terazhan addressed the newcomer, "Where have you been?"

"I am sorry, brother, I lost track of time," she replied.

"Cute!" Aunt Melandri rushed forward to hug her.

Solar bent over to whisper in her ear, "Your Aunt Vallerielle, the goddess of time."

Lykinnia chuckled, understanding the jape. *Maybe she will be fun. Aunt Melandri seems to like her.*

"Take your places!" Father said brusquely.

His sisters hurried to comply.

"Melcorac travels this way. He would not follow me into the portal. I have promised him an attempt to restore his body using the altar." Terazhan stared off into the horizon.

Solar grumbled under his breath.

"So, then, it has begun?" asked Uncle Dilantro.

Father's gaze refocused, and he locked eyes with her for the briefest of moments. "It has. I expect everyone to prepare for their part and not to deviate from what we agreed to."

All heads were nodding and shifting side to side to check their neighbor's response.

Uncle Jakarrak leaned toward her father and whispered.

Terazhan eyes fell upon his daughter, then he said, "We will meet back here in a fortnight."

The council members disappeared as fast as they came.

"Uncle Jakarrak!" Lykinnia called.

He paused in front of an open portal.

"Lykinnia, you are with me." Father's tone did not offer any leeway.

Uncle Jakarrak glanced between them, then smiled. "We will talk later, Princess." He stepped through the portal and disappeared.

20

Friends

Cymm

For three days, Cymm holed up inside Stoneheart Silver in Delge, since returning from the Plane of Tides. Brogan remained oddly absent, and Grendella's mood soured as they waited.

The dwarven cleric launched into a new tirade this morning about healing the injured and feeding the starving in the dungeons. It lasted for an hour before she abruptly left. She aimed most of her rant directly at Solar, who had promised her a solution for destroying the ebony shard, which she still carried and protected.

Cymm sat in a chair—the same chair in which he had fallen asleep the first night—contemplating Grendella's mood. He had not known her long enough to discern how much the shard affected her. *If Dego is truly imprisoned in there, he must be trying to get out. I wouldn't want that burden for myself.*

"Cymm, watch the shop. I have to run to the market." Ibor disappeared before the young man replied.

Brogan was not the only one avoiding Cymm. He had not had any contact with Feldarius or Azreala since he had rescued her on Fire Island. Nor had he heard from Lord Terazhan or Solar. The absence of Lykinnia upset him the most. *She should have arrived at Delge by now or at least had contacted me. Maybe she can't without the altar. Where are my friends when I need them.* Cymm's breath caught in his throat. *Jenaleya must think the same of me. If only I had recognized her sooner. How could I leave her there?*

It will take me four or five moon cycles to travel there by horse, and once I arrive, I will have to battle through Ledaedra's entire dragon horde to save her. Not to mention, I need to kill them all, otherwise they will harry me the entire trip home. Where is Feldarius or Azreala? Or even Lykinnia! Any of them could open a portal for me.

The door to the shop opened. Ibor returned quicker than expected. "I found a friend of yours in God's Hammer Square, creating quite a disturbance."

"Who?"

The ethereal form of Lykinnia floated past the doorsill.

"Lykinnia!" Cymm rushed forward to hug her, then paused with the absurdity of the action. "Why aren't you here in person?"

"It is a long story, and I do not have much—"

"Then create a portal and walk through," said Cymm.

"No…I cannot do that," replied Lykinnia.

"Not even for a minute?"

"Cymm Reich, are you trying to get me in trouble? Solar would be very upset."

"I just want to see you in person."

She issued a deep sigh. "It is not a good idea."

"Please."

"Oh, ho ho, if I get caught, you are in big trouble. Lykinnia inspected the room. "Do not move."

Cymm's lips pursed, and she disappeared, only to be replaced by an ovular doorway a moment later.

Lykinnia walked through.

They rushed toward each other and embraced for several seconds.

"Tell me what happened." Cymm clutched her tightly.

"The short version is we were attacked on our way here."

"Is everyone all right?"

Lykinnia's face scrunched up. "Camak was seriously injured but will make it."

A loud pounding on the door brought Cymm's head around and caused Lykinnia to squeak before she turned invisible.

"Who are you talking to in there?" yelled Grendella.

"Lykinnia." Cymm glanced about unable to locate her.

The dwarf peaked her head in from the back room. "Well, keep it down."

"Sorry, I didn't realize you were—"

Lykinnia grabbed Cymm's arm, turning him invisible too. "What a grumpy goose."

"Lykinnia? Are you there?" A vaguely familiar voice echoed through the shop.

Cymm's head craned in every direction. "Who is that?"

"I am not certain," whispered the young miss.

"Lykinnia! It's me, Zaph—ZaphMordakai."

A knot formed in Cymm's gut.

"Zaph? Where are you?" asked Lykinnia.

"The Plane of Ashes. Ledaedra has taken me prisoner and plans to execute me. Please, help me."

"My last visit to the Plane of Ashes did not go so well, Zaph. I warned you this would happen." Lykinnia rubbed her temple.

Cymm glared at her. "You don't need to help him. He made his choices."

Lykinnia returned the stare with pursed lips.

"Ledaedra is coming. I have to go. They are moving me to Fire Island, to a prison. Cymm knows where. Please Lykinnia, I should have listened to you. Please, save me," pleaded Zaph.

Ledaedra's distinct voice called out, "What do you think you are doing?"

Zaph screamed in agony, followed by a long wailing moan. Lykinnia terminated the spell cutting off Zaph's pain-riddled roar.

21

The Dark Council

BrimStrakenstone

The colossal red dragon landed on the sky platform near the pinnacle of Fire Mountain. In no rush to enter, he folded his wings methodically. BrimStrakenstone chanced a glance at his destination within—the portal to the Plane of Ashes.

Brim sighed heavily. He despised using the portal and the angst it created in his bowels. At a snail's pace he shuffled forward, past the entrance to the prisoner's cavern. His head craned to the side, and he leered at ZaphMordakai, currently being held by an adamantine rack. The distraught look on the dark elf's face brought Brim much joy and relieved some of his distress.

I guess he would change positions with me in a second. With a final deep breath, Brim entered the portal. His first step out of the corridor and onto the plane landed in six inches of ash. It billowed up around his legs with each step, sucking the moisture from the air and his body. He coughed, but out of habit or necessity he was not sure.

Brim would have taken flight to cover the distance to the meeting, but the cloud of ash created at liftoff and landing would have been unbearable.

Even the Dragon Queen did not fly near her altar, the only thing visible in the area besides the looming volcano. Several figures huddled around it in eerie silence.

As the red dragon drew near, he could identify everyone in attendance, save one. The twin princes, Malekai and Marekai, were present, as well as Hymnoch, the god of chaos. Harendread, the surly giant, had not arrived, but a draconian priest stood comfortably in the group. Ledaedra remained motionless, talons held high, in a trance, possibly communicating with Harendread or Bardonril, both of which she expected to join in the near future.

BrimStrakenstone came to a halt, eyeing the acolyte suspiciously.

The glossy, scaly skin of the draconian glinted in the starlight, and seemed impervious to the incessant ash fall. "I am Rakai, mighty dragon."

"You are not welcome here. Return to Fire Island and your duties," the red dragon bellowed.

Rakai took a half-step backward with a smile but otherwise did not move.

An overwhelming despair filled Brim, and he knew Ledaedra's mind had returned to her body.

The queen will take care of this. It isn't my place anymore. BrimStrakenstone shuffled back into his position.

Ledaedra's eyes sprung open and navigated to each individual present, then came back to Rakai. "Did you introduce yourself?"

"Yes," replied the draconian acolyte.

"To everyone?" Dragon Queen persisted.

Rakai cleared his throat. "Everyone? Are you certain?"

Ledaedra blinked. "BrimStrakenstone, have you met the newcomer?"

"Yes, why is he here?"

Malekai leaned forward, resting his forearm on his brother's shoulder, the edge of his smile sharp as a blade. "Spy."

Ledaedra joined in. "Brim, meet our double agent, Jakarrak the Trickster."

Rakai's radiant skin shimmered with shreds and sprinklings of tangerine light, and he transformed into a nine-foot-tall humanoid. "I do not like that nickname," he rumbled, but with laughter in his eyes.

22

Twins

Azreala

The Plane of Spirits and the Plane of Shadows were neighbors in the space-time continuum, but distinct regions of existence, the master and denizens of each as unique as the terrain contained within. Since the awakening of time, a disturbance had always existed, a small partition of overlap between the worlds. No bigger than a breath, no smaller than an exhale, this tiny wedge of reality occurred twice each day—right after dawn and right before dusk. An instance that allowed both spirit and shadow to dance side by side or on top of one another. On a rare occurrence, one or the other would become trapped in the wrong plane or intentionally escape and would need to be retrieved. A long-standing agreement between Azreala and Malekai, Lord of the Shadows, existed and allowed her to cross into the Shadowlands to rescue any lost spirit.

Azreala could not remember how many spirits she had retrieved and had lost track of how many shadows she had chased back to where they belonged. Her current quarry proved quite difficult to find. It had eluded her for the past day and a half, but now she had it cornered.

She considered once again the misconception of this place as one of total darkness. *Without light, there can be no shadows.* It seemed so obvious to her. *Why do others not understand?*

Her pace slowed as she peered around the craggy tree in front of her. The crimson glow of the rogue spirit pulsed from behind a shattered onyx boulder.

Shadows trimmed in a violent haze flitted about her, observing as usual and preparing to report back to their master. A stinging sensation radiated through her left shoulder as one bumped up against her. Dozens of tiny, ice-cold needles pierced her skin simultaneously in a compact area. Not deep, but she wanted to scream. She clenched her teeth. *If I scream, I'll be chasing this spirit for another day and a half.* The pain dissipated within seconds as the creature moved on.

Azreala gazed toward the horizon and smiled. Phoenix—the giant crimson moon as well as her talisman and holy symbol—rose as quiet as a thief. With a deep breath, she crept forward on cloven hooves, navigating silently through the rubble and thatch.

Another shadow brushed against her right side, and she pulled up abruptly, barely avoiding a collision with a third.

Her eyes blazed a fiery red and her talons extended from the mini sheaths they were housed in. Red-hot waves of anger coursed through her mind while leaping upon the third shadow. Her talons ripped through the creature's neck and torso with lightning-fast strikes. Its violet shimmer pulsed once and faded before it hit the ground.

Hissing erupted all around her. Shadows emerged from every nook and cranny, their agitation obvious from the more brilliant shade of violet.

Azreala bared her fangs and crouched. She turned in a slow circle. "Do you want to join that one?"

She actually had no idea where *that one*—the one she had decapitated—had gone, but she doubted it was a nice place. The spirits and shadows were waiting in a sort of purgatory on their perspective planes, awaiting the decision of Feldarius as to which branch of the river they could travel down. He seldom varied from the presort she did. *Maybe they went into oblivion.*

Three rushed her in a frenzy, and she dispatched them with precision rakes.

Her tail and buttocks went numb when a fourth shadow stealthily attacked from the rear. Before the paralytic effect traveled down her legs, she leaped onto the onyx boulder. Dozens of shadows were charging and more appeared in the distance. She glanced down quickly, surprised the crimson glow from the spirit had not moved, and gasped.

The spirit lay prone, struggling against ethereal ropes, while tiny shadow wraiths assailed it. Every time a wraith pierced the spirit's ghostly body, it shuddered, and its crimson glow took on shards of violet.

I must help it!

Shadows clambered up the front of the boulder and ravaged Azreala's hooves. She kicked out at them and knocked several backward into each other. With numb legs she shifted positions, preparing to jump down. *Will I be able to free the spirit before the shadows overwhelm me? I will imbue it with strength so it can break free.*

Crimson tendrils snaked off the ends of her fingers, winding their way down toward the spirit.

Two large convulsions racked the spirit's form, causing it to moan. Its eyes snapped open, and its normally blank stare fixed on hers with a penetrating intelligence. It howled like a banshee.

"No. Stop!" She hurled herself at the wraiths and drained them of life and essence with a single pass of her tendrils.

Too late. The spirit's substance had been compromised. Its soul infused with the inky tar of a shadow. One of the ethereal bindings broke free, no longer holding its arm in place.

Azreala vaulted back to the boulder, but midleap an ice-cold hand latched onto her leg just below the shank. An icy chill rapidly spread through the appendage rendering it useless. She hit the side of the rock hard, knocking the wind out of her lungs.

Shadows swarmed the boulder.

The goddess of death slammed her free hoof into the face of the abomination, then scrabbled up the side of the onyx rock. Each talon seeking purchase as she clawed her way to the top. Her lungs heaved in the brief respite, knowing they would come. She had worked herself up to a seated position when the first heads appeared. Talons flashed, then she twisted and severed two shadow-heads as they crested the boulder's edge.

The swarm closed in, creeping up after her, clubbing and clawing her legs. Before she knew it, a numbing sensation infiltrated her body from the waist down. The chill crept toward her heart, which raced with panic.

"No!" Her lungs and lips continued to function, but for how long? She could no longer feel the pummeling her body took.

The fog in her mind made it difficult to concentrate, and she held onto one reoccurring thought. *If I die here, I won't be able to retrieve lost spirits for two hundred years. No! I can't die.* The atrocity committed on the spirit lying below her amplified her anger but did not enable her to move.

Without warning, the shadows receded.

She scanned her surroundings, struggling inch by inch.

A giant shadow cat appeared, the flat of its back six feet from the ground. Malekai's favorite form to assume. He prowled around the same craggy tree she had hidden behind a short time ago. Shadowy tentacles erupted from his ribcage to his shoulders and undulated in the air. Each time one snapped back in the opposite direction it initiated the release of a tiny bolt of shadow magic. The dark violet fur, short and sleek like that of a panther with lighter shades coursing through it.

"Thank you, Prince of Demons. Although, you cut it a little close."

Malekai stepped towards her as his head resumed its natural form. "I would not thank me yet."

From the other side of the craggy tree peeked the head of a hellhound—a crossbreed between a horse and a dog—its hooves burning with indigo flames. Malekai's twin brother—Marekai, Prince of Devils—had arrived. As you would expect from twins, their bipedal forms were more similar.

A savage howl from the distorted spirit startled her.

Her paralysis faded with each passing second, and she glanced over the edge of the rock. The side of the spirit head was caved in from where she had kicked it, but its metamorphosis had continued to advance. A dark indigo skin had enveloped the creature, and black horns had erupted from its head. As it rolled and writhed on the ground, a barbed tail sprouted from its rump.

Azreala swallowed hard. "Devikin," she mumbled, then pushed herself up on hands and knees, and finally staggered to her feet atop the boulder. *How is this possible? Devils and demons were banished from all planes of existence except their own.*

The brothers now stood ten paces away.

"Your visitor's pass has been rescinded," Marekai projected into her mind.

"So tough when your brother is here to protect you. Last time we met, you cowered behind your devils," replied Azreala only to him. *If he were alone, I might have a chance, even if he is three thousand years older than me. This is not his plane, but with Malekai here to shield him in his home world, I will be demolished. If I could locate his altar and lead him away from it, but it could be the craggy tree or this onyx rock I stand on, or a hundred other objects.*

Marekai, the hellhound, pounced forward. *"I will eviscerate your body and gorge on your heart!"*

She ignored him. "Malekai, my dear, are you going to let your brother take charge in your home?"

The shadow cat spun in a circle and transmuted himself back into the lord of this domain. Malekai, resplendent with a flaming halo arcing from one shoulder to the other above his head, brushed unseen dirt off his lapel. "Do not play me for the fool. I tired long ago of your petty squabble with my brother."

Azreala's strength returned with every second. "I expected you to take his side, just like the old days, which is why our relationship never had a chance."

With a cold calmness, Malekai said, "It could have worked. It can still work—"

"Just the two of us?" she asked.

"As I said before, I share everything with my brother." Malekai motioned toward his twin with a flourish.

"With the Lord of *Pain* and *Suffering*? I don't think so." Azreala nonchalantly scanned the vicinity for an escape route.

Marekai dropped his hellhound form and stood next to Malekai with a hand on his brother's shoulder, licking his lips.

The devikin roared. After completing its transformation, it proceeded to snap yet another ethereal band.

Now or never. Azreala punched her fist into the air. "Sinati avay drachma." A black cloud of smoke billowed forth, and her summoned hellsteed, coincidentally a gift from Malekai when he courted her, shrieked from the void. The plume of darkness concealed her beast until the very last second when it emerged with fiery red eyes matching her own.

Azreala took two half steps trying to time her leap onto his back, when a second portal materialized and her hellsteed disappeared. She flailed her arms, trying to stay atop the rock but only delayed the inevitable. She crashed to the ground only a few feet from the devikin.

The tainted spirit rushed her, launching itself at her face. Its razor claws swiped the air and her shoulder. Four thin red lines appeared. The final ethereal band had held, otherwise the damage would have been significant.

"Did you really think I wouldn't consider that?" Malekai glanced at his brother for approval, his halo sparkling vibrantly.

Marekai could not contain his glee and practically curled in a ball.

Azreala hurled herself at the lord of this plane before he turned back toward her. She hit him hard in the chest with a punch enhanced by necromancy.

Malekai's soul flew out the back of his frame. It flailed and clawed to maintain contact with his body and avoid almost certain death. Full separation would have occurred if his twin brother, Marekai, had not intervened.

Without hesitation, she turned and summoned her hellsteed once again while running straight for the onyx boulder, a dozen strides away. She jumped onto the side of the rock and pushed off with one leg, leaping onto her mount.

Simultaneously, the devikin broke its final bond and leapt over the boulder with horns and fangs gleaming. Time seemed to slow as the devil descended with snapping jaws. Its caved-in face causing its teeth to click and scrape in an eerie fashion.

Her hellsteed bucked and sent two flaming hooves into the devikin's chest, hurling it backward, then took off at a canter.

Howls and roars behind her inflamed her adrenaline. The twin brothers had transitioned back into their four-legged forms. The chase began.

Azreala dared to glance back. They were closing the gap, and the devikin outpaced even the twin brothers. *What do they want?* Something gnawed at her gut. She had argued with these two knuckleheads many times, but never had she worried about them killing her. *Why would Malekai revoke my permission to visit his plane?* She scoffed. *So, they can create more devikin.*

Time to leave, but not to the Plane of Spirits. If I flee to my home, they will follow, but they would never attack me if my brother were here. "Feldarius, I need help!"

Moments later, a portal blossomed in front of her, and she raced through it. Her heart jumped into her throat, making it difficult to breathe. A quick scan of her surroundings revealed a nightmarish land of fire, and the oppressive heat caused sweat to run down her neck immediately.

I am a fool! The portal was Marekai's, not Feldarius's. Azreala attempted to contact her brother again when he appeared before her.

"What's going on?" he asked.

"Why does your home look this way?" She dismounted and ran to embrace him.

"Your hellsteed entered first. You're shaking. Are you—" but he never finished his question.

Azreala turned to find all three of her pursuers exiting the portal.

Feldarius waved his arm parallel to the ground. "You are not welcome here!"

Flames shot up around all three of the trespassers.

The devikin howled and danced in a circle, lifting alternating feet, then sailed back through the still open portal.

Marekai, the devil prince, reverted to his natural form and stood unmoving as the soles of his boots caught fire and disintegrated to ash. With a devilish glare, he approached them. His skin and flesh scorched and attached to the ground with each step, and he ripped his foot free, leaving gruesome remnants behind. His foot appeared to regenerate before it struck the ground again.

Azreala would expect nothing less from the Lord of Pain and Suffering. She launched her chattering skulls screaming toward him, trailing wisps of crimson smoke.

Meanwhile, Malekai, her ex-boyfriend, burst into a cloud of bats and swarmed past his twin, intent on their position.

Streams of fire shot forth from the river at Feldarius's command and wrapped around him and his sister. Several bats were singed, a few more were scorched, and the rest broke off and flew toward the portal.

Marekai fought feverishly to keep the skulls at bay; Azreala had drained him once before. Somehow, he managed to summon his quartet of ghoulish apparitions and ordered them forth.

Two of her skulls latched on to his shoulder and calf, and she immediately engorged the wisps.

He ripped the one violently from his leg, then screamed, "This is not over! If you dare come back—"

"It's not your home, and you have no say," Azreala replied. "Besides, I hold the power to send all souls to my home and none to your brother's."

Marekai continued to scream profanities as he jumped through the portal. It closed behind him.

Feldarius shook his head. "This relationship you're chasing had better be worth it."

"He still wears the necklace we gave him. This will work," she replied.

"Then tell me we chose the right side." Her twin fixed her with a glare she knew well after spending one thousand, seven hundred, and eighty-two lifeyears together.

Azreala could only stare back in silence.

23

Truth

Lykinnia

The air above the Altar of One shimmered as heat rose off its surface. No surprise after baking in the sun all day.

Lykinnia sat on the platform, under the altar, contemplating her next actions. Terazhan clearly set expectations for her contribution to the master plan. After Delge, her travels would take her to City of the Mystics to seek an audience with Archmage Kazkackarus. Together, the two of them would determine how to free her mother from the chain running through her body.

If the prisoner even is my mother. Solar, Uncle Jakarrak, and my father all saw her. So, why did I see myself? If I use the altar to travel back in time and view the prisoner like my father did, would I see Mother or myself?

She glanced over and saw feet at the edge of the platform. Leaning out, she discovered they belonged to Solar.

"Is everything all right?" he asked.

Lykinnia returned to her former position without a word.

Solar dropped to his knees, then crawled under the altar. He rested his back against the other support leg, his head grazing the underside of the tabletop. "A little tight in here for someone like me."

This brought a smile to her face.

Solar leaned forward with his hands on his knees. "A lot has changed in a short time. How are you handling it?"

The young miss shrugged. "Do you think the prisoner is my mother or not?"

"I have no reason not to. Why?"

"Going to City of the Mystics could be a big waste of time. I have friends that need help, and I still have not been able to confront Uncle Jakarrak." Lykinnia interlaced her fingers and placed them under her chin.

"I see. What if we involve your father to deal with Jakarrak?"

"Perhaps. What about my mother? We need a plan to determine the truth."

Solar gently squeezed her leg above the knee, a tickle spot. "I think the plan is simple. Save the prisoner and hope she is your mother."

Lykinnia pursed her lips and gave him a do-not-do-it-again look. "Hope is never a good plan. Besides I am almost out of hope."

"We have no other choice at this point. Now, what about these friends who need help?"

She paused, unsure how much she wanted to share, then blurted out, "Ledaedra has imprisoned Zaph."

Solar pondered this information for a moment before shrugging. "Good riddance. He has been a nuisance from the beginning."

With a crinkled nose, Lykinnia replied, "You can be a nuisance, too! But I would never leave you to the whim of Ledaedra. Cymm and Grendella just rescued Azreala, maybe the four of us can release Zaph."

"This is more important than saving your mother? I cannot support this endeavor. Why would you do this?" Solar folded his arms over his muscular chest.

"Zaph's time is limited, and he may be dead already. Ledaedra has not killed my mother in four hundred years. I do not think she plans to kill her any time soon."

Solar raised his eyebrows and nodded. "Fair, but…"

Footsteps rang off the platform and stopped at the center of the altar.

Solar lifted his index finger to his lips.

Lykinnia giggled, a feeling of nostalgia washing over her as they recreated a childhood memory.

"I know you are under there," said Terazhan, "and you both have assignments you should be working on."

The young priestess placed her palms flat on the underside of the altar and teleported herself to Delge, leaving Solar to deal with her father. She immediately appeared in the last place she had seen Cymm.

Grendella screamed, stumbled backward into a chair, and unintentionally took a seat.

Lykinnia placed her hand over her open mouth. "Sorry."

Ibor and Cymm burst into the room moments later.

"Lykinnia? Why are you back so soon? I thought I wouldn't see you until tomorrow." Cymm returned DragonSin to his scabbard.

Dusting herself off, the dwarven priestess exited the room, pretending a scream never came from her mouth. With a huff, Ibor followed.

"I wanted to see you again." Lykinnia took a hesitant step forward.

Cymm rushed in and embraced her, lifting her off her feet.

She responded with a kiss on the cheek. "We have a lot to talk about. Have you eaten yet?"

"A while ago, but I could eat again," he replied.

Lykinnia started to clear off the table in the room and Cymm joined in.

She wiggled her fingers and chanted "Trevli mana byvar" to produce bread, cheese, strawberries, and a carafe of wine.

Cymm pursed his lips. "Wine?"

She handed him a glass half full. "I have a surprise to tell you and a favor to ask. Wine seems appropriate."

"Alright." He gently tapped the glass on the table and extended it to her.

"No, that one is yours," Lykinnia said, taking a sip from her own.

Cymm's mouth hung open with his glass in the air, but he shrugged and sipped his wine. "What did you want to talk about?"

"We need to rescue Zaph."

The young man froze mid drink. "He chose his own path. You said so yourself, and besides, it would be too risky."

"If you and Grendella were able to save Azreala, the three of us and Solar could save Zaph."

"Is that what this is about? Azreala?"

Lykinnia placed her hands on her hips. "No, but the circumstances are similar—"

"No, they're not. Azreala chose to fight with us and was taken prisoner. Zaph stood by Ledaedra's side as they chased us back to Feldarius's plane, then she took him captive." Cymm set down his wine chalice. "Although, it would be nice to release all the prisoners."

Her eyes narrowed. "Yes…it would be, but there is something you are not telling me."

"I know one of the other prisoners, Princess Jenaleya from Norfolk, but I have no idea what they want from her."

"The girl you saved from the dragon's lair?" Lykinnia nibbled on a cube of cheese.

"Yes. Why?"

"That means they have taken her captive twice. She must be a Descendant of Twilight. How many others were there?"

Cymm scratched the side of his head. "Um…four. What's a Des—"

"Descendant of Twilight. It is someone who has a demi-god parent and a mortal parent. There are several of us Ledaedra is trying to capture. She wants to drain our souls to increase her own power." Lykinnia sipped her wine and glanced at Cymm above the far rim as he started to babble. "Are you practicing that second language again?"

Cymm's mouth hung open, and his face had gone ashen. He soundlessly mouthed the word "us" as if it were a curse.

Lykinnia's heart raced, and she mentally berated herself. Butterflies swarmed her stomach. "I did say we had a lot to talk about." She placed a lock of hair behind her ear. "Terazhan—is my father."

For a moment, only silence, then Cymm's face contorted. "How could you keep this—"

She cut him off, voice trembling. "I never meant to keep it from you. It's just… there never seemed to be a good time. I was afraid of what you would think."

He shook his head. "Afraid? Of me?"

"No, of what it would mean—for us."

Cymm's head continued to shake slowly.

Lykinnia had already considered the ramifications for many months. Cymm would have labeled her a friend and run off with a princess given the newness of their relationship.

"What else aren't you telling me?" Cymm raised both hands above his shoulders.

Several responses ran through her mind, but none she could share. She cleared her throat. "Well, Azreala is my aunt."

Cymm burst out laughing.

Lykinnia joined in hesitantly.

He continued to chuckle, wiping the tears from his eyes. "This is crazy!"

"Cymm, calling your girlfriend crazy is not very nice," she said, trying to calm him down, even though his body language clearly indicated she had a snowball's chance on the Plane of Fire.

She slowly twisted her hips back and forth, clinking her mithril skirt. "I am still your girlfriend, right?"

Cymm choked on his own saliva and lurched for the glass of wine he had set on the table. He sipped it and stared at her. "We never really finished that conversation at your lifeday celebration. Setting aside your lineage, we still have a huge difference in life expectancy. I will grow old and die, and you will look as beautiful as you do today."

Lykinnia beamed at the compliment. "Azreala is almost twice my age and that does not seem to bother you."

"Because we are friends. We aren't talking about spending the rest of our lives together."

The young priestess lifted both eyebrows.

Cymm smiled. "Well, I'm not. Besides, I could never love a priestess of the Phoenix. Our philosophies are too different."

Satisfied, Lykinnia said, "I still have the surprise to share with you. Well, another surprise."

"I'm not sure how much more I can handle."

Where do I start? The butterflies returned and panic took hold within her.

Cymm rose and gently grabbed her hand and held it. "What is it?"

"Do you remember I asked you if you could live for two thousand years would you want to be with me?" she asked.

"Yes."

"You said you loved me."

Cymm gazed into her eyes. "Yes, and I still do."

Lykinnia reached out with her other hand to grab his free one. "Now, we can be together. I extended your life using my own essence."

Glowering, he forcefully withdrew his hands.

Her smile faded. "This is a good thing. Now we can—"

His face hardened. "You had no right to do this without asking me!" He retreated several steps and leaned against the table. "No right," he whispered.

For a long moment, neither spoke.

This is what we both wanted. How can he be angry? Lykinnia could feel tears pooling, but she refused to let them fall. *I gave this gift freely and asked for nothing in return.*

"How do I explain this to my household?" Cymm muttered, more to himself than Lykinnia. "I will have to watch them all grow old and die, along with their great grandchildren, and I will have barely aged."

With an outstretched hand she approached, intending to caress his arm.

Upon contact, Cymm flinched. "Lord Terazhan will be furious when he finds out."

Lykinnia remained an open-mouthed statue for several moments. "He already knows."

Cymm's hands shot to his head. "No. This can't be happening."

"My father is angry with me, not you. Now, how are we going to save Zaph and the rest of the prisoners."

Cymm's face registered no emotion. "I can't go. Lord Terazhan has asked me to perform a few miracles in the dwarven squares to improve his image and convert some of Bardonril's followers into his own."

"Then we will go tomorrow. I will calculate—"

"Lykinnia! I am not going to help you save ZaphMordakai. He is a vile, evil creature. Not to mention, an idiot."

"Were he evil, the altar would have taken his life when he arrived at the Peak of Power." Her gaze bore into his. "And he is my friend."

"Then you have poor taste in friends." Cymm's eyelids flared wide open.

In all the turmoil, she had forgotten Zaph's promise to kill Cymm. *Maybe Cymm is right, we should focus our energy elsewhere.* "Cymm—"

The young man cut the air diagonally with both hands. "No, I am done arguing. Leave."

Trapped energy coursed through her body, and Lykinnia's face flushed. "But I was going to—"

"If you won't leave, then I will." Cymm stormed out of the room.

With an ear-piercing scream, Lykinnia summoned a portal, then disappeared a moment later.

24

Miracle Worker

Cymm

God's Hammer Square filled quickly as news spread.

Cymm detached himself again from the little boy's grasp and stepped three paces away.

Brogan pushed through the crowd with ease. "What in the nine hells are you doing?"

"I thought you were avoiding me. Where have you been?" asked the paladin.

Grendella corralled the little boy and escorted him to his mother.

"Cymm, it is not safe for you to be out in the open. There are many who would see you dead for killing the assassins and starting a war in their city. Not to mention, a rumor has sprung up in the taverns of a hefty bounty on your head," said Brogan.

"I'm not surprised. Bardonril promised to get revenge. I think his exact words were—*I will hunt you down and kill you. All of you!*" replied Cymm.

Brogan wrapped his massive arm around Cymm and pulled him. "Come on. Let's get you somewhere safer or at least easier to defend."

Cymm shrugged off his arm. "Not yet. After this I'm leaving. I need to check on my household and home and make sure they are aware of what might be coming."

The pitter-patter of little feet preceded a giggle, then a groan. The young boy held fast to Cymm's leg again.

Cymm glanced down with his own groan.

"Why is he doing that?" asked the big man.

The crowd grew in size and volume, a mixture of excitement and anger. A rotten fruit splattered the ground near them.

"Up until this morning, he had never walked normally before, let alone run. He had a crooked back." Cymm knelt and gave the boy a final hug. "You need to go to your mother."

Brogan shook his head slowly. "I don't get you, Cymm."

"What's to get? People need help and I can help them."

"You ready?" asked Grendella.

Cymm nodded to the female cleric. "Let's get everyone in position."

Grendella's voice boomed like thunder above the excited chatter. "Anyone who wants to be healed needs to form a line here." She walked a straight path pointing at the floor. "If you are blind, deaf, paralyzed, or diseased, you need to stand here." She walked the same route backward.

The line grew quickly as dwarves guided or carried their loved ones to the appointed location, then stood behind them. Others came on their own, limping or crawling.

Brogan seemed physically shaken. "You can heal all these people?"

The paladin's shoulders lifted. "I'm going to try."

"He can't heal anyone if you're in the way!" Grendella placed two hands on his thigh and pushed. She might as well have been pushing against the trunk of an ancient tree, its roots buried deep within the ground.

Brogan seemed not to notice. He continued to stare at Cymm with an expression of amazement, then he turned abruptly and repositioned himself several feet behind Cymm. He drew his sword and put the point into the stone floor.

Cymm took a knee and began to pray silently to Terazhan.

Grendella had nearly toppled over when the big man moved, but she quickly regained her composure. She inspected those gathered and pointed at a woman. "You, come here."

The woman approached with her hands held wide by her hips, fingers spread, and frozen in place. She had pigtails and bulging biceps. "If I move them the skin cracks and bleeds. I burned them on—Oww!"

Grendella grabbed her hands roughly, cracking the blistered skin. Blood dripped upon the floor. "Terazhan, Father of Healing, please heal this woman's hands and provide her with comfort, so that she may return to her normal life." Grendella fixed her with a reassuringly glare.

Golden light blazed between them and quickly vanished, the agonizing pain on the woman's face with it. She remained transfixed as she wiggled each finger.

A boot flew through the air and struck Grendella in the face.

"Your false god is not welcome here!"

"These are the lies and the tricks of a shaman!"

Blood trickled down the dwarven cleric's cheek as she shook Cymm by the shoulder. "We need to start now," she said glancing at the crowd tentatively.

Agitators pushed through the line of sick dwarves and approached from the sides, but they avoided the rear where Brogan stood.

A hand grasped Cymm's wrist and a punch landed on his hip—nose-high on a dwarf.

Grendella staggered as a meaty fist from the crowd caught her temple. She crumpled as bodies crashed into her from all sides, driving her to the cobbles.

Cymm lurched to help her, but his adversary's grip on his arm held firm.

The sound of marching boots and clanging metal echoed from the far side of the square. Over the top of a sea of dwarven heads, he identified a squad of Red Axes as the source. He exchanged a worried glance with Brogan, then turned to address his own assailant.

Brogan sheathed his sword, grabbed a dwarf on top of Grendella, and threw him to the side like a sack of potatoes.

The newly healed dwarf with pigtails joined Brogan and dragged another dwarf off Grendella by the leg, but two more opponents tackled her from behind and drove her into the pile.

Cymm now had five adversaries upon him.

The Red Axes joined the brawl, and in the distance more dwarves were rushing into the square.

The protestors were successfully subduing them: Grendella lie unconscious, the pigtailed woman restrained, and Cymm driven to his knees. Only Brogan remained standing, but dozens of citizens and guards swarmed him.

The captain of the guard stood eye to eye before the kneeling paladin. "Cymm Reich, you are under arrest for the murder of—"

A boot hit the officer's back.

Seething, he spun to address the crowd. "I will have the head of who—"

Another boot hit him in the chest, followed by two more.

Cymm could hear another platoon of guards approaching from the opposite direction.

"Leave him alone. Let him heal these people," someone shouted.

"Arrest him, and anyone else who supports these blasphemers," replied the captain.

"They are heroes of the colosseum!" shouted another citizen.

A guard rushed over to make the arrest, but two more citizens had already voiced their anger.

Citizens were sounding off left and right, overwhelming the number of protestors. The forty guards from the first platoon were all engaged when the second platoon arrived.

"Cymm, the guild is here." Brogan gestured with his head toward the back of the square.

The newly arrived captain stared at Cymm twirling a finger through his beard. "Didn't I warn you?"

The young man stared back defiantly from his knees. The arrogant glare the captain returned infuriated Cymm further, yet something seemed familiar about him. Cymm focused on the twisted, braided pattern of his beard, and a smile came upon him like sunrise.

"Finally. I told you they would hunt you down in the city like a cave rat," said Captain Stormaxe, the guard from the front gates, the one who helped him get into the city. "If you still want to do this, get ready. Your window will be short."

Cymm took stock of his surroundings. Already the new squad cleared the area of citizens—sympathizers and antagonizers—and the original platoon of Red Axe guards.

Everyone complied, and a semicircle formed.

"Terazhan, use this disciple of yours as a holy vessel to show those gathered your power." Cymm rocked his head back, waiting for his lordship to arrive. However, only solid rock existed above; no light shafts were cut in the ceiling like other squares.

Brogan carried unconscious Grendella to stand next to the paladin.

The assassins are attacking, said DragonSin.

Help as much as you can. Cymm continued to search the far reaches of the square for a sign of Terazhan.

Guild members were writhing in pain on the stone floor alongside the guards they stabbed in the back.

A golden shaft of light streaked in through a tunnel.

Cymm tried to ignore the screams of agony all around him. He breathed in deep and braced himself a moment before the light entered him—not from above but from the side. The powerful impact bowled him off his feet without the ground to reinforce him. He rolled to his back, stunned.

Bones creaked and cracked. Muscles stretched and tendons groaned. Cymm's body stretched to nine feet tall, towering over the dwarves and even Brogan. As in the past, he had a difficult time viewing anything through the golden liquid pooling in his eyes. He caught glimpses of battle but naught much else.

In prior bindings, he could hear with total clarity, but as this sense faded, his vision returned like never before. He glanced down at his hands, greyscale and misty.

"No!" said Terazhan in a panicked voice. *"If our bodies separate, we will both lose consciousness. Do not move. Let me maintain control. For this spell to work, we must become ethereal yet remain consubstantial."*

Cymm had no idea what that meant, but he chose to limit his movement. The transparent golden liquid in his eyes allowed him to focus on the scene before him, an unusual delight. Captain Stormaxe and his guards were losing. Half of his men were already wounded or dead, and they fought against not only the assassins, but the other Red Axe guards.

Terazhan forced the avatar to walk through the first inflicted body, a blind young boy who had not moved since his parent placed him there. A pure white shimmer engulfed the inflicted and periodically gave off radiant bursts. The avatar passed through a second and a third patient, both paralyzed, followed by an identical response.

Within moments, four more suffering from an ailment were radiating light beams, and eight more after that.

Terazhan moved fast and resembled a firefly. The battle ground to a halt. Everyone stared in wonder at the spectacle. White beacons were springing to life throughout the square, not just in the line of the infirm.

With a final ear-popping, eye-burning burst, the lights went out.

For a heartbeat, no one moved.

A child screamed, "Mama, I can see!"

Guards near the brink of death were rising to make a full recovery.

Parents wept, hugging their rehabilitated children.

The healed pressed forward, reaching for Cymm, trying to touch him.

Miracles were everywhere: the blind could see, the deaf could hear, the paralyzed could walk, and the pain-stricken could smile.

Guards from both platoons were rejoicing and celebrating together. The two captains shook hands, then turned as one to face the real enemy: the assassins lurking in the wings.

Cymm's begging, praying, and demanding in the past had come to fruition. He smiled when a guard's sword impaled the first of many assassins.

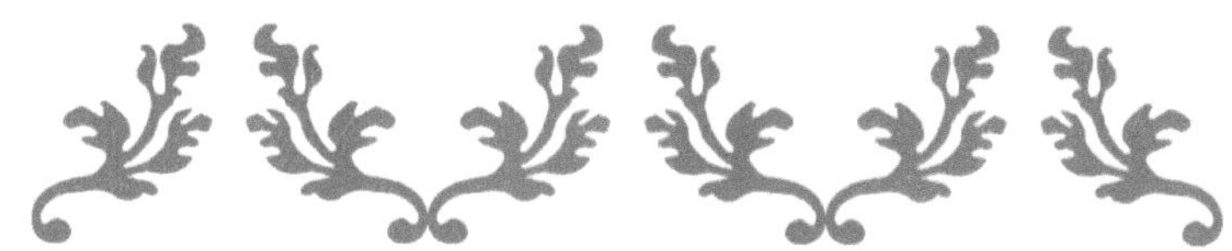

25

Blue Sunrise

Lykinnia

The sun peeked over the Knife-Edge Mountains, sparkling off each ice coated peak. A spectacular view that usually made Lykinnia dance, but today she felt sad.

How did everything get so messed up? Lykinnia shuffled her feet on her way to the altar. *I was about to apologize or at least agree with him. Did he want me to chase him out the door?* She sighed. *I should have chased after him. No! I am the daughter of Terazhan. He had no right to act like that. To be so…so…what? Jealous—envious—hateful?*

The tips of her toes came to rest at the edge of the platform by force of habit. Her head rocked up to find Father and Solar staring back. "What?"

"Is everything all right?" asked Terazhan.

The winged man ruffled his own feathers. "No singing or dancing? Did you eat a rotten tomato last night?"

Lykinnia gave him a sour face. "What is going on here?"

"I asked Lord Terazhan to assist us with Jakarrak. He is willing to question him," replied Solar.

The young priestess stepped onto the platform and stood before her father. "Why are you not upset with Uncle Jakarrak?"

"He is my brother," said Terazhan, as if the answer were obvious.

"But he manipulated you!"

"His deceit was not without benefit." He fixed his powerful gaze on her.

Lykinnia's face screwed up in confusion.

"You. My brilliant, beautiful daughter."

She tapped her foot as the sides of her mouth curled up.

"He is who he is. To expect him to be anything else is folly. It would be like him asking me to stop healing or trying to save the world."

Lykinnia and Solar scoffed simultaneously, then glanced at each other with a smirk.

Solar stomped off into a portal and disappeared without a word.

Her father's portal buzzed behind him. "I hope you are making progress on your task."

"I will figure it out," she replied, her chin high.

"I know. I believe in you. If anyone can figure it out, it is you." With a nod, her father vanished.

Lykinnia patted the altar with alternating hands to burn off her nervous energy. The drumbeat echoed hollowly in her ears. "I have to do this." Her conviction sounded weak. She cleared her throat. "I have to do this. Much better."

She closed her eyes, focused her mind, and cast her invisibility spell. After a deep breath, she exhaled and called out, "Mother."

"Mother? You must want something. What is it?"

"I have been thinking about your offer—"

"And?"

Lykinnia gritted her teeth. "And, if you release ZaphMordakai, I will listen to your plans about how we can work together."

The creature tsked. "How weak. You need not worry about him. He is a traitor and will not be with us much longer."

Lykinnia sighed in relief. *He is still alive.* "If not a deal, how about a trade?"

"You have nothing I desire."

"Oh, but I do." Lykinnia paused for effect. "I have a very powerful spell book—"

"I will kill Jakarrak, too," the creature hissed.

"So, do we have a deal then? ZaphMordakai's freedom for the book."

"Fine. Bring the book here and—"

"Nice try." Lykinnia shook her head. "You will release ZaphMordakai, and when he arrives here at the Peak of Power, I will open this portal and deliver the book to you."

"You do not trust me, yet you expect me to trust you. That is something your father would do."

The priestess's head tilted to the side and the matching shoulder rose. "I will take that as a compliment. Well?"

At length, the creature agreed.

Lykinnia closed the portal a moment later and returned to her abode. She had a lot of transcribing to do this evening.

26

Lamira

Azreala

The animal figurines lay neatly arranged on the nightstand, glittering and sparkling in the low light. Fifteen hundred years ago, Cavendar commissioned the finest gnome and dwarven artisans to carve them from the deepest, richest vein of tanzanite and they remained a vibrant violet hue. Azreala sat on the edge of her bed blankly staring at them. Over a dozen of these prized possessions existed—a pegasus, a hippogriff, a hippocampus, a chimera, and a faerie dragon were all present—but the griffin remained her favorite. This proud and majestic creature had always caught her fancy.

These precious heirlooms had come into her possession. Originally, Father had given them to her sister, Lamira—a millennia older than Azreala and charged with the tutelage of her and her brother. If she did well in her studies, she could play with them, and when she did extremely well, Lamira would summon one of the beasts—Azreala always selected the griffin. The figurine would grow to epic proportions and transform into a life-sized creature with tawny fur and white and hickory feathers. She had sat astride her friend and soared high into the sky many times, but that was a long time ago. Now, the carefully guarded power words to bring forth each creature were lost.

The demi-goddess shifted her position, then hoisted her favorite piece. One thousand years, and she could still remember the way the air ruffled her hair and fluttered her tail. A smile flitted across her features before disappearing an instant later.

Azreala shook off the dregs of the ill memory and tried to determine how long since she parted ways with Cymm—more than a couple of days, closer to a week—she could not be sure. *After he saved me, he returned to the city of Delge. I'll begin my search in God's Hammer Square.*

She retrieved her mostly untouched goblet of wine and swirled it, in no apparent rush to leave. *With him to boost my power, I could bend Marekai and Malekai to my will and end these demons and devils hunting me.* She sighed forcefully and took a sip of wine. *Power breeds independence. Even my reliance on Cymm will diminish and eventually fade away.*

Her mother's face came unbidden to her mind's eye. "Mother?" A sudden, vicious death had befallen her mother, according to her father, who chose not to share the details. *Lamira tried her best to raise us…if only I had listened, she would still be alive.*

Azreala squeezed the tanzanite statue, and it bit deep into the flesh of her palm. *Why did I follow Father?*

It was not the first time, either.

Azreala considered it a game. One at which she excelled. She would follow her father to his laboratory and observe him from her favorite hiding spot. After hundreds of successful missions, she assumed she would never get caught.

On this particular day, her father had summoned a hulking black beast—twelve feet tall, a stooped back, and its girth as wide as an ancient tree. She had seen him perform this task many times, after all, he was the Lord of Spirits—the original Necromancer.

The creature, a Balor—once used by her father to guide the evil spirits to the afterlife—carried a dark wooden staff and emanated an aura of power. Spikes erupted from its back amongst scraggly fur, which would spontaneously ignite and send glowing embers into the air.

One mighty combustion scorched most of its hair, and Azreala gasped in surprise.

The Balor groaned as its bulk rotated to spot the intruder. The pungent scent of sulfur and scorched hair wafted through the area in a thick haze.

Azreala froze, a result of her father's disapproving glare. She knew she had gone too far this time.

With surprising speed, the monstrosity whirled back around and struck her father with the staff so hard, he died instantly. His phylactery had not protected him; his altar inconsequential.

"No!" Azreala had screamed.

The creature turned hesitantly, unwilling to test the boundaries of the protective wall her father had erected.

Azreala scrambled to get away, but the glamor of the summoning circle faded. The Balor flashed an evil grin and charged. She crab-walked backward, whining and whimpering, her little hooves slipping and sliding. Her efforts proved futile, within a dozen steps the monster overtook her.

It stood tall and menacing, then raised its staff to pummel her. "Nothing should last forever, little one."

Azreala raised her arm to shield her face, cringing and shaking in terror.

Lamira raced into view in a blur of motion, striking the side of the creature's knee with a vicious kick that caved one into the other with a sickening crunch. Her sister had taken a defensive position between them with her sword, Dark Morning, in hand.

The Balor brought the staff down in an arc and pointed it at her. A long blade materialized at its tip.

"Return to your duties!" commanded Lamira, glancing back to ensure the safety of her sister.

The staff shot forward with speed the lumbering hulk should not possess, and Lamira barely dodged it by rolling to her side. She quickly returned to her feet and inspected the fresh gash on her arm before crouching. Dark Morning pulsed, sharing her sister's fury.

Azreala, now standing, noticed Feldarius approaching stealthily from behind the enemy combatant.

Sparks flew as magical blade rang against magical blade.

Thrust, counter, parry—Lamira's movements were quick and deft.

Lunge, advance, press—the enemy's were powerful and daunting.

This deadly dance continued back and forth with no advantage gained by either.

Lamira parried again and finally scored a successful hit on a riposte, lacerating the creature's forearm, then quickly ducked and rolled under its return swing. She beat a heavy cadence, driving it back, then pressed the attack again with several feints and reprises. After scoring several more hits the beast stumbled.

The Balor retreated and successfully defended a barrage of swipes and lunges, then stomped its back foot, magically drawing everyone's attention.

The battle paused, and the enemy's blade erupted from her sister's back.

The Balor lifted her several feet off the ground, smirking as she hung from the end of its polearm.

Once again, Azreala cried, "No!" She could not remember a time when she had felt so powerless. She hated and feared this feeling. It left her overwhelmed and bereft of any desire to go on.

Dark Morning fell slowly from her sister's limp hand, but before it struck the ground it arced and flew into her brother's grip. From behind, he cleaved spikes and hide, driving the sword through the monster's shoulder blade and into its chest.

The memory haunted her still, a great source of sorrow and a harbinger of wet cheeks. She quaffed the remains of her goblet. *No child should ever have to observe the death of a parent or sibling or endure the guilt of having caused it.*

Azreala gently returned the griffin figurine to its original resting place. In remembrance of her sister, she claimed the tanzanite statues, just as Feldarius had claimed Dark Morning for his own.

She dried her face with her palms and prepared to search for Cymm.

27

Origins

ZaphMordakai

The black panther padded softly up the winding trail, leaving the stream and occasional tree behind. His heart raced, but not from exertion. A fortnight had passed since he last saw Lykinnia, although it seemed longer, and he feared their reunion.

ZaphMordakai's rear paw lost traction on a loose stone. *How will she react when I arrive? Normal. She has no reason to suspect me, making my job easier.* His stomach churned. *Easier? Will it really be easy to turn her over to the Dragon Queen?* For his mother, he could do anything. How many times had she protected him, refused to leave him behind? How many times had she given him everything he needed to survive—food, shelter, and love? A stabbing pain lanced through his cranium, causing him to squint his right eye. *I will do this.*

He doubled his pace and before long arrived at the crest of the trail. The two sphinxes circled overhead like vultures. Neither had made an aggressive maneuver, but he had not yet stepped onto the plateau. He glanced over at the altar, then scanned the vicinity. *You would think their security would be a little tighter. What if I was*—he cleared his throat—*I am the enemy.*

After hesitating a moment, he transitioned back into his dark elf form, rubbing the scar on his neck. "Lykinnia?" He called twice more, then took a tentative step toward the stone breakfast table. "Maybe she is eating."

A sharp shove in the back sent him reeling.

"I doubt it. She ate earlier this morning," came a reply.

Zaph corrected his posture, slightly perturbed. "How much earlier?"

"Early enough to follow you from the woods to the stream, and up the mountain pass." Lykinnia materialized in front of him. "I wanted to make sure you were not followed."

Fear coursed through his body as he replayed the past couple of hours in his mind. *What did I say?* He had a bad habit of thinking out loud. "Thank you, Lykinnia. You are a true friend." Again, a pang of guilt racked his gut. *If I were a true friend, I wouldn't be doing this. Let's just get this over with.* "The Dragon Queen told me to remind you of the spell book."

Lykinnia hugged him awkwardly. "Of course, onward to my abode." She took the lead and glanced back.

I'm following. He forced a smile.

They walked side by side in silence for several moments.

ZaphMordakai glanced over. "It is good to see you."

"Is it? If you were truly concerned for your own wellbeing, you would not have gone back." Lykinnia's voice rose an octave. "You could be dead right now."

Zaph nudged her gently. "You sound like my mother."

"I am old enough to be."

"Ha ha." Zaph remembered back to a time not so long ago when they wagered lunch over who was the oldest.

"Actually, I am old enough to be your great grandmother," she quipped.

As they approached the door to her lair, Zaph's stomach gave another churning protest. A groan emanated from his belly.

Lykinnia peered at him quizzically. "Are you hungry?"

"I haven't eaten in a couple of days, but let's get this done first." Zaph made a distinct gesture toward her room.

She opened the door and entered.

The dark elf fell in line behind her and quickly rubbed his left elbow, validating the presence of the patch.

A tome rested on her table as a centerpiece.

"Is this the book?" asked ZaphMordakai.

"Yes. It belonged to my mother." Lykinnia stared down at her feet.

Zaph blinked twice. "Your mother's? How can that be?"

"She was a very powerful mage and the author."

"Oh," Zaph chuckled. "I thought you meant the Dragon Queen was your mother. She claims someone stole this spell book from her."

Lykinnia stared back at him blankly. "Possibly."

Zaph waited for more, but she said nothing else. *I don't have time for this.* "May I look at it?"

Lykinnia raised her shoulders.

He hoisted the tome with one hand while peeling the cantrip patch off his elbow with the other. His fingers trembled as he palmed the magical adhesive Ledaedra had given him, the sweat on his brow threatening to betray him. Fortunately, Lykinnia's gaze fell elsewhere, lost in thought. He took a deep breath and pressed the glamour to the spine. *This is for my mother,* he told himself repeatedly, but why then did he feel like a coward.

"So much fuss over this," he said, forcing a smile again. His thumb stroked the deep, rich leather of the cover. Its hickory brown binding had several patterns engraved in it—astrological, geometrical, and images of nature—that glittered a crimson red. Balancing the book on his palm, he waved his free hand over its surface casually.

Laughter burst from Lykinnia's mouth. "That's not how you check for wards or glyphs, silly. Do you think I would let you burn yourself?"

The dark elf finished his minor incantation and lifted the cover. "I know, just practicing. You should open the portal."

Her face quirked, but she flicked her wrist. "Travor makii lek."

The portal sprung open, and Lykinnia disappeared.

Zaph gasped and glanced behind him. "Where'd you go?"

"I am still here. This is part of the spell."

"I am here as well," came Ledaedra's voice from the void. "I have been waiting."

He thrust the spell book toward Lykinnia's last known position. "Here." Zaph's heart hammered. He felt her grasp it and tug gently, but his hands would not release, then grudgingly he let go, and a small part of his soul went with it.

Dread snuck up on Zaph. Now, Lykinnia will realize he is a traitor. Her disappointment will hang in the air like a fog, and the tone of her judgment will cut like a knife. At least her invisibility, a welcome boon, would spare him seeing the look in her eyes.

28

Home

Cymm

Stallion Rise rose above the sea of tall grass, resting on top of a hillock. The stalks nearest them swayed and bowed with the breeze, but they did not bend. Nor did they relinquish any of the seeds in their head and would not for a couple more months.

Cymm glanced at Grendella. "I can smell the—"

"To the nine hells with your berry bread!" interrupted the dwarf, but her stern mask melted into a smile.

"I really am looking forward to sleeping in my own bed." Cymm imagined his head sinking into his pillow.

"Two days and we head to Armak, no matter what," said Grendella.

Walking next to his mount, Brogan said, "And I get a new horse—a bigger horse."

"If you weren't so darn big, you could be riding right now. Maybe I will leave my pony in Stallion Rise and ride on your back to Armak." Grendella's head bobbed to emphasize her point.

Brogan rolled his eyes. "I can't wait to head home myself. It's been a while. After Armak…"

Cymm returned to his silent brooding, a habit he had acquired these past five days. He knew his friends were worried, but there was no cause for concern. This last battle in Delge had unsettled him. It had been somewhat balanced between the guards and the assassins, but the citizens had had enough. Once they joined in, the skirmish turned into a slaughter.

In the end, the torn and mutilated bodies of the guild members lay strewn across the square. Cymm could not purge the image from his mind of one citizen using the arm of a cutthroat as a club. After ripping it free, he had beat the other senseless and bloody, then the wild-eyed attacker spun and charged his next victim covered in blood and gore.

Each subsequent attack he witnessed did not compare, but they were all brutal and primal. A release of pent-up anger and fear. A need to protect their children and provide them a safer environment to grow up in. A desire for change.

"Ter—a—zhan!"

The hundreds of survivors had dropped to their knees in prayer and supplication, forsaking Bardonril. The power of the chant had rocked Cymm to his core.

"Ter—a—zhan!"

The god of healing remained in Cymm's body, basking in the devotion.

"Many innocent people died today. I wish it didn't have to happen this way," Cymm had shared with the deity.

"Do not blame yourself. I did not plan for this to happen. The revolt was inevitable. Think of all the innocent lives that will be saved with the elimination of the nightly assassin missions," replied Lord Terazhan.

Cymm could sense his lord's happiness; he had many new disciples. He also detected overwhelming fatigue, a frailty that had never been there before. When Terazhan had finally terminated the avatar connection, the evacuation occurred agonizingly slow. The final overlap of their bodies and souls had refused to let go. They had stretched and clung to each other until a reluctant snapback transpired and they separated.

Terazhan had floated away toward the exit tunnel swaying like a drunken sailor.

Brogan, Grendella, and Cymm had fled the city while DragonSin had serenaded them with his awful voice. The death of scores of assassins had invigorated him. The strength of their mental connection, the power of his life-draining force, and the intensity of his green aura all seemed to grow with the extermination of so much evil.

Cymm's lethargy after their separation caused a deep desire for sleep, but no more so than usual. He had leaned heavily on Brogan at times, especially up the Great Stairs to the front gates, and the big man had practically carried him to the stable and lifted him up on his horse.

Azreala could have rejuvenated me, or maybe not, it hasn't been a new moon cycle yet. Our miracles in Armak are going to be limited each day without the avatar form. They had decided to replicate the healing event in Armak, with the intention of converting new disciples.

They began the final approach to Stallion Rise, an abrupt climb in the dirt road.

Brogan remounted, and he shot Grendella a glare when his horse groaned. "Don't."

The dwarven cleric stared straight ahead, apparently oblivious to the groan and the comment, then blurted out, "Poor horsey."

Brogan sighed, Cymm laughed, and they entered the village center near the tower bell. A short trek brought them to the Reich farm barnyard, and they dismounted in the midafternoon sun.

From the porch a voice called, "Cymm Reich, get over here and give your auntie a hug."

"Does my favorite auntie have any berry bread for a beggar?" Cymm wrinkled his nose at Grendella.

"I sure do, although I baked it yesterday."

Cymm smiled at his friends and hustled over to the doorway where she waited. "Auntie Nové."

She hugged him back. "Well, come on in, all of you. You must be hungry and thirsty."

A whine, a whimper, and a growl emanated from around the corner of the house, then repeated, with some of the noises mixing to form new sounds.

"Maybe you should wait to come inside." Auntie Nové stepped inside quickly and closed the door.

A flurry of fangs and fur raced around the corner of the house and barreled into Cymm, knocking the wind out of him and driving him to the ground.

Jalko dispensed licks between whimpers, attempted to lay on Cymm, then rolled to his back on top of him.

Cymm groaned. "Get—" He groaned again.

Brogan rushed over to push the dire wolf off, but he only succeeded in getting Jalko's rump to the dirt.

Two high pitched whistles followed by a click froze Jalko in his tracks, then the wolf rolled to his feet.

Cymm struggled to his knees, then gained his feet while holding his ribs. "You taught him the horse whistles?" he asked, a moment before Talo crashed into him.

"Yes. He needs discipline, and he enjoys it." Talo eased up on the force of his hug. "We both missed you."

"I can see that, and I have missed you." Cymm pushed past him and gave Jalko a big hug around his neck. He proceeded to scratch behind his ears and migrated to the tickle spot on his ribs, the one that made his leg involuntarily kick like a jackrabbit. He finally grabbed Jalko's jowls and forced their eyes to lock, so he could push an image of love into his mind.

A lick from chin to forehead disrupted the communication.

"Cymm, we have a lot to talk about." Talo glanced around. "By Melcorac's hammer you're tall," he said to Brogan.

"Talo, this is Brogan, and you already know Grendella."

Auntie Nové opened the door. "People inside and wolves outside."

Cymm wanted to question why, then stopped. "What have you been eating Jalko? You stink."

While everyone took a seat, Cymm's cousins set plates of bread and cakes on the table, along with pitchers of ale and water.

Uncle Daro entered through the front door. "Am I the only one working today? …Cymm! I didn't realize you had returned."

"Hi Uncle. This is my friend Brogan. We are passing through on our way to Armak," said Cymm.

"And to Stormcrest," added Brogan.

"It is nice to meet you, and welcome back, Grendella." Uncle Daro shook both of their hands in turn.

"Well, sit down Daro and join them." Auntie Nové found herself a seat and a sweet cake.

"I am starting to get worried. What is going on?" asked Cymm between bites of berry bread.

Talo set his mug of ale on the table. "You told me to keep an eye out for anything strange, especially concerning Dirk."

Grendella wiped crumbs of berry bread from her mustache. "What'd he do now?"

"He has been acting very weird and stopped by several times looking for Cymm. He refused to tell me what he wanted, but I think we all know. Also, his interest in Jalko has increased because he thinks the wolf can track Cymm." Talo lifted his eyebrows to solicit feedback.

Cymm glanced from Grendella to her knapsack and back again. "We need guidance from Lord Terazhan or Solar. The sooner we destroy the ebony shard the better."

The dwarven cleric grunted, then pulled on the backpack straps. "Solar promised me a solution weeks ago. This package seems to get heavier every day."

"I could carry it for a while," offered Cymm with his hand stretched out.

"No! This is my burden to bear," barked Grendella.

Cymm's hand retracted as if burnt.

Grendella hung her head. "I'm sorry Cymm, but you in particular can never touch the dark shard. Even holding the backpack could put you at risk."

"At risk of what?" asked Uncle Daro and Talo simultaneously.

"I don't know, but Lord Terazhan specifically said Cymm should not touch the shard," replied the dwarf.

"Yet another burden to bear. Uncle Daro, we had an encounter in Delge again that did not go well for our enemies. Specifically, the followers of Bardonril, and there is a large bounty on all three of our heads," said Cymm.

His uncle rubbed his face with both hands. "You need to be more careful. Why do you continue to upset them?"

Cymm raised both hands. "We did not intend to. Our beliefs contradict Bardonril's. It's the same as last time—"

"Except this time Cymm healed dozens of suffering people with permanent ailments!" exclaimed Brogan. "It was a…it was a—miracle! The blind could see, the deaf could hear, crippled beggars that I have passed hundreds of times could now walk, and—and…well, lots of other things. It was amazing!"

Auntie Nové gasped and clasped her hands to her chest. "Oh, Cymm, how wonderful. Your parents would be so proud."

Talo smacked him on the back.

Uncle Daro smiled warmly. "I guess that more than makes up for a few upset dwarves."

Cymm shifted uncomfortably. "Anyway, you need to be on high alert. We were careful to make sure no one followed us, but any dwarves in Stallion Rise should be considered hostile and dangerous."

A low growl emanated from the barnyard.

Cymm and Talo locked eyes.

"Jalko, it's me, you silly wolf," came a nervous voice. "Cymm, it's Dirk, can we talk?"

"So much for sneaking out of town tonight." Cymm rose from the table. "Jalko, come here, boy!"

Jalko came immediately to the doorway, circled around behind Cymm, and walked at his flank.

"Hello, Dirk. Talo told me you need to talk to me. Is everything alright?"

A shiver went through Dirk's body. "Can we talk in private?"

Cymm glanced back to find at least seven heads peeking out of the doorway. With a sigh, he waved for Dirk to follow him toward his father's old barn.

"Where are you going, Cymm?" asked Talo.

"I'll be right back."

Grendella raised both palms. "Cymm—"

"I'll be right back." Cymm strode to the barn door and flung it open.

Dirk entered, followed by Jalko, and Cymm brought up the rear, leaving the door open.

"What is going on?" Cymm kept a reasonable distance between them.

Dirk spun with crazed eyes. "I need help. Only you can understand what I am feeling."

Cymm recoiled from the man who no longer resembled his friend. His eyes bulged and now appeared bloodshot. His clammy white complexion a stark contrast to his jet-black hair. He had also developed a facial tic.

Jalko growled and stepped forward menacingly.

"See, even your wolf senses something's wrong with me. I can't sleep and I barely eat." Dirk pulled on his own face.

"Jalko, come." Cymm pushed an image of when they first met at the River of Binding into the wolf's mind to settle him.

The dire wolf sat at Cymm's side, his head reaching several inches higher than Cymm's six-foot-three stature.

Dirk motioned with his chin. "You could be the Guardian."

"Do you see a war dog around here?" replied Cymm cynically.

Dirk took another step closer with sweat beading on his brow.

Cymm raised one hand. "More talkin' and less walkin'. What's going on?"

"It keeps calling to me. The black crystal I held in my hands. I think it is trying to tell me something. If I could hold it again, maybe this noise in my head would go away." Dirk smacked the side of his head as if trying to expel his demons from the opposite ear.

"Dirk, it doesn't work that way. It will kill you. Besides, we don't have it any longer."

Dirk inched closer. "The great Cymm Reich has never lied to me before. The intensity of the call and my discomfort have increased as you drew closer to home."

Cymm sighed. "I'm sorry Dirk. I'm trying to help you."

"Do you remember the thing that happened when we were younger that we never talk about?"

After clearing his throat uncomfortably, Cymm said, "Yes."

"I think it has something to do with that. I see blazing red eyes in my dreams, and I swear the voice is the same." Dirk shifted to pulling on his hair.

Cymm nodded slowly. "You might be right, which is another good reason to leave it alone."

"I don't know if I can, Cymm. Sometimes the urge takes over me."

Cymm blanched. *Takes him over. Does he mean like an avatar?* "You need to fight against this urge. Remember what happened the last time it entered your body?"

No response came.

"I have had many encounters with this creature, and it never turns out good for the person he enters. Most die. You were one of the lucky ones, and I don't think you will get lucky again."

Dirk kicked at the dirt floor.

Cymm squinched up his face. "Are you wearing my boots?"

29

Roots

Lykinnia

Lykinnia grasped the spell book, neither too big, nor too heavy, and certainly not cumbersome, with two caring hands, nonetheless. She always did, to ensure she did not drop it, but the tome had never leapt into her hands before. It was a strange feeling and left her unsettled, almost as if her hands and the book were magnetized.

"Give me the book," commanded Ledaedra.

"Not yet." Lykinnia set her mother's spell book on the table to peruse through it one last time but could not release her grip. After several moments it became clear that her fingers were not the problem.

By Melandri's good name, she grunted, *what is going on here?*

"Give it to me," Ledaedra said again.

The tome's leather binding, no longer content with sticking to her palms, stretched and engulfed her fingers one by one until both hands disappeared.

Lykinnia attempted a desperate spell—nothing. With a snarl, she tried again, summoning a tiny, searing light that fizzled, choked out by the queen's dweomer of anti-magic.

Ledaedra's green arm reached through the portal, palm up. "The spell book—now."

I have no choice but to lop off her arm again. "Trivoli lek manaca!"

Lykinnia became visible, but the portal did not close.

"Are you trying to deceive me? Abscond with the book and the prisoner." Ledaedra's green talon latched onto the other end of the book with lightning speed.

"Help me, halfwit!" Lykinnia's gaze bore into Zaph's.

ZaphMordakai stared at the ground and mumbled, "…my mother."

The leather cover now engulfed her wrists and half of her forearms.

Ledaedra jerked her toward the portal with one mighty heave.

Digging her heels into the floor, Lykinnia cried, "Zaph, help me this instant!"

The dark elf walked slowly toward her and grasped her around the waist. "I must save my mother." He pulled her back into his body.

Lykinnia found comfort in Zaph's initial heave, even though he delayed in responding. Her struggling renewed in earnest against the spell book and Ledaedra's pull.

ZaphMordakai hoisted her up, then drove her forward like a battering ram into the portal.

One—two—three—four—five steps and they passed through the chilly tunnel of ether and crashed to the ground. Ash billowed up around her, filling her nose and mouth. Lykinnia rolled to her back, covered in dust. It was deeper than she realized, and the six-inch deep layer made it difficult to move.

Zaph rose to his feet first and extended his hand.

"Get away from me! What did I ever do to deserve this?" she demanded.

His breath caught and he struggled for words. "Nothing. If your sister were still alive, I would have..."

Lykinnia sat up and flung the hair from her face. "You are not making any sense. I do not have a sister, and your mother is dead."

Zaph's eyes went wide, and his face paled as he stared into the distance over her shoulder. "Is that a—"

A powerful gust of air struck the dark elf in the chest and launched him back into the yawning portal.

Lykinnia lurched to grab his flailing arm.

The portal closed and she whipped around.

Ledaedra posed in front of her altar leafing through Sendaria's spell book. Behind her, a six-legged creature disappeared into a second portal, and immediately a third portal opened.

A ball of fire materialized in Lykinnia's hand. "What have you done with Zaph?"

"I thought you were a genius. How clever is it to attack me in front of my altar?" Ledaedra leaned forward and lifted her eyebrows. "Now extinguish your flame and come here."

Lykinnia doused her spell but remained unmoving. Her eyes drifted toward the captive still chained to the pillar beside the altar. Uncertainty besieged her mind. *Could it really be my mother? Why did everyone else see her, but I saw myself? Maybe Ledaedra had played a trick on me. Maybe she played the same trick on Zaph. My ethereal form could have changed my perception or allowed the demon to fool me.* She sighed. *Or ten other reasons and justifications to make it okay to believe that is my mother. With twenty strides I could be standing next to her, pushing back the sweaty hair covering her face, and settling this right now.* The muscles in her legs twitched uncontrollably.

The Dragon Queen followed her gaze. "Would you like another glimpse?"

Lykinnia withdrew from the precipice that would have allowed her to run to the captive seeking the truth. A truth that could be both liberating and condemning. "Where is Zaph?"

"He is at the Peak of Power, as we—"

"No! That is a death sentence. When they find me missing, they will kill him."

Out of the third portal came three robed figures with deep cowls to hide their facial features. A strange metal contraption hovered in the air before them, resembling the spine of a monster.

Ledaedra's nod brought them to a halt. "We had a deal. You turn over this spell book, and I deliver the traitor to the Peak of Power. The transaction is complete."

"You know that was not the intent of our agreement!"

"What do you care? He is a traitor, and not just to me but to you. He staged the entire hostage situation and brokered the trade. Now, what's your decision? An alliance or…" Ledaedra gave a flourishing gesture toward the metallic device. "A prisoner."

Lykinnia turned toward the three acolytes. *Zaph is a traitor. He just stood there and watched her take me until I yelled at him.* She shook her head with a sharp nasal exhale. *I thought he was going to help when he grabbed my waist, but he pushed me in.* Her gaze came up, and her eyes locked on Ledaedra's for several moments before turning back toward the three robed figures.

"So predictable," cooed Ledaedra.

The young miss spun back around with clenched fists, then bit her tongue and continued back in the same direction.

"Something to say, daughter?"

She spun again with her finger wagging. "Did you tell Zaph you were his mother, too? Is that why he is acting so irrational?"

Ledaedra set the spell book down on the altar, a shadow flickering behind her eyes. "His mother? What in the seven heavens are you talking about?"

"Here come the lies," said Lykinnia.

"Oh, I lie. I lie often and enjoy it. I lie about lying. In fact, I'm such a good liar, some might say I've perfected the art of lying. And yet, I still have no idea what you are talking about." Ledaedra growled the last sentence with her jaw clenched.

"Zaph's mother is dead. Why does he think she is alive?" asked Lykinnia.

"I don't know." Ledaedra walked through her altar and turned.

Lykinnia's body froze and only her eyes moved, shifting from side to side. "You are lying."

"Maybe. This conversation has become a bore and so have you. Last chance to work together."

Lykinnia had had enough. A fireball instantly appeared in her palm, and she rocked back to heave it at the demon and her altar. Cold metal clasped her wrist and her neck from behind.

him kill her, get my mother back, and finally kill Cymm. Might as well kill you, too, Lightning Finch.

The birdman's shoulders settled several inches. "If I had not seen the portal and you flying out of it, I would not believe your story, but you are leaving out an important piece. I know you were a prisoner. How did you escape and why did you come here?"

"Lykinnia told you?" Zaph gulped. "She made a deal with Ledaedra to trade the spell book for my freedom."

"Anything else?"

"That's everything," replied Zaph.

"This is madness. Come with me." The winged man waved for him to follow as he exited the room and turned to the left.

ZaphMordakai took a step to follow, then a more hesitant step. He could not fathom their destination. After two more steps he peeked around the door jamb to find his escort waiting.

"Are you coming?"

"Where are we going?" asked the dark elf.

"One door down. We need to talk to someone else," replied the winged man.

Zaph considered this for a moment, and his confidence returned. He fell in step behind him for ten strides or so. *How am I going to find Uncle Deton? Maybe at Fire Island?*

"Right here," the Lightning Finch indicated an open door with a wave of his hand.

If I can find the necklace and put it on, my uncle will come soaring after me. I wonder if his lair is still—

The door slammed behind him.

He charged the door and threw himself into it. "Let me out of here!"

Through a peephole wide enough to accommodate only three fingers came the Lightning Finch's voice, "As soon as you are ready to tell me the rest of the story."

"I told you everything. Let me go!"

His captor paused and waited. "No, you have not. I will be back."

ZaphMordakai's eyes flared wide open, and he called upon his magic. *After I blast the door, I'm going to blast you.* Not even a spark or a flicker came to his hands. He kicked the stone floor. *If I transform back in this small room, I will suffocate.* He found a seat against the far wall where the daylight from the peephole struck. The light conveniently hit him square in the right eye when he settled into position.

He drummed his fingers against the floor, covered in a thin layer of ash and soot. *I need to get out of here. She could be killing my mother now. What can I say that he will believe? I can't tell him about the deal I made with Ledaedra, which means I can't mention my mother, or that I tackled Lykinnia and drove her into the portal. How does he even know that there is more to the story?*

Now he drummed both hands against each side of his body. *Everything I have told him so far has been true. A few lies by omission, but I doubt his spells of truth detection would sense anything. Oh, by the seven heavens! He asked me if there was anything else, and I said, "that's everything."*

A guttural growl escaped his lips. *I need to get out of here! I have to give him something. What part of the story can I tell him? Or maybe I can distract him with tales of espionage. Yes! I will give him some of the Dragon Queen's plan.* Zaph fought back tears. *I'm sorry mother. I tried. I know you wanted me to be a general in the Queen's Army, but saving you is more important.*

Zaph desisted from the drumming and rested his head back against the wall. For the first time in his life, he began to hum.

ꝏꝏꝏ

A ruckus startled ZaphMordakai awake several hours later, but in his groggy state, had no clue of the source. He waited, listening. Moments passed until nearby shouts rang through his small chamber. Approaching footsteps beat a steady pattern. He jumped to his feet, with the intent of gazing through the peephole, when the thick wooden door exploded inward. Shrapnel struck the dark elf and flung him against the back wall with significant force.

The growls of the sphinx brothers reverberated through the room and grew louder with each passing second.

Zaph struggled to his knees.

In the failing light of day, a large skeletal figure loomed in the doorway, holding a massive, two-headed hammer. "What in the nine hells are you supposed to be?"

"What am—have you seen your own reflection?" asked the dark elf with a furrowed brow.

With clenched teeth, the skeletal being asked, "Where is the woman who lives here?"

"I have no idea. I'm a prisoner." Zaph glanced at the remains of his cell door.

The intruder hoisted his hammer and stormed away.

Zaph scrambled to his feet. *At least I was a prisoner.* He cautiously made his way to the entrance and scanned the area. A sphinx lay on the ground nursing a broken wing. The other sphinx and the winged man—already injured—were trying to keep him at bay.

The voice of the Terazhan boomed forth, "Melcorac, stop this nonsense, at once!"

With the snap of three fingers, the dark elf transformed into a black panther. *I would love to see this battle, but…* Without hesitation he slunk away.

As soon as he entered the safety of the orchard, he sprinted for the trail heading down. The sounds of the conflict rang out behind him as he started down the path. He gained the first switch back and scanned for pursuers but found none. When his gaze came back in front of him, he slid to a halt.

Coming up the trail were two humans in regal attire.

A wordless stare-down occurred for many seconds.

Finally, one of the men whispered to the other, "What do we do? Do you think this is one of the inhabitants Cymm spoke of?"

The other replied, "It's a panther. Cymm said people live up there."

Zaph transformed into a dark elf with a quick look up the mountain. "What do you want?"

They both retreated several steps and turned as if to flee.

"Wait. How do you know Cymm?" asked Zaph.

"King Varacek—Guardian of the Southern Border and Protector of Jannibar Pass—has sent us to the Peak of Power to deliver a message to Lord Cymm Reich," replied the first messenger.

"That's not what he asked. We traveled here with Lord Reich three fortnights ago to deliver the head of the dragon. He warned us that the people who live here do not like visitors. We apologize for the intrusion, but we are in desperate need of his help," added the second messenger.

Probably the head of BelCharius. If I had time, I would kill you both slowly. "Well, you will not find him here. Do you know where Stallion Rise is?" Lavender lightning illuminated the tips of Zaph's fingers as he peered up to the plateau. The sounds of battle no longer drifted down the mountain side. "I have to go."

"Thank you, good sir. Yes, we can find Stallion Rise."

Zaph froze mid snap of his transfer. "You can? We can travel together then, but we must hurry, my friends up there are very angry right now."

With looks of horror on their faces, they turned and sprinted down the switchback trail at breakneck speed.

Zaph completed his change to panther form and easily caught up to them. *It looks like we will have a happy reunion after all, Cymm.*

31

Descedants

Lykinnia

The manacles chaffed both wrists and ankles and the large vein in her neck throbbed against the collar. Lykinnia's limbs were going numb after only one day of captivity. Her arms were held out to her sides in a crucifix position but angled backward to push her torso forward—her legs were no different.

She tried to summon her magic, but the restraints glowed and sparked, counteracting her control of the spell. The adamantine shackles also drained her energy. A slow incessant drip she could not resist. The lethargy they created made it difficult to complete a thought. She found herself repeating the same phrase multiple times and struggling to recall common words. This alone could cause a failed spell to go horribly awry.

She glanced about the inside of a large cave with five other prisoners, who were also being held in metal contraptions. Immediately to her right slumbered a young, blonde female, approximately her age—well, not her real age. Given the others present, this had to be Jenaleya, the princess Cymm rescued. As she continued around the semicircle in the same direction she discovered: a half-orc human boy, an empty rack, a large gap before a stocky young man with fancy clothes, then a muscular dark-skinned man of middle age wearing only a breechcloth, a giant creature akin to an ogre, and finally a second empty rack.

Even though the sunlight streamed into the cave from the massive gap in the wall to her left, every captive slept. Beyond the opening a stone platform extended into the sky.

Her head bobbed and she quickly shook the haze out of her mind. She blinked twice and scanned the room again. Everyone floated knee-high above the floor. Her eyes fluttered closed, then snapped open. *I must be seeing things. I need sleep.*

The exhaustion overtook her, and she lost consciousness.

ထထထ

Lykinnia awoke minutes, hours, or days later—she could not be sure. Although, from the excessive amount of saliva on her chin and pooling on the ground below her, it had not been minutes.

A few prisoners were awake and in a subdued state, barely lucid.

The two from the Silver Dragon Order—that held Zaph prisoner—believe Ledaedra intends to drain our lifeforce to gain power. Is that what this is? She surveyed the diverse group. *Could all these people be Descendants? I doubt it. Besides, this is where Cymm rescued Azreala, and Zaph was being held, and they are not Descendants.* She glanced across the semi-circle at the empty rack. According to *Cymm, Azreala occupied an end location—that one or mine. He also said Zaph chased him out of here. I should have listened to Cymm.*

Lykinnia heart rate accelerated. *I thought the traitor was checking for glyphs and wards. What a fool I am. A blind, stupid fool. If anyone else activated a cantrip in front of my face, I would have recognized it immediately.*

Her anger counteracted her drowsiness. "Jenaleya, are you awake?"

A mumble.

"Shake it off," said Lykinnia.

Jenaleya turned her head toward the sound, her long locks falling into her eyes and mouth, muffling her response. "How do you know me?"

"I am Lykinnia, Cymm's…"

"…girlfriend. So, you're Lykinnia."

The priestess replied in kind, "And how do you know me?"

Jenaleya spit the hair from her mouth. "Cymm may have mentioned your name once or twice."

This brought a huge smile to Lykinnia's face. "I heard ZaphMordakai was here. Do you know him by that name?"

"Yes. He is the one who brought me here. It was very strange. He came and went as he pleased for a while, but a week ago I awoke to find him in that holding rack over there." Jenaleya motioned with her head toward the right and the empty one two slots away. "He wouldn't talk to anyone and cried out for his mother when he slept."

Lykinnia cleared her throat. "Anything else?"

"Yeah, he has issues. He—"

"We all do!" Lykinnia snapped. *You have no right to judge him.*

Jenaleya froze for a moment. "I can see that! As I was saying, he is trying to be two people. He saves me and my city by lying to his commander, then days later he threatens to kill me and Cymm…hmm, actually he promised to kill us. ZaphMordakai is obsessed with Cymm—with *killing* Cymm."

Lykinnia sighed. *Tell me something I do not already know.*

"Did you know he is a dragon?"

Lykinnia smirked. *I said something I do not already know.*

"What?" asked Jenaleya, confused.

"Sorry, this entire thing is outlandish. Do you even know why we are here?" Lykinnia's voice rose and garnered attention from others in the cavern.

"Because we idiots and got captured," said the big ogrish-looking captive.

Jenaleya whispered, "That's Ronks. He has no problem giving his opinion on…well—everything."

"For ransom, I say. My father will pay handsomely for my safe return," said the well-dressed man.

Ronks rolled his eyes.

"Leighton, I no highborn. No one pay copper to me," said the half-orc boy next to Jenaleya. He leaned his head out and looked past the princess to Lykinnia. "You's pretty. I Haskins."

"He says that to all the ladies," said Jenaleya.

"He never say to Leighton." Ronks let out a bellowing laugh.

Leighton shot the half-ogre a glare. "Ha ha. You're so funny, I almost wet myself from laughter."

"No, that was the drool from Lykinnia's chin." Jenaleya looked like a cat who had swallowed a mouse.

Lykinnia's tongue cramped from shock. Finally, she sputtered, "Oh, is that how things work around here?"

The wild cackling from Leighton mixed with the chittering from Haskins disappeared in spurts as Ronks's guttural, booming hoots overwhelmed them and gave Lykinnia a clear answer. She did take note that one prisoner—the dark-skinned warrior next to Ronks—did not participate or even look at anyone during the entire exchange.

"What is his story?" Lykinnia's chin pointed toward the silent captive.

Jenaleya glanced to the other side of the semicircle. "He doesn't talk much. All we know is that he is a prince from Toragan, and his name is Naterion. We call him Nate."

"Two princes and a princess, I am sure I can come up with a decent jape," said Lykinnia.

"I'm sure you can, but maybe we should focus our attention on getting out of here," Jenaleya said with a wrinkled nose.

Lykinnia tucked her chin and stared back at the hypocrite.

A raspy voice startled her.

"More talk of escape? If I withhold your nourishment, you will be too weak to escape." A cloaked figure materialized from the shadows of the far recess behind Leighton.

"No!" roared Ronks.

Jenaleya whispered, "He likes food."

"Shut up, Jena, or I eat you when we get outta here." Ronks thrashed against his bindings.

Another robed captor appeared with a large woven basket filled to the top with whole loaves of bread.

The original captor said, "Someone share the consequences of trying to escape with the new girl." He waved his index finger in a circle above his head and orange magical energy darted to Ronks's right wrist.

The clasp enlarged—more than double in size—so he could pull his hand through and grab bread from the basket.

In her mind, Lykinnia immediately began researching the components of the spell she just witnessed.

32

The Barn

Cymm

Brogan fed the cinch strap under the warhorse to Cymm, then returned to the head of the horse. He stroked the beast's head and scratched behind the closest ear. "I've never seen a horse this big in my life. I am going to name him Claymore."

Cymm grunted.

"What? You don't approve? What name would you give him?" asked Brogan.

Cymm gave the strap one last pull with his knee in the horse's ribs. "I don't need to approve. He is now your horse to care for. Come on, let's get the rest of our gear loaded."

"You should name your horse, Falchion, to match mine." Brogan came over to help with the loading.

With a dour expression, Cymm said, "You know we don't name our horses."

"And why is that again?"

With a huff of exasperation, Cymm replied, "We teach them whistles, and calling them a name confuses them. It definitely slows their learning process."

"I could call him Clay(whistle)more(whistle)." At the end of each syllable, Brogan actually whistled.

Before Cymm could respond, Grendella entered the barn with berry bread hanging from her mouth.

The young man visually inspected the contents of her hands and found two laden sacks. "Are you kiddin' me? You didn't bring me a piece?"

Grendella shrugged. "Last piece."

"Aww!" exclaimed Cymm.

"Besides, it tastes best warm. So, I had to eat them before they got cold." The dwarf set the sacks down near her pony.

"Them?" Cymm voice squeaked, then he stomped back to the pile of provisions.

Talo entered the barn with a backpack slung over his shoulder and Jalko at his heel. "Ma said to give this to you while it is still warm." Talo handed a half-loaf of berry bread wrapped in a cloth to Cymm.

Grendella and Brogan burst out laughing.

Brogan took a seat on a haybale holding his gut. "You should have seen the look on your face!" Another chortle escaped his lips. "Them?" he mimicked Cymm's voice as best he could, squeak and all.

Talo froze in a state of confusion, his eyes the only thing moving as he glanced from friend to friend. "What'd I say?"

Grendella approached Talo to collect the bread.

Cymm ripped it out of both of their hands. "What did I do, to deserve friends like you?" His eyes narrowed. "Why do you have a backpack?"

Pretending not to hear him, Talo drifted over to a far stall and led his horse out, already staged in the barn.

Jalko slunk over next to his cousin and would not look at Cymm.

"You're not coming," Cymm said brusquely to Talo.

He shrugged. "Then you don't get the other half loaf of bread."

With his hands on his hips, Cymm said, "Talo, it's not safe to travel with me. Ask Brogan."

Brogan stepped back two paces with his hands held up in peace. "Oh, no, you don't. I'm not getting involved."

A unique whistle sounded, followed by three short bursts, and Jalko rushed to his cousin's side, fangs bared. "I have a dire wolf that says otherwise. I'll be safe."

Cymm dropped to a knee. "Jalko, come here. Talo, you don't know what he went through. He starts to shake at the sight of blood."

"Not anymore. We've been training every day. Why do you think he smells so bad, and what do you think has stained his muzzle brown?" A slight tremor had entered Talo's voice.

A storm of images traveled from Cymm's mind's eye into Jalko's and a flurry of images returned. He sent another barrage, trying to convince the wolf to stay here and guard his family.

Jalko remained steadfast. He did not want to be left behind.

The barn door swung open again, and Uncle Daro entered. "Cymm there are three strangers here to see you. No dwarves, but one is a dark-skinned elf."

Cymm rose slowly. "Did you tell him I was here?"

His uncle swallowed hard. "You said to watch out for dwarves."

"Get these horses packed and slip out the back door, now! Talo, take everyone and my horse to our family rendezvous spot. I'll meet you there. Uncle Daro, tell him I will be out in a minute, then casually go inside and get everyone out the back door to safety," Cymm barked out the orders.

Brogan laid his hand on Cymm's shoulder. "There are only three of them. I think we can take them if there's a problem."

"Even if one's a black dragon?" asked Cymm.

Brogan turned slowly away. "Talo, it is not safe to travel with your cousin."

"Get moving, now," ordered Cymm. He himself helped finish the packing, then approached the barn door. With a deep breath, he heaved it open.

33

Bloodhound

Azreala

"This way!" yelled a dwarf, waving for others to follow.

Over two dozen dwarves trudged past Azreala, carrying common everyday items as weapons. A butcher's cleaver, chisels, wooden chair legs, and masonry hammers were only a few of the weapons being wielded.

A few moments later, their intent became apparent. From her lofty—almost seven feet—vantage point, she glimpsed their quarry, a dwarf in a long, stone-grey cloak. She tracked him for a couple of seconds until he disappeared into a wall.

Hmm, how strange. This should be interesting. She paused to watch.

Members of the chasing group called out for support. Several dwarves with polearms rushed over from the other side of the square, forming a semicircle around the section of wall where the grey-cloaked dwarf disappeared. The polearms dug into the stone and scraped horizontal trails at multiple heights.

A savage beast emerged from concealment, swinging wildly with a short sword in his right hand and stabbing with the dagger in his left. He injured two of his assailants and killed a third before the throng pummeled him to the ground, ending his life.

The goddess of death did not hesitate, sending his soul to the Shadow Plane—not yet ready to implement her threat to the knuckleheads. She dispatched the other soul and moved on.

She encountered similar events on every street. This vigilante militia combed through the city searching for members of the Assassin's Guild, likely driven underground by now.

Azreala paused outside a temple of Bardonril, intrigued by the commotion. A raid. The avengers drug several priests out into the street.

"Where are they?" one vigilante yelled into the face of a priest.

None of the priests spoke, even after the dead body of an assassin dropped in front of them. All three were beheaded.

After assigning their souls, Azreala moved on.

The atmosphere in the city of Delge—a dichotomy of hatred and happiness—continued to evolve and change for the past two days. She witnessed brutality interspersed with joyful celebrations.

Azreala roamed through the chaos, finding Cymm's trail at every turn. She inquired about him several times and numerous stories of his miracles bombarded her, as well as his extraordinary impact on the populace.

She checked everywhere—except for the dungeons—and she could not find him. *Maybe he is hiding with The Guild,* she japed. Her chuckling drew even more attention from the crowd in the form of stares and gawks.

The Maker's Square sprawled out before her, bustling with activity. She walked carefully to avoid kicking any dwarves or stepping on the children.

She squatted in front of a teenage child dancing fervently, although somewhat clumsy. "And why are you dancing?"

"Cuz I couldn't three days ago. Cymm and Holy Terazhan done fixed up my legs. So, I dance cuz I can."

Of course. "And do you know where Cymm went?" she asked.

"Terazhan done took him to the heavens to be with the other angels," replied the boy.

Hmm. Maybe back to the Peak of Power. She turned around and came to an abrupt halt.

A dwarven priestess knelt before her. "Are you the goddess of death?"

"Yes. Who wants to know?" she replied.

"Valmar Redforge. I renounce my former deity and wish to follow you." The dwarf gazed at the floor.

Azreala blinked twice. She had never had a dwarven follower before. "Why?"

"I no longer agree with the direction of my faith. There are others, too."

Bardonril is banished for two hundred years and losing followers every day by death and desertion. The thought alone made Azreala chuckle. She could only imagine his anger. "Up and follow me. We are looking for a young human called Cymm Reich."

"How shall I address you?" asked the priestess.

"Mistress, will do," replied Azreala.

"Mistress, Cymm has not been seen in four days. Many believe he has left the city."

Azreala's tail snapped whiplike in the air. "Shall I assume you were searching for Cymm to pledge your services, as well?"

Valmar swallowed hard.

"Not to worry. My path is currently aligned with Cymm's. Where did he go?" asked Azreala.

Valmar shrugged. "I have no idea, Mistress. Where do humans go when they leave the city?"

"Hmm. Good point. I need you to gather the *others* you mentioned and find out what they know. Be quick about it. You will find me here, in Maker's Square." Azreala stared off into the distance, watching the citizens climb the massive staircases. *Not even two moon cycles ago, I walked those stairs with a legion of dead at my side. A fortnight later and not too far from here, Dego showed me how weak I truly am.* She mulled her capture over for a moment. *I hate this city.*

She actually despised weakness, the feeling of powerlessness, and someone telling her what she could and could not do. She gritted her teeth at the thought. *Cymm is only one piece of the puzzle. He can help me gain control of the council and place the Mantle of the Gods on my shoulders—the two missing pieces—then no one will be able to challenge me, and I can begin my tour of revenge on the balor. Terazhan is a weak leader, he could use the power of the mantle to destroy Ledaedra and the dragons, bend everyone else to his will, and bring harmony to the planes.*

My reign will be different. There is no need for Seven Heavens and Nine Hells. The Material Plane should be hosted by sixteen planes of coexistence. One united realm of beauty and chaos, where souls roam free and experience a balance of joy and suffering based on the choices they make. Each plane's landscape appreciated for its uniqueness, and all threats and opposition crushed. I would create growth and harmony within the planar universe.

Azreala beamed with pride as she strutted around the square. *I wonder what Lamira would have thought of my plan. Her and father never appreciated my perspective, but Feldarius does.* Her pace slowed and her tail twitched. She opened a summoning link, but before she could contact her brother, a gaggle of priests pushed through the crowd toward her. She gazed across the square from four feet above the citizens and decided to meet them halfway.

Valmar led the group of over a dozen priests. "This is everyone I could find on short notice."

Azreala nodded, impressed. "These dark silver robes will never do. You will don robes of crimson, like the moon Phoenix."

Several dwarves glanced at each other.

"You've never seen the moon, Phoenix? It's the big red one in the sky." Azreala motioned toward the ceiling of rock.

Comprehension rolled through the group, and they began nodding.

"Forge Ember," exclaimed one.

"Yes. Forge Ember. Bardonril's great forge in the sky," said another.

Azreala's eyes burned a fiery red. "No! You will not call it that."

Valmar stepped forward and bowed. "Forgive us, Mistress. We will make the transition more seamless in the future. No one here has seen Cymm in two days. We'll ask around, but I doubt he shared his destination with anyone."

"I need to be on my way. You will pray to me four times each day until we form a bond, then I will decide what abilities I will share with you." Azreala shooed them away.

Now where was I? The only two places Cymm could've gone are the Peak of Power—where I'm not allowed—and Stallion Rise—which I can't find. Maybe Feldarius can help me track him. Hopefully, Cymm didn't get himself captured again. He never did answer my question about how he escaped from Ledaedra's grasp.

Another dwarf stood before her.

She rolled her eyes. *They're like stirges. They just want to suck you dry.* "What do you want?"

"You don't remember me?" asked the dwarf.

"Should I?"

A flash of anger washed over his face, and he turned to leave.

"Wait!" Azreala commanded.

The dwarf did not break stride.

Rage welled inside her, and crimson skulls circled her open palm. She cocked her arm back to hurl them at him and paused. "Ibor."

The dwarf froze midstride, casting a glance over his shoulder.

"Cymm's friend," said Azreala.

Ibor turned and faced her. "I hear you've been looking for him."

Azreala tucked her chin and grinned.

34

Departure

Cymm

Although not a bright, sunny day, Cymm squinted nevertheless when he stepped through the doorway. He scanned the barnyard and found the three men closer to his uncle's house than the barn. Two wore the garb of Norfolk sentries, causing Cymm to shake his head.

The other man was ZaphMordakai.

Cymm halted and called out to draw them away from his fleeing family. "What are you doing here?"

The three visitors approached.

One of the sentries replied, "Lord Reich, King Varacek sent us to find you. Princess Jenaleya has been taken hostage. He hopes you will help to rescue her—again."

ZaphMordakai performed a proper bow. "Lord Reich, it has a certain ring to it. Don't you think?"

"What are you doing here, ZaphMordakai?" asked Cymm again.

"Please, conclude your business with these dedicated guards, who helped me find my way here. I can wait."

Cymm accepted the gift of time. He recognized sentries, his travel companions Delemere and Trewellyn, knights for King Varacek. *I dare not mention they helped me transport the green dragon head from Norfolk to the Peak of Power or Zaph will kill them.* "I've already located where they are holding the princess."

"Wonderful news! We will help you rescue her," said Trewellyn.

Cymm shook his head. "I know you are both very brave, but there are hundreds of dragons guarding the princess. I need you to return home and tell the king that I am working on it."

Delemere shifted uncomfortably, looking to his partner for support.

"What is it?" asked Cymm.

"Forgive me, Lord Reich, but King Varacek expects us to return with you or with the princess," replied the sentry.

ZaphMordakai sniggered under his breath, "*Lord* Reich."

Cymm's eyes flared at the dark elf's comment, but he checked his anger and addressed the sentries. "Neither is going to happen. You need to trust me and leave now."

The sentries were not convinced and floundered where they stood in indecision.

Standing between them, ZaphMordakai roared, "Enough! He tried to save your lives—and failed." Instantly, he transformed into a black monstrosity, his sheer bulk hurling them in opposite directions.

Trewellyn smashed into the side of the barn with a crunch, leaving a bloody smear behind. Delemere hit the ground and slowly rose to his knees, fear etched in the whites of his eyes.

Cymm hastily unsheathed DragonSin while he inspected his enemy. The black goliath was about the same size as TetraQuerahn, the green dragon who had killed his family. A surge of confidence filled the young man.

The sword stirred with frantic energy. *"Cymm! I cannot protect you from the black dragon's breath. The lightning bolts will kill you!"* A long pause followed. *"And he intends to kill you."*

ZaphMordakai stretched his wings. "I told you your days were numbered, didn't I? Now you won't have time to save Jenaleya or Lykinnia."

Cymm lunged forward, hacking at the dragon, then continuing to run between his front legs and out the right side. The resulting laceration—much smaller than expected—caused his confidence to waver. *Where is Lykinnia?*

DragonSin launched his mental barrage with maximum intensity, attacking ZaphMordakai's psyche.

A deafening roar trumpeted forth from the dragon's maw, sending a shiver down Cymm's back. ZaphMordakai attempted to spin and chase his attacker, but the young man proved to be too elusive.

The paladin leaped over the dragon's tail and sliced his back in the process, then continued to circle around to his side and under his wing.

A whisper on the wind, barely audible, called out in agony, "He's over here. Kill him!"

Cymm had played this game before with the evil dragon spirit trapped in his sword—DraKarrion.

With one mighty swish of his tail, ZaphMordakai took half the roof off Otec's—now Talo's—barn, the same building Cymm had just exited.

The blade barely penetrated the dragon's right flank as Cymm drove it forcefully into the rugged scales. He pushed again—harder—and it pierced the hide a little farther. *I must keep moving.* He withdrew the sword and continued to circle, staying one step ahead of the dragon. He rushed through the tight space between the monster's front leg and the split rail fence and ran headlong into Delemere.

Cymm clipped the Norfolk messenger mid swing, knocking them both to the ground. A miracle neither had impaled the other.

Scrambling to recover his footing, Cymm stood, then spun into the snout of ZaphMordakai. They locked eyes, and the paladin retreated a half-step with an uneasy feeling in his gut. The hair stiffened on the back of his neck and a twinge of panic set in. He stared into pools of hatred, unable to break away, but continuing his slow retreat. The snap of lavender lightning arced between the monster's teeth.

A battle cry from under the dragon reverberated off the buildings nearby, and Delemere rammed his sword into the monster's belly with no effect.

ZaphMordakai whipped his head around, breaking the Cymm's trance-like state. The paladin's retreat abruptly ended as the upper bar of the split-rail fence pressed into his back. He scanned the ground, searching for DragonSin, then quickly glanced over his shoulder to where it lay, a few yards beyond.

A chill washed over his entire body. His sweaty palm reached for his chest as it tightened and squeezed the air from weak lungs. Inside a prison of ribs, his heart thundered and fought against the constriction. Crackling energy vibrated as it crawled up his spine and slowly dissipated in the muscle surrounding his neck, leaving him petrified.

As he recoiled from the monstrosity, bending backward over the fence his mind churned. *This is not rational!* He screamed at himself. *Jump the rail and grab your sword.* His body would not respond. *Maybe ZaphMordakai has turned me to stone like a basilisk.* Although, if that were true, his jaw would not be trembling, nor would the sharp painful seizing of his heart occur with every beat. He tried to swallow, but his dry mouth would not allow it. *If I can't break free of this dragon fear…*

Cymm's eyes fell upon the faded, blood heart painted on the fence rail. A parting gift from his mother prior to being murdered by TetraQuerahn. His vision began to tunnel, and the heart went in and out of focus.

A hiss drew Cymm's attention. His eyes came back around to find his attacker uncomfortably close, once again. The oppressive weight looming in the air and the acrid scent of decay washed over him in undulating waves of despair with each steamy breath. Blood dappled the dragon's fangs, presumably from the brave Norfolk messenger.

A raucous howl emanated from behind the dragon's bulk. Snarling and snapping filled the air.

No! Jalko, what are you doing? Cymm inched closer to breaking free of his paralysis. The ferocious attack continued, and he became more concerned for the safety of his canine friend.

The barking and growling abruptly ended with a *thump.* Then came a whine and a whimper.

"Jalko!" Cymm screamed.

"You finally regained control of your tongue. Any last words?" A brief chortle escaped ZaphMordakai's maw, followed by the sharp intake of air.

The weakness had not left Cymm's extremities yet, and he sighed. *How ironic. I will take my last breath only a few feet from where my parents drew theirs.* He gazed at the blood on the fence again and half-whispered, "This is where my mother died."

A catch abruptly ended the dragon's inhale.

Cymm clenched his jaw, rocked his head back, and glared at the dragon. "What is taking so long?" *Lord Terazhan, where are you? I need help.*

ZaphMordakai's eyes narrowed to mere slits. "What did you say?"

Cymm bellowed, "Get this over with!"

"Before that," growled the dragon.

Unconsciously, Cymm's gaze drifted toward the heart, which his mother had painted with her own blood. A message of love to her son in her dying moments. "Nothing that concerns you!"

ZaphMordakai furtively glanced toward the red spot on the fence. "What happened here?"

A tear meandered down Cymm's cheek unbidden. A tremor, originating from deep inside, blossomed into a full-blown body shake before he exploded. "This is where he murdered my family! Your friend tortured them, played with them, then killed them slowly. Can you imagine having to watch your mother die? Watch her bleed uncontrollably and there is nothing you can do about it. Or to promise your sister…" He trailed off unable to continue.

The black dragon's front talons pounded the ground in unison, almost knocking the paladin to the ground. The monster inhaled, gulped, inhaled further at a sharper pitch, then exhaled. A roaring screech and snap of power.

Cymm's skin prickled, and his hair stood on end. He closed his eyes involuntarily as hot air assaulted his eyeballs and streamed across his face. The predecessor of the lavender lightning.

35

Frog Face

Lykinnia

The mountain shook and dust drifted down from the ceiling. Outside, thunder rumbled and everything shuddered again. Shrieks of pain and roars of anger flooded the room through the massive opening to the sky.

Lykinnia blinked twice as the remnants of her drug-induced sleep faded away.

A dragon soared in and out of view in a flash.

"Did you see that?" Lykinnia asked a sleeping Jenaleya.

Ronks cleared his throat, half-awake. "I sees it."

"What is going on out there?" Lykinnia's gaze quickly shifted to the half-ogre and back.

Ronks shrugged as others began to stir.

The body of a blue dragon crashed onto the sky platform, smoking and exhibiting deep cuts along its flank and neck. Its eyes were glazed, and its tongue hung loosely to the ground.

Several more cries rang out from a distance and were immediately answered by a deafening roar nearby. A second round of threats and challenges went back and forth before an eerie hush ensued, replacing the previous madness.

A new commotion from inside the cavern caught Lykinnia's attention. Down past Jenaleya and Haskins, in the previously empty metal rack, a newcomer in a hunter green robe joined the party while they slept.

The young female, definitely an elf and a devout follower of Sehaleah, had unfamiliar mystical runes on the cloak. Still in a mental fog, Lykinnia could not determine if they were magical, clerical, or even druidical.

"Hey Frog Face, wake up!" yelled Ronks.

"That's mean!" Leighton yelled back.

Lykinnia's eyebrows knit together. "Aww."

"Frog Face?" asked Jenaleya, confused.

"He is not talking to you—this time." Lykinnia winked at the princess, who wrinkled her nose in return.

The new girl examined her surroundings in a daze. "Sehaleah, protect me."

Leighton stared at her, across the gap in their semicircle. "It's all right. You're safe for now. Look at me. No one is going to hurt you."

"Where am I?" she asked.

Leighton replied, "We are all prisoners in Dragon Mountain."

"Fire Island," corrected Ronks.

"Fine, Fire Island. I'm Leighton. What's your name?"

"Myra from Breezeport," answered the elf.

Lykinnia had a newfound respect for the Prince of Bruc. "Leighton, you are so kind and caring."

"Unlike ogre-breath over there," added Jenaleya.

"Hey," said Ronks with a scowl.

Leighton puffed like a peacock. "Well, she looks so lost, and scared, and—well…hot."

Jenaleya shook her head. "You're a pig!"

"More like a dog," said Lykinnia.

Ronks bellowed out a honking laugh.

Haskins finally stirred awake. He inspected the new girl next to him with a smile. "You's pretty."

Everyone joined in the laugh, including Naterion, their silent companion.

Unabashed, Leighton carried on. "So, Myra, how did they capture you?"

"Fazekas and I were out hunting for herbs and mushrooms when we became separated from my guards. They descended on us from nowhere. I didn't even have a chance to release a spell," Myra replied in a quiet voice.

Jenaleya's eyes rolled up into the back of her head. "Wait, guards? Why do you have guards?"

The elven girl froze with her mouth open, then clammed up.

"Are you royalty by chance? Maybe a princess?" Leighton asked with his eyebrows raised.

Haskins shot him an angry glare. "Give a rest. She's—"

"Yes," squeaked Myra.

"Ah ha," exclaimed Leighton. "This is not a coincidence."

"No, that doesn't make sense," said Jenaleya.

"But what do they want from us?" asked Myra.

Naterion, who normally stared at the floor, glanced up, his interest clearly piqued.

"Hear that, Haskins, you and me's royalty," Ronks said.

"No. No. No. It has nothing to do with the nobility," said Lykinnia.

"Do you know something we don't, Lykinnia?" asked Naterion.

His penetrating gaze caught Lykinnia off guard. *What should I share? No matter what I say, they will wonder how I know, and I am not ready to share who I am.* "Well, we are prisoners due to our lineage, but not what you think. One of each of our parents had a special ability they passed on to us. That is why we are being held."

"And how do you know this?" asked Leighton.

Lykinnia cleared her throat. "ZaphMordakai told me. The one who brought me here."

"What else did he tell you?" asked Jenaleya.

"He said he had to save his mother and that I have a sister, which does not make any sense," replied Lykinnia.

"He information make no sense. Maybe he wrong 'bout everything," Ronks grumbled.

A hush settled over the group as the draconian acolytes entered from the shadowed alcove with another large basket of bread.

Ronks's stomach rumbled.

Haskins giggled.

Lykinnia prepared to watch the spellcaster intently.

Once again, the acolyte waved his index finger in a circle above his head, but this time Lykinnia caught the slight flick of his little finger before a dark brown aura bloomed around his finger.

36

Thoughts of Weakness

ZaphMordakai

ZaphMordakai flew in a circular pattern, climbing above the smoke rising from the Reich Farm. His inner turmoil so fierce, his brain felt split in half and controlled by different entities.

"I shouldn't have done that. Why did I do that?" For as long as Zaph could remember, these cruel and haunting thoughts had plagued him, coming unexpectedly and definitely unbidden.

His mother had always calmed him afterward. "It's alright, Zaphling," she would say. "I have thoughts like these, too. In time, you will learn to control or hide them."

I do not like these thoughts. They make me different. They make me weak. At least that is what Uncle Deton had told him over and over.

He had tried to hide them from his uncle unsuccessfully. During one of his first training drills, they manifested, causing him to freeze with indecision. He expected the severe punishment he received that night and the entire next day.

Zaph balked at the reunion, but he needed to find his uncle and tell him about the trellbac. Ledaedra had fooled them all. Or at least everyone except his uncle.

Together they could save his mother and Lykinnia, assuming they still lived. But what would he say to her about his betrayal? And what would he tell her about Cymm?

37

A Trap

BrimStrakenstone

BrimStrakenstone's blood boiled. *How dare he attack our stronghold! He made me look like a fool.*

The colossal red dragon's body continued to quiver uncontrollably as the adrenaline coursed through him.

XanChilxakxus—the giant blue roll-call sergeant—flew up alongside him. "Why aren't we pursuing him?"

"He wants us to give chase, so he can lead us into a trap and attack with advantage!" boomed Brim.

"I don't care what he wants! He can't kill all of us, and he needs to pay for killing my son." XanChilxakxus replied in kind.

"Go ahead. Get yourself killed." Brim banked hard to the left, ending the conversation.

He landed heavily on the sky platform and roared in frustration. The carcass of the recently slain blue dragon partially blocked his path and destination—the portal to the Plane of Ashes. Without hesitation, he pushed it over the edge with one mighty heave to fall a thousand feet and hit the side of the mountain below.

Brim entered the main tunnel off the platform, avoided the prisoner chamber, and growled at a robed lizardman when he attempted to engage him. He paused before the portal and stretched his back in three directions, then entered the gateway.

"Who dares to enter? BrimStrakenstone, I did not summon you." Ledaedra gawked, unmoving.

A six-legged creature waddled and slithered into a portal on the other side of the altar behind Ledaedra.

Brim mirrored his leader in frozen consternation. *A trellbac. Why is she conversing with a trellbac?*

After an awkward silence, Ledaedra beckoned him forward with a wave of her green arm. "Come. I will explain. I've been trying to negotiate the release and safe passage of the remaining dragons from your home world."

It took exceptional effort for Brim to find his voice. "Even the elemental dragons?"

"No. They have already fled. Only your brethren, the prismatic dragons remain. The trellbac continue to hunt them mercilessly. If we can get them to the portal, they will be safe in this world," she replied.

"And the ranks of our army will swell. Are you close to succeeding?" Brim's eyelids lifting, waiting.

Ledaedra made a noncommittal movement with her head. "Yes. Now why did you come here?"

"DetonKonraber attacked Fire Island, killed a blue dragon, then fled, but there was no urgency in his flight." Brim drew in a deep breath and exhaled.

"You suspect a trap?" she asked.

Brim's eyelids flared. "Yes, and I fear several are planning to take the bait. Should I let them, or make a statement? There are a few I could make an example of."

"No. We need to set a trap of our own. Send two squadrons, but only to harass him. Tell them to drive him toward the Kharnal Mountains. I will have several trellbac waiting for him there." A sinister smile bloomed upon her face. Her needle-like teeth gleaming in the false daylight.

Brim roared and expelled a gout of flame. "No!" *What is going on? Why would the trellbac obey to her?*

"No?" The Queen of Dragons sported a strange expression.

"We cannot let your daughter's mad-scientist creations into this—"

Ledaedra lunged to strike and barely missed raking her claws across his snout. "You will not speak about my daughter that way!"

BrimStrakenstone knew he had gone too far, but he had made many sacrifices to ensure his offspring would have a better place to live. "There must be another way."

Ledaedra appeared to ponder this for a moment, or maybe she tried to determine how to punish him. Finally, she said, "We will trick him, but it will require a sacrifice—a red sacrifice."

Brim hesitated. *Sacrifice one for the many? As long as she doesn't think I'm going to—*

"There is a chance that only DetonKonraber will die if everything goes as planned." The queen chortled. "We will design it into our imminent attack."

Brim sighed in relief and conceded. "I will find a willing *sacrifice* and begin assembling the army, so they are prepared to leave immediately."

38

Unexpected Visitor

Talo

Talo invoked a mental prayer to Terazhan for Cymm's safety, a common occurrence this past year. However, he stayed true to his word and waited for his cousin. The family rendezvous overflowed with people and animals. Everyone had made it here safely, thanks to Cymm's quick thinking.

While pacing back and forth, Talo absently plucked his bowstring. His eagle eyes continued to search the horizon for a sign. He understood why, but he had effectively been left behind again—they all had. This was Cymm's battle, but it did not make it any easier to accept.

A loud, terrifying roar punched through the silent grassland like a warhorn, making him jump. The horses reared as the crack of thunder peeled through the cloudless sky.

A few moments later a plume of smoke appeared above the Reich Farm, drawing gasps and moans from his family. The din hushed as a massive black form lifted above the barns and silos and glided toward the bell tower before returning the way it had come, circling the column of billowing smoke.

"Jalko?" He glanced briefly over his shoulder at the rest of his party, then sprinted ahead. "Jalko!" He wove through the stalks of grass until he found a natural path, then bore down to accelerate his speed.

The bell tower clanged, grating his nerves.

The source of the smoke came into view; his demolished barn blazed like a bonfire. He continued at breakneck speed toward the inferno—its howl increasing with every step, and the heat washing over his face—until he rounded the corner and entered the barnyard. His steps gradually slowed to a stop as he tried to process the scene before him.

Cymm sat in the middle of the yard cross-legged with Jalko's head in his lap. He stroked the wolf's head and flank in an automaton state. Ash and blood streaked his face.

"No!" Talo lurched forward and flung himself onto the ground next to Jalko.

Cymm blinked slowly, dazed and confused, then recognition finally settled in. "Talo? It is not safe."

"What happened? How did he…" Talo sobbed.

Cymm glanced down, then back up. "The dragon threw him off his back and our buddy hit the ground hard."

Jalko licked Talo's face.

"But he should make a full recovery with a little more healing."

Talo continued to cry with interspersed bouts of laughter. He hugged Jalko fiercely. "I thought you were dead, buddy."

One of the messengers who arrived with the dragon joined them, his right arm hung limp and useless, and blood ran down the side of his face from a gash in his head. It dripped onto his armor in a steady cadence.

Cymm detached himself from Jalko carefully, then rushed to help the sentry to the ground. "Delemere, you do believe in Terazhan, don't you?"

The injured man stared back blankly.

"Probably not the best time for a sermon. Lord Terazhan, Lord of Healing, please grant me the power to heal this man's wounds." As Cymm recited the prayer, the air grew cold and still. A sphere of pure white light appeared, then engulfed them, returning warmth to the immediate area.

Talo had never seen his cousin perform this awe-inspiring feat before. Visible beneath the light's veil, the blood no longer dripped, and the wound closed. A droning hum filled his ears, then subsided with the aura.

Grendella and Brogan entered the barnyard cautiously with weapons in hand.

"Is everything alright?" asked the dwarf.

"What in the nine hells happened?" asked Brogan.

Cymm rose and pointed to Grendella. "Heal Jalko. I'm going to check on Trewellyn."

"He's dead," said Delemere. "He was dead before the barn collapsed on him."

Brogan stared into the sky. "What makes you think the dragon isn't coming back? We should get out of here."

Cymm slowly shook his head. "I don't know. I have no idea why I'm still alive. He had me pinned against the fence but took his anger out on the barn. His head snapped back around to lock eyes with me, and he roared in my face, then left without a word. I have never been so scared in my entire life. Even after I had accepted the fact I was going to die, I could not shake the fear. It felt like a parasite inside me."

"It is the way of dragon fear. You can't fight it naturally. The priests of Azreala and Feldarius have spells to combat feelings of terror." Delemere dusted himself off.

The tolling of the bell tower ceased, and villagers arrived with questions and concern.

Cymm met them with patience. "The attack is over. You can go back to your homes."

Many lingered, whispering amongst themselves in smaller groups.

A speechless Vena, still shaking, made her way over to hug her husband, Talo.

His father and Head of Household approached Cymm with a haggard appearance and a lack of energy. He clamped a meaty hand on his cousin's shoulder. "They're scared, Cymm. Dragons, magic swords, and dark elves. When will it end?"

"I wish I knew. It might get worse before it gets better." Cymm made to leave.

A firm grip on his cousin's arm brought him back around to face Talo's father, away from the blazing barn. "You're dragging him into this."

Cymm pulled his arm free. "No, I'm not. Talo's pushing himself in."

"I don't want him to go with you. He just got married, and he has responsibilities here." His father's voice cracked, and he ran his fingers through his sweaty hair.

"I agree, and I told him he should stay here with Jalko where—"

"But he's capable of making his own decisions." Talo had heard enough. He gently separated himself from Vena's embrace and moved to join them. He could feel the energy coursing through his body, and a new spine of steel had formed. He was ready for this argument, but from the glares of his father and cousin, so were they.

Talo attacked. "I'm tired of being told—"

Daro and Cymm both followed Talo's gaze to find Dirk Darkmane entering the barnyard. All three issued a collective sigh.

"Is everything ok, Cymm?" asked Dirk.

"Now is not a good time." Cymm waved his arm in a circle, indicating the mess.

"I just wanted to make sure you were alright." Dirk's shoulders twitched up and down twice.

And steal the dark shard if he wasn't, thought Talo.

"Yes, everything is good." Cymm stepped out of a cloud of smoke, a gift from the shifting wind.

"You can leave now," said Grendella, joining the group.

Dirk's brow furrowed. "Very well. If you need help rebuilding, let me know."

The villagers of Stallion Rise gasped, shrieked, and moaned, drawing everyone's attention. A mother grabbed her child and ran for the far corner of the burning barn.

From the smoke-shrouded alley between the two main barns came a figure taller than any man—a nightmare. Her horns gleamed, her goat-legs crushed cinders underhoof, and her eyes like twin forge embers swept the crowd.

Talo strung his bow in seconds. "Cymm, what is that?"

"No!" Vena collapsed to the ground, shrieking. "No."

His father took a half step back. "By the nine hells…"

Cymm charged, but Brogan and Grendella delayed.

With a grunt, Talo released an arrow and nocked a second.

The arrow bore down on the creature's head but at the last second her tail slapped it from the air.

"Talo, stop!" Cymm turned to face him, weaponless, and waving his hands.

Crimson skulls of smoke appeared in her hand, and she hurled them at Talo. They chattered and howled as they raced toward him. The sneer on her face transitioned to ecstasy when the skulls struck their mark.

Talo's eyes flitted and he began to shake. His notched arrow released and flew skyward over the blazing barn. "It burns…it burns!"

"What are you doing?" Cymm shouted at Azreala. He lunged through the insubstantial crimson tendrils, waving his arms to break them apart.

A bead of sweat trickled down Talo's temple, and his knees buckled. "What is going on? What is that thing?"

"Not what, who. This is Azreala, the goddess of death." Cymm rushed to help his cousin regain his feet.

"Maybe you should have gone with the Necromancer or the Lady Taker," said Azreala with a grin.

"You could have hurt him! You can't attack anyone here. I shouldn't have to tell you this," scolded Cymm.

"Fine. I wouldn't want to end up a prisoner in a horse stall. Speaking of prisoners, how did you escape from Ledaedra's shackles?" she asked.

Cymm cocked his head. "Shackles? I was never her prisoner."

Grendella joined them, but Talo took note that Brogan did not.

Azreala scowled. "I saw you chained to Ledaedra's altar on the Plane of Ashes before I was taken prisoner."

Cymm shrugged.

The Head of Household, Daro, approached Cymm from behind. "Most of your family and fellow villagers are huddled together, cowering, and those that had any sense have already fled. This is what I was talking about. Now we add demons to the list."

Azreala addressed him directly. "I'm not a demon, but several are headed this way."

Talo placed a reassuring hand on his father's shoulder, as a wash of anger flooded Daro's face.

39

Tougher

ZaphMordakai

Sleep would be a sweet relief from the nagging thoughts running through his waking mind, but he could not afford to rest yet. He wanted to find DetonKonraber. He would start searching in a place he knew well, his uncle's lair. At least four days of hard flying would bring him to the heart of the Scorpion's Tail Mountains. His destination lay hunkered in the deep bend.

Clouds and wind whisked by ZaphMordakai's wings. *Why did I allow Cymm to live? I could have killed him a dozen different ways. A massive lightning bolt would have ended it quickly but biting him in half and tasting his blood would have worked too. Or I could've raked him with my talons, eviscerating his—*

He roared into the sky.

I need to stop this. I chose not to kill him for a reason. He did the same thing I would have done if given the chance…avenge the death of my mother. In fact, if I'm honest with myself, I'm jealous he succeeded. I wanted to kill DetonKonraber that day in the cave, but he assured me he didn't kill my mother. I thought he meant the other dragon—the dead dragon—had killed her, but maybe he knew all along she wasn't dead.

His brain hurt, an intense pain forming behind his right eye. He did not like change; he abhorred change. For over three hundred years he had intentionally avoided this place. He could not comprehend where all those years had gone, some sections of time were a blur. However, the days of his captivity all came rushing back. His detainment had lasted nearly seventy-five years, all while wearing that infernal collar with the magical tracking device. The collar also had the capability of transferring a soul rending jolt of energy, conspicuously similar to the pain the goddess of death had dealt him, but far less potent.

The days with his uncle were horrendous, filled with physical abuse, but paled in comparison to the mental manipulation. His lips curled into a sneer.

There were some good days, though. Zaph's inner eyelid glazed over…

He had recently turned fifty lifeyears, marking a point in time where he had spent more than half of his life with his uncle. No longer a wyrmling, he was considered a youngling. Which apparently did not matter to his mother who had recently called him "Zaphling" as an adult of four hundred lifeyears.

His uncle had proclaimed, "From this day forward, you will hunt for your own food. I don't want you to eat from my leftovers anymore. If you can't hunt, then you will starve."

Zaph had spent the next few days unsuccessfully scouting. Most of the prey in the vicinity had already been eaten or frightened away, at least in his area of confinement between the mountains and the river.

On the fifth day, with his belly rumbling, he came across a monstrous owlbear—bigger than him. After crossing the river, the creature paused momentarily to shake the collected water from its feathers and fur, then charged through the forest.

Still airborne, Zaph continued to follow at a distance. Eventually the owlbear slowed and crawled into the dense underbrush. He took note of his shadow and landed downwind of his prey. Not much larger than a horse with a long tail, he crept up to the thicket and entered, planning to attack from the rear. He bumped into the hard, smooth surface of a beak instead of the expected fur and feathers in the rear and lost the element of surprise.

The owlbear lunged and grazed his head. Before Zaph could clear the brush, three claws raked down his flank.

Once in the clearing, the fleeting thought to flee flooded his mind, but he shook it off. He breathed in deep and launched a lightning bolt straight into his adversary, then charged. Unfortunately, so did the owlbear.

They collided with grunts and groans, shrieks and roars.

Zaph lost his footing and the owlbear drove him into the ground. He slithered out the proverbial backdoor and found himself behind his enemy. With a savage growl, he ravaged the hindquarters of his prey with tooth and talon, then fired off another lightning bolt as the bear turned. In its final death throes, it inflicted several more gashes, then slumped to the ground.

To cook the meat further with a crispy coating, ZaphMordakai expelled one more bolt of lightning at the owlbear.

The terrain around him rumbled as a large body touched down behind him.

Beaming with pride, Zaph turned. "Uncle, I did…"

A dragon, not DetonKonraber, approached.

The stranger's red scales glinted in the sunlight. "Move along, wyrmling. I've been tracking this bear for days."

Zaph stood his ground. The right side of his face twitched, revealing his upper fang.

The big red dragon chortled. "Easy killer, or I might eat both of you." He lunged and his jaws snapped shut, barely missing Zaph's neck. He then pounced and pinned Zaph on his back, one large claw digging deep into his chest scales.

Zaph bit down deep into the talon inflicting pain upon him. His attacker withdrew his paw hastily, allowing Zaph to roll free and recover his balance before swiping the air in front of him. He connected with the huge dragon's snout, drawing blood.

The red dragon's face registered shock, then anger as he began to shake. He bellowed in Zaph's face until his eyeballs quivered.

Another dragon landed, heavier than the first. DetonKonraber sent tremors through the ground.

The red dragon inhaled deeply.

"KorEmberstrike, you better hope that kills both of us," Uncle Deton said. "Otherwise, your dead."

The intake caught in the red dragon's throat, while his eyes scanned side to side. He exhaled slowly. "The owlbear is mine, not your son's. I've been tracking it for days."

"He's not my son. Did you kill it?" asked Uncle Deton.

The giant red returned a wordless glare.

"I killed it," replied ZaphMordakai.

"I didn't ask you." DetonKonraber turned to the red dragon. "My nephew might be much smaller than you, but I guarantee he's tougher."

Zaph replayed those beautiful words over and over again in his mind while puffing his chest.

KorEmberstrike bristled, both nostrils flaring. "Watch it, snake."

Many dragons believed their species evolved from snakes, and the less intelligent individuals possessed an unevolved reptilian brain. After twenty-five years of angering his uncle, ZaphMordakai could detect the nuances in his facial features.

The shadow passed from DetonKonraber. "Let's see who is tougher." The large black dragon brandished a long, razor-sharp, solitary talon. "Who will submit to the removal of a digit."

"I'm not playing your stupid game," red dragon replied promptly.

"I will!" ZaphMordakai placed his paw upon a boulder without thinking.

Uncle Deton nodded, and Zaph detected a hint of pride in his smirk.

KorEmberstrike's head slithered down in front of the youngling with a menacing stare.

DetonKonraber said, "Don't hold it against him. Fire dragons aren't known for their courage or toughness."

When the red's head snapped back to his uncle, three talons raked deep across his face. "If you ever hunt my land again, I will kill you."

They stared at each other, issuing throaty growls.

Zaph anticipated a battle—in truth, he desired it—and retreated a few steps. Although equally matched in size, his uncle's fighting prowess could not be matched.

The red dragon acquiesced and side-stepped to leave.

Uncle Deton fired off one more remark, "And no one touches my bloodline except for me."

After two steps KorEmberstrike leaped into the air and hit several tree boughs as he fought for elevation.

When his mother died, his life became one bad day after another, strung together for years, but the memory of this day always made him smile. A better day would not occur for many years, until he liberated himself from his uncle, joined the Queen's Army, then finally made captain.

So, now what do I do? Continue to my uncle's lair, dredging up the life I escaped from. I have no other options. I need my uncle's help to save my mother. Lykinnia would have helped me…

Her words burrowed into his mind, *"This is why you have no friends, Zaph. Even when you finally get one, you betray them."*

ZaphMordakai fiercely clenched his jaw, and a fleeting thought came to him. "No, that is a ridiculous idea. We are not friends either."

After a moment's consideration, he said, "Although…he does owe me his life. Would he help me?"

He exploded in anger. "He has no choice! I will make him help me."

"But how could he possibly make a difference?" Zaph sighed extravagantly. "He was able to rescue the goddess of death from Fire Island. Maybe together, we could figure out a way to save mother."

"Yes! And I could tell him about Lykinnia. We could save them both."

The black dragon wheeled about and headed back to Stallion Rise to find Cymm Reich.

40

Following

Cymm

The parade of characters demanded attention as it drew near the gates to the city of Armak. Farmers, merchants, and other travelers merged with the band, but no one dared to harass or harangue them. Most gave them wide berth.

The giant woman on a hellsteed—its hooves aflame—garnered the most attention, which had nothing to do with her own cloven hooves or the horns sprouting from her head.

"Azreala, dismiss your mount." Cymm glanced nervously in several directions.

The goddess of death did as requested. "I thought you liked attention. Should I expect to see a statue of you in this city also?"

This caught Brogan's interest, the second tallest and largest member of the group. "What's this?" He encouraged his warhorse to inch closer.

Cymm shook his head. "I have no idea what she is talking about—yet again."

"I haven't slept, eaten, or prayed in over a day. I don't have the patience for this." Grendella closed her eyes while riding her pony, whether to pray or sleep was not obvious.

Which left Talo in the rear. He dismounted and summoned Jalko with a sharp, shrill whistle. The dire wolf immediately trotted up next to him, and Talo gave his scruff a pat.

With a sour glance at the dwarf, Azreala continued. "I visited the town of Copper Rise on my way to find you, and I did—find you—in the town square. A statue as tall as a hill giant with your sword raised over your head and your foot planted firmly on a dead gnoll's body."

Cymm groaned. "They didn't."

"Oh, yes, they did, and the town bard was more than happy to sing me a song about your heroism," replied Azreala.

Brogan belted out a chuckle. "I'm going to be a bard when I return home. Maybe you could teach me the song."

"Now you're talking to me again?" Azreala glared at the big man.

Cymm grit his teeth but understood the strife between them. The party had hastily left Stallion Rise the same night ZaphMordakai had attacked, in search of the demons and devils chasing Azreala. They planned to hit the flank of the fiends hard and lead them away from the village…

∞∞∞

Azreala led the way, retracing her path. Everyone sat up straight in their saddle peering into and over the tall grass, but even on their mounts, spotting the enemy would be difficult.

Cymm slowed the group to a trot as the sun sank lower in the sky. Longer shadows were dancing through the grass, and everyone's head swiveled every time the wind rustled through the stalks. He examined his cousin, who had a short sword unsheathed to inspect it.

Cymm had decided to let Talo borrow the magical sword from the green dragon's lair, where he rescued Princess Jenaleya.

"Stop," Grendella called out in a low voice. "What is that?" She pointed toward the southeast and a dark patch.

Everyone stared, but no one answered.

A growl precipitated Brogan's grunt. He crashed to the ground—knocked clear of his horse—with a purplish horror on top of him.

"Ride!" shouted Azreala to the others.

Cymm glared at her, then issued three short clicks and a long whistle.

His warhorse retreated and kicked, delivering a powerful blow that collapsed the creature's ribcage.

Brogan rolled to his feet with a few deep scratches and rubbed his shoulder. He stormed toward Azreala. "You were going to leave me again?"

The goddess's face contorted. "No, I was—"

"More of those things are coming!" yelled Talo with his bow already strung.

Brogan sounded his own unique whistle, and his warhorse approached with a snort and muscles twitching. He swung his leg over quickly and glanced about.

"Let's go!" urged Cymm. His warhorse lurched forward.

Within the span of ten breaths, Grendella's pony fell behind.

"Keep riding!" yelled Azreala.

Cymm's face took on a red hue, if the heat were any indication. "What is wrong with…"

Ghostly skulls of crimson floated in the air cackling and chattering around Azreala as she whirled her hellsteed about.

In confusion, Cymm called out, "Keep riding!" However, he spun around backward to watch. *What in the nine hells is she doing?* As he stared at her retreating form, a thought flitted through his mind, *Why does the grass not catch fire from the hellsteed's hooves?*

Skulls danced all about Azreala and her mount, more than he had ever seen her deploy. Her hands shot down to her sides, slashing the air diagonally. The chattering apparitions sailed forth wailing at their targets. They never seemed to miss.

He could not count the swooping skulls swarming the Necromancer like angry hornets until they zipped straight forward leading a thin crimson fishing line. Cymm shook his head in disbelief—there were ten. *Her power is growing quickly.*

The violet-skinned creatures barreled forward at an impressive speed. All six of them ran like apes, arms forward, knuckles on the ground. Some of them were hit by two skulls, and one by three. The impact hurled them backward, flailing.

Azreala guided her mount around to follow after Cymm, dragging the creatures through the grass behind her. Waves of energy pulsed down the wispy fishing lines and into her body. One creature, then another, bounced off the ground and stretched the skyward limit of its tether.

As the bodies blackened, the thrashing of limbs diminished.

Before the goddess of death returned to the group, the first desiccated corpse disintegrated and blew away in a cloud of dust and flakes with the wind. She pulled even with Cymm. "Turn around. We need to get to Armak as quickly as possible. There are at least a hundred back there…maybe more."

"We can't stop for the night—can we?" asked Cymm.

"If we do, we will never awaken," Azreala replied without hesitation.

"What were those things?" he asked.

"The weakest of the demons. Calendri. We should hope their stronger brethren do not join the hunt."

Cymm pushed his mount to the head of the column. "Slow the pace. We're riding straight through. Grendella…we will need light spells to guide our way."

"I'm on it. I have already cast a spell to help our mounts, especially mine," replied the dwarven cleric. "One of us needs to heal the singer." She motioned toward Brogan.

Cymm chuckled. "I got it. You keep a steady pace, so your pony makes it through the night."

However, the pony's endurance waned, and they had to pause, then walk.

Everyone glanced about apprehensively and jumped each time the wind made the grass whisper.

Azreala did not linger long. She galloped the perimeter on patrol, feeding her hellsteed with the energy drained from the calendri. Her exceptional speed slightly blurred her appearance around the edges.

The shifting lunar positions indicated midnight approached. With only the moon Phoenix currently illuminating the sky, Cymm could easily trace Azreala's path around them, because the hooves of the hellsteed lit the surrounding grass like a lantern.

After Azreala completed her third loop with a significant arc, Cymm began to relax, but wailing and snarling soon drew his attention. He expected to see the familiar skulls orbiting her head, but not this time.

Two calendri ran in a berserker-like frenzy, howling and hooting. First left, then right, and several other seemingly random directions before finally sprinting back the way they came.

Azreala returned to the group. "We need to pick the pace up or kill the two demons I sent running. They will return."

"Why didn't you drain them?" asked Cymm.

"I can't use that power again today, unless I'm in you." She gave him a double eyebrow lift followed by a wink.

Cymm quirked his red cheek while shaking his head. "Must you make everything so brazen?"

"Relax. I'm just trying to have a little fun. You know…turn your face the color of Phoenix. Have I told you how cute you are when you blush?" Azreala put on a little pouty face to antagonize him.

Cymm ignored it. "Your power has grown significantly since the last time we fought."

Her eyebrows both raised in affirmation.

He lifted his voice, "Alright let's get going. We still have many hours till Armak."

The rest of the journey had been similar, with one more rest, and they all had breathed a sigh of relief when the walls of Armak rose on the horizon with the sun.

∞∞∞

Cymm dismounted and walked beside Azreala. "What a chaotic night, huh? Hey, are you taller?"

Azreala smirked. "As you said before…I am *growing* more powerful."

The young man issued a groan.

"What? That was a good one," she said in response.

Grendella abruptly dismounted her haggard pony. "What was a good one?"

Cymm rolled his eyes. "Azreala made a jape about—"

"Oh, never mind then," Grendella responded quickly.

Cymm attempted to stifle a laugh and spittle flew from his mouth. "Now that was funny." He continued to chuckle, flaming the intensity of Azreala's eye color. "Relax. It's not personal. The competition to be funny in this group is quite intense."

"We will see who's funny when I visit you tonight while you're sleeping," Azreala said coyly.

Cymm's face scorched red. "You will do no such thing!"

Grendella burst into laughter, and Brogan joined in.

"See, I *am* funny!" Azreala tossed her hair about.

Leading his warhorse, Talo ambled as close as he could with Jalko on his heels. "What's going on?"

"Apparently I'm the butt of the jokes again," replied Cymm.

"Ahh, and I missed it?" Talo smirked devilishly, and Cymm punched his arm.

The guards at the gate wanted nothing to do with the formidable-looking group and passed them through unchallenged.

A few unkempt children were playing in the street, and Cymm recalled almost trampling one of them during his last visit to Armak. "We should continue to walk our mounts."

One of the young boys gaped at him with wide eyes, then took off running. "Cymm is coming! Cymm is back!"

The other children hurried after him.

One glanced back. "Are you sure?"

Another chimed in, "How do you know?"

Brogan glanced at Azreala. "Not one statue—two statues."

"Whatever," said Cymm amongst the many snickers. "Let's just get to the Broken Horse Inn."

The band of travelers turned onto the packed main thoroughfare.

Kids were dancing and skipping through the crowd.

"Cymm is back!"

At first there were six.

"Cymm is back!"

Then a dozen.

"Cymm is back!"

"Cymm will save us!"

The number quickly swelled to over a score.

"Cymm is back!"

"Look how big and strong he is."

It was hard not to let all this attention go to his head, but he was determined to try. He glanced around at his friends to gage their reaction, and his jaw dropped.

The children swarmed around Brogan.

"Did you kill any more dragons?" asked one girl.

"Of course he did, stupid," retorted a cruel boy.

"They probably flee when they see him," shared a third child.

Brogan locked eyes with Cymm and shrugged.

"You *are* going to save us from the dragons, right?" asked the cruel boy.

Brogan shifted uncomfortably.

Cymm shared his friend's discomfort. *I couldn't even defeat one black dragon. They have no idea…*

A middle-aged woman corralled one of the youngsters and paused, inspecting Brogan up and down. "Huh, I thought you'd be bigger." She turned and pulled the child along after her.

"Cymm, can I pet your horse?" asked a teenaged girl.

"Where's your wolf and your war dog?" asked her friend.

Two guards pushed through the crowd. "Make way. Make way for the Swords of the King."

One of them pointed at Brogan. "You there, keep moving! You're blocking the street."

"That's Cymm," said a boy to the guard.

"I don't care if its Melcorac. Let's go!" yelled the guard.

A tug on Cymm's hand drew his attention. The original boy at the city gates who started the commotion said, "You're the real Cymm, aren't you?"

Cymm winked and pulled his hood up. "Yes, but don't tell the horseflies."

The little boy nodded and snickered. "I'm Orts."

Traffic flowed again, but the crowd had not dispersed. The bottleneck in the street had morphed into a parade centered around Brogan. Onlookers cheered and some joined in the march.

Another pair of patrolling guards approached the mass. They spun about and escorted the group only a few feet in front of Cymm and Orts.

"That isn't Cymm," said one guard to the other.

"I know. Isn't he like nine feet tall?" asked the other.

"No. Where did you hear that nonsense?"

Cymm tousled the little boy's hair.

"My wife's cousin's family saw him in Tent City when he killed the black demon."

"Well, I saw him in the King's Court many moons ago, and he isn't nine feet or even seven like this guy, but he *was* taller than you and me," said the first guard.

"Let's break this up then."

The first guard grabbed the other by the arm. "No. We'll have a riot on our hands. Let's just get him to his destination."

The parade continued right to the front door of the Broken Horse Inn, at which point the guards barred the way to anyone else entering the building.

Orts took the reins of Cymm's warhorse. "I got him."

The Paladin of Terazhan let go reluctantly with a nod from Talo.

Jalko received a pat on the rump from the boy. "The wolf, too."

Cymm had forgotten that wolves and war dogs were not allowed inside the taverns in Armak.

Grendella also followed the boy, while Azreala simply dismissed her steed to whence it came.

While Brogan bid farewell to his adoring fans, Cymm entered the building. It took a few moments for his eyes to adjust to the dim light.

The tavern had only half a dozen customers, but three of them rose immediately and stared at him.

Cymm froze. *How did they find me?*

41

Scarface

BrimStrakenstone

The cathedral geode pulsed and groaned with a life of its own. BrimStrakenstone shifted his bulk but remained silent, awaiting an answer.

KorEmberstrike's inner eyelids were glazed over as he stared into the center of the geode, his three scars catching the firelight dancing off the gems. His wings twitched and his head rotated. "One misstep, and I'll die for it, Brim." Yet the hunger for vengeance in his golden eyes spoke volumes. He nodded.

Brim knew he would volunteer for this suicide mission. DetonKonraber had given him those scars hundreds of years ago, at a time when they were more evenly matched. Now, the black dragon towered over Kor, and no one—not even Brim—could match his fighting prowess. This was Kor's only chance for revenge.

He scanned the area, inspecting his brave warriors from a distance. *I have lost enough soldiers lately. The queen's carelessness has cost us many lives.* The senseless death in the battle with Terazhan and Melcorac still burned in his gut. He had killed many insolent drakes and even more that fancied themselves a general, but he had lost two of his best captains in that meaningless attack.

The heat from nearby lava vents caused the air to shimmer above the Septragons—the generals of the Queen's Army—as they approached. They were assembling to discuss the next assault. The queen appeared in a flash and summoned a scrying window. Through the haze, the city of Armak came into view.

The mammoth red general recently discovered that his brood contained two hatchlings. He had finally achieved the title of Grandsire. *Is this the type of world I want for them or anyone in my line? Even the rest of the dragon species do not deserve to raise a wyrmling in this environment. I will never live to one thousand lifeyears at this rate.*

"BrimStrakenstone, care to join the discussion?" asked Ledaedra.

"My Queen, yes, forgive me. The attack on the city of Armak should draw DetonKonraber to the battle. KorEmberstrike has volunteered to sacrifice himself, if need be, to trap our enemy. He has also been assigned to watch for his arrival."

"Scarface?" asked the shadow-dragon general.

The three black dragons in the circle sniggered, but three red dragons did not.

Lashing out like a scorpion's tail, the shadow dragon on Ledaedra's back struck the other shadow dragon with lightning speed. It bit deep into the top of its neck, invoking a roar of pain.

"Would anyone else care to disrupt my meeting?" asked the Dragon Queen. After several moments of silence, she continued. "Many of the humans north of the city are now followers of the Peak of Power. Our first strike will be here." She pointed to the massive grouping of tents outside the city walls.

Brim found it disconcerting how his species and all dragonkind had transformed into savage beasts in this world. His warriors hungered for this next attack, and strangely, so did he.

42

Reunion

Cymm

Cymm remained frozen in place, trying to comprehend the likelihood of their presence being a coincidence. The smallest member of the group charged straight for him, the other two close behind.

She wrapped her arms around his waist and buried her face in his side. "Cymm!"

Cymm patted her back. "Hello Tanya. How did you find me?"

Zecarius offered a broad smile and his hand. "We didn't. We were heading to your village when this one," he swiped a thumb in his daughter Tanya's direction, "heard a merchant claim 'the Broken Horse Inn is Cymm's favorite place to stay when he is in town.' I guess they were right."

Katara, Tanya's aunt, embraced him from the other side, and kissed him on the neck—which she could barely reach on her tiptoes. "Did you finally bathe that horse of yours?"

Azreala ducked slightly as she crossed the open doorway. "He has no need for your services, trollop."

Katara took a step back and her hand went to the hilt of her short sword. "You'll have need of his healing services if your tongue continues to wag."

Cymm quickly grabbed Katara's wrist. "If you unsheathe a weapon in this city, they will arrest you."

"That's a good girl. Go curl up by the fire," taunted Azreala. She walked between Cymm and Katara, muttering, "I thought you had a girlfriend."

The tavern had gone quiet, and everyone stared at the spectacle.

"Don't!" Cymm hissed back at the goddess with fire in his own eyes.

Tanya, the little girl who begged him to teach her to be a paladin, said, "I've been training, Cymm, just like you told me to."

A low din returned to the room, and the young boy returned, followed by Talo, Grendella, and finally Brogan.

Talo rolled his eyes at Cymm. "He's the stable boy."

"And the dishwasher!" added Orts.

Cymm tousled his hair again. "No wonder you knew who I was."

Brogan and Zecarius embraced with a hearty greeting.

The young boy pushed Tanya back away from Cymm with grunts and groans.

"Orts, where have you been?" asked the tavern owner, a middle-aged woman that Cymm had met many times.

"In the stables," replied the young boy.

The owner scoffed. "For two hours? I doubt it. Where's your brother Dregs?"

"I don't know, Ma" Orts returned to pushing Tanya.

"Stop!" instructed Tanya, switching to Cymm's other side.

"Let's go. There's work to do in the kitchen." The owner turned to look at Cymm. "Find a seat. Will you be wanting food?"

"Yes, and a couple of rooms," replied Cymm.

Tanya, following close, slid into the seat immediately on his right. "Everyone in the city is talking about you!"

"Apparently, you are nine feet tall and can fly." Katara chuckled, taking the seat next to her niece at the head of the table.

"And you kill dragons, cut their heads off, and eat their brains!" added the young girl.

Zecarius frowned. "Tanya…"

"What? That's what the merchant told us," she said.

Brogan, sitting at the other head of the table, leaned in heavily and the wood creaked. "That's not all. They kept asking me where my war dog was. I'm supposed to have a horse, a dire wolf, and a war dog."

"They think I'm the Guardian in the prophesy?" asked Cymm.

"What prophesy?" asked Grendella, sitting between the two bigger men.

Talo, listening quietly, gawked at Cymm. "Yes—that makes sense!"

"No, it doesn't. I'm not…the story clearly shows—this is foolish." Cymm scratched the back of his head.

"What prophesy?" asked Grendella angrily.

Brogan leaned over and whispered to her.

"Wouldn't it be wonderful if you were Cymm? Do you remember when I use to pretend I was the Guardian, calling my countrymen to battle and summoning The One." Talo's eyes glimmered.

Cymm chuckled. "I remember that."

"Are we done with the fairy tales?" asked Azreala.

The tavern owner reappeared from the kitchen struggling with platters and tankards. "Sorry, we are a little light on help for the next couple of hours."

Orts set a mug in front of everyone except for Tanya and gave her a baleful glance.

Zecarius jumped up to help the owner unburden her load.

"Thank you." She wiped her hands on her apron. "Everything has been covered. Enjoy."

Cymm shook his head. "You don't have to—"

"I didn't. You have an anonymous benefactor. Let me know if you need anything else."

Zecarius returned to his seat next to Katara. "So, Cymm, what are you doing in Armak?"

"I have begun a new mission, and I may not be back to Stallion Rise for a few weeks. You are welcome to stay there until I return." Cymm began helping himself to the food.

"Can I come?" asked Orts with a small voice from behind him.

Cymm offered a smile, not realizing he stood there and hesitated.

"No. It's a dangerous mission not for little boys," replied Tanya.

"I'm not little." Orts cast a glance at Brogan. "Well, maybe a little little, but I can…"

"Orts, can you ask your mom to bring us another round?" asked Zecarius.

"Yep." The boy disappeared.

"That was not very nice," Zecarius said to his daughter.

Tanya hung her head.

"Where are you heading?" asked Katara.

Cymm picked at a nick in the table. "Honestly? We're not sure. We came here seeking advice from the local wizards," replied Cymm.

Azreala sat on the opposite side of the table in a semi-catatonic state, but her eyes slid open. "We did?"

"It was a pilgrimage originally, to heal the sick, but we have more pressing matters now." Cymm shifted uncomfortably.

"Ones that should not be discussed openly in a tavern," said Grendella, sternly.

Cymm glanced around at the relatively empty room. He remembered how the assassins had stood behind Lord Barrister, invisible, waiting to attack. "Agreed. Why are you here, Azreala?"

The deity's face quirked. "You saw the horde of hellions chasing me."

Brogan scanned the room with exaggerated movements. "So, then you're leaving now?"

Azreala shot up, forcing her chair against the wall behind her. With blazing eyes, she said, "What is your problem?"

Brogan rose as well and pointed his finger at her. "I heard you tell everyone to leave me to die. Again."

"No, you heard what you wanted to hear. I told everyone to keep going, because my hellsteed is faster than your mounts," replied Azreala.

Brogan tried to respond, but she cut him off.

"I said the same thing the second time, and I took care of the demons. I rode circles around the group to keep you safe, patrolling the entire night."

With a harrumph, Brogan sat down heavily and folded his arms over his substantial chest.

This seemed to satisfy the Lady Taker. "I can handle a dozen or two, but there are thousands of demons and devils. If the Princes of Hell send their hordes after me or Cymm, we will be safer together."

"By Terazhan's good graces," Grendella muttered.

Brogan stared through the shuttered window slats.

Katara and Zecarius glanced at each other in concern.

"Maybe we should stay together, too," said Tanya.

Cymm chuckled. "That would be more dangerous for you. It isn't a very nice world we have inherited, is it?"

Tanya shook her head.

Everyone ate and drank in reticence for a while.

Cymm pondered their next steps. *How do we get an audience with one of the mages in Armak? I don't even know where they reside. Maybe I should start with the priests of Terazhan. They might have good insight into our next steps.* He turned to Grendella on his left. "Maybe we should start at the Temple of Terazhan."

"Not a bad idea. Just you and me though." Grendella gazed over the rim of her mug at Azreala.

"Of course. Let's finish up here and head over. They tend to lock the doors early these days." Cymm quaffed the rest of his ale and grabbed a large chunk of meat. "Brogan, make sure the three rooms are as close together as possible. We will be back as soon as we can."

Azreala shifted in her seat. "You know, the temple won't collapse because I walk through the doors."

Cymm gave a half-smile. "There is no reason to distress the priests who live there. We won't be long."

"You can leave your packs here. I'll get 'em up to the rooms," said Brogan.

Grendella eyeballed him, slung her backpack over her shoulder, and headed toward the door.

Cymm left his but knew why the cleric would not relinquish hers. *The continued burden of the ebony shard weighs on her.*

They walked side-by-side toward their place of worship, and Cymm clapped her on the shoulder.

"What?" Grendella's tone and visage drained of friendliness.

Realizing he had overstepped a boundary, he pivoted. "I'm worried about Lykinnia. We haven't spoken in six days."

The dwarf rubbed the back of her neck. "Terazhan has not responded to my prayers in three days."

"Now that you mention it, same here. It can't be a coincidence." Cymm finished his walk to the temple in quiet. *ZaphMordakai's comment continued to bother him. "I told you your days were numbered. Didn't I? Now you won't have time to save Jenaleya or Lykinnia." Was he trying to tell me Lykinnia is a prisoner with Jenaleya, or like Jenaleya, or just trying to get under my skin?*

43

Charisma

Talo

Everyone piled into Talo's room once the paladin and priest had returned from the temple.

Talo could not shake off the effects of last night's chase. He gazed at Cymm with admiration. They had always been close, but this past year had taken a toll on their relationship. They had never spent more than a couple days apart when one of them had an illness. Now, they spent months apart, and rarely did they spend more than a couple of days together in a row.

He sighed heavily. *I can't remember the last time we went hunting or fishing. I thought this would be one long hunting trip—instead, we are the ones getting hunted. This isn't what I expected. I should have listened to Vena.*

Even though Talo had two lifeyears on Cymm, he had always looked up to his younger cousin. The only thing he had ever accomplished that Cymm had not was winning the archery competitions at Hot Springs. *Why did I force them to bring me. Everyone in our party is powerful and has their own special talents. Brogan has his massive size and strength, Grendella has Semper's magic warhammer and casts spells, and Azreala…well, she's a deity. What do I offer? I can shoot a bow—big deal.*

The three new strangers entered the room.

"Find a comfortable spot. We have a lot to discuss." Bria's ring banged against Cymm's chest and sparkled in the lamp light.

Talo wrinkled his nose. *Why is Cymm including them?*

Azreala wore a strange expression as she scanned the room. "What are they doing here?"

Talo placed a hand over his mouth to cover his grin. *Maybe she isn't so bad, and after all she did enchant Bria's ring for Cymm.*

Cymm patted the air. "Just settle down, and I'll explain everything."

Talo scowled at his cousin. *How can you take all this in stride?* He recalled a conversation his mother and father had with Uncle Otec late one night after everyone had gone to bed. Talo had come to the kitchen for a mug of water and overheard…

ꝏꝏꝏ

"Cymm isn't even eight lifeyears yet. How can you possibly know?" asked Daro, an edge to his voice.

Uncle Otec's voice boomed, "It isn't just your boy!"

"Shh!" said Talo's father and Auntie Shay.

His mother, Nové, quickly looked over her shoulder.

With a softer voice, Uncle Otec continued, "It's every boy in the village—Softtails, Darkmanes, Sempers—and it doesn't matter how old they are either, they listen, and they follow."

"Well, look at the size of him," said Nové.

"Yes, that is part of it, but other than with the Darkmane boy, he doesn't use his size to his advantage," replied Uncle Otec.

Talo attempted to lick his lips with a dry tongue from the shadowy recesses of the dark hallway.

Auntie Shay's soft voice joined in, "The boys are thick as thieves. They might as well be brothers. I don't think this will cause a problem."

Daro cleared his throat. "That may be, but this is not normal."

"I know, and hopefully we have decades before anything needs to change," said Uncle Otec.

"By then, Talo may prove to be more confident, less fearful, and someone we can trust to lead this family," said Daro.

His words stung, but the way his father said them hurt even more. A mixture of longing and hope existed, but no real belief it would ever come to fruition. To make matters worse, the other three adults, including his mother, had sighed and agreed.

Young Talo stumbled back to bed in a daze, confused and still thirsty. The tears running down his face and into his mouth would have to do.

ꝏꝏꝏ

Talo had only been ten lifeyears, before they had even joined the militia with Old Man Semper. Now at over twenty, the memory lingered.

Prove to be more confident, Talo thought. Since then, he had tried to emulate Cymm and followed him everywhere. He realized this only made it appear worse, but how else could he learn the skills he needed to know to make his mom and dad proud? *Can someone learn to be more magnanimous? More charismatic?* He continued to try, but this did not bother him so much as the ending. *Someone we can trust to lead this family.* The words rang out like a clarion call in his mind.

Households did not survive without trust. Entire villages could be destroyed from a lack of trust either from within or...

"Talo." Cymm gave him a stern look, ending his reverie.

Grendella crinkled her nose. "As I was saying, they recommended that we travel to see the priestesses of Vallerielle. They are the keepers of the Enchiridion, a compendium of magical items and artifacts. The tome contains details about the creation of many items. If that doesn't help, Vallerielle's followers can cast a divine spell to look back in time."

Cymm turned his gaze on Zecarius. "Are you familiar with Bard Keep?"

"I know exactly where it is—not too far from where we live. Why?" asked Zecarius.

"That's where we need to go," replied Cymm.

"You live in the Knife-edge Mountains north of the pass?" asked Grendella.

Katara glanced from her brother to her niece. "Cymm, I hope you're not asking us to go with you. Demons and devils are chasing you."

Brogan cleared his throat. "I live in the same mountains. If you draw a map, I'm sure I will find it."

Zecarius and Katara stared at each other until Tanya stood up.

"For the past three months, all we have talked about was Cymm's bravery. How great it was for a stranger to help us and others, and how many lives he saved. If it isn't safe between Armak and home, then our people are not safe, and we need to warn them. So, we travel with them or by ourselves, and I prefer to travel with them." Tanya returned to her seat.

No one spoke for a time.

Talo elbowed his cousin and whispered, "Reminds me of your speech to save Old Man Semper. Although, she missed the legendary part at the end, 'and who will answer the call?'."

Grendella and Cymm laughed first, but eventually the others joined in.

Cymm rubbed his hands together. "It's settled. Tomorrow morning, we head out."

During the confusion and noise of people departing, Azreala slid up next to Cymm. "Where is your girlfriend? Shouldn't she be buzzing around here in a jealous fury by now?"

"I've been wondering the same thing, but why would you care?" asked Cymm.

Azreala shrugged, but Talo caught her quick glimpse at the departing Katara.

44

Dragon Queen's Army

BrimStrakenstone

BrimStrakenstone surveyed his host with great pride and satisfaction. More was not always better, but in this case Ledaedra had agreed with his decision to bring a significant portion of the horde from Fire Island. This would be the largest assault they had mounted in the war thus far. However, the majority of his army still roosted with their mates, trying to fulfill the queen's mandate to produce offspring. He planned to leave a large presence behind to defend and maintain their military base.

Brim scanned over the dozen ice dragons with craggy white hides. They could not endure these temperatures for long periods, so most of them remained north in the ice lands awaiting the queen's call for The Final Conflict.

The behemoth general considered the battle to come, not the attack on Armak but the one on City of the Mystics. *That will be the battleground for The Final Conflict, the battle Ledaedra's entire plan revolved around, and the one she foretold for years. Many of the Mystic wizards were aligned with the metallic dragons, in fact, many silver dragons lived in the city disguised as humans. With the removal of both the stronghold and the meddling metallic dragons, nothing would stand in our way. We can continue to eradicate the races who worship the other deities, and Ledaedra's power would soar.*

Brim's inspection of the army continued with the green dragons. There were several dozen present. Their potent, poisonous gas could effectively target the humanoid races and eliminate mass populations. Ledaedra believed the primary source of Terazhan's recent power surge emanated from this city, and she intended to rectify the situation.

The blue dragons on the island remained behind to guard the stronghold at Fire Mountain. Their abilities could best be utilized near large bodies of water, and they were usually positioned near the coastline. All the civilizations near the oceans, including City of the Mystics, would see a large concentration of the blue dragons, but not Armak.

Six dragon species comprised the Queen's Army, of which only five came from his home world. The shadow dragons were somewhat of an enigma. Although Brim knew how many had pledged their allegiance to the Dragon Queen, he did not know the size of their total population. It did not help that they hailed from the Plane of Shadows, and Malekai would not share this information. Brim had selected ten to reinforce the ranks.

Without a doubt, the co-existence of the black and the red dragons created an enormous problem in the Queen's Army. The two species did not cooperate well with each other and were known to intentionally sabotage one another. Not to mention, they individually had an inflated view of themselves and exaggerated their own importance. To keep things civil and to avoid affecting the mission, BrimStrakenstone usually selected an equal number of each species if he intended to include both, and this time he had chosen ten.

Brim's image replication ability required him to be quite exceptional with numbers, but a simple roll call did not. Including himself, there were exactly eighty dragons—or sixteen phalanxes. He had a solid battle plan, but not without its flaws. The city defenses could not be overlooked. Situated on the outer walls were many trebuchets and ballistae and inside the towers were wizards. Even with scores of his brethren, the initial attack wave would be very dangerous. Every scouting report indicated the city of Armak had the third largest population of magic-users and the fourth largest garrison of soldiers.

With pride in his gut, he allowed himself to enjoy the scene a moment longer. The spectacular force arrayed before him with the peak of Fire Mountain rising to its full glory behind them etched into his mind. *Will any of the new hatchlings remember this day?* The weight of expectation brought him hope, and yet, its burden almost too much to bear. *Or will they, too, live and die by the whims of a queen whose plans run deeper than dragonfire?*

The colorful display of dragon hides immediately reminded him of the Dragon Queen. He found it bizarre and unsettling that six different dragons and six different colors comprised her body—all of which swirled together on her torso in a kaleidoscope of color. Not to mention, she possessed the innate abilities of every dragon, the immunity to dragon breath and most spells, and understood the nuances of each dragon society. She had to be the Mother of Dragons—as many called her—but where had she come from?

Brim's father told him she had appeared at the same time as the trellbac, and many proclaimed it a miracle and her a savior. His father, a stalwart supporter along with all his brood, had never said enough to remove the tickle at the back of Brim's mind, and now it had grown into an itch. *Why did Ledaedra appear so comfortable with the trellbac when I caught them together? Her story's plausible, negotiating the release of the remaining dragons, but it isn't likely. The math isn't mathing.*

Seventy-nine pairs of eyes bore into his, and he realized they were still awaiting his command.

It is time. He prayed to Ledaedra, and she reached out to establish a telepathic connection. *"It is time, My Queen. Open the portal."*

45

Capture Stories

Lykinnia

A veil drifted across Lykinnia's eyes while she slept. She blinked several times, trying to clear her foggy vision, while her body delivered a status report. Everything ached, as if a blessing of unicorns had trampled her in the night. Ronks groaned low, then abruptly paused—all sound disappeared momentarily—only to repeat the on-off pattern like the flash of a lightning bug.

How long have I been out? A headache pulsed between her eyes. It took a while for her senses to function properly, as well as her mind. She slowly glanced about.

Ronks, the first to awaken as usual, fared no better than her. His cross-eyed, woozy appearance indicated as much.

There is an obvious hierarchy, because I am always second to awaken. Naterion and Leighton should be next, followed by Jenaleya and Haskins. If my theory is correct, Myra will slide in before Haskins, the half-orc boy. Lykinnia cleared her throat. "Ronks, how long were we out for this time?"

"Me not know. Head hurt bad," replied the half-ogre.

Naterion grumbled himself into consciousness, and the rest of the captives awoke in the exact order Lykinnia had predicted.

However, before Myra's first twitch of wakefulness, she yelled, "Fazekas, I'm over here!" Whispering ensued for several moments. "Hide, they're coming. Don't let them see you." Her eyes finally opened, and she cast bleary-eyed glances all about her. She proceeded to strain against the shackles with concern upon her face.

The robed priests had not appeared yet from the shadowed alcove to attend to them.

Lykinnia practiced the finger movements for releasing the manacles. She should have had it worked out already, but the drug in the food constantly fogged her mind. *Besides, all I can do is practice anyway until the manacles come off.*

The new captive whimpered.

"Myra, are you ok?" asked Leighton.

"I can't find Fazekas," she replied.

"It was just a dream," added Jenaleya.

"Who is Fazekas?" asked Lykinnia.

"My friend. He watches over me and protects me," replied Myra.

Ronks chuckled. "Bad job he did. You—"

"Ronks!" three of them reprimanded simultaneously.

"What? It's true." The half-ogre bared his teeth.

"Ignore him," said Jenaleya. "I would like to meet your friend."

Myra shook her head violently. "No. You can't. He only talks to me, and you can't see him either."

Haskins pursed his lips. "Tee hee hee. Myra, Haskins meet him? Me no have friends."

"No. He's very shy," she replied.

Jenaleya glanced over at Lykinnia and whispered. "An imaginary friend?"

"Probably. I feel bad for her," Lykinnia whispered back.

Ronks waved. "I sees him. He right behind you."

"No. Only I can see him." Myra glanced over her shoulder anyway, toward the alcove.

Leighton sighed. "That's not funny."

Several dragon calls drifted in on the wind. The creatures were active this morning.

Lykinnia intentionally changed the subject. "Haskins, how did they capture you?"

The half-orc boy shifted uncomfortably. "I just caught."

Lykinnia shrugged. "Did I say something wrong?"

Ronks hooted. "He volunteered."

"He didn't *volunteer*," said Leighton.

"He went willingly with big smile on face," replied Ronks.

"Hold back, Ronks. You're being mean even for you today," said Jenaleya in disgust.

"He right. No one want Haskins. I taught dey friends," the half-orc boy stared at the floor.

Ronks bellowed with laughter.

"I suppose you have a more interesting story, Ronks. You were the first one here. Did you fight your captors? Slay scores of the enemy before you were taken." Lykinnia did not hide her disdain.

A visceral change washed over the half-ogre's face and his jaw moved as if he were chewing on something. A darkness dwelled behind those stone-cold eyes. "Me and Haskins is here long before princes and princesses arrived. Us half-breeds do the best we can."

Two draconian priests entered with the basket of bread and began the normal routine.

"Story time later, Princess." Ronks's playful demeanor had returned.

Everyone here is losing their minds. Or they were already lost before they arrived. I need to get out of here before I join them, thought Lykinnia.

Ronks grabbed his usual two loaves of bread, then wavered and grabbed a third by holding one in his teeth.

The acolytes moved to Lykinnia next—which logistically made no sense to cross the circle—released her hand and offered the basket of bread.

Jenaleya and Haskins followed, then the priests moved on to Myra.

Lykinnia immediately used her free hand to execute the spell movements she had been practicing. The manacle expanded and she slipped her hand out. With a devious grin she waved to Ronks across the chamber.

The half-ogre's eyes went wide, the bread fell from his mouth to the floor, and he squawked.

The priests glanced over past Naterion to Ronks, then to the fallen loaf.

Time froze, forcing a lump into Lykinnia's throat. In a whirlwind of motion, she returned her wrist to the manacle.

The acolytes' heads swiveled, tracing the source of the expression on Ronks's face. After staring at Lykinnia for several seconds, they returned to dispensing the loaves of bread.

After her captors had departed, Lykinnia could not contain her glee.

"What are you grinning about?" asked Jenaleya.

"Ask Ronks, he saw," replied Lykinnia.

"I asked you," said Jenaleya.

Lykinnia whispered, "I can remove our manacles."

"Are you kidding?" Jenaleya exclaimed.

"What?" asked Haskins and Leighton.

Jenaleya glared at Lykinnia sternly. "Don't say it." She turned and whispered to Haskins.

His eyes grew wide, and when he told Myra, she gasped.

Leighton choked on his bread, and Naterion's jaw dropped before he turned to Ronks.

"I already know!" The half-ogre glared at Lykinnia. "Then what? Ride off on dragon?" He motioned toward the opening in the cavern and the hubbub below.

Everyone glanced at the alcove in apprehension.

Leighton grimaced. "Keep it up and none of us will eat for a week."

Ronks grumbled to himself quietly.

Naterion had a sparkle in his eye. "What does this mean?"

Lykinnia answered, "We have only begun. We need to figure out an answer to Ronks's question."

46

Three Waves

BrimStrakenstone

A javelin tore through the soft membrane of BrimStrakenstone's lower wing, and several others whizzed past his head and body. He had included himself in the second attack wave because the first had failed so miserably. An entire phalanx of green dragons wiped out before they even made it to the wall—javelins and chain shot ripped them apart. He had underestimated the effectiveness of their defensive weapons. Brim's tactics had pivoted immediately from covering the city in a cloud of toxic gas to destroying the walls, fortifications, and defensive engines.

A black dragon raced ahead sending a massive lightning bolt careening into the outer wall. Rock shrapnel flew in every direction. Brim and several others weaved and twirled to circumvent the projectiles hurled at them and the flying debris. Most made it through and released their own breath weapons.

The black dragons are trying to prove their species is superior again, Brim thought, but he also put a little extra effort into his first fiery detonation.

A trebuchet along with its operators flew off the ramparts on fire, followed closely by sections of the wall. In the aftermath of his passing, a large crater appeared in the western defenses.

BrimStrakenstone banked and raced back toward the original gathering point where the missiles could not reach him. He streaked past a black dragon writhing on the ground with two javelins piercing its body.

Several other explosions echoed through the air behind him, but the bulk of his body blocked his view. When he arrived at the rally point, the big red general spun to inspect the battle scene.

Three large breaches in the outer wall created the appearance of an ogre's smile.

Brim grinned back at the fortification and prepared to launch the third wave. He paused a moment; three new dragons littered the battlefield—two blacks and a red. One of the bodies resembled a porcupine with a half dozen javelins protruding from its body. The enemy fired at the downed dragons to finish them off.

"Third wave…attack!" hollered Brim.

The shadow and the white dragons sailed forward.

Movement from the south caught his eye, and he quickly sent scouts to reconnoiter.

One of the white dragons plummeted to the ground with wings of stone. The mages had joined the battle, hurling their magical orange darts at the dragon's wings.

The remaining white dragons released their frosty, breath attacks—a wedge of white tinged with blue. Some of the metal fractured, more of the stone cracked, and all the flesh hardened.

The shadow dragon's breath weapon—black with tiny motes of brilliant pink—interlaced with the white dragon's creating a dichotomy of color. The diameter of the black cylinder never changed and appeared to be no thicker than the nose of the dragon from whence it came. This column instilled fear within those struck, far greater than even a red dragon's natural fear. Every creature struck reacted violently and immediately. Many ran off the top of the wall in a frenzy, while others ran into a structure nearby, knocking themselves out or causing an injury.

As the dragons swung back to the rendezvous another white dragon went down with stone wings.

A brilliant flash drew Brim's attention. A column of golden light shot up from inside the city and intercepted a shadow dragon. It struck him mid-wing at the bend, and half of his wing disintegrated. The drake screeched—in pain or fear, Brim could not tell—before plummeting to the ground. Another blast ended its wailing.

"By the seven heavens!" Brim cursed. "We have already lost more warriors than I anticipated."

"One more pass will eliminate the rest of the defensive engines. Then the green dragons won't get shredded," replied a black general.

Brim growled in response, preparing to launch the fourth wave.

One of his scouts returned in a huff. "There is a small army of fiends approaching the city. I estimate their number to be five hundred."

Brim's brow ridge raised. "We'll let them overrun the breaches and swarm the city, then we will take out the mage towers. Pass the word."

"Yes, commander." The black general departed without another word.

47

Divine Quest

Cymm

Cymm watched his doppelgänger accidentally bump into Terazhan's elbow. His imaginary twin cringed and stepped forward to glance into the small window carved into the door. He rushed ahead to also view the contents of the room. A skeletal being sat on the floor with its shoulder blades against the wall. Its skull rotated to gaze back at him, and a chill tweaked the muscles in his neck.

"What is it?" asked Cymm from the Divine Quest.

Terazhan gently laid a hand on Twin Cymm's shoulder. "Not what—who. That is what remains of Melcorac, the Holy One."

Cymm took note of the sadness creeping into Terazhan's voice.

Cymm's doppelgänger asked, "How did this happen?"

"It is a long story, but I need your help to restore him and end his suffering," replied the deity.

"The New Moon is still far off. I didn't think we could bind again until Terazhan's Twilight has come and gone."

"You are correct, but you will not be binding with me." Terazhan glanced back over his shoulder and Twin Cymm followed his gaze.

Cymm's eyes bulged from their sockets. He had not noticed the two women standing there, each one registering shock for different reasons. The first women—the embodiment of purity and beauty—had a halo of miniature stars orbiting her head, and she emanated a cobalt blue aura. He had never seen a more beautiful woman. The presence of the second woman on the Peak of Power registered even more shock because his friend, Azreala, stood there.

His ethereal form rushed over the mountains, woods, then plains and merged with his corporeal body in his room at the Broken Horse Inn. He thrashed his covers and sat upright in bed, having no concept of how much time had elapsed.

Talo moaned in the background.

Cymm's mind churned. He could not determine how long ago his last Divine Quest occurred—five or six months. *Apparently, Terazhan wants us to travel to the Peak of Power.*

He glanced toward the shuttered window—no light peeked through—hours of darkness remained. *How can I possibly sleep now? I can't believe Azreala stood upon the Peak of Power. Her past prohibition appears to be lifted. Terazhan must need me to bind with her to help Melcorac. Or maybe I am binding with the other woman, or both. I wonder who she is. I'm sure I will find out when I get there, and maybe I'll learn why Lykinnia hasn't contacted me in seven days. Not that I'm counting.*

With a huff, Cymm laid back down, his arm hanging off the bed. He slept fitfully for the remainder of the night.

In the morning, Cymm and Talo were the first ones down the stairs, as expected.

Brogan would have been last if not for the dwarven cleric on his heels, yawning and sleepy-eyed.

"Good morning, it's about time." Cymm greeted them. "Grendella, I need to speak to you."

She glanced around the table. "Not now."

Cymm stared at her in bewilderment but honored the request.

Everyone had risen somewhat early to begin the journey north. Not as early as Cymm would have liked, but no one besides Talo understood the life of a farmer.

Tanya tugged on his arm. "Can we start my training today?" She wore a pouty face assuming what the answer would be.

Cymm knelt in front of her, so they were eye to eye and mimicked her face. He then pumped his arms up and down and snorted.

The little girl giggled. "Well?"

He tapped his finger on his chin. "If we can find some time during our ten-to-twelve-hour ride…"

"Cymm, come on," she whined.

The door swung open and Azreala entered the inn followed closely by Jalko. "Are we ready?"

Cymm picked a strand of grass bedding off her minimal clothing. "Did you sleep in the barn? Why didn't you use the bed?"

With a flutter of her eyelashes, Azreala responded, "I don't use beds for sleeping."

Cymm sighed as the heat rushed to his face, ignoring her, he turned to Jalko. "Hey buddy, you can't be in here."

"I meant human beds are too short. Get your mind out of the sewer," Azreala beamed with pride.

Most of his companions had consumed a light fare or had skipped breakfast and were hoisting their packs. Cymm used the diversion to escape. "Tanya, let's go—grab your pack."

The departure from the inn began as people made their way to the stables.

Cymm put a shoulder to the door and held it for Tanya. *I need to catch up with Grendella.*

Once outside the building, Katara fell in next to Cymm and slid her hand into his. "Hello, stranger." She smiled warmly at him. "So, you have a girlfriend? When were you planning to tell me?"

He slowly pulled his hand away. "I did not have a girlfriend when we met—"

Azreala grabbed Katara by the neck, lifted her off the ground, then slammed her into the outside wall of the stables. "Do not think you are my equal, fool."

Katara's blades were already unsheathed and poised to attack, but they clattered to the ground from limp wrists. Her face turned blue, and a red wisp danced around her head.

A massive bicep wrapped around Azreala's neck. Brogan struggled to pull her away and continued to try unsuccessfully.

Zecarius rushed over to defend his sister, but a tail whip knocked the sword from his grip. Isochronously, he lunged to grab it, and she stepped upon it.

"Azreala!" Cymm managed to wedge himself between the women. "Stop this immediately!"

The goddess of death locked her fiery gaze on him and the flames smoldered. She released her grip and allowed Katara to fall to the ground, where she collapsed with body racking coughs.

"What in the nine hells was that? We are not each other's enemy!" Cymm's arms flailed as he stared up at her, trying to yell in her face.

Grendella knelt next to Katara, praying.

"I won't let anything, or anyone, get in the way of my plans—or our plans." She scowled back at him menacingly.

Cymm took half a step back. He had never seen this side of her before and had always felt in control of the relationship. "Azreala…we are friends with a mutual goal, but I still have someone."

A smile flickered across her face briefly then disappeared. She stepped around him and opened the door to the stables.

Jalko growled.

"A little late, buddy," said Talo.

Cymm's eyebrows knitted together, and he surveyed the area. "No, he isn't growling at her."

"You need to control that monster!" Zecarius said, assisting his sister to walk with her arm draped over his shoulder.

Brogan gave Cymm a stern "I-told-you-so" look.

Cymm stared him down.

"Fine! I will fill them in on who she is." Brogan followed them into the stables.

With the group turmoil subsiding, Grendella brought up the rear of the procession.

"We need to talk," they both said at the same time.

Cymm closed the door to the stables and nodded for her to go first.

"I had a Divine Quest last night," she half whispered.

"So did I!" Cymm blurted out, then pulled her back toward the Inn. "Is this your first?"

"No, I had several when I was in the Dungeons of Delge in order to meet up with you," replied the dwarf.

"Are you comfortable with the plan changing?" asked Cymm. "I know you were hoping to rid yourself of the shard."

"What in the nine hells are you talking about? Lord Terazhan wants us to head to Bard Keep and figure out how to destroy this thing," replied Grendella.

Cymm's head shook vigorously. "No, we need to return to the Peak of Power so I can help him heal Melcorac."

"Melcorac!" Excitement lit the dwarf's face, but it did not last. "No, there's a reason we received different quests on the same night. Our paths lead us in separate directions."

"Are you sure?"

Grendella considered the options for a moment. "Yes."

Cymm glanced back at the stables. "This is going to be hard. How do we split the others up?"

"This is going to be easy. Who did you see in your quest?" asked the dwarf.

Jalko's throat rumbled again.

"I only saw…wait a minute, that doesn't mean anything. Talo and Jalko are coming with me."

Grendella cast a doubtful look. "Everyone else was in my Divine Quest, even the little girl."

The door to the stables swung open and Brogan's head peaked out. "You two comin'?"

They glanced at each other and shuffled toward the door.

Jalko sniffed the air and ground but fell in next to Cymm.

"Talo's coming with me," whispered Cymm.

"He should make up his own mind," she replied.

"I agree." Cymm smiled, showing all his teeth, as he held the door open for her.

Inside, the horses and pony were pulled from the stalls and saddled. Zecarius Stormcaller, his sister, and daughter gathered in a small group without a mount to ride.

"What were you two doing?" asked Brogan.

"We're ready to go," said Talo.

Jalko circled behind Cymm, placed his muzzle under his elbow, and with a quick flick had his bonded companion's arm over his back.

"There's been a change of plans," said Grendella gruffly. "We need to split the party up."

"What?" asked Brogan.

"Why?" asked Talo.

Tanya rushed forward to grab her mentor's leg. "I'm coming with you."

Cymm shared a glance with the dwarf. "Grendella and I both received messages from Lord Terazhan last night. He intends for us to complete separate quests that are equally important."

"I'll be continuing north to Bard Keep. Brogan, you're with me," said the dwarven priestess.

"Azreala, you're with me. We'll be heading south to the Peak of Power." Cymm's gaze drifted to Talo. "I'll let you decide where you're going, but I would prefer you travel with me."

Without hesitation, Talo said, "Fine by me."

Zecarius shot Azreala a cold stare. "Cymm, we won't be going with you. We'll meet you back at Stallion Rise in a couple of months."

Tanya's mouth opened wide in a silent scream, then she yelled, "No!" She raced over to her father. "No, Daddy. Please."

"You are welcome to travel with us. The images I received from Lord Terazhan included all three of you." Grendella checked the saddle straps on her pony.

Zecarius hugged his daughter. "Thank you for the offer, but I need to focus on the safety of my family."

The skin on Katara's neck already formed large red welts intermingled with purple blotches. She stood off on her own and would not look up from her boots.

"Alright, let's move out." Cymm walked toward his warhorse.

"Hold on," said Talo, not moving. "Was I in your vision or quest thing?"

Cymm and Grendella stared at each other long and hard.

Talo shrugged off the arm his cousin tried to wrap around his shoulder. "Well, was I?"

"No, but it doesn't matter. You can still come with me," replied Cymm.

Talo shifted his gaze to the dwarf. "How about yours?"

Grendella nodded.

Jalko snarled low, with his scruff up and his ears perked.

No one moved.

Finally, Talo asked, “What is that sound?”

There were many sideways glances, but no one answered.

Brogan threw open the stable door.

A commotion rose above the city din, getting louder by the second.

Everyone issued out into the street.

Orts ran down the road toward the inn and swerved at the last moment in their direction. “Dragons! Dragons are attacking!”

48

Broken Silence

Lykinnia

At least two days had passed since Lykinnia removed her wrist restraint. Each time she awoke, lethargy persisted a little longer, the distinction between foggy dreams and reality dissolved a little more, and the rate at which the protective walls guarding her emotional stability disintegrated a little faster.

An unusual clamor caught her attention. It came from outside and from a distance but not clear enough to distinguish.

"Fazekas, hide. They are coming…" Myra faded off into mumbling, then shouted, "Leave him alone!"

Anger flooded Lykinnia's mind. "Oh, shut—"

Jenaleya gave her a stern glare.

"—the door, I feel a cool breeze rushing in." The daughter of Terazhan—a priestess of good—found herself struggling to be nice to her fellow captives. She wanted to leave them all behind and save herself. *What would my father think of me if I did that? What would Cymm think?* A sharp pain seized her chest, making breathing difficult for many seconds. *I know what they both would think and what they both would do.*

"Hey, Princess, that not nice," said Ronks.

Lykinnia ignored the half-ogre but caught a quick glimpse of Naterion's expression. He shook his head slowly with a frown. She implored him with her own expression to forgive her, although she did not know why she cared.

Naterion gave a curt nod.

Ronks took possession of his rations.

"How did you get captured?" Lykinnia asked Naterion before he looked away.

Anticipation flitted through the room briefly until the dark-skinned warrior shook his head once.

"Nice try, Princess," said Ronks between chews.

"Come on, Nate. It cannot be that bad," Lykinnia urged.

Half of his face wrinkled. "Yes, it can."

The noise outside continued to increase, likely the culmination of many sources. The dragons were gathering.

"Please." She flashed a big smile.

Naterion sighed, then took a deep breath. "They chased me through the woods, howling and grunting. There were hundreds of them, but they could not catch me. I continued to dodge them and hide—sometimes I used tricks to confuse my pursuers—but eventually they caught up to me."

"That's it?" asked Jenaleya.

Leighton huffed. "I thought you were a prince. Where was your personal guard?"

"Yeah," added Haskins.

"They…they—it was not possible for them to be there," Naterion replied.

Lykinnia wanted to scratch her head. "Wait a minute. 'They caught up to you' is not the same as they caught you. Did you escape?"

The gathering outside grew loud enough to distract everyone, including the Ledaedran priests, and all fell quiet for a moment.

After a long pause, Naterion said, "Yes."

"How?" asked Haskins excitedly.

"I ran up a tree."

"What?" asked Leighton.

Jenaleya's face quirked. "You mean you climbed a tree."

"No, I ran up a tree, then transformed from a jaguar to a hawk and flew away." Naterion nervously glanced from one captive to another.

Lykinnia mindfully continued to eat. "You are a shapeshifter?"

"Yes, but not how you mean."

"You're a druid," Myra stated boldly.

"I am, but that is not how I changed forms…" Naterion hesitated, holding something back.

"Out with it," said Ronks with a mouth full of bread.

Naterion's eyes flitted side to side. "It was a dream. They chased me every night for weeks until they caught me, and I awoke here."

A raucous roar erupted from Ronks. "What? A dream?"

"Hmm," Lykinnia said more to herself than anyone else. *What is going on here? Is every deity involved in this conflict?*

"What is it?" asked Jenaleya in hushed tones.

"Dreams should not leave bruises," Lykinnia whispered. "What did the creatures chasing you look like?"

"They were…they had—demons, they were demons with skin darker than mine. They rose to twelve feet tall. Their stooped backs were wider than a wagon, covered in spikes, and speckled with mossy hair. The strangest thing would happen; its hair would unexpectedly…"

"…burst into flame." Naterion and Lykinnia said simultaneously.

The draconian priests offered the breadbasket to Leighton.

"What does this mean?" asked Jenaleya.

"It's a very powerful spirit or shadow creature from the underworld called a Balor, but that should not be possible," replied Lykinnia.

"Why?" asked Jenaleya.

"An incident occurred over a millennia ago, and they were banished from the sixteen planes and this world. I believe they were confined to the outer planes of existence." Lykinnia took a large bite of bread to block any more questions so she could think. *If the Balor are involved in this, then Feldarius is involved—either directly or indirectly. Father believes he is on our side, but if he is on Ledaedra's…*

Inside, a hush fell over the room. Everyone seemed consumed with their own thoughts.

Outside, an eerie stillness drifted in through the giant opening in the cave.

49

Homesick

BrimStrakenstone

Demons and devils swarmed through the gaps in the outer wall and were met by soldiers charging forward to intercept them. The defenders thwarted the initial surge of indigo and violet bodies. No one seemed to gain ground in either direction, but the pile of bodies filled the gaps, creating a makeshift barrier.

BrimStrakenstone lost interest in the battle below. He had to restrain himself for now. Malekai and Marekai would not take kindly to their minions being slaughtered by dragon fire. Besides, he planned to capitalize on the huge benefit of waiting. Once the defenses were broken and scattered, he would lose far less warriors in the next wave of the assault.

He scanned the vicinity and the horizon in every direction. Everyone held their position, awaiting his command. An eyesore near the gates caught his attention. Three dragon skulls were displayed in a grotesque fashion. His blood began to boil, an easy feat for a red dragon.

"Destroy those skulls!" Brim shouted at a black general.

In the distance, KorEmberstrike patrolled the northern front, the path DetonKonraber would most likely take when approaching. The black dragon had yet to arrive. Maybe, a blessing in disguise, since many of the younger drakes believed the exaggerated stories about his battle lust and prowess. DetonKonraber the Devastation, at least two centuries older than him and considered ancient by their kind, grew up in the old world with his father. A mutual respect existed between the two older dragons, an oddity for red and black, but everything changed when they came to the new world.

Deton should know better. We need a new home, where we can multiply and thrive. Why does he resist? Can the rumors about the death of his brother and a confrontation between him and the Dragon Queen be true? There is too much bad blood between them to recover now. He needs to be dealt with and eliminating him and destroying this city would be two huge steps forward in the war for this world.

His thoughts drifted. *I would have preferred to reclaim our home world, but the trellbac have multiplied like lice, and we have no defense against their vocal weapon. Ledaedra must be immune to their caterwaul. Why would she allow them to step one claw into this world, or even onto the Plane of Ashes for that matter. Unless she can control them.*

Excitement swelled within him. *We could let them swarm this world and return to our own. Invite them in and close the portal. It would have to be all of them or at least most of them.*

BrimStrakenstone longed to see his own world again. At a young age he fled to this world with his family, but he could still remember it vividly. The smell is what he missed most. This world was wet, dank, and full of rot. His own body decayed from the outside in. His arid homeland had the scent of…cinnamon. The closest example he had come across—sweet, dry, and aromatic.

I need to share my idea with the queen. She will—

"General! KorEmberstrike is signaling."

50

False Expectations

Cymm

Cymm's nerves prickled all through his neck and upper shoulders. "Do you know how many there are and what color?"

Orts's face quirked. "A lot! Red ones and some black ones, too."

Cymm shuffled his feet. "Listen, kid—"

Brogan grabbed the paladin's arm at the bicep. "Don't." He turned to the boy. "We are in a hurry."

Grendella, with a stern visage said, "Orts, go tell your mama what 's happening and get to safety."

Orts waited until Cymm smiled, then he ran off.

Before Cymm could blink, they hauled him back into the barn.

"Mount up, we're getting out of here!" ordered Grendella.

Brogan released Cymm's arm with a push. "I don't want to hear any of your pious blather either."

"If Terazhan wanted us to help, he would have waited to send us the Divine Quests," added Grendella.

Everyone mounted their steed except for Cymm. "Wait a second!"

"Oh, here we go," said Brogan.

Cymm scratched the back of his head. "No, *here we go.* I know we can't fight these dragons. How are we getting out of the city, and how do we avoid the dragons picking us off while we flee?"

No one responded.

He turned his gaze on Azreala. "Can we portal to your home?"

"Yes, but then what? If only you and I made the request, my brother would open a portal for us."

"I've been there," Grendella asserted.

Azreala scoffed.

"She has, but not by invitation." Cymm tapped his toes rhythmically. "Feldarius kind of owes me. Can he portal us ten miles to the east? In and out of the Plane of Tides."

He only received a sideways glance from her.

He extended his head and neck toward her. "We have no other option." Glancing around at the others he asked, "Do we?"

"Standing here staring at each other is not a plan. Let's make our way toward East Gate, away from the sounds of battle." Brogan did not wait for a response and urged Claymore, his warhorse, through the doorway and into the street.

Cymm sprang into his saddle. "Maybe a better idea will present itself along the way."

"Feldarius will only open his realm to you and me. So, we need to find an alternative route with safe passage for them," said Azreala.

Talo's warhorse pulled alongside Cymm's. "I'm going with them."

"I don't have time for this."

"You don't need time for this. My decision is made. This is what Terazhan wanted. He must think I can help," Talo said.

"First, we have to find a way out of here, then we'll talk," Cymm said to his cousin's back, who had already turned away. He pulled hard on the reins as a mother with two children ran in front of him. "Watch where you're going!"

"They're frightened. They know what happened to the other cities," said Grendella with an admonishing glare.

Cymm sighed. "What are we going to do?"

"I don't know. Are there any tunnels or sewers that lead into the countryside?" asked Grendella.

"Nah. There is a small gatehouse in the southeast corner, but they would never open it willingly." Cymm peered at Azreala, intently listening to the conversation.

The Necromancer said, "That will not be a problem. I can make them comply with our wishes."

"No. We will not injure our allies. Can't you do something? Like make a section of the wall disappear for a short time or turn us invisible or something," asked Cymm.

DragonSin stirred. *"I can levitate us over the wall, as long as I can see the object and the destination."*

Azreala replied, "No, my magic is—"

"Yes, that's it!" Cymm blurted out, startling the dwarf.

"By the nine hells, Cymm. What's your problem?" asked Grendella.

"DragonSin can help us get over the wall. We need to find an appropriate exit point. Let's go!" Cymm issued one sharp whistle, and his warhorse took off at a canter. He led the group, yelling frequently, "Clear the way!" He kept the speed reasonable so he could react quickly if someone ran out of an alley or a doorway, and so the Stormcallers could keep up on foot.

Within minutes they were approaching the eastern wall.

Azreala pulled even with him astride her hellsteed. "I will scout ahead and make sure the other side of the wall is safe."

Before Cymm could reply, she lurched ahead. Fifty feet from the base of the wall, her mount leaped and cleared the thirty-foot high, crenellated top.

Gasps of excitement and horror escaped the lips of everyone in the group.

"I'm glad she's on our side!" exclaimed Brogan.

"Is she?" asked Zecarius, dubiously.

Brogan squirmed in his saddle.

"I'll go first," said Cymm.

"You can't go over the wall. We need to land on top so we can move everyone safely up and down," said DragonSin. *"Moving anything fragile, including humanoids, requires more concentration and visual cues. So, do not break contact with me, and try to keep a constant eye on the target."*

Cymm replied, *"Very well."*

Brogan recalled everyone from the bailey, and they hid in a side street.

A foot off the ground and his warhorse spooked. He kicked, whinnied, and blew forceful breaths.

"Stop! This isn't going to work," said Cymm to the sword.

They returned to the ground and Cymm dismounted. After many soft clicks, the warhorse finally nuzzled its head against his.

Talo rode out to meet him. "Everything all right?"

"No. We'll have to do the horses separate from the riders." Cymm handed the reins to his cousin.

Talo took a deep breath while scanning the sky.

"I know. Send people over to the base of the wall one at a time." Cymm unsheathed his sword and gripped it tightly, and the world lurched. The ground dropped away as he rose—fast and dizzying—until his boots scraped atop the stone battlements. From here, the chaos of the city hit him in the face, citizens screaming, dragons circling, magic burning the air.

Azreala stared up at him from the other side and gave a curt wave.

A hundred horse-lengths to the north, the eastern gate houses loomed and in between were a half-dozen ballistae. Each one had soldiers with their eyes trained on the sky. He hoped they would stay that way, and their passage would go unnoticed. He continued his inspection behind him and found the same scene, except in the distance to the south he could see the corner tower rise above the defensive weapons. To the west, dragons dotted the sky. A maelstrom of agony rose above the battle din. Clouds of dust and smoke covered the far wall obscuring his vision.

Grendella waited below, alone upon her pony.

Cymm prepared to yell down to get off, but DragonSin did not wait.

Her mount barely reacted when its hooves lifted off the ground. As she passed Cymm by, she smirked. "Some mounts are trained better than others."

"Careful, or I might drop you." Cymm grinned back.

With Grendella safely on the ground outside the wall, he turned to find Talo and two warhorses below.

Once again, his warhorse reacted violently, but this time—since he had no rider—they persisted. Cymm issued several soft clicks as he passed to lessen his fright, but it had no effect. He took a couple steps back to ensure the horse could not reach him with a lunge or kick. When his hooves hit the ground, he took off at a gallop.

Cymm could not worry about that now and immediately lifted Talo into the air. As he drifted by, he made a funny face but did not say a word. Talo's horse was less jittery but blowing hard. His owner quickly grabbed the reins and clicked to ease the beast's nerves.

The Stormcallers went next—Katara, then Tanya, and finally Zecarius. They went much faster since they had no mounts. As Zecarius floated by him, he expected some form of salutation, but instead his friend's eyes went wide.

Cymm resisted the temptation to shift his gaze, and he focused on returning him safely to the ground. When he turned, his heart sank. Five dragons had circled around the far side of the city and were approaching quickly. Three of them were as white as snow and the other two were a mix between black and gray—their bodies made of smoke.

While ducking low, Cymm glanced down to the bailey, where Brogan and his horse waited.

"DragonSin, bring Brogan up to the battlement, then send his horse over the wall."

Brogan's feet lifted off the ground, and he had the appearance of someone about to lose their balance. He touched down next to Cymm. "What are you doing?"

Cymm did not look at him; he kept his eyes on Brogan's warhorse while he pointed toward the north. "Look what's coming. I'm not sure I can do this."

"Do what?"

"Leave them to die." Cymm followed the horse through the pinnacle of its path.

Brogan surveyed the sky again. "I don't see any green dragons, which means those people are going to die with or without your help."

A steel shaft whizzed over top of their heads. The ballistae were firing, which meant the dragons were in range.

Cymm huffed. "I can't. I am going to force Azreala to help me."

"That's madness!" yelled Brogan.

"Listen to me. Take my horse, get everyone mounted, and by Ledaedra's bones get out of here. Push east until you hit the War Dog Tribes, then head north. I will try to catch up." Cymm did not wait for a response. *"DragonSin, move him."*

51

The Ruse

BrimStrakenstone

The black form continued to approach at a rapid speed from the east. Given DetonKonraber's last known position, it was reasonable to assume he would have arrived from the north. KorEmberstrike adjusted his position to intercept.

BrimStrakenstone reached out telepathically, *"My Queen, we are ready for the portal."*

The fiends still swarmed the western gate.

He turned to the general on his right. "Send a phalanx to attack the backside of the city."

A few moments later, the gateway to the dragon's birth home appeared. Nothing unusual caught Brim's attention except for the size. A full-grown dragon could barely fly through, let alone DetonKonraber, and its color blended perfectly with the blue sky, except for the hazy shimmer around its edge.

With the trap in place, Brim contemplated flying through it himself. The scent of cinnamon called to him, to escape the stench of burnt flesh, smoke, and rot of this sodden world. His tail lashed in frustration. *Why do we fight for this place? It will never be home.*

The portal would need to be closed quickly after Deton went through to prevent him from escaping. Brim had no concern about the trellbac pouring out of it. The queen had somehow devised the gateway to prevent the creatures from using it. He remembered using one when his family fled their home world. The portal remained permanently open, but only dragons could pass.

KorEmberstrike recalled his replicated images—which he created using the natural ability of a red dragon—and they converged from different directions on the portal. Four additional warriors soon patrolled the sky under the control of KorEmberstrike.

BrimStrakenstone observed the approaching dragon with interest. *Deton has slowed his speed. Maybe he is counting how many warriors I brought. He could not possibly have sensed a trap. Or could he? How does he even know where and when we are attacking?* Brim felt foolish. *This trap was a bad idea.*

His adversary had shifted his trajectory southeast instead of east.

Brim's head began to ache from the contemplating. *This is not like him. What am I missing? He should be charging in his normal berserker-like frenzy.*

His entire retinue gazed toward the east, hoping Deton would take the bait.

Enough of the games. There is no way he can defeat ten of my best warriors. The losses will be great, but I may not have another chance like this. No, I will send fifteen.

Brim had to shout three times to the general on his right to get his attention.

When the black general finally looked his way, his eyes darted up and went wide. "Brim, watch out!"

A massive lightning bolt struck him in the back, moments before DetonKonraber did the same.

52

Bold Attack

ZaphMordakai

ZaphMordakai stared in disbelief at the dragons attacking the City of Armak. He did not have to count the wyrms in the sky to acknowledge the largest offensive the Queen had ever mounted. The huge red dragon before him he knew well, even without the three long scars across his face. KorEmberstrike, the drake who had tried to steal his first kill. Zaph slowed his pace considerably.

She is attacking Armak. I knew it was coming. Zaph buffeted the air, holding position. He no longer had any desire to join the city raids, but he wanted to observe the carnage. *Ten dragons could devastate this city; fifty plus should be a massacre.* However, he decided to avoid the confrontation with the red dragon, even though he believed they were evenly matched.

A sudden thought sprang forth, *Will Uncle Deton arrive? That alone would be worth waiting to see.* He changed his plan immediately as four more red dragons joined his old nemesis. Zaph turned toward the south, away from Stallion Rise, and moved along.

He gazed sideward, across the city to inspect the main body of the dragon army. Primarily blacks and reds flanked BrimStrakenstone, while the green, white, and shadow dragons gathered at a slightly lower elevation. As he distanced himself, an eerie chill swept through his body. *Why are most of them staring at me?*

Before he could turn away and flee, an immense black form emerged from the clouds above the army, diving straight for its leader. The scene developed slowly in Zaph's mind, as he tried to comprehend the unfolding scene. A white flash escaped its maw and brought Zaph out of his trance. The lightning bolt exploded upon impact with Brim's back, moments before the two behemoths collided.

BrimStrakenstone issued a primordial roar—driven by an unknown emotion of pain, fear, anger, or surprise—in the aftermath of the incredible damage done.

Their wings flapped with a frenzy, but neither could avoid the inevitable. They plummeted toward the ground, slowly at first, then with increasing speed. They ripped and tore at one another, slashed and bit. Neither yielded, nor tried to break away. Flame and lightning continuously flashed in the sky. The speed and intensity of the attacks grew more vicious and primal.

Zaph could not look away—both horrified and mesmerized by the epic battle long in the making.

Every dragon's head turned to witness the struggle; no longer did they peer his way.

The colossal combatants released and caromed away in a tight circle. Brim's left wing only extended partially, indicating severe damage.

The spectators froze in position, in shock or uncertain how to proceed.

DetonKonraber banked around and raced back to reengage with a thunderous roar. BrimStrakenstone circled with difficulty, but by the time he exited the loop, seven of his friends had joined him.

His uncle's fervor never waned, and he closed the distance. Everyone understood a red dragon's innate ability to replicate itself.

Zaph had no love for his uncle, but he hoped he had the ability to detect the real one.

A brilliant flash of light ignited between them. Deton screeched, and angled his body at an absurd angle, then disappeared.

Brim and his simulated cohorts raced through the same area a moment later. Bloodied and torn, BrimStrakenstone released a victorious gout of fire.

53

Pent-Up Energy

Cymm

Far below the dragons, standing on the walls of the city, blood red orbs blinked on Azreala's avatar. Ten engorged tendrils snaked back to grotesque hands with blood-red talons splayed. Crimson energy raced through them in pulsing bursts. Occasionally, a bulge would form and balloon until the mounting pressure from the river of energy forced the blockade to clear. These sudden rushes of power were almost unbearable, and caused Cymm to reel in ecstasy or agony, he could not be sure which. The ever-present passenger, knowledge of their fears, arrived bundled with the energy, but no fear coursed through their minds. However, death and destruction ran rampant.

Cymm had lost track of how many demons the avatar had ripped apart and could not count the number of devils they had drained, but he knew he could not hold much more.

"Azreala, we need to release this pent-up energy. What's the plan?" Cymm asked.

Twenty horse-lengths away, the top of the wall exploded, showering the necromantic avatar.

"Wait!" Azreala replied with a strain.

The citizens who had previously amassed in front of the gate, hoping to flee into the countryside, now fled back into the city.

From on top of the fractured battlement, Cymm gazed through the red haze in his eyes. At least three dragon corpses littered the battlefield, and one had crashed into and partially through the battlement. Demon and devil carcasses lay strewn everywhere and very few remained alive in the area.

In the sky, more dragons approached.

Cymm clearly heard Captain Beckwith calling out orders in the beginning, but his voice had gone silent. The paladin said a quick prayer for his wellbeing. The King's Guard had still not arrived, and he hoped Lord Barrister and Lord Grom were protecting the king in his castle, or they had already escaped.

Azreala closed the avatar's eyes and lifted his arms above his shoulders. When they began to twirl in independent circles, he knew what came next—moans, groans, and undead wailing.

The avatar's eyes flittered open, but the demon and devil corpses did not move. There came a singular, low, raspy growl followed by a substantial chunk of the battlement crashing to the ground. Another tremor went through the twitching dragon carcass embedded in the wall. By the time it disentangled itself, three other animated dragon corpses had joined it.

The sluggish undead creatures almost formed a line in front of the avatar as Azreala maintained control and waved his arms in the air above his head.

Cymm vividly observed every detail of the living dead; his vision crystal clear. The spikes on their heads, wings, and backs gleamed with an eerie radiance.

Now, the moaning began, louder than the surrounding sounds of battle, more urgent and more fervent. The former dragons were angry—angry to be complying with the commands of necromancy.

Azreala turned his head, so she could gaze into the sky. She shot the disformed arms forward toward a squad of approaching dragons. "Attack!"

Slowly at first, wings began to flap. The confined area did not allow for unimpeded movement. One creature snapped at another, and in turn it snapped at two more. They spread out and finally took wing.

"Now do you feel better?" asked Azreala.

Cymm's pain had dissipated, a significant reduction, but he could not remember when. The eminent rupture of whatever stored the drained energy no longer concerned him.

"Azreala, we have exceeded my expectations. We need an exit plan," said Cymm.

"No, not yet," she replied.

"I know you're enjoying this, but we need to go."

In response she cast an additional volley of life-draining wisps at the few remaining hellions.

"Why do you seem to have an endless supply of these tendrils now?" asked Cymm.

Azreala almost purred in response, *"I told you, binding together breaks that limitation, and the energy I drain can be used for many creative things."*

"Well, this vessel has had enough. We—"

A lightning bolt detonated within a sword's length of where they stood. The base eroded beneath their feet, and Azreala commanded his body to jump out over the bailey.

Below them red and blue eyes blinked into existence. Some angry, some gentle, but all obeying. The spirits floated up and formed an invisible platform beneath them. Transparent hands grasped the avatar's ankles, and they rocketed forward on a simulated magic carpet.

The wind whistled in his ears during the fast crossing of the bailey. They barely made the edge of the closest building before their ride began to dissipate. Cymm seemed to know instinctively that Azreala released or commanded them to report to a different plane.

A screech up above drew Azreala's attention in time to witness the midair collision between two dragons. They clawed and scratched each other, and blood fell like rain drops all around the avatar. The cloud of fury drifted over them, and the undead dragon finally lunged for the throat.

The once living dragon's wings ceased flapping and it dove into the dirt. The beast did not move again.

Another squadron of dragons had arrived, and chaos erupted.

Two of Azreala's animated corpses immediately plummeted to the ground.

"I think it's time to leave," Azreala said.

Cymm would have laughed if the circumstances were not so dire. *"Yeah."*

"We need to retrieve my body first." Azreala dug the avatar's crimson talons into the side of the building and slowly fell twenty feet to the ground. They entered the warehouse through the same door they had broken into. "Feldarius, I need help. Open a portal."

"No! Transfer back to your body. I need to make sure they escaped." Cymm struggled under her control of thc avatar.

"Honestly, Cymm. You're not only predictable but annoying." Azreala took a deep steadying breath, then heaved her lifeless body over the avatar's shoulder.

Before Cymm could resist the movement of his arm, the avatar's hand caressed Azreala's lifeless butt cheek. *"Talk about predictable and annoying. It will be easier if you transfer back to your own body."*

Azreala had them running out the door they entered through. *"Currently, there is nothing more powerful than us on the battlefield, but if we separate…"*

"Fine. What's the plan?" asked Cymm. *Once again, I'm just a passenger in my own skin.*

"Watch." Azreala scanned the vicinity and altered their course toward a large fissure in the wall. She leapt up and grabbed the broken edge with one claw, then scrabbled up the steep incline to the top of the battlement while carrying her body.

A quick survey of the vicinity revealed more squadrons of dragons approaching from the western gate, and none of Azreala's dragon minions remained. With a huff, she shot crimson wisps out and struck several plainsmen trying to escape the city.

"No! What are you doing?" Cymm shouted.

"We need the extra energy."

"No. Find another way."

The smokey tendrils evaporated, and finally Azreala trumpeted her satisfaction. New tentacles raced toward her latest target, a black dragon on the ground in its death throws. Deep claw marks covered its body and javelins had pierced it. It stared back with venomous eyes as its life force traveled back to the avatar.

Azreala wasted no time converting the sapped energy into necromantic power. The same dragon began to twitch and rose clumsily on unsteady legs. It shook its head as if something had crawled into its ear, then shrieked in their direction.

The shrill sound drew the attention of the three dragons in the immediate area, and they broke off their chase of the escaping humans. They banked around and headed straight for the newly risen dead.

The numbers were mounting against them. Fifteen dragons from the west, three dragons from the east, and a quick glance to the south revealed more. They were surrounded.

"Azreala!" cried Cymm.

"I know! This isn't going to work." Azreala ran halfway down the broken wall, retracing her way up, then leapt to the ground. She summoned her hellsteed and vaulted onto its back, placed her limp body across the beast on the avatar's lap, then raced toward the eastern main gate.

They were halfway there when an enormous red body dropped into the bailey before them, gliding below the battlement.

Azreala forced the hellsteed to make a severe left turn, so sharp, her unconscious body began to slip, but not sharp enough to avoid the approaching wall.

If Cymm had control of his eyelids, they would have grown wide in apprehension. *We are going to hit the wall. "Azreala!"*

Azreala did not respond, and the mount did not slow.

Cymm gasped.

The radius of the curve took the hellsteed up the side of the building eight to ten feet before it arced back down to the ground. Their speed never dropped; it might have even increased.

Azreala glanced back, and Cymm's stress diminished. The red dragon had not gained more than a dozen horse lengths.

"Terazhan be blessed!" Cymm said exuberantly.

Azreala laughed, but her mirth ended abruptly when their vision returned to the front, a black dragon had swooped down into the bailey barreling straight for them. Trapped between two dragons.

The avatar pulled hard on the hellsteed's neck, veering to the far side of the bailey—the outer wall.

"Cymm, I have no idea how much damage this body can sustain. We can't take on these two dragons directly," said Azreala.

Cymm could feel the acceleration of the mount beneath them, and he anticipated her intention to leap the outer wall again. A quick glance to both sides revealed the black dragon closing fast. Too fast. The creature would arrive before they jump.

Azreala placed the avatar's hand on her lifeless body's bare skin. *"Goodbye, Cymm."*

The black dragon breathed in deep and expelled a lightning bolt.

54

Hard Truth

Talo

Talo glanced back over his shoulder for the hundredth time. He could easily see over the top of Katara's head, who had her arms wrapped around his waist. There did not appear to be any dragons following them, and they had not seen a demon or devil for a while. He had no idea how long their flight for freedom lasted, but the towers of Armak were no longer visible.

A tall stand of hollow grass loomed ahead. Ranging from ten to fifteen feet tall, it would easily conceal them from those above.

Talo urged his warhorse forward, taking the lead and entering the grass. Some of the stalks approached the width of his hand and would not budge, but most were pliable and shifted around the horses and pony.

"Why are you stopping?" asked Grendella.

"We need a plan," said Talo.

"We *have* a plan. Let's keep moving." Brogan tried to push past him.

With two clicks, Talo halted Brogan's warhorse. "We need a better plan."

Brogan eyeballed him with a cocked head. "Cymm told me to keep moving until we get to the War Dog Tribes, then turn—"

"He can't defeat that many dragons. He's going to die, if we don't help him." Talo ran his hand through his hair.

No one said a word.

Zecarius, riding Cymm's horse with Tanya in front of him, shifted uncomfortably in the saddle.

"I'm going back." Talo urged his horse forward.

This time Brogan blocked his way, and he stared at Grendella.

The dwarf sighed. "Talo, think about what you said. If Cymm can't defeat them, how could we possibly help? If any of us return and die, it will lessen the value of Cymm's sacrifice."

"*Sacrifice?*" Talo wailed. "So, you think he is going to die?" Talo's chest tightened. He tried to grip the reins tighter, but his sweaty palms made it difficult.

"I think he knew what his chances were, and he did it anyway to save us and as many inhabitants of the city as possible. That is who he is," replied Grendella.

Katara rubbed his shoulder. With a raspy voice she said, "It's what brings him happiness."

Everyone seemed to be nodding in his direction.

"How is it possible that all of you know him better than me, and I have known him his entire life?" Talo hung his head.

Jalko issued a low growl toward the direction they had come from.

Talo's head snapped up in alarm. "Something is following us."

55

The Wizards

BrimStrakenstone

The western gate of Armak lay in utter ruin. After the demons and devils had won through the outer defenses, they progressed to tracking and killing the humans manning the ballistae. With the war machines eliminated, the dragons proceeded to sack the western side of the city while the fiends swept through the streets toward the eastern gate.

BrimStrakenstone barely remained aloft. DetonKonraber's talons and teeth had torn large gashes in his torso, but the lightning bolt delivered the most damage, severely wounding his back and left wing. Every flap of his wings generated a burst of pain that radiated through his body.

Brim took care to ensure his eagerness to end this raid did not end with a bad decision. He did not have ZaphMordakai's innate ability to heal, but his wounds would mend, and maybe the queen would assist him. He glanced nervously at the point in the sky where the portal had materialized. DetonKonraber possessed the same uncanny ability to heal himself, and he would avoid a rematch until fully recovered.

On the other side of the city, Brim discovered a full-blown skirmish underway. To his great surprise, dragons were attacking dragons.

"General!" he called to the black dragon on his right and second in command. "What is going on over there?"

"I have no reports yet."

"Find out!" Brim grimaced through the command, unsure how much longer he could endure this pain. They had accomplished their main goal and killed thousands, maybe even ten thousand in the process. *I need to deal with Deton's decoy before I go. It would appear there is a traitor amongst us.*

At this distance no distinguishing features had stood out—other than black scales. He scanned the horizon for the culprit anyway. Nothing. The three phalanxes now enroute to the eastern gate blocked part of his view. Suddenly, a thought sprang to mind, *what happened to all the wizards? Are they setting a trap?*

Brim held the green dragons in reserve for the final wave. Even with the ones he lost, there were enough remaining to blanket the entire city in a green fog.

No longer would he question the effectiveness or the usefulness of Marekai's and Malekai's horde. Five hundred hellions had made an obvious difference. The Twins of Terror claimed to have over twenty thousand more in their legion, as well as hundreds of higher-ranking hellions at their disposal.

"General!"

BrimStrakenstone emerged from his contemplating. "What?"

"There are dragons attacking our forces," said the black general.

"I know that. What I don't know is why," growled Brim.

"Our own dead warriors are fighting against us."

It must be the work of the wizards. They are behind this. BrimStrakenstone flinched as another surge of pain radiated through his coracoid. "I think we found the magic-users."

Although his second in command hid it well, he smirked at Brim's pain and wrinkled his snout in contempt. "Everything seems to be centered around one creature. Come, I will show you."

"Come, I will show you," Brim was not so naïve to think he would not be attacked by his own army, especially an ambitious general. In his current condition, he needed to be prepared for anything, and he could not show any weakness. "Lead the way."

BrimStrakenstone followed, but at a distance, keeping an eye above and behind him.

56

The Withering

Azreala

The wind whipped Azreala's hair across her face and her stomach lurched. As she fell, she second-guessed herself. The hasty decision to abandon the avatar's body—to abandon Cymm—had nullified years of planning. So many unknowns and too many possibilities for her to take a chance or for things to go wrong. The lightning would not have killed the avatar, but a possibility existed when adding the damage from the fire drake barreling in. What if the phylactery's ability to protect her soul did not function when she using an avatar or what if her soul could not find its way back to her body? The phylactery had not worked for her father. The risk exceeded the reward. She would need to find a new way to accomplish her ultimate goal.

Azreala hit the ground hard and rolled, searching for an escape route. The lightning bolt had sailed over their heads, delivering no damage to her body. She had not intended to banish the hellsteed, but it instantly disappeared when she transferred back to herself, causing them to fall.

Her body tingled with exhilaration from the extraordinary amount of power she had just wielded. Endorphins coursed through her brain like a living creature, making it difficult to concentrate. She had never harnessed so much raw energy.

A massive body hit the ground behind her, causing her to spin and discover the red dragon. She backpedaled three or four steps with crimson magic dancing between her fingers. Her arms reared back to release her most powerful spell—the withering—but the red dragon skidded to a halt. Its eyes were blank, and its tongue hung from its mouth. The brilliant red scales covering its body were missing from the left side of its face, neck, and torso, blackened by the lightning bolt.

"Azreala!" Cymm yelled from above her.

The black dragon had him in its talons, carrying him away. Or, so she thought, until he banked around quickly, heading straight for her.

He survived! I can't believe he survived. She readied her spell again and took care not to hit Cymm. A little closer and the wrym would not have time to dodge the shadow bolt.

Cymm waved her forward with a peculiar smile on his face.

Before she could analyze the meaning, the dragon released him and swooped away. The young man landed on the battlement after a short drop.

"Azreala, get up here!" called Cymm.

She easily made the ten foot jump up to get her claws in the damaged crevice, then scrabbled to the top of the sharp incline onto the battlement.

They both began talking simultaneously.

"Why did you say goodbye?" asked Cymm.

"Why didn't the dragon kill you?" asked Azreala.

Both waited for the other to answer, then assessed the approaching dragon horde.

"We do not have time for this!" Azreala scanned the perimeter outside the wall.

"Summon your fire-hooved beast and let's be gone," replied Cymm.

"Without the excess energy to feed him, he will not be fast enough, especially with two of us riding." Azreala's face lit up. "I have a better idea!" Her arms shot up above her head and whipped around in circles. She noticed the black dragon returning with the dragon horde close behind.

Her most recent undead dragon lifted its black body above the edge of the battlement, startling Cymm, who fell backward in shock.

Azreala made an impressive leap onto the dragon's back. "Come on. Let's go!"

Cymm regained his feet, but after three near attempts he had yet to jump.

"Time to go. Move it!" Azreala could feel the skin and flesh of the dead beast wrapping itself around her hooves.

After retreating half a dozen paces, Cymm turned back toward the crumbling battlement, and sprinted as Azreala swooped in.

The creature's wings made it impossible to get close, but Azreala tilted the undead dragon as they approached, dipping its closest wing.

Cymm's boots slipped on the ragged edge as he launched himself into the air. He hit the dragon's side with a groan.

Wind howled in her ears as they raced away, drowning out most of Cymm's moaning.

Azreala shrieked, "Hold on!" She pitched the dragon in the opposite direction to help him climb up on the undead dragon's back.

Cymm could not climb the rough black scales. His fingers, slick with blood, clung to the bone-hard spikes.

She dropped to all fours and reached down to hoist him up. Her smile disappeared. Two dragon spikes had impaled him.

With white knuckles wrapped around a spike, Cymm barely hung on. "I can't move my leg."

Like an acrobat, Azreala dropped down next to him using the spikes for hand and foot holds. "You're not going to like this," she said with a devilish grin, then forced her body between Cymm's and the dragon's. "Wrap your arms around my neck!" The warmth of Cymm's skin against hers made her pause.

The undead dragon's body rocked from a massive collision, then continued to shutter as wisps of shadow magic danced through the air.

"Dragons are attacking! Hold tight!" yelled Azreala.

Cymm cried out in agony as she pushed her hips, tail, and buttocks back into him.

The spikes withdrew with a sucking *slurp* from his muscular leg.

She climbed back up with ease and settled him in place before wheeling their undead mount at a sharp angle to the left, then dove with her crimson magic crackling in the air.

"Not the black one! He's on our side," yelled Cymm between groans of pain.

She held her spell, the magical energy awaiting her command, but it dispersed when a cone of frigid air hit them from the blindside. The white dragon swooped past them raking the undead dragon with its talons.

Back on the main side, the shadow dragon released its bolt of shadow magic while their backs were turned, but the magic called to Azreala. Her eyes blazed red, and she grinned. *He obviously doesn't know who I am.*

The goddess of death reached out with both arms and funneled the energy into a ball before absorbing it.

Dozens more dragons were trailing them.

"We may need to bind again," shouted Azreala above the wind.

Cymm bled profusely from one of the puncture wounds. "We can't until the new moon."

Azreala scoffed. "That rule does not apply to me. I don't know why, but I can feel your body calling to me."

Cymm mimicked her scoff. "My body is not *calling* to you. I need to heal myself. Can you steady this creature?"

"I'll try. Their closing in again." Azreala angled away and glanced back to gage the distance.

The black dragon split the two dragons as he raced between them, buffeting them off kilter.

Cymm took advantage of the opportunity. "Lord Terazhan, please heal this faithful servant of yours."

The undead dragon emitted an ear-piercing shriek and plummeted.

She swallowed hard, the endorphins racing through her body for a second time. Finally, she pulled up, and its wings filled with air. "Don't do that again!" Azreala commanded, even though the exhilaration had made her hooves tingle.

"That was crazy! I almost flew off the back." Cymm still clung to large spikes with bulging biceps to avoid falling.

Azreala offered her hand and assisted him to his feet. When he rose, his body came within inches of hers.

"Quickly! We need to leave this place," the black dragon growled as he pulled even with them.

Cymm said, "That is ZaphMordakai. He is—"

"Cymm, bind!" Azreala tried to lock eyes with him.

"I'm telling you; this isn't going—" Cymm went silent.

Azreala mentally commanded the avatar to grab her body before it collapsed. She lowered it down onto an enormous spike, sending it through her abdomen, to ensure it would not fall off the dragon. After turning to ride backward, she could feel the scales conforming around her hooves. *I love this avatar form. I am unstoppable, I am…invincible, I am a juggernaut!*

With a bellowing war cry, she released her crimson tendrils.

The white dragon banked to avoid them, but they slammed and embedded into the dragon's flank. The beast reared and pulled but could not free itself. Its movements became frantic, and it roared in pain or fear or both.

Another bolt of shadow magic hit the avatar full in the chest.

"Shadow dragon, you did not learn from the first time. You will learn soon enough who I am," Azreala said. She absorbed the energy without even flinching.

The thickness of the wisps attached to the white dragon grew into tentacles as they pumped the life force from the white dragon. Its thrashing and ability to fight were waning.

"Azreala! You do see the other dragons, right?" asked Cymm nervously.

She did. Fifteen came on fast and had cut the gap in half. *Just a few more moments.*

The shadow dragon lurched forward with a burst of speed. Its smokey face ephemeral, but its teeth were bone-white needles.

Azreala's right hand released the energy draining tentacles and slashed at the dragon with astonishing speed.

The dragon roared in pain. The shadowy smoke on its face revealed deep grooves.

"I can see it in your eyes. You finally know who I am. Don't you?" hissed Azreala with the avatar's voice.

"You are no one!" the dragon hissed back.

The white dragon crashed to the ground below, only to rise moments later.

"You would have never done this to my father," screamed Azreala.

The shadow dragon sneered. "You are not him. Cavendar, would be ashamed of you."

Azreala trumpeted in rage as she cupped the avatar's hands together, then violently ripped them apart. The avatar's eyes blazed brightly, blinding her briefly.

The roar of the shadow dragon ended abruptly, replaced by a groan of pain which transformed into a shriek. Struggles morphed into gurgles before it exploded into motes of shadow magic. She collected each one like a shepherd gathers his flock, calling to—

A lightning bolt blasted into the avatar's chest, causing its right arm to hang numb and useless.

Azreala, Cymm, and the avatar all screamed at once.

"Azreala! Pump some energy into our mount," Cymm pleaded.

The hair on the avatar's head stood at attention and tiny electrical bolts jumped from one clump of hair to another. As the undead dragon picked up speed, the wind whistled in his ears until a raging inferno roared towards them.

The undead dragon dove and banked right, but not before the skin on the avatar's forearms and calves blistered, scorched by the fire.

Cymm said with terror in his voice, *"We're going to die. My body can't take all this damage. We're going to die."*

"Relax. Did you see the thrashing Bardonril took before he died?" Azreala felt warm and tingly.

"You might be safe when we separate, but my body will be left damaged and broken. More energy. Go faster! Look back. Are we losing them?" Cymm's hysteria had not abated, and he forcefully took control of the avatar's neck.

They were pulling away from the chase pack and starting to catch up to ZaphMordakai.

Cymm forced the avatar to glance down toward the ground.

Azreala encouraged it by releasing some of her control. She could feel his heart racing, and it fanned the flames of her excitement. From two hundred feet in the air, the droves of refugees were incredible.

"Do you see our group? Do you see Talo?" asked Cymm.

Azreala pulled gently on a wisp tethered to the undead black dragon, feeding it energy. It slowly adjusted course, heading south.

"Cymm, if we want to save these people, we need to redirect the dragons following us."

After a long pause, Cymm replied, *"Yes. We should save them."*

The dragons chasing them tried to cut the tangent in a futile attempt to close the distance. They hung on for half an hour, then disappeared.

"ZaphMordakai, we are landing," said the avatar.

The black dragon glanced back over his shoulder, then nodded.

"As soon as we separate, heal yourself. If that doesn't work, I will encase your soul again, so it cannot leave this world," said Azreala.

Upon landing, the avatar grabbed Azreala's body and leaped down to the ground. The transference began immediately.

Azreala dropped to a knee in pain. In addition to her soul, she had taken half of the bodily damage with her when she transferred.

In fits and starts, Cymm called out, "Terazhan, the One-True-God…heal me—please!" When he finally recovered, he rushed over and extended his hand to Azreala. "You're injured."

"I'm all right. Did you feel the raw energy running through us? I have never felt so powerful. No one can stop us." Azreala peered up into Cymm's bright eyes and smiling face. Their gazes locked. She drew a deep breath that caught in her throat. When he hoisted her to her feet, their bodies came within inches of each other, and she sensed a palpable heat coming off his body. She wanted to embrace him, squeeze him, and feel his heart pounding against her chest. Hot fire coursed through her veins, and she could not catch her breath.

"No, you're not all right." Cymm reached out to grab her shoulder while praying to Terazhan.

Azreala took a hesitant step back. "No, *He* can't heal me." *Let Cymm touch you.* She gently bit her lower lip. *No, this is not what I want. I only pretend it is.* She could sense the horror on her face, but she lunged toward him anyway, hoping he would wrap his arms around her.

Instead, he seemed to take it as permission, and his white healing light expanded quickly.

Her wounds closed rapidly, but a beast deep inside had awakened. The endorphins running through her body amplified tenfold, and her body burned with desire. When Cymm began to pull away, she grabbed him roughly, lifted him, and kissed him forcefully.

The revulsion on Cymm's face struck her harder than a slap. *How dare you look at me that way. I am a goddess.* She blinked several times. *But why do I care? I need his help—his power—not his love. He promised me the death of—*

"What are you doing?" Cymm sputtered. "Why did you do that?"

Azreala had no answer for him. In fact, she wanted to ask herself the same question.

57

Tracker

Talo

Jalko took two slow steps back toward the city of Armak with his head sunk low. He issued a warning growl to whatever approached. The dire wolf had everyone's attention, and they turned their mounts in the same direction—back the way they came.

"Is it a dragon?" whispered Brogan.

Talo's shoulders lifted once. "Should we ride hard?"

The stress and uncertainty bubbled over in the murmured voices.

"Quiet! Katara, scout it out." Brogan issued the commands quietly.

Talo silenced Jalko and sent the wolf with her.

The setting sun cast long shadows in the tall grass grove. The wind, absent most of the day, creaked even the thickest of stalks, creating an unsettling atmosphere.

Time passed excruciatingly slow, and Talo worried at his lip while straining his ears. "Someone is coming."

Panting heavily, Katara burst out of the thicket and into their midst, followed closely by Jalko. "A single rider following our trail through the grassland." She offered her hand to Talo to pull her up.

"No. We stand here." Brogan dismounted. "Spread out. We'll surround him when he enters this area."

Talo found his position and glanced about. A six-inch thick grass stalk did little to conceal a warhorse. He shook his head—no one was really hiding—but prepared to converge on their pursuer.

A long, drawn-out creak from nearby increased the tension as their pursuer's horse pushed past one of the thicker stalks. Moments later the clearing exploded into action.

After surrounding the horseman, Brogan unceremoniously ripped him from his saddle. The stranger struggled and fought but conceded when his face hit the dirt. Katara relieved him of his weapons, then Zecarius and Brogan hauled him to his feet.

"Unhand me!" cried the stranger.

Brogan gave him a shake, and his hood fell backward.

Talo gaped.

Dirk Darkmane glared up at them.

58

A Convincing Offer

ZaphMordakai

A boulder protruded from the ground in the middle of a short-grass field. The white, black, and pink speckled stone stood out in stark contrast to the field of green and brown. Cymm Reich sat upon it brooding.

Azreala stood statuesque with her eyelids fluttering.

ZaphMordakai, still in dragon form, lounged nearby side-eyeing them.

Cymm removed his necklace, a ring attached to a leather thong.

The dragon had an aptitude for detecting valuable treasure, and this did not appear to be of any value.

With slow, methodical movements, the ring spun around the cord, gradually picking up speed. The air around the human's hands began to distort and a turquoise haze sprang to life, then coalesced into an image of a little girl.

Zaph's head slowly spun, and his eyes bulged. He had not expected this. *By the seven heavens, this Cymm is full of surprises.* The color of the magic had him flummoxed. He had never seen turquoise magical energy before. *What is the source of this dweomer?*

After completing the sequence with the ring twice, Cymm returned it to his neck while staring at the ground, then fixed a menacing gaze on Zaph. "So let me get this straight. First, you want to kill me, and you have the chance, but you let me live. Then, you help me escape back there by killing other dragons, which is exactly why you wanted to kill me in the first place. What do you want, ZaphMordakai?"

Azreala's eyes rolled from the back of her sockets. She stared intently at Zaph, listening.

Energy percolated through the dragon's body, forcing a wave of heat across his brow. "I already told you. My mother is being held captive, and I need to save her."

"Yes, and how does that apply to me?"

Zaph shook his head briskly in disbelief. With a quick glance at Azreala, he said, "You saved her."

"Oh, no…no…no. We were lucky. No one expected we were coming," replied Cymm.

Zaph rose and lunged. "You owe me!"

"Easy, dragon!" Azreala already had crimson fire flickering off her fingers like candlesticks.

A low grumble escaped Zaph's open maw.

Azreala guffawed. "In this body, I could kill ten of you. Would you like to join your black undead friend over there?"

Zaph clamped his mouth shut. Her ability to heal herself surpassed even his own. He turned back to Cymm. "I want to save my mother, and you are going to help me. As a bonus, you can save eight others including your beloved, Lykinnia."

"What?" came the surprising, explosive response from Azreala.

Cymm fixed her with a bizarre gape.

Zaph's gaze flicked away. "She was taken days past and chained up—same as you." Zaph indicated Azreala with his snout.

"We need to save her!" Azreala's eyes flamed anew.

Excitement ran through Zaph's body. "And my mother!"

Cymm finally spoke, "That would explain why I haven't heard from Lykinnia in almost a week. Why is your mother a prisoner?"

"Ledaedra is using her as leverage over me."

"Then she is dead," said Azreala without emotion.

ZaphMordakai's stomach twisted in pain. "No! Not yet. If we act fast, we can free her."

"What aren't you telling us? Ledaedra told you she would kill your mother, and yet you still helped us. Why?" asked Cymm.

Zaph barely heard the human, and he mumbled to himself, "She can't be dead. When I left her, she remained chained to the pole."

"Chained to what pole?" asked Azreala.

Zaph shifted uncomfortably. "It's not important. Let's get moving and save Lykinnia and my mother."

"What pole?" Azreala's eyes were catching fire.

"A stone pillar next to Ledaedra's alter, but the Dragon Queen is not always there. We will wait for the right moment to strike," replied Zaph, speaking rapidly.

Zaph did not like the way the goddess's eyes narrowed, but she did not speak her thoughts.

Cymm stared off blankly into the distance until the white undead dragon landed heavily next to the black one. He rose from the boulder. "We definitely need to save Lykinnia and the others, if possible, but I am heading to the Peak of Power first."

"No, that will take too long," said Zaph.

"I agree, we need to act fast," added Azreala.

"Terazhan must know Lykinnia is missing, and he wants me to come to the Peak of Power. Maybe he already knows how to save her, and besides, if we fly the rest of the way there, we can arrive by morning." Cymm looked at the two undead beasts.

Zaph did not care about the abominations that had once been his brethren. He did not care about any of the dragons that willingly followed Ledaedra, and he could sense his opinion of his uncle changing rapidly. "We need to help my uncle too. He battled with the red general."

"We don't have time to save your entire family. Let's go." Azreala stomped toward the undead dragons.

Cymm fell in line. "Zaph, what happened to your uncle?"

"It looked like he disappeared into a portal, probably created by Ledaedra."

"A portal? To where?" asked Cymm.

Azreala waved her arm. "Come on, let's go."

Zaph stretched his wings. "I don't know. Not to Ledaedra's plane. I would guess she sent him back to our home world."

Cymm mounted the undead dragon behind Azreala. "Maybe a little kindness."

Azreala rolled her eyes and stitched her brow. "We should be there by noon."

"I have made this trip before. We will arrive by midmorning," Zaph corrected her.

"You'll need to wait at the bottom of the mountain, Zaph. We should not be too long," said Azreala.

"I've never had to wait before," replied Zaph, lifting into the air.

"Before? You've been there before?" Azrcala's grumbling drifted away behind him.

Every fiber in ZaphMordakai's body screamed for him to forget this madness and rescue his mother on his own, but Cymm was willing to help, and he seemed to always succeed.

And he had better succeed this time too.

59

Crucial Conversation

Azreala

With the rising of the sun came a clear line of sight of the surrounding mountains. The Peak of Power rose hundreds of feet higher than the next highest summit, and a sparkle crowned its top. The entire mountain range wore a blanket of snow except for their destination.

The breeze whistled in Azreala's ears, providing some distraction from the anxious rumbling in her gut. *Am I really going to be allowed to visit? To tread on hallowed ground. Will I be treated as an equal?*

Azreala could recall several invitations in the past, expecting to visit, only to be denied. She would not tolerate her emotions being toyed with this time. This caused her to feel the highs and lows more acutely and created the bitter resentment she currently harbored.

She could now distinguish four unique cascades splashing down the side of the mountain and collecting at the bottom in a large pool ringed by boulders.

Cymm pointed over her shoulder toward a large open space on the plateau. "We should land there."

"Alright." Azreala guided their mount in the direction indicated.

ZaphMordakai glided up next to them. "You two aren't very bright."

Azreala, unfazed by the comment, glanced back at Cymm poised with a jape.

Cymm's sharp intake of breath indicated he felt otherwise. "What are you talking about?"

"What do you think will happen if those undead creatures land on the holy ground below?" asked the black dragon.

Azreala's eyebrows went up. "Good point."

"I'm not even sure I can land there in my dragon form. I usually land at the bottom and transition into a drow or panther, then make the climb," said ZaphMordakai.

"Lead on," replied Azreala.

"Fly over the top, and I will levitate down. DragonSin can control my descent." Cymm pushed back from her so he could swing his leg around and ride sidesaddle.

"What for?" she asked.

"So, I can prepare the way and make sure I haven't misconstrued anything."

Azreala gritted her teeth. *Here we go again.* "Cymm, don't do this."

Long seconds of silence drifted by. She could sense his gaze boring into her back, but she dared not look. She had no intention of revealing any more of herself than her previous sentence—her vulnerability to raw and sensitive. She allowed herself a deep, steadying breath.

"Fine. We go together." Cymm swung his leg back around and even patted her on the shoulder.

ZaphMordakai swooped in closer. "Everything alright with you lovebirds?"

Cymm groaned.

Crimson fire leapt from her hand and singed the dragon's nose before he dove.

Cymm smacked his hand on his thigh. "You know he will tell Lykinnia a distorted version of the truth."

"I promise you he won't say a word about my momentary lapse of judgement."

When they landed a minute later, ZaphMordakai transformed instantly into a black panther. He lurched for the trail after a moment's glance but not quick enough.

Azreala vaulted from the dragon's back, crimson skulls rocketing forward before she hit the ground. All five smacked into the side of the panther, hurling him into the rock wall. A small pulse of energy snaked back to her, and she took a tiny taste.

The cat shimmered and groaned as it transformed to its true nature.

Cymm rushed up behind her. "Stop!"

"Go on ahead, we will catch up." Azreala lowered her voice to a whisper, "I won't kill him, yet."

"No, I will make sure this doesn't get out of control." Cymm grabbed her arm. "We agreed to go together."

ZaphMordakai's bravado returned with his dragon form, and he lunged with an open maw.

Azreala took another taste, freezing him in place. She sniggered.

"What...do you want?" the dragon asked with gasping breaths.

With a mocking smile, she said, "I have worked too hard and yearned for too long to allow someone like *you* to ruin my plan. You will not mention my indiscretion again, to anybody, including Lykinnia. Especially Lykinnia."

The dragon raised his head defiantly. "Don't you think she deserves to know?"

Azreala's eyes flared hot and crimson. "Do you remember the pain you felt in the Plane of Tides when you and Ledaedra came uninvited? Imagine dealing with that every day, every minute of every day."

ZaphMordakai scoffed. "Why not every second?"

"Because the rest of the time you will be watching your mother's soul writhe in agony from the same pain. All because you ran your mouth when you shouldn't have," said the goddess of death.

"Well, that—I am certain…" The dragon railed against his restraints. "You had better not touch my mother!"

"Then we have a deal?" *He really thinks his mother is still alive. Ledaedra's ruse is very convincing, even I thought I saw Cymm being held captive. I wonder how many she has tricked.*

ZaphMordakai grumbled but nodded in agreement, and the crimson tendrils evaporated immediately.

For individual reasons, no one spoke the entire trek to the top. At first, Cymm refused to ride double on her hellsteed, but he quickly changed his mind when he began to fall behind.

The black panther crested the final rise in the trail first, but Azreala hesitated, then alit and dismissed her mount. ZaphMordakai had already taken on his drow form and now walked beside Cymm heading toward the altar.

Azreala's first steps were tentative. *The council meets here, and Feldarius and I have never been invited to attend. Even Bardonril attended before he took a darker path.* The two sphinx guardians circled low overhead, ignoring her. A wry smile formed as her confidence built.

In the distance, stood several individuals near the altar—Terazhan among them.

She inspected him closely. *He's wearing it!* Her eyes sparkled in delight rivaling the gleam from the gemstones on the Mantle of the Gods. *Everything is coming together exactly as Jakarrak said it would.*

60

War Dog Territory

Talo

They had not seen a dragon in the sky for almost two days, although the groves of tall grass made it impossible to see the horizon in any direction. The group continued to head east but after the first day, they had slowed the pace to keep the horses fresh in case they needed to sprint.

"Dirk, quit your bellyaching," growled Grendella Ironcore.

Talo shook his head. "I agreed to you coming if—"

"Quiet!" said Katara, barely above a whisper as she sprinted back toward them.

Brogan raised his hand, and everyone stopped.

Talo picked out only one word as Katara updated Brogan, "horns."

A savage brawl broke out in the direction from which Katara had returned. Snarls, shouts, and howls mixed with yelps and cries of pain.

Concern and urgency rapidly replaced Brogan's confusion. He turned his horse sharply to the left. "Quickly, this way."

Everyone but Jalko followed. With a grumble, he rocketed forward toward the noise.

"No, Jalko!" Talo urged his warhorse after the dire wolf, chasing him through the endless tall grass until they popped out into a field of the knee-high, wide-bladed variety.

Surrounded by men and dogs, two monstrous creatures with violet skin and pitch-black hair stood steadfast. These things from nightmares had to be demons.

The men in the skirmish went by the moniker hackles—from the War Dog Clan—and one already lay upon the ground thrashing from a grievous wound. Deep claw marks raked across his belly, through his leather jerkin, revealing his bowels.

Jalko ravaged a demon from behind while engaged and distracted. Talo's horse crashed into the other trying to trample it and causing the demon to fly several horse lengths away from the mighty collision. Talo raced away, stringing his bow in the process.

A war dog pounced on a demon only to be backhanded and sent soaring into his bonded partner. Another dog's yipe ended abruptly before the beast fell to the ground motionless.

With back bent, a demon loomed over a fallen man butchering him with both claws. An arrow struck it in the neck. It wavered, on the brink of death from the damage the dogs had done to its body. Talo's second arrow hit within an inch of the first, and the demon went down.

"Joharie, to me!" called one of the hackles. He glanced over his shoulder. "Joharie?"

Two men, a dog, and a wolf surrounded the last demon.

Talo lost the opportunity for a clear shot at its face and released his arrow into its back.

From five horse lengths, a second war dog hobbled to join the fight, yelping every time he put pressure on his front leg.

A fury possessed Jalko, the likes of which Talo had never seen, as if this demon were king of the jackrats. He paired proficiently with the war dog as they supported each other's attacks and defended each other's flank.

The demon swung in a circle and drove its elbow into the chest of a hackle, impaling him with the long spike protruding from it. Its howl of glee quickly turned into frustration when the body of the dead man continued to hang limply from its arm after repeatedly trying to dislodge him.

Talo's bow creaked under pressure, waiting to deliver its payload. The demon paused to sniff the air, gazing past Talo toward his friends. He sent his next arrow through the creature's eye.

The surviving hackle decapitated the demon. He grunted and his short sword rose in a defensive pose, facing Talo's companions. They remained at the edge of the tall grass, observing.

Brogan had his arms crossed over his chest, and Grendell's typical dour face seemed even more sour.

"It's alright, they're with me." Talo dismounted and approached the stranger slowly.

The war dog sniffed at Talo and decided Jalko was more interesting. Both sniffed each other's hindquarters while walking in a circle.

The man sheathed his sword and ran his fingers through his hair. "They came at us out of nowhere. What are these things?"

"I think they were—"

"Look at what they did. How am I going to explain this to the elders?" The man gazed into the distance, rubbing the back of his neck.

Talo did not attempt to answer his second question, having learned his lesson from the first. A whimper to his immediate right drew his attention.

The injured war dog nuzzled under Talo's elbow while standing on three paws. His fourth hung in the air, dangling back and forth.

Talo gave the male dog a scratch on the head. "It looks like your shoulder's out of joint, friend. I can help you if you lie down." He received a tilted head in response from the war dog.

"Talo, let's go!" called Brogan.

"Can you lie down?" asked Talo.

The dog panted rapidly.

"What are you trying to do?" asked the hackle.

"I've put many horse legs back in their socket, and I think I can help him," replied Talo.

"Joharie, lie down," the hackle commanded.

The war dog hesitated, then flopped over without putting any pressure on the injured leg. His impact with the ground made a resounding *thud*.

"This is going to hurt," Talo warned the hackle. "I need you to hold his neck or collar tight, so he doesn't bite me."

"I'll try. I'm not sure how long I can hold him for." The hackle knelt next to the back of the war dog's neck.

Talo sat with the dog's injured leg between his legs, and it reached past his crotch. He placed both feet on the dog's chest—one on each side of the injured leg—and bent the dog's good leg under him to avoid being kicked. When he grabbed the injured leg at the shank, Joharie whimpered and tried to squirm away, but both men held him tight.

With a firm grip and a quick pull, the bone slid back into the socket with an audible *pop*.

A high-pitched yelp escaped the dog's jowls, and with a powerful surge, he rose to his paws.

Talo rolled and quickly moved to avoid his snapping jaws, then retreated several horse lengths.

The war dog stared at Talo for several seconds—unmoving and unblinking—then walked gingerly without whimpering to his deceased master.

A rustle in the grass to his right, alerted Talo to Grendella's presence.

She patted him on the back, and said, "We need to keep moving."

Joharie lay down next to his master and placed his massive head on the lifeless man's chest.

Turning to leave, Talo almost ran into the dwarf. "Isn't there anything you can do to heal the hackles?"

She shook her head.

Brogan snorted like a bull. "You're not Cymm! Stop trying to save everyone."

"I know. I was trying to save Jalko." Talo glanced at his heels. *Where is he?*

As if the recent battle had never happened, Jalko and the other surviving war dog romped through the grass chasing each other.

Talo sounded his unique whistle for Jalko, commanding him to come. *What has gotten into him?* Jalko appeared very comfortable with the war dogs. *Cymm did say he ran away from his wolf tribe for a couple of years. Who knows where his travels took him.*

After a brief hesitation, Jalko came running.

61

Leighton

Lykinnia

The sun hung low on the western sky, ushering in a new day, but which day was uncertain. In her foggy mind, Lykinnia lingered at the precipice of her abode, holding the door open. A glorious morning awaited her outside. She yawned and shifted to rub her sleepy eyelids.

"Wake up, Princess!" Ronks's guttural voice called.

Lykinnia's current predicament came rushing back to her in a tidal wave of reality. "How long?"

"I not know. Three days?" replied the half-ogre.

The priestess of Terazhan sighed heavily. *It has been half a fortnight at least. Father must be worried, and Cymm knows even less. Solar has probably scanned the seven heavens and the nine hells by now. Do they know where I am? Are they coming?*

With a deeper sigh, she scanned the chamber. *I need to make a plan and save them too if I can. I am supposed to be trying to free my mother, not myself.*

The draconian priests assigned to watch over them entered the prison with their cowls in place. It was impossible to tell them apart, except for slight skin variations in their hands when they extended the baskets of bread. However, many lizards could change color and maybe these creatures had the same ability.

"No, Fazekas! Wait." Myra struggled against her bonds as she began to stir. "Uncle Jack said to wait." A short pause followed. "Soon…"

Ronks's amusement boiled over with a belly laugh.

All the captives had awoken, and the meal service had begun.

Lykinnia's eyes flared with anger. "I am still waiting for that story, Ronks. The legendary capture of—"

Something firm struck her on the forehead. She scanned the floor in shock and found a chunk of bread.

The half-ogre's raucous laughter bounced off the walls.

A gooey residue remained on Lykinnia's skin. "Why in the nine hells would you do that?" She could feel her ears overheating. "I *will* get even."

Two acolytes approached, one with a basket of bread. The manacle on her left wrist glowed with a shade of hickory before loosening.

"The story of my capture is interesting. Care to hear it?" asked Leighton.

The acolytes moved on, and Lykinnia gazed blankly at the floor.

"He's talking to you. I've already heard it," Jenaleya whispered in her direction.

With her mouth half-full, Lykinnia said, "Oh, sorry, Leighton. Yes, I would love to hear your story."

Leighton cleared his throat. "Very well. I'm from the city of Bruc, north of City of the Mystics. My father is the king, as you have probably guessed. When I awoke on the day in question—"

"Bah! We not have all day. Get to good part where you almost die," grumbled Ronks.

"No skip breakfast. Me likes quail eggs," said Haskins.

The prince rolled his eyes, then peered at Lykinnia. "About midday, and after eating quail eggs, my city was attacked."

Haskins beamed.

After glancing at the boy, Leighton continued. "By four black dragons—each one bigger than the next—and an enormous red dragon. We had no warning. Thick, ancient, stone walls were sundered by lightning and melted by fire. Hundreds of my people died within the first five minutes."

Lykinnia gasped. "Leighton, how horrible."

His story had obviously captured Myra's attention.

The prince pursed his lips and continued. "I was in the practice yard and sent soldiers to deliver messages to the castle and the wizard's tower. By the time the mages arrived, a thousand people were already dead. The first black dragon crashed to the ground with wings of stone, destroying a city block. I mustered the remaining city defense…"

The acolyte arrived to loosen Leighton's manacle.

He paused the story to grab two loaves and bit into one of them. With his mouth half-full he continued. "The dragon was not dead but severely injured. We hacked, stabbed, and sliced the beast until it finally died."

"We?" asked Lykinnia dubiously.

Ronks cackled. "Yeah, this is good part!"

A small chunk of bread hit Ronks on the side of the head.

"Leave him alone," said Myra, her arm still raised in a throwing position.

The entire room went silent for several seconds, then everyone burst out laughing, including Ronks.

Leighton took another bite and chewed thoughtfully. "Yeah, I was right there with my father's men…my men. We climbed over and through the rubble to get at the thing. Our weapons could not pierce the thick hide, but we attacked its wounds, driving our weapons deep into its body. When the dragon stopped moving, I climbed up on its torso to rally the remaining royal guard. My war cry lasted only a second before I was tail slapped into the nearest building."

"And?" asked Ronks with eager eyes.

Leighton sighed. "The structure collapsed on me."

Ronks hooted and howled. "They brought him here half-dead."

"No funny," said Haskins.

"He almost died several times. They cared for him and healed him in a separate room for several turns of the moons. He claims he was the first to be captured," said Jenaleya.

"I don't *claim*, I *know* I was," replied Leighton.

"No. Ronks first. Haskins second," said the half-ogre.

"Enough!" shouted one of the draconian priests. "Finish eating now."

Only Ronks heeded the warning immediately and began chewing furiously.

The others mostly grumbled, apart from Haskins. "Eat, eat."

Lykinnia's confusion continued until the manacle latched around her free wrist, then wrenched her arm out straight. She allowed the remaining, useless loaf of bread to fall to the floor.

Myra cried out in pain.

Ronks looked like a fat, happy chipmunk with swollen cheeks.

Naterion roared in frustration.

"No, Fazekas! No!" Myra's eyes were wide with fear.

One of the priests paused and searched over both shoulders before exiting the chamber.

Lykinnia scanned the area as well and met Jenaleya's gaze.

"How did Cymm get in and out of here?" asked the Princess of Norfolk.

One side of Lykinnia's face squinched. "I am not sure, but I would assume he used a portal."

"Can we?" whispered Jenaleya.

"I have no idea where we are, and no one else knows I am here, so it is unlikely." *I cannot even contact my father.* Lykinnia's head tilted. *However, if I could contact him from somewhere in this mountain…*

"What are we going to do?" Jenaleya voice cracked, the first sign of stress she had exhibited.

After glancing around conspiratorially, Lykinnia whispered, "Do not worry, the answer will come to us. I know how to release the restraints."

Jenaleya did not respond and became reticent.

Lykinnia's stomach grumbled. *I should have eaten more.* She glanced down at the floor below her. The chunk of bread was gone.

62

The Patient

Cymm

Cymm stared at the skeletal figure entwined in the tree near the altar. Lykinnia's favorite tree. She had shared numerous memories with him—memories that mostly included Solar—and were centered in the area surrounding this tree.

I can't imagine Lykinnia will be happy to learn it has become a prison. Cymm scrutinized the prisoner. *Is this the same skeletal creature Lord Terazhan showed me in the cell? Could the Divine Quest be so wrong?*

ZaphMordakai also stared at the captive with his dark elf eyes. "I wish I could return the favor and release you, but I can't."

Azreala wore a foolish smile as she joined them at the tree. "What is this thing doing here?"

"I am not a thing!"

Azreala jumped.

Cymm chuckled. "Didn't realize he was alive, did you? This is Melcorac, the Holy One."

"And how do you know that?" asked the skeletal being.

The gaze from the empty sockets sent a shiver down Cymm's spine; he glanced away toward the altar.

Lord Terazhan floated down from the back of the platform, catching Cymm by surprise with his appearance. His normally stiff, upright posture had a curve to it, and his squinty, wrinkled eyes were those of a man who hadn't slept for days. Even his energy level concerned the paladin as the deity walked the hundred feet to join them. The slow walk of an ancient man, and he appeared to have shrunken since the last time Cymm saw him.

"Hello, Cymm," said Lord Terazhan.

"Hello, my Lord. Is everything alright?"

"The battle at Armak has taken its toll. We lost many supporters to our cause, but everything will be fine." Lord Terazhan pointed toward the skeleton. "This is our patient, Melcorac."

ZaphMordakai snorted. "He looks more like a prisoner."

Lord Terazhan stared back pointedly. "His rage has not diminished in the past week since you fled here." He shifted his gaze. "Cymm, Azreala join us at the altar."

"Yes!" Azreala answered, her eyes still on the Mantle of the Gods.

Cymm turned and walked next to the deity. "Lord Terazhan, why is Melcorac not in the cell like I saw in the Divine Quest?"

"Scrying into the future has become less reliable. I have been having problems for a while now. Lykinnia should have been in Armak with you during the attack. Instead, she was taken prisoner by Ledaedra. Strange happenings are afoot." Terazhan continued at a slow gait.

The skin on Cymm's arm prickled, and his breath caught momentarily. "If the accuracy of the Divine Quests is an issue, is my cousin in peril?"

The three of them stepped onto the platform and joined four others. ZaphMordakai—who tagged along in the back—did not follow them any farther.

Cymm recognized Solar and had seen one of the women in the Divine Quest—the beautiful goddess with miniature stars orbiting her head—but he did not know the giant man towering over Terazhan, or the other woman dressed in green with her hood pulled up.

Terazhan turned with an open hand. "Cymm, this is my brother Dilantro and my sisters Vallerielle and Sehaleah."

They acknowledged him with a nod.

With butterflies of uncertainty, Cymm dipped his head in response.

Vallerielle crossed the gap and grabbed Azreala's hands. "Sister, I am glad you finally joined us."

Azreala's stoic expression finally transformed into a smile. "Thank you."

"I know the council reconvenes in a few days," began Lord Terazhan, "but the gathering of this subgroup is necessary. I believe I have determined a way to restore Melcorac, but it will require our combined power. Cymm, the stress of this process will put your life at risk and age you considerably, enough to kill a normal human. I know what my daughter did to you, so the unnatural aging will have little effect on you, but the stress to your body is real. You must be willing to help Melcorac or I will find another way."

Cymm considered this a moment. "I want to help. I don't believe you would put my life at risk if not important. What do I need to do?"

"You need to be a willing avatar like you have done for me, except this time many of them will need to use you, one after the other." Lord Terazhan stared intently at him.

There's that word again: use. Still, Cymm confirmed his acceptance.

Lord Terazhan continued to stare at him for several seconds. With an affirmation of finality, he addressed everyone, "When we are done here, I will leave for my home plane to recover and gather my strength."

Cymm glanced at Azreala, but she did not make eye contact. Her gaze locked onto the mantle.

"Do not respond to anything Melcorac says. He gets agitated easily, and this process will be hard enough when he is calm. I will guide us through each step of the process. Is everyone ready to begin." Terazhan responded to the silence with a clap of his hands.

Dilantro and Sehaleah left the platform headed toward the bound patient. When they arrived, Sehaleah began to chant, and the tree reacted at once. The strands holding Melcorac fast began to throb, then slither, and finally released their grip on the skeletal being.

A vortex of wind shot forth from Dilantro's thrust hands and swirled around Melcorac, controlling his movement and lifting him into the air. With slow, deliberate motions, the giant deity paraded the captive toward the altar.

Melcorac endured the treatment quietly, his face of bone revealing no emotions. When they arrived at the platform, he glided out over the Pool of Age, hovering at the same height as the altar.

Lord Terazhan switched his attention back to the group. "Vallerielle, we need as many seconds as you can capture."

"I know, I will do my best." Vallerielle stepped toward Cymm and paused. "Are you ready?"

Cymm swallowed hard and his head bobbed, then he croaked, "Yes."

Stars of cinnamon drifted out of Vallerielle's eyes, swirling in a steady pattern as they approached Cymm. Unlike Terazhan or Azreala, nothing hit him—no impact, no moment of entry, and gentler than his mother's embrace. His self-awareness gravitated toward his surroundings and the group dynamics, and finally his mind evolved. The stars revolving around the goddess's head were not stars, but galaxies, and within the swirling pattern of each were thousands of stars. He understood the inner planar dimensions and why they were divided the way they were. Even the outer planes of existence became clear as well as their structure. The words plane, dimension, and galaxy were new to him and yet, they were not. Their existence and purpose seemed obvious. His curiosity piqued, *I wonder what other knowledge I have access to because of this union.*

The world turned cinnamon-brown and opaque, as Cymm's eyes filled with a thousand spinning stars. He could only hear the blood rushing past his eardrums; he could only feel the concussive pounding of borrowed magic against his soul. Naught else.

"I am almost through. Hold on a bit longer," Vallerielle's mind reached out to him.

"How can that be. We only just begun." Cymm quickly realized the concept of time no longer had the same meaning. A heavy weight settled on him—exhaustion, an overwhelming fatigue. His head swam with self-doubt. *Who am I? These are not my words or thoughts.* He wanted to ask Vallerielle, but her exit from his body had gone unnoticed.

The weary goddess stood next to him, glistening in sweat.

Cymm bent over and placed his hands on his knees. "What…did…we do?"

"We stopped time. I can usually do it for only a few seconds," replied Vallerielle.

In confusion, Cymm scanned the faces surrounding him.

Solar motioned toward Melcorac. The vortex of wind no longer swirled, and the skeletal creature hung suspended and unmoving.

Cymm caught a quick peek of ZaphMordakai frozen with a hand in the air.

"Quickly! We have two minutes," added Lord Terazhan "Ready yourself, Cymm. Azreala, you need to drain Melcorac's life force completely, and any second life force, as well."

Azreala blanched. "A second life force? That's not—"

"We don't have time. Begin!" commanded Lord Terazhan.

The goddess of death's eyes flared, but she complied. She placed her hand on Cymm's shoulder. "You need to stand up straight so I can see your eyes. Don't worry, this will rejuvenate you. Remember?" She retreated five steps and launched her crimson arrow of energy.

Cymm welcomed the pain. He had bound many times with Azreala—as many as Terazhan—and it hurt every time, but a comfortable pain like working all day in the fields.

Before Azreala's real body hit the ground, she threw her wisps.

Through the avatar's bloodshot eyes, Cymm could only estimate the number of crimson lines to be ten, but the influx of energy came fast and furious. His power and strength returned at an accelerating pace.

"Can you feel it?" asked Azreala.

An involuntary shiver of delight ran down the spine of the avatar, reacting to Azreala's euphoria. She withdrew slowly, reluctantly, and took the excess energy with her.

Azreala had the same insidious gleam in her eyes as when she had kissed him. She ran her fingers from one shoulder across his back to the other.

"Don't do it!" Cymm hissed.

"I won't. It was the power, not me, I promise," Azreala replied sheepishly.

"Azreala, do you see Melcorac's spirit, or any other spirits or shadows?" asked Terazhan.

The goddess of death paused and glanced about. "Only Melcorac's, but it has a strange glow."

"I knew it! Sehaleah, work your magic," said Lord Terazhan, showing some vigor for the first time today.

The goddess with the green cloak stepped within an arm's reach of Cymm and lifted her hand. Her skin turned green, her feet rooted in the ground, and parts of her body sprouted, including her fingers. The tiny vines coiled forth and smacked into Cymm's face before entering his eyes, then they became thinner, more supple, tethering them together.

His body stretched and groaned to eight and a half feet tall while green liquid collected within his eyes. The avatar's body lurched forward to the edge of the platform on the side of the altar. Patches of skin hardened into bark across his body, which creaked as he moved like a tree blowing in the wind. The avatar lifted both arms and all ten fingers shot forth, snaking toward an empty space above the Pool of Age.

Ten vines divided into twenty which multiplied into forty, and the process continued. A sphere large enough to contain a human started to form as the vines surrounded an area.

Cymm caught a quick glimpse of a ghostly form within the cage of vines.

An electrifying green field pulsed to life and the immobilized spirit moaned. Several deities gasped as they stared in rapture from their fixed locations. The moan built into a wail, then ended abruptly with a horrifying shriek.

The vines slithered out of Cymm's eyes and the pools of hunter green drained from top to bottom. He slumped to his knees.

"We are so close—twenty more seconds," said Lord Terazhan.

"What do you think you will be able to do?" asked Azreala. "Melcorac's spirit is out of his body."

The Lord of Healing froze. "Can you help?"

"Only if I bind with Cymm again," replied Azreala.

Terazhan hung his head. "Then all is lost."

Azreala strode toward Cymm. "No, I can bind more than once. On your feet, quickly!"

Cymm glanced up but never rose, and a crimson dart struck his eyes.

With renewed vigor the avatar extended its gaunt forearms, the blood-red talons still growing to their full extension. A cloud of crimson mist engulfed the invisible spirit, the red film in his eyes allowing Cymm to see the undead creature.

"Quickly, Azreala, time is running short," cried Vallerielle.

Task completed, Azreala withdrew from his body like the shadows flee the sun, but this time Cymm felt powerful. A raging river of energy flowed through his body.

Lord Terazhan eyes searched for an answer to an unknown question. Golden lightning bolts descended, striking only the deity. A radiant burst of golden light surrounded him and drove him to his hands and knees. "Why is it not working for me?"

Anger flooded Cymm's mind, but not his own emotion. A presence inside him forced him to glare at Terazhan. *How dare you try to bind with me!*

"Stick with the plan, brother!" yelled Dilantro.

The Lord of Healing summoned golden balls of energy into each hand and lobbed them at Melcorac, even as he rose. As soon as a globule left his hand, another began to grow in its place.

A shimmering vortex of wind engulfed Melcorac while ligaments formed around every joint, and muscle grafted itself directly to the bone through tendons.

Vallerielle yelled with a strained voice, "I can't hold it any longer."

"Father, forgive me." Lord Terazhan ripped a gemstone off the Mantle of the Gods and crushed it between his thumb and forefinger. It exploded in a shower of sparkling dust. His hands shot beams of golden light at the partially formed cadaver. He focused the rays on Melcorac's chest, and the heart and lungs popped into view.

The vortex creaked and groaned, then suddenly snapped. Dilantro struggled to maintain control of the cyclone as it lurched forward, flinging Melcorac's body out over the edge of the mountain.

Muscle and tissue continued to divide and multiply, wrapping around bone and tendon. A liquified skin enveloped the entire body and solidified as he drifted back toward the altar. Melcorac's feet touched down next to ZaphMordakai, and the hair on his body finished growing into place.

Sweet relief rushed through Cymm's mind.

A feeling of great exultation descended upon all those present as they rejoiced in their shared accomplishment

Cymm's smile faded when he turned to inspect the results.

Melcorac stared back at him menacingly, prepared to pounce.

63

The Forest

Talo

The adventurers wove through the War Dog Tribe's territory the past two days and intentionally avoided the villages after trading for food in the first two they came upon. The group relied more on silent brooding than communicating apart from the youngster, Tanya.

"We should turn north like you agreed to with Cymm," said Talo to Brogan, who glanced at him sideways but did not reply.

Talo continued, "Cymm won't be able to find us if we don't follow the plan."

"He knows where we're going. Do you see that forest ahead? When we reach that tomorrow, we'll be safe from dragons overhead." Brogan leaned toward him as if awaiting a rebuttal.

Talo understood the logic, to some degree, he even agreed with it, but Cymm had survived worse odds. By the grace of Terazhan, he lived, and he would find them.

ꝏꝏꝏ

By early afternoon the following day, they entered the outskirts of the forest as Brogan had predicted.

Talo had never been in a forest before or even seen one. Some of the grass in the plains reached up twenty feet into the sky, and some even provided shade, but nothing compared to this. He stared up at the first giant sentinel in awe and almost fell off his horse trying to crane his neck back far enough to see the top.

The group continued deeper into the woods before turning north, then kept the woods line in sight on their left as they trekked under the cover of the leaves.

A loud groan then a creak made Talo jump. "What was that?"

Tanya giggled. She rode on Cymm's warhorse in front of her father. "The trees, silly. They move when the wind blows."

Trees can't move. They have roots. Talo inspected the rest of his companions' faces and most were amused.

In particular, Brogan, who continued to shake his head accompanied by a sigh.

The trees creaked again, and Talo quickly glanced side to side.

ꝏꝏꝏ

The setting sun made it difficult to see the edge of the forest and out into the plains.

Brogan put his arm up. "That's it for tonight. I don't want to get lost in here."

"Can we start a fire?" asked Dirk.

"Yeah, and we'll need to set a guard," replied Brogan.

Talo smacked Dirk on the back. "Come on. I'll help you gather some wood."

The left side of Dirk's face wrinkled, his eye squinted, and his neck spasmed, turning his head in the same direction. "Is there something you want."

With a wave of his hand, Talo walked further away from the group. After gathering a few sticks, he asked, "I'm curious, how were you able to follow us through the city and escape."

Dirk's taciturn behavior continued while he gathered branches. "I didn't enter the city, and I wasn't following you."

Talo scoffed. "Explain."

"I can sense the stone that Grendella carries." Dirk glanced over his shoulder, then whispered, "It calls to me. It makes my body twitch and quiver the closer I am to it."

Dread spread through Talo, and he dropped his sticks. Before he could turn and flee, Dirk grabbed his arm.

"Wait!" he hissed. "Cymm knew my secret and kept it. You can't tell the others."

"I must."

"Why?" Dirk's left elbow spasmed and kicked out to the side.

"Because, if you could track us using the shard, so can others." Talo broke free of his grasp and ran.

Shuffled steps and panting bore down on Talo from behind, then something struck him.

ထထထ

Talo awoke with foggy vision and foggier thoughts. He slouched on his back next to a snapping campfire.

"He's awake."

"Talo, are you alright?"

He groaned. His eyes fluttered open to blurry vision. He could not identify the speaker, but someone diligently washed his face. *Why does the back of my head hurt?* Everything came rushing back. "Dirk hit me from behind."

"No, I didn't!"

Someone or something washed Talo's face again. Or was it a lick?

"Jalko, is that you?" Talo opened his eyes again, and they came into focus. Two furry faces stared down at him. He identified Jalko immediately, but the other seemed less familiar. He sat up, rubbing the back of his head. "A dog. Joharie?"

"Yes, it's the war dog you helped," said Dirk excitedly.

"Were you expecting someone else?" asked Zecarius.

Talo smirked. "When I first opened my eyes, I thought it was Jalko and Grendella."

Hearty laughter and some hooting followed.

Grendella snorted. "Let's see if I heal you again when your dog knocks you out."

"Hey, come on. Cymm's not here. We have to pick on someone," replied Talo.

Dirk grinned with a twitching upper lip.

"What are you smiling about?" asked Talo.

"What do the legends say about the man who becomes a horseman, a wolfer, and a hackle?" asked Dirk.

"Are you mad? You think I'm the Guardian?" Talo slowly rose to his knees. "I'm a simple horseman. The wolf is Cymm's, and the war dog is following us." Inside he smiled, knowing a younger version of Talo would be beaming right now at the thought of someone calling *him* the Guardian.

"Who is the Guardian?" asked Tanya.

"Who, indeed," replied Dirk. "The Guardian will save us all from the return of an ancient evil barely defeated the first time—"

"Bah! If you're not going to tell the story right, then I'll tell it," said Grendella, putting her pony between them.

Dirk relented with raised hands.

"There is a prophesy at the core of our belief system—the followers of Terazhan—that tells of an event in the distant future called The Rending. The return of the Dark Lord is inevitable. The One True God defeated him and locked him away in a magical cell, but the energy required to maintain such a prison is significant."

"Who is the Dark Lord?" asked Tanya.

Grendella's face quirked. "He has gone by many names—"

"No, no, no. Now you're messing up the story. His name is Antas Abaddon, and only the Guardian can summon the One True God to defeat him again," said Dirk with a satisfied nod that turned into a neck twinge.

Tanya had a half-smile as she glanced from one adult to the next. "But where did the One True God go?"

Katara rushed into the circle of light. "Keep it down. Something is out there."

64

Special Council Meeting

Azreala

True to his word, Terazhan immediately left the Peak of Power, followed closely by the rest of the deities. Solar and the sphinx brothers remained as expected, and after all his grumbling, ZaphMordakai stayed as well. Azreala had planned to visit her brother, Feldarius, on the Plane of Tides, but the glare of death from Melcorac to Cymm had made her reconsider.

Melcorac's free rein of the peak followed the explicit instruction not to leave until after the special council meeting in two days' time.

Azreala had used the time to catch up on her spirit and shadow evaluations while keeping a hawk's eye on Cymm. Both nights, during the wee hours, Melcorac had wandered over as quiet as a wraith, stood a dozen paces from Cymm, and stared. Azreala remained unmoving but watching, and by the time she had processed a hundred souls, he would walk away. The goddess of death had become the night's watch. She could go days without sleep and had done it before. This newcomer would not be allowed to interfere with her plan. She would eliminate him if necessary.

Cymm awoke oblivious to the night's activities and proceeded to the altar to pray.

ooooo

The Council prepared to convene near the Altar of One and the Pool of Age while nervous energy ran rampant through Azreala's body.

Seven deities were on the platform along with Terazhan's solar. They spanned an arc from one corner of the altar to the other.

Melandri winked at her, but no one else acknowledged her presence, not even Jakarrak.

Azreala glanced back to locate Cymm, and he scowled back at her.

ZaphMordakai and Melcorac drifted closer after being absent most of the morning, and now the drow paced impatiently, waiting for this meeting to begin.

Terazhan passed his hand over his neck and shoulders, and the Mantle of the Gods appeared. "The Council shall commence."

The chatter died down.

"When last we met, a fortnight ago, everyone had his or her assignments. What did you learn?" asked Terazhan.

Jakarrak jumped to speak, "The Silver Dragon Order will not fight with us, but they will continue to spy."

Terazhan sighed. "And the golden dragons?"

Sehaleah coughed and stared flatly back at him as if the answer were obvious.

"We cannot count on the Cabal of Copper Dragons either. They do not see any benefit in getting involved," said Dilantro.

"Then there are no dragons who will fight with us?" asked Vallerielle.

ZaphMordakai replied from a short distance away, "DetonKonraber the Devastation has been fighting for centuries. Maybe *you* could join *him*."

"No one has asked for your input," said Solar.

Terazhan waved his hand parallel to the ground to silence the assembly. "And what do you know of this DetonKonraber."

"He is my uncle, and I know him very well. He despises Ledaedra for past actions, but it might go deeper than that." ZaphMordakai pulled up short of walking onto the platform.

"Do you have a means to contact your uncle?" asked Terazhan.

"No. I think he has been exiled to our home world, the same world your so-called *good* dragons came from. The creatures there, known as trellbac, will hunt and kill him."

Vallerielle tsked. "And we are back to no dragons."

"Not necessarily," Azreala said. "I can animate the dead dragons to fight for us, once we start killing them."

"Really! How many?" asked Melandri.

Azreala beamed with pride. "Only one on my own, but once I enter Cymm, ten or twelve."

"Enter him?" Melcorac shot Cymm another death glare.

Melandri clasped her hands with wide eyes. "Amazing."

"And the dragons killed by the undead dragons can be reanimated, creating an endless cycle potentially."

Melcorac's gaze bore into Cymm. "You…have my aura?"

Cymm hesitated and forced a half-smile. "I have *my* aura."

ZaphMordakai pushed between the two humans and walked back to the edge of the platform. "We should focus on killing Ledaedra, not my brethren. Many of them were not given a choice like the *good* dragons."

"Your brethren support Ledaedra and make her more powerful," said Terazhan.

"Can you influence any of your ilk to renounce Ledaedra?" asked Dilantro.

The dark elf shook his head. "No. I do not have that kind of influence, but my uncle does."

"He is apparently unavailable," said Solar.

Undaunted, ZaphMordakai said with excitement, "Yes, but we could rescue him. After we rescue my mo—Lykinnia, from Ledaedra's prison."

Hope filled Terazhan's face. "Do you know where my daughter is being held?"

"Yes. On Fire Island, in one of the upper chambers," replied ZaphMordakai.

Solar's wings flared with tiny blue bolts of electricity. "Why are you here?"

The dark elf became introspective before he responded, "I have personal reasons, but suffice it to say, Ledaedra has lied to us all, and my uncle has known from the beginning."

"Are we done here?" asked Jakarrak.

The stars above Vallerielle's head pulsed. "Do you have somewhere to be?"

"Most of us do not have all the time in the world," Melandri quipped.

"Terazhan, I need to be going as well. Can we conclude this session?" asked Dilantro.

What a dysfunctional group. We do not have a chance of winning this war. Maybe if Terazhan used the Mantle of the Gods we might. Azreala resisted the urge to mention the artifact.

Terazhan shifted back into his position in the semicircle, and his shoulders slumped. "You know your assignments. Keep pushing ahead. We will reconvene in half a fortnight to provide updates. Hopefully, Lykinnia will be with us by then."

ZaphMordakai's face lit up like a beacon, but Azreala knew it concerned the rescue of a different woman—his mother.

Deities disappeared one after another until only Terazhan, Solar, and Azreala remained on the platform. They sauntered over to join Cymm, Zaph, and Melcorac.

"The five of you will form the rescue party for Lykinnia. We need to discuss the limitations of the mission and how to best accomplish this task."

"Limitations?" asked ZaphMordakai incredulously.

Terazhan's eyes revealed his sadness. "I love my daughter very much, but we cannot afford to lose any of you." His gaze passed over each member.

Azreala noted the fleeting glance he gave the dark elf, which spoke volumes. However, the lengthy stare she received pleased her immensely.

"The three of us have been there. As I mentioned, it is one of the top chambers, and there is access by both tunnel and air." Lavender lightning snapped between ZaphMordakai's teeth as he spoke, emphasizing his excitement.

He won't be happy to discover that thing chained by the altar is not his mother. Azreala had no intention of telling him. *But what then is it?*

"We need a plan for removing the shackles from Lykinnia and the other prisoners." Cymm glanced at the goddess of death. "The only reason we successfully rescued Azreala is because she shrunk in size, and we used the drained energy to increase the avatar's strength to snap the neck restraint."

"Agreed. If we can figure out the manacles, we can portal to the platform outcropping and get in and out quickly," said Azreala.

Solar knitted his brow. "We can just snap them all off."

ZaphMordakai chuckled.

Azreala waved him off. "I expended all of the stored energy just to break one."

"They are made of adamantine. The entire rack is," added ZaphMordakai.

Terazhan rubbed his chin. "I can provide an open spell, but I cannot guarantee it will work."

"There is nothing to open. The draconian acolytes did cast a spell to enlarge the rings. They never opened them," said Azreala.

"An enlarge spell is quite basic. Why does that sound too simple?" asked Solar.

Azreala's eyebrows lifted. "You reminded me of something. Any spell I tried to cast was…negated…by the shackles."

"If you can't enlarge the metal, then shrink the people," said ZaphMordakai.

Cymm pursed his lips. "We need to be able to save them all, and we should leave right after midnight, when the acolytes are sleeping."

Solar exchanged glances with Terazhan before saying, "I will be ready with both spells."

"Anything to add, Melcorac?" asked Terazhan.

"No."

Terazhan shook his head, before disappearing, he said, "No Divine Quest this time, Cymm. You are on your own."

"I will return." Solar took his leave.

Azreala stepped off the platform and grabbed Cymm's arm. "We need to talk."

65

Dirk Darkmane

Talo

Howls echoed through the woods a moment before the creatures burst forth from the underbrush. Running on all fours like the animals they were, four devils bore down on their hastily assembled defense.

Talo released his arrow. It caromed off the side of a devil's head and stuck in its rump.

Jalko and Joharie intercepted one of the creatures and worked together to drive it back.

Brogan and a third devil exchanged wounds in the initial flurry, then locked into mortal combat with each other.

"Stay back!" Zecarius yelled at his daughter.

The remaining devil bowled into the right flank of the defense, sending Zecarius and Katara flying. Grendella clipped the same monster with her warhammer, allowing them to regain their feet.

Dirk and Talo separated to keep their enemy between them, and both scored minor hits immediately.

A sword plunged into a devil's chest, and Brogan smiled ferociously. It flailed its arms as he twisted the blade, then quickly withdrew it before its limp body fell to the ground.

A devil lunged for Grendella, but Katara drove her short sword into its back. It whirled to attack her, and Zecarius slashed its side with his long sword.

The dire wolf and the war dog drove their devil back into a tree. The creature returned their vicious snarls with similar vigor.

Talo's foot caught on a root as he back peddled, causing him to fall to his back with the weight of the devil on him. Pinned to the ground, he could not bring his sword to bear. He reached to his boot, grabbed his dirk dagger—the one Old Man Semper had given him—and plunged it into the devil's side repeatedly.

The devil gasped and its tongue rolled to the side of its mouth. With its dying breath, it raked its claws across Talo's neck. Blood spurted everywhere and pain exploded in his mind.

"Grendella!" came the panicked cry from Brogan, who stood over his wounded friend after throwing the devil's corpse to the side.

The dwarven cleric arrived instantly with a reassuring smile and a golden glow around her hands. The severe lacerations on his throat began to close instantly.

"No!" Tanya screamed over and over.

"Grendella!" Brogan's voice boomed again.

Talo attempted to sit up, but Grendella forced him back down. "I'm fine!" He tried again and propped himself up on his elbows in time to see Brogan run his sword through the last devil.

Next to Brogan lay Zecarius, torn to pieces, and next to him sat Katara, dazed and clamping her hand over a severe laceration running the length of her arm.

Tanya sat with her father's head in her lap, sobbing. "Grendella, help my Daddy."

The dwarven cleric rushed over, kneeling over Zecarius. She scanned him up and down and froze in indecision.

Katara's eyes rolled up into the back of her head, and she collapsed to the ground.

Grendella crawled to Katara and immediately began her prayer of healing.

Talo stared at Zecarius's broken body. He snorted, jaw clenched. *The real hero of prophecy will be able to save his friends*. He wanted to laugh or cry or shout in anger.

"Where's Dirk?" asked Brogan.

Grendella's eyes went wide. She quickly rose and jogged to her pony.

"What's the matter?" asked Talo.

She stared back at him. "Dirk's gone and so is my backpack."

66

An Optional Flight

ZaphMordakai

Azreala pulled Cymm along with her as she headed off to the side of the platform and the plateau. Zaph's irritation escalated, and he wished Lykinnia were here to see it. They resembled a married couple in the middle of an argument. He wanted to mind his own business, but their volume made it impossible.

"Why did you scowl at me?" asked Azreala.

"I didn't scowl at you. Why did you keep looking back to see if I was still standing there?" asked Cymm.

How are we going to save my mother? ZaphMordakai's excitement tempered with realization. *If Ledaedra is there we won't stand a chance. We need a diversion.* He stroked his chin. *Maybe this group can be the diversion. Once we are in the Transference Chamber, I will tell the acolytes to summon Ledaedra to prevent the prisoners from escaping, then I can slip through the portal to the Plane of Ashes.*

"I still don't know why you kissed—"

"This again!" Azreala fumed with her arms flailing.

Cymm tried to drop the volume of his voice, "You promised to never lie to me."

"And I haven't."

"Good. Then tell me, with all the flirting you do—" Cymm paused and glanced at Zaph.

When they saw him eavesdropping, they moved farther away.

Be careful, lovebirds. I promised not to mention the kiss, nothing else. Zaph broke off his gaze and found Melcorac staring at him. "What?"

"I cannot understand how you are here," replied Melcorac.

"What's that supposed to mean?" asked Zaph.

Melcorac hefted his massive warhammer, it shimmered with a golden aura. "I cannot get a good read on you, or your intentions, but I have heard you are a black dragon."

"Is that a problem?" asked Zaph.

"Only if your thoughts and deeds are evil." Melcorac shifted his gaze to the head of his hammer. "Warsong was crafted specifically to deal with evil. In fact, I killed one of your kind outside my tomb. They attacked for no other reason than to kill, and now I am learning your master is the one that plagued me."

ZaphMordakai rose from the lounging position he had taken. "Ledaedra is not my master! At least, not anymore."

"Let's hope that is true. I will have my eye on you," replied Melcorac.

"Maybe you should keep an eye on yourself. Only a fortnight ago you were here like a raving madman, smashing doors, clobbering sphinxes, threatening Terazhan with your hammer. How do we know you won't snap again?"

"I was ill, thanks to your former liege lord, but I have been healed. It will not happen again. I will assume you were ill as well, and now your brain is functioning properly." Melcorac turned and walked away.

Given enough time, eventually everyone hates you. This had become his mantra. *Why does this happen to me every time? Cymm, Solar, Azreala, and now Melcorac—none of them will have my back if things go bad.* Zaph glanced at the sun and sighed. *Why is it so hard to make a friend—to keep a friend?*

Many hours remained until the rescue mission began. He decided to take advantage of the opportunity to sleep.

ထထထ

Primordian, the only moon in the night's sky, blazed bright at its zenith, showering the Altar of One and the platform with mystical light. Terazhan and Solar huddled near the altar making final preparations.

"Are you ready?" Azreala asked Cymm.

"I think so," Cymm replied with an unconvincing tone.

Without hesitation, the goddess of death entered him, a crimson dart in each eye. Her body collapsed to the ground.

The necromantic avatar grabbed her lifeless form and moved it off to the side.

Terazhan stepped to the edge of the platform. "We are ready to begin. The location has been calculated based on input from Cymm, Azreala, and ZaphMordakai, but precision at this great distance is difficult. Solar will enter first. If our calculation is wrong, and we miss the outcropping, he will be able to fly to safety."

Blue lightning zipped through Solar's wings as he flexed them. "I am ready."

"ZaphMordakai." Terazhan motioned for the dark elf to follow him toward the back of the platform. "Remember what my daughter did for you on top of this mountain, not too long ago, when you were a prisoner of the Silver Dragon Order. She believes in you."

Zaph's stomach clenched, and he turned away. *That was a lifetime ago. Her feelings have changed.*

The portal opened, and Solar raced through in an instant.

Time ticked by, at least a dozen seconds, and he did not return. An equivalent amount of time elapsed and still nothing.

Terazhan stared at the remaining group, at a loss for words.

"I'll go. I can transform back to a dragon quickly if I need to fly," offered Zaph.

"Swiftly then!" Terazhan waved him over.

Zaph jogged to the portal, hesitated for a moment, then plunged in.

67

Ronks

Lykinnia

When Lykinnia awoke, her belly groaned and quivered. Her face grimaced from starvation. A ravenous pang stabbed through the right side of her abdomen. She tried to breathe through the sharp pain but could not until it finally subsided.

"No feel good, huh, Princess?" asked Ronks.

Lykinnia fixed her gaze on the half-ogre.

"The belly pain. Every time I wakes that how I feel."

The wave of anger inside of Lykinnia disappeared when she saw the sincere concern on his face. "I did not know. How do you endure it?"

"I don't. That why me so angry. Ronks much smaller than before."

Naterion stirred.

"Will you ever tell the story of your capture?" asked Lykinnia.

Ronks shook his head. "No. It too embarrassing."

Lykinnia considered his response.

"Why not you tell your story?" asked the ogre.

"No one asked me to. Someone I considered a friend, betrayed me. It is a sad story that only shows my desperation for friendship." Lykinnia launched into her story before everyone had woken.

She left out a few parts but otherwise bared her soul, and by the time she finished with Zaph pushing her through the portal, all the captives were listening intently.

"That is very sad," said Jenaleya.

"If Haskins see him again. Haskins kick him in shins," added Haskins.

"And I will have Fazekas clobber him," said Myra.

Ronks took a sharp intake of air. "Fine. I tell a story about love."

"Love?" Haskins chittered.

Everyone burst into laughter.

Leighton cleared his throat and deepened his voice. "The ogre and the princess—part one."

Even Naterion smiled. "This is less embarrassing than your capture story."

Ronks growled as the laughter continued, then hung his head.

"Quiet!" commanded Lykinnia. "Ronks was about to share something personal with us."

After glancing up, the ogre shook his head.

A thought sprung forth and Lykinnia grinned. "Ronks, have I ever told you I can conjure food and water?" She left the part about escaping first unsaid.

The half-ogre lifted his gaze and assessed her, likely searching for a trick.

"And ale…" Lykinnia added.

"When I still wearing sheepskins, I met Rebrugala at fish camp. She a couple years older than me and very beautiful." Ronks paused and glared at everyone, daring them to make a derogatory comment.

Haskins giggled. "Keep goin'."

"Rebrugala very smart, not like me, but very smart for an ogre. My mam always tells me I got my wits from pa, who left before I born. Anyway, everyone at fish camp tease me for half-breed blood, calling me pointy nose or baby cheeks and others. Rebrugala called me Ronkie, and I follow her everywhere."

The draconian acolytes appeared from the back alcove with the usual basket of bread.

Ronks stared with mouth agape, forgetting all about the story.

Leighton cleared his throat. "That's it?"

"Huh?" The ogre's attention remained locked on the basket of food.

"Give him a minute," encouraged Lykinnia.

Nothing broke Ronks's concentration—not the acolyte in front of him or the unlocking of the manacle on his wrist—until he took his first bite from the loaf of bread. "What?"

"We are waiting for the rest of the story," said Leighton.

"Fazekas, come back. You aren't allowed in there." Myra searched frantically over both shoulders.

Lykinnia and Jenaleya shared a concerned glance.

"Where I was?" Ronks chomped and slobbered some more. "She identified at young age to be priestess of Hymnoch." He paused again to eat.

Lykinnia and Naterion munched their bread, while Leighton licked his lips and reached for a loaf. The daughter of Terazhan had wisely grabbed three this time.

"So, I join temple to serve Hymnoch and be near her but only allow females." Ronks finished his second loaf. "She would spend next ten years behind those walls, and I not know what to do."

The ogre scanned his audience suspiciously, holding on to some secret. "So, I dress up as female and join the temple of Hymnoch."

Two heartbeats of silence ensued, then the chamber erupted in raucous laughter.

"You did not," said Leighton.

Ronks nodded slowly while chewing.

"I'm crying," claimed Jenaleya.

"Oh, Melandri help us. That is too funny," said Lykinnia.

Naterion shook his head in disbelief. "Did you get in?"

"Not only get in—made it through first year," said Ronks proudly.

"You're kidding, right?" asked Leighton.

"Nope. I not make further cuz year two has sterilization process. Boy, were they surprised." Ronks grinned from ear to ear.

Everyone laughed heartily except Haskins. "What surprise?"

Now Ronks roared and choked. He covered his mouth so no food would escape.

Myra paused her search for her invisible friend. "What did they do?"

"High Priestess say, 'Since you so smart, you be attending the High Towers of Sorcery in the City of the Mystics.' I shackled and delivered as prisoner." Ronks finished eating quickly, his eyes on the basket of bread.

"So much for that love affair," said Leighton.

"No, I saw her again. I graduate as mage and return home. When I find her, I cast charm spell so she love me," replied Ronks.

"Huh. The Ogre and the Priestess. Who would have known?" asked Leighton.

"And they lived happily ever after," said Jenaleya.

As the acolyte with the basket headed toward the back room, Ronks asked, "Can I have one more?"

"No."

Lykinnia twisted up her courage. "Give him another one."

The acolyte with the bread departed.

"Ronks." Lykinnia threw him her last loaf of bread with a gentle underhand lob.

In his excitement, the ogre bobbled it, but he clutched it to his chest with his one free arm. "Thank you! Thank you, Lykinnia."

"Not Princess?" Lykinnia smiled. "You are welcome."

"Hey, Lykinnia. Rebrugala was my ZaphMordakai."

Lykinnia smiled warmly, but her insides were churning. *How sad. I cannot imagine how I would feel if Cymm turned on me.*

68

Identity

ZaphMordakai

ZaphMordakai stepped into a cloud of dust, which billowed around him. His eyes were stinging and watering, and he could not see, but his feet were on solid ground.

A hand clamped over his mouth. "Shh," came a whispered voice.

Zaph's mind worked overtime. *It's Solar.*

"Follow me." The winged man slowly moved away.

In hushed tones, Zaph said, "No, we need to return."

"The portal is blocked, or it is a one-way door. Follow me." Solar led the way.

Zaph had no choice but to follow. *Where in the seven*—but before he finished his thought he knew—*I'm on the Plane of Ashes.* "What's going on?"

"We are on the Plane of Ashes. Wind is gusting through the portal, so I know it is still open, but we cannot go back through. It must be a trap with no exit."

"There's usually a portal near the altar that takes you back to the island."

They escaped the ash storm, and Solar found an outcropping for them to hide behind. He pulled Zaph to the far side and pointed. Fire Mountain loomed in the background, but only twenty dragon lengths away stood Ledaedra's altar. The Dragon Queen could not be seen anywhere.

Zaph gasped when he glimpsed the prisoner. "Mother."

"What?" Solar's perplexed stare was comical.

"Nothing. Let's get over there and find the portal while she is absent." Zaph began walking around the outcropping.

Solar reached out, blocking his path. "Hold. We need a plan."

Zaph turned to face him. "I have been here several times and there is always a portal back to Fire Island. It's actually very close to the Transference Chamber where the prisoners are being held."

"Perfect. I should be able to contact Terazhan from there. Can you sense if she is present?" asked Solar.

"You mean invisible? No." Zaph began walking quickly toward the altar.

"Then we need to be careful. Slow down," said Solar, following at a slower pace.

ZaphMordakai wanted to see his mother's face, ensure her wellbeing, and reassure her of her future freedom.

After taking a dozen steps, Solar asked, "What are you doing? You cannot go anywhere near the altar. You will trigger a ward and summon her here."

With clenched fists, Zaph growled, "I need to see the prisoner."

"What for? She is none of your concern," said Solar harshly.

Taken aback, Zaph answered in kind, "She is *my* mother. Of course, she is my concern."

Solar chuckled. "Unless you are Lykinnia's long lost brother, that is not your mother."

Zaph's face turned hot. "Do not laugh at me, Lightning Finch! I have seen her here before. I spoke with her. That woman chained to the column is my mother."

"Lightning Finch? It would appear we are two sides of the same coin, unless your wings are permanently gone," replied Solar.

The anger died in his chest as Zaph realized the irony of his nickname. With a calmer tone, he said, "That is my mother. Come, I will show you."

"We dare not get much closer. We need to find the portal you mentioned." Solar scanned an arc in the distance. "There it is, over there."

Zaph followed his line of sight and pointed finger. "That's not where it usually is." Zaph scratched his head. *That's the portal the trellbac used.*

Solar grabbed the dark elf's arm. "This is close enough."

After a look of disdain, Zaph called out, "Mother!" He paused. "Mother, it's me, Zaph."

The prisoner's head came up, and the hood fell back. It *was* his mother. "Zaphling, is that you?"

Solar gasped and sputtered.

Zaph whispered. "See, I told you." Aloud he said, "Yes, mother. I am here to save you."

Behind the altar the air shimmered, and the Dragon Queen materialized. "How sweet, but how will you save her when you can't save yourself?"

"You promised to release my mother," Zaph shouted defiantly.

Ledaedra stifled a yawn. "Only two little fish in my net. I thought there'd be more. Solar, did you like my double-portal trap? I learned that trick from my daughter."

Solar began a slow retreat.

Zaph, on the other hand, marched toward the altar. "You have a daughter? Let's see how you feel when I take her from you." He motioned toward the prisoner. "I want my mother back!"

The dark elf captive gazed up at him with hope in her eyes. "Zaphling, why are you upset?"

He dropped to his knees and grabbed her hands. "I'm not, everything is fine." His next breath caught in his chest, and he paused, thinking. He turned her one hand over and examined the smallest finger. "How did it grow back?"

His mother glanced back at Ledaedra.

"It doesn't matter anymore. You have done well, Ariata. They will both be dead momentarily."

Solar's distant voice yelled, "Ariata?"

Zaph barely noticed the shock in Solar's voice. He could not comprehend why his mother's hand had changed color. When he peeked up at her for an explanation, he rocked backward as if struck a heavy blow. "What…what are you?"

Ledaedra cackled, apparently enjoying every second.

The prisoner no longer appeared as a dark elf. She had become something akin to a human, although her ears were still pointy.

A bolt of shadow magic ripped through the air and blasted Zaph as he tried to rise, reminding him of his immediate danger.

"Goodbye, ZaphMordakai. You have been my greatest disapp—" Ledaedra froze as if listening and vanished a moment later.

Blood streamed out of Zaph's nose and ears, and he could taste the metallic flavor of his own blood dancing across his tongue. His left arm hung—nearly torn from his body—limp and useless.

The prisoner rapidly changed back to his mother. "Zaphling, you look unwell. Do you need a hug?"

Tears streamed down his face as Solar wrapped a strong, supportive arm around him. "We need to leave before she returns."

"That portal is not an escape route. I believe it leads back to my home world and therefore certain death," said Zaph, but he allowed himself to be led in that direction. He refused to look back.

"How are you not in pain?" asked Solar.

"I do not experience physical pain like others," Zaph replied.

From behind them the prisoner called out, "Solar, don't leave me."

Solar glanced back and stopped. "Sendaria?"

The prisoner replied, "Don't you still love me?"

"I will always love Sendaria, but you are not her," whispered Solar. The winged man resumed pulling Zaph along. "We have no choice. She is trying to delay us."

ZaphMordakai's right knee clicked, then buckled from the increased pace. He glanced down at his destroyed joint—bone grinding on bone—and leaned heavily on Solar. He fought back the tears and focused on his severe limp, each step like trudging through water. His mental anguish worsened. The lies, the loss, the gnawing sense that nothing in his life mattered—no mother, no friends, no purpose.

He finally cracked and glanced over his shoulder at the woman he previously believed to be his mother. A body-racking sob overtook him, and he would have fallen if not for the winged-man's support.

Solar pulled him close and did not let go until the portal's light swallowed them both.

69

The Monthly Sacrifice

BrimStrakenstone

A dozen humanoid creatures milled about the stone-pebble beach. They were not chained and shackled or even bound with rope, but they did not dare to stray far. The diverse group included humans, orcs, ogres, and gnolls—split evenly with males and females. Most wore expressions of fear and peered at the dragons surrounding them with apprehension.

BrimStrakenstone had to contend with his own anxiety as he waited for the portal to open. Ledaedra could not open a gateway to the Plane of Fear without the consent of Marekai, who had yet to reply to her request. He hated going to this place more than the Plane of Ashes but tightened up his own resolve an hour ago. However, as the minutes ticked by, his angst threatened to return.

His wounds healed slowly, even though the Dragon Queen had allowed her acolytes to provide him some magical relief, but after three days, the pain lingered. She could have drained one of these sacrificial offerings and provided him more assistance with his recovery.

Marekai's delay would have been considered normal except for today—the twenty-fifth day of the month. On this day only, the moon Plover appeared in the sky by itself, and the Prince of Devils eagerly received his new sacrifices. As if on cue, the portal snapped open with an indigo hue.

The enormous red dragon swallowed the lump in his throat. "Let's go!"

The prisoners ran for the portal, trying to escape the throng of dragons and the fear inside themselves, not realizing they fled toward terror.

Brim led the procession into the doorway, knowing what awaited him on the other side. The short trek through the hollow void to the Plane of Fear swallowed all noise—the scuff of a boot, the deep breathing caused by the short run to the portal, the gasp of those few individuals that realized they had gone willingly to the slaughterhouse.

The dismal lighting allowed shadows to dance on the periphery of one's view, a mere dragon's length away.

Something vine-like and damp slithered over Brim's front paw, causing his tail to involuntarily flick. Although he had no desire to hear the voices, they spoke to him anyway.

"Have you forgiven yourself yet?" came a cold, harsh voice.

BrimStrakenstone knew the speaker, he knew him very well, as well as the details of his death. The former owner of the voice had raised him using severe mental and physical disciplinary actions for minor infractions. When Brim had arrived to take his seat at the general's table, this individual, his father, had been one of the two dragons to flee. Rightfully so. He planned his sire as his primary target. He had no intention of serving as a general or as the commander of this army with his childhood tormentor sowing seeds of discord and weakness. The constant stories of his wyrmling and youngling years would have undermined his position and authority.

As a general in the Queen's Army, his father's act of cowardice brought him much ridicule and isolation, a deadly combination with a hunter about. DetonKonraber had caught him alone and unaware.

Brim ignored this apparition of the past and pressed forward.

Marekai and his altar materialized in front of him. A completely unorthodox altar to say the least, and he used it more as a multi-level lounging, partying, and torturing structure. "The Unholy Commander, to what do I owe this honor?"

"I won't be staying long. I have brought this month's gift. The queen claims you will particularly enjoy the female gnoll because she is immune to pain and unbreakable."

"Hmm," Marekai scoffed. "We shall see. Would you like to stay for the show?"

"As I already stated, I won't be staying long," replied Brim.

"This won't take long. I insist." Marekai motioned toward him with fingers spread on both hands.

The vines crawling all over the floor reacted violently, winding around his legs with an iron grip. The reaction of the prisoners behind him indicated they were experiencing similar treatment.

BrimStrakenstone immediately released his breath weapon directed at the floor and spun in a circle, disintegrating anything moving, including one of the prisoners accidentally. "I will stay of my own volition, but do not try that again."

"I make no such promise. If this gnoll doesn't live up to the hype, you will fill the gap." Marekai walked around his altar toward the sacrificial offerings.

"My Queen, the delivery is going as planned, but the Dark Prince is acting unusually bold." After waiting for a few seconds, and not receiving a response, Brim glanced back at the portal to ensure its presence. The queen knew he would want to test the gnoll's pain limits immediately and instructed Brim to stay and watch if allowed to. *"My Queen, can you hear me?"*

Marekai strolled through the mewling, cowering prisoners and paused at the charred corpse—the one Brim had killed. "I hope this wasn't the individual."

"That would be your fault!" Brim sidled to his left, keeping an eye on the portal. *Burn the Seven Heavens! I will not be trapped here.* The lightning burns on his back flared in pain, reminding him of his vulnerability.

"Ah, this one." Marekai ran the back of his finger down the length of her arm, beginning at the shoulder. He offered his hand and froze when she accepted it.

The red dragon smirked in satisfaction. *The queen said she would not break easily.*

Marekai escorted her up to the front of the altar, then turned her to face him. He grabbed her other hand, and they posed as if they were to be married. He flinched slightly before his eyelids fluttered and his face took on the glow of ecstasy.

Brim discovered a thin silvery shaft had penetrated the side of the gnoll's left leg—closest to the altar—and continued out and into the right leg, effectively tying them together. His gaze shifted to Marekai and found him similarly wounded.

The female gnoll had not even flinched.

Both had small rivulets of blood trickling down their legs when another thin spear pierced an arm on each of them. Neither made a sound or a movement. The third came quickly and penetrated the right side of the chest, and the next two through the lower abdomen.

The prince approached and leaned in close, his nose almost touching her. He sighed. "Ahh, intoxicating." He glanced at the prisoners and came to rest on one. "But nothing compares to human's blood."

The captive wailed.

Marekai quivered with delight. "Ready for more?"

A barely perceptible nod came from the female being tortured.

"Oh, I like you. I like you a lot," exclaimed the Prince of Devils.

Brim could not determine the origin of these lancets, but the next pair materialized and struck right under the collarbone and exited out both of their backs.

Marekai cackled like a madman. "No one has ever made it this far without crying for mercy. If you make it to ten, I will grant your last reasonable request."

A smile flickered across the female's visage but disappeared before Brim could be certain.

Number seven went through her mouth from cheek to cheek, and the eighth behind her kneecap. Marekai no longer participated in the piercing.

Brim could not comprehend the mental fortitude required to stay so calm, even if she could not sense pain.

"You are quite a specimen. We'll have to let you heal so we can play this game again," said the god of pain and suffering.

The tortured female glanced up meekly.

A ninth miniature lance appeared low and parallel with the ground. It slowly pushed into the biggest toe, under the claw.

The gnoll wavered and almost lost her balance. "Is that ten?" she asked with the spike lodged between her teeth.

"No. There is one more." Marekai paused mid-gesture. "You already know what you want, don't you?"

Her eyes closed slowly, and she nodded.

Marekai hooted triumphantly. "I knew it! What is it?"

The gnoll replied in a whisper, "I wish to see my homeland."

"An unacceptable request. You can't leave this place." Marekai pointed to the ground next to his feet.

Brim grew bored and located the exit portal once again. *The queen never said how long I needed to stay.*

"No, just see with my own eyes," she replied.

The tenth lancet materialized in front of Marekai and hovered in space. "I intended this next one to pierce your eyeball." He sighed extravagantly. “I can choose a different target, or…” The demi-god’s face lit up. “I can honor your request now and not change my sequence.”

With a whirling motion of his arm, the Prince of Devils opened a portal behind him, keeping himself between it and the prisoner.

Brim began backing toward the doorway, trying to avoid crushing the remaining sacrifices.

The severely wounded gnoll shuffled forward with small steps, the spear through both legs preventing a normal gait.

Marekai put his arm out when she drew even with him. “This is far enough. You can see from here.”

She stopped and leaned on him heavily. “Is that my village?”

He stared at her arm on his shoulder with amusement. “No, but they are all the same.”

A shadowy appendage erupted from the prisoner’s back.

Brim paused his departure and stared in disbelief as it snaked around them both holding the prisoner fast.

As the gnoll grew to epic proportions, Marekai turned to face her. “What do you think you are doing?”

No response came, only a tightening of the trap.

The red dragon gawked at his liege lord, now standing eighteen feet tall, more than double the height of Marekai.

“Not even you are strong enough to attack me in front of my own altar,” screamed Marekai, power enhancing his voice.

Ledaedra grinned and they both glanced at the open portal simultaneously.

“No!” wailed Marekai grasping for the edges of the portal as Ledaedra hurled them both through.

The sounds of battle drifted through the opening. Brim inched closer to get a view, but before he covered half the distance, a pervasive silence emanated from the gateway.

An implosion pulled him toward the portal, then an immediate explosion sent a torrent of shock waves in his direction. His talons flexed and he dug deep grooves into the floor.

Ledaedra hurtled through the portal with wisps of smoke rising from her body and landed with a thud. She scrambled to her feet and fixed BrimStrakenstone with gleaming eyes. "We should be gone before he returns. This will be his prison for the next two hundred years."

"My Queen won't Marekai pull all of the devils from our army?" asked Brim.

"No, I don't think so. Ariata has been taking his image and directing his minions on and off for two months. They won't even know he's missing." Ledaedra cackled in delight.

70

Invisible

Talo

Talo sounded his unique whistle, and Jalko came running, his muzzle coated with blood and gore. He grabbed the dire wolf's jowls and put their faces close together.

"Jalko, I need you to find Dirk Darkmane. Find Dirk!" Talo pushed him away.

The dire wolf stared back.

"Go!"

Jalko took off like an arrow.

Joharie gave chase momentarily, then returned to Talo's side with a grumble.

After several soft clicks and a scratch on the neck, Talo swung up in the saddle. "I'll be back." He whistled sharply, and his steed trotted off.

"No, I'm coming." Brogan fought to gain control of his warhorse.

Talo slowed his horse to a walk and noticed Joharie plodded along next to him. "I can't see anything. What was I thinking?" He whistled for Jalko to return.

Brogan pulled up next to him. "Why didn't you wait for me?"

"I lost Jalko," replied Talo. "I have no idea which direction—"

"Shh!" Brogan hushed him.

Before the big man could explain, Talo heard it too. Something large crashed through the forest, heading their direction.

The dire wolf returned and stood side by side with Joharie, facing back the way they came. The pair issued low throaty growls.

Talo strung his bow, and Brogan drew his sword.

The stampeding creatures stormed into view—five more devils. They stopped and stared menacingly. The leader sniffed the air repeatedly, then lurched and bolted past them, howling without another glance.

Brogan and Talo shared a look of stunned confusion.

"What in the nine hells just happened?" asked Brogan.

Talo's head continued to shake slowly side to side. "I don't know."

Brogan massaged his temple.

"The dark shard!" they said simultaneously.

Grendella joined them astride her pony. "You're not going to believe what happened. Five devils barreled through our camp and barely glanced at us."

"Same. They ran through here one minute ago. They must be tracking the dark shard," said Brogan.

"Where are Katara and Tanya?" asked Talo.

"They would not leave Zecarius's body. Tanya still clings to it," replied the dwarf.

Tako took another gut punch, another reminder of the dangerous game they played. "We need to help them bury Zecarius. Come on. Let's head back."

"When we are done, I'm going after the shard. The artifact is too dangerous to allow our enemies to possess it," replied Grendella. "I will not fail in the mission assigned to me by Lord Terazhan."

Brogan harrumphed. "We barely survived the battle against four of them. There's no reason to get ourselves killed."

"Dirk could be ahead of us two miles or more if he is pushing his horse. He rides a courser. We could never catch him on our warhorses." Talo gave his horse's neck a rub and a pat.

"Will the demons be able to catch him?" asked Grendella.

"Not a chance. They couldn't catch us when we rode to Armak." Talo spotted Katara and Tanya up ahead, in the same place.

Brogan threw both arms in the air. "If we don't go after the dark shard, where does that leave us? The entire purpose of going to Bard Keep was to destroy the shard."

"Well, I'm going. Talo, you know Dirk best. Where would he head?" asked the dwarf.

Talo shrugged. "I'm going, too. Jalko can track him."

Katara tried to detach Tanya from her father.

"We need a plan if we catch up with the pack of demons," said Brogan.

"Let's head back to the plains, and we can ask for help at a war dog village." Talo unstrung his bow.

"And they would help you, too," came a voice from an unseen owner.

Jalko's hackles bristled, and he growled menacingly.

Joharie joined him.

Everyone swung his or her mount to face the intruder.

Out of the shadows stepped Dirk Darkmane. "If the Guardian asks for your help, you do not deny him."

71

Trespassers

ZaphMordakai

Almost four centuries had passed since ZaphMordakai fled this world with his parents, and his return felt anything but a homecoming. Nothing seemed familiar. The color of the sky, the scent of the air, and the utter lack of background noise, all made him feel out of place. He was trespassing.

Solar groaned. "Where are—"

"Shh!" With his head on a swivel, Zaph surveyed their surroundings. "There are creatures here that can kill from a distance with noise from their mouths."

Solar joined in the search for unseen enemies. "What is the plan?"

"We need to find my old home, my uncle's lair, and the portal back to our world. If we can find my old home, I think I can find the other two."

"Do you know where to start? Or do we need to explore the entire planet?" asked Solar.

Zaph's nose twitched. "There were only three mountain peaks, and we lived in the shortest. I remember fleeing through a canyon and on the far side was a forest of gargantuan mushrooms."

Solar scoffed. "How tall could they be?"

"Hmm…ten dragons."

"Seriously? Are they edible?"

Zaph made a sour face. "First, yuck. Who eats mushrooms? Second, they are probably poisonous."

"Let me take a look at those wounds. I can heal them," said Solar.

A caterwaul echoed in the distance as Solar amber glow receded.

Zaph swallowed hard. "That's them. They may have detected us. Can you cast an invisibility spell?"

"No. I am not a wizard. I can polymorph into another animal, as small as—"

"Stop! We don't have time. Fly straight up as fast as you can and do not slow until I tell you to." Zaph transformed instantly and lifted off the ground.

Solar soared into the sky with a mighty squat thrust.

ZaphMordakai, the little wyrmling, fled with his parents from the trellbac all over again. Throughout his body, muscles quivered uncontrollably. Between the first and second cloud layer, he flew by the winged man, and still he raced on. When he passed completely through the next layer he slowed his pace.

Hyperventilating, he called out to Solar, "We—are safe—now."

Barely winded, Solar asked, "Is there nothing that can kill them?"

"They're not immortal. Many things will kill them, and fortunately for us, they are highly susceptible to lightning."

"Good. Now, where are we heading? With all this cloud cover it is impossible to see anything below." Solar tucked his wings and prepared to dive.

ZaphMordakai's fear dissipated, replaced by melancholy. "Hold on a second. I'm still trying to understand what happened back there. Who is Ariata?"

"Terazhan's first daughter, who died during childbirth. If that truly was her, maybe the better question is *what* is Ariata?" Solar's perplexed expression never changed for several seconds.

"I don't care. My mother is dead." Zaph sighed heavily. "I have destroyed my relationship with Lykinnia for nothing."

"Let us focus on getting out of here alive, then you can worry about repairing friendships. Lead on, and I will follow." Solar waved toward the sky before them, putting his entire body into the motion.

"Very well. Once we put a few miles in, we can pop in an out of the clouds to determine if we are heading in the right direction based on the terrain below." Zaph turned with the wind so he could glide along easily while he tried to recall as many details about this world as possible. *Over four hundred years have come and gone. Will I still recognize my home? And will Uncle Deton actually be in his lair? I doubt it. He would not want to get trapped in his lair; there would be no escape. If we do find my home, I am confident I can find the portal back to the other world. The ravine we used to escape points directly toward the portal.*

Solar flew up next to Zaph's head. "You all right?"

"We should take our first peek at the terrain below."

With a glance at each other, they dove.

Zaph had no intention of losing the challenge, and he raced through the second cloud layer. He pulled up as he entered the clear air, then banked hard to the right narrowly missing a mountain top and plowing into Solar.

The winged man grunted heavily and clung to a spike protruding from Zaph's neck. "Why in the nine hells did you do that?"

"Are you looking ahead of us?" asked Zaph.

Mountain peaks erupted through the first cloud layer across the horizon.

Solar continued to grunt and groan as he crawled up onto the dragon's back and leapt into the air.

"Be more careful next time. If you strike me again, you will wish you hit the mountain instead." Solar descended, taking his smile with him.

ZaphMordakai had never been able to fly in this world before they had fled and found himself enjoying it immensely. The clouds were thicker, had more substance, and fluttered even the smallest flaps on his ears. He sighed contently as he exited the lowest layer of clouds.

Mountain peaks of various sizes surrounded them. Many had a steep pitch and were rocky and craggy, but others sloped more gently toward the ground and had vegetation growing on them. All were dappled with patches of snow.

"Does anything look familiar?" asked Solar.

A valley between two very large peaks presented itself before them.

"No. It was a long time ago and it is hard to see anything in the middle of these mountains," replied Zaph.

A roar of pain echoed off the nearby peaks. The final death throes of a beast. It could have emanated from anywhere.

Zaph's nerves caught fire, a tingly sensation with no relief. None of his senses gave him any more information, and he flew through the mountain pass on high alert.

A small ledge swung around the backside of the peak on the left and broadened into a small plateau with a cave entrance on the backside. Movement within the shadows preceded a body emerging from the cave.

Zaph's heart burst from his chest. "Climb!" *These things are everywhere. Did it see me?* He glanced back to see if Solar followed and if the trellbac had reacted. To his utter surprise, neither had happened.

Two more trellbac emerged from the shadows, working with the first to haul a dead red dragon from his home. They had the drake halfway out of the tunnel.

To Zaph's dismay, Solar charged the enemy, blue lightning collecting on his wings.

72

Portal Inspection

Cymm

Seconds ticked by and no one reappeared through the portal. Terazhan, Melcorac, and Azreala's avatar all stood rooted in place, seemingly statues from a lost time. The stillness was daunting, and the nervous energy palpable.

In a panic, Terazhan turned toward the altar and waved his hand. An enormous scrying window materialized, and in it an image of land and sea from high above. They raced toward the ground, toward an island off the coast, a very large island with a volcano in the center of it.

Fire Island—Terazhan is checking on Solar and ZaphMordakai. The blood red haze in Cymm's eyes made it more difficult to see but this seemed obvious.

The scrying window sped forward until the huge stone outcropping came into view. With no one around, Terazhan intently studied a portal—presumably his portal—from all angles.

To Cymm, it appeared to be a normal portal. He laughed at himself. *What in the nine hells do you know about portals?*

After an excessively long investigation, Terazhan spun the scrying window around, turning his back to the portal. He stared at an opening in the rock wall, then slowly approached.

Upon entering, Cymm recognized this place. The chamber across the hallway held the prisoners. To the left, another portal shimmered in a dead-end hallway, and they had fled to the right after rescuing Azreala.

Terazhan pushed further inside and into the prison chamber, then halted.

Cymm and Azreala breathed a collective sigh. They had found Lykinnia shackled and sleeping, but alive.

Azreala stepped the avatar forward. "We need to rescue her now."

"That's what I was going to say." Confusion tainted Cymm's happiness. *Why does she care?*

"I know," she replied.

Terazhan turned toward them and closed the portal, but not the scrying window. "No. If there was one trap there is a good chance there are others. The Dragon Queen is always a step ahead. I need to figure out where Solar is."

"So, what are we going to do?" asked Azreala.

"We will watch," replied the deity.

"What trap?" asked Cymm.

Azreala relayed the question.

"The Dragon Queen placed a second portal up against mine, indicated by the two different colors, gold on one side and dark brown on the other. Solar did not have a choice and walked right into Ledaedra's portal, and I have no clue where it sent them." Terazhan became reticent in obvious contemplation.

The avatar's lip curled. "A second portal? Impressive, she placed one gateway against another."

Both Terazhan and Melcorac scowled at her.

"What? I'm just admiring her intellect. I'll talk to Feldarius. His portals may still work," said Azreala.

Terazhan exhaled forcefully through his nose. "Yes, do that."

Cymm stared through the scrying window at Lykinnia. He knew her father would never allow any harm to come to her. His thoughts shifted to Talo and the others. *I hope they survived.*

73

The Missing Backback

Talo

Dirk Darkmane urged his horse forward. It complied with nervous energy and wide eyes, dancing equally in a lateral direction.

"This is the last place I expected to see you Dirk," said Brogan.

The would-be thief of the dark shard did not answer, but a calculating smile bloomed across his face.

"That's not Dirk," whispered Talo. All his twitches and idiosyncrasies had vanished.

As if on cue, Jalko and Joharie sprang before Talo's warhorse baring their teeth.

"He has released the demon," added Grendella.

"I am not a demon. Do you think me an agent of Malekai?" replied the creature in Dirk's body.

"What are you then?" asked Talo.

"I am beyond your comprehension, but some of you have already met me." Dirk's head swiveled to Brogan and back to Grendella.

"What do you want, Dego?" asked the female dwarf.

"The same thing I've always wanted. Where is your friend?" asked Dego.

Grendella quickly glanced around the circle at her companions. "We don't know. He—"

"I don't believe you. This vessel says he traveled north with this group." Dego's eyes flared red, as bright as Azreala's.

"That is true, but we separated four days ago when we left the city," replied Talo.

The glare from Grendella silenced him. "That's close enough, Dego. I'm sure you remember my other friend." The cleric raised her warhammer in his direction.

Dego pulled on the horse's reins.

"He didn't go anywhere. He stayed behind to help the people and fight the dragons." Brogan set his sword blade across the back of his warhorse.

"No. That fool! Then we are heading back to find him." Dirk Darkmane twitched and rubbed his ear.

Talo wondered if anyone else had noticed the brief window of Dirk regaining control.

Grendella shook her head. "That was four days ago. He's either dead—"

"Or he is on his way to the rendezvous point," finished Brogan.

Talo's head went side to side in amazement. *Did these two rehearse this lie? What are they…?* His eyes focused on Grendella's backpack hanging loose from the horse's saddle, and he understood the ruse. *Very clever. If we can't carry the shard there, get this creature to take the shard there for us willingly.*

"Terazhan would never let him die. Where is this rendezvous?" asked Dego, back in control of Dirk's body.

"The High Towers of Delagor," replied Brogan.

Dego gazed at them suspiciously. "And what is there?"

Grendella had returned the warhammer to her shoulder. "Nothing. Simply our meeting place before we pass into the Realm of Dragon's Bane."

A second shadowy head materialized from Dirk's left shoulder. It screamed, "And?"

Using Dirk's mouth, Dego said, "If you don't provide better answers, some of you are going to die."

"We're traveling to the east coast, to Fire Island." Grendella stroked her wispy beard.

Dego smirked. "You're lying!" He paused and cocked his head, listening. Dirk's body convulsed. "I need a stronger vessel."

"That's not going to happen." Grendella brought her weapon to bear, yet again.

Unfazed, Dego panned the group until he reached Tanya. "If only you were a few years older."

Katara pulled her niece behind her.

Dego said with a sniff, "Although, I—" His head tilted again to listen.

Talo could hear it, too. The fiends were coming.

"Why won't these things let me be?" growled Dego.

Brogan's face had gone white. "Form a defensive line. We will run through them and keep running."

"We need to head for the plains where the horses can run faster," said Talo.

Brogan waved him off. "Grendella put your pony behind the three warhorses. You too Dirk, or Dego, or—"

"Where'd he go?" asked Katara.

"He was just here." Something on the ground caught Talo's attention. "Oh, by the nine hells! Grendella, is that your backpack?"

74

Lorelei

BrimStrakenstone

Ledaedra opened a scrying window with BrimStrakenstone by her side. The cathedral geode blazed to life, each gemstone sparkling with a light of its own. The Dragon Queen delved deep under the mountains where the true dark elves lived. In underground caves and tunnels, they practiced their dark magic and offered sacrifices to their patron god, Marekai.

"I would have preferred if you went," Ledaedra hissed as the image finally solidified.

Of course you would have. You care not who dies if your objective is met, Brim thought, but instead said, "I have every confidence they will succeed, and besides, the bulk of a dragon is not suited for that environment." *Especially a red dragon, but my legion of black dragons can infiltrate their domain and possibly their society in the form of a dark elf.*

Ledaedra scoffed, "Then why did you send a second team?"

Brim had sent eight black dragons to capture the dark elf priestess, Lorelei, and deal with her three handmaidens. Two squads of four with the same mission, but he sent the second group late the following day to ensure the successful extraction of the target.

"There are too many unknowns and possibilities. It seemed prudent to send a second team for backup." He shifted uncomfortably. The second group had contacted him earlier this morning with news of a delay. They had encountered the denizens of an underground lake, and to avoid conflict, backtracked themselves into a significant delay.

The Dragon Queen and Brim both stared in muteness as the first group took position and waited.

ReiStratakai, the leader of the first group, stared across the massive cavern from behind a stalagmite at the priestesses congregating around an altar. Above the flat surface, floated a golden-skinned creature captured within an intense indigo globe of energy. The chanting and synchronized movements of the worshipers indicated a sacrificial ritual.

Brim cast a sideways glance at his liege lord. "The globe will interfere with their night vision." All the natural drow had their cowls in place, shadowing their faces. "Do you know which priestess is the target?"

"She will expose herself."

The extraction party stealthily surrounded the platform, JalRaknar first in position. The other two had yet to reveal themselves, or maybe they were obscured by the energy source and the craggy stalagmites.

ReiStratakai crept forward to a better viewpoint but still waited in the gloom.

The four priestesses now surrounded the altar and the sacrifice, rocking back and forth in a state of meditation. The large globe of energy pulsed in response, and small indigo spheres appeared, revolving around each caster. Their chanting grew in volume.

Ledaedra's arms shifted, and the angle inside the window rotated, creating an unobstructed view of the altar.

The priestess with the brightest and largest aura emanating from her raised her hands. She had twice as many orbs revolving around her. They had found their target.

JalRaknar climbed over the edge and crouched behind a priestess.

He sent ReiStratakai a signal, and she snuck over to the broad staircase. She took them two at a time until her eyes peeked over the edge.

All four members of the capture party were moving into position.

This will be easier than I thought. Brim's head drew closer to the scrying window in excitement as TorSarkath pulled himself over the rim and into position.

Brim's breath caught in his throat. In the fourth position, an indigo ball of energy descended from above. It crashed into SarMirabain as she crept up behind their intended target. Her limbs contorted abnormally, bending and cracking audibly.

With a gleaming dagger in hand, JalRaknar rose and pulled it across the throat of the priestess in front of him. A thin red line quickly became a torrent of blood.

Lorelei's chanting faltered, and her eyes popped open. She turned, eyes blazing indigo, and locked gazes with ReiStratakai. "You will not have me. Not while I breathe." Her hand waved at JalRaknar. Three indigo spheres struck him immediately, sending convulsive spasms throughout his body. A moan escaped his lips before she slammed him into the altar with brutal force. His body, twisted and broken, fell to the floor.

Rei broke free of the bonds of indecision and slashed the priestess in front of her, not once but twice in a decussate fashion. Her enemy collapsed on the ground, and the spheres orbiting broke from their revolution and returned to Lorelei.

TorSarkath plunged two short swords through the back of the drow cleric in front of him and they erupted from her chest.

Pounding footsteps echoed off the walls of the cavern. Reinforcements were coming.

Rei sprinted across the gap toward the target.

Two indigo orbs crashed into ReiStratakai, knocking her to her knees only a few steps from Lorelei. With a roar she transformed into herself—a beast—a monster, then released a second deafening roar. Stalactites were ripping through her back, fanning her fury. This chamber was not meant to house a leviathan.

The large globe containing the sacrificial offering exploded. Purplish plasma flung in every direction, covering friend and foe indiscriminately. Brim could see nothing in the dismal light, but he assumed the eyesight of those in the chamber had switched to night vision.

Lorelei summoned the remaining indigo orbs from around the chamber and constructed a shield in front of her. The remaining priestess had not been so lucky; the plasma clung to her in thick patches. Her wails of agony were abruptly ended by TorSarkath's sword. Her body hit the floor a moment after her head.

Guards swarmed up both sets of stairs, the steel in their hands an inky blackness in the infrared spectrum, which Brim forced his vision to shift to.

ReiStratakai swept the platform with her massive tail, killing two guards. Her enormous talons raked across Lorelei's shield in a shower of sparks.

A retaliation of indigo whips thrashed out from behind the shield and struck Rei in the face. Her left eye burst, and the contents spilled down her face. In a berserker-like frenzy, the black dragon lurched forward, biting down on the shield and Lorelei and pinning her against the altar. Teeth scraped across the priestess's body in several locations, but the shield protected her from further damage.

The guards hacked and slashed at the dragon's back, inflicting many lacerations with their unusual weapons. Once again, the black dragon brought her tail to bear and swept the floor clean behind her.

Rei slammed Lorelei into the altar two more times in rapid succession, and the priestess went limp.

More dark elves were surging up the stairs, screaming and waving. Four of them had formed a perfect line.

ReiStratakai dropped her victim and breathed in deep, then loosed a massive lightning bolt. It struck the leader in the line with significant force, throwing him into the ones behind him. The bolt forked and hit all four plus two others.

Another stalactite dug a deep groove across her neck before snapping and falling to the ground, and other pieces were raining down from the ceiling.

The fighting paused, and the drow began running for the exits with their eyes trained above them.

Rei's head spun back and forth, attempting to see with her remaining eye.

Only four dark elves persisted, everyone else had fled. The same four she had hit with the lightning bolt. They were singed—wisps of smoke rose from their skin and clothing—but otherwise uninjured.

Two dark elves shot their own lightning from their hands into Rei's face and neck, while the other two slipped around her to shield the helpless body of Lorelei.

ReiStratakai charged in a mindless rampage…

"No!" bellowed Brim.

…never realizing whom she attacked.

In the cramped space, two of the drow transformed into black dragons. One clamped onto her neck with its maw while the other shredded her body. They ripped her apart in mere seconds. They transformed back into their dark elf forms and immediately fled the chamber with an unconscious prisoner in tow.

Crestfallen, Brim shook his head, "The second squad has arrived."

"If Lorelei is dead, I will kill them all." Ledaedra fumed while creating a portal for the second team to return home.

BrimStrakenstone continued to stare into the scrying window at the pools of blood on the platform. He lingered there, long after the screams died out.

75

Disciple of Terazhan

ZaphMordakai

ZaphMordakai slowed before he entered the clouds shielding him from discovery but also obscuring his view of the chaotic event taking place. Solar had already covered half the distance between them, and the trellbac remained oblivious. So confident in their own safety, they had no reason to take precautions.

You fool! You will get us both killed. Zaph continued to hover at the edge of the first layer of clouds.

The air around Solar shimmered with a golden haze, causing all three lizardmen to glance up in surprise. Before the winged man could cover much more distance, the first trellbac released its caterwaul.

Zaph's eyes widened. He heard it then felt it in rapid succession even at this distance. The power in the waves had dispersed before they hit him, but a slight ache in his chest lingered.

Solar's charge had ceased, and Zaph mentally said goodbye, but before he could climb into the clouds, massive blue thunderbolts careened off the finch's wings. The lightning raced toward the ground and struck all three trellbac, but not before they caterwauled.

The trellbac danced about in a circle as if playing a childish game of hotfoot. Their feathers caught fire, and their golden skin turned dark brown. With a final jerk, the enemy collapsed around the dead red dragon.

While scanning in every direction, Solar cautiously descended. When he touched down, he immediately crouched and waited.

Awestruck, ZaphMordakai, drifted closer. He could not think in complete thoughts. *How? He should be…more enemy.* Working against every desire to flee, he plummeted toward the ground.

After inspecting the first body, Solar moved on to the second with his golden shield enduring.

Zaph landed heavily and unsheathed his talons to ensure the death of the third trellbac. "Unholy Terazhan! How did you survive?"

Lightning crackled along Solar's feathers. "Do not ever say that again."

"Fine." Zaph swallowed hard. "Did this shield protect you?"

Solar hoisted his left arm. "This blocked the sound waves from touching me."

This could be the difference! It could balance the power and allow us to take back our homeland. Zaph's body tingled with excitement. "Can you teach me this spell?"

"It is not a spell—"

"Do not lie to me! You wish to keep this power to yourself," Zaph's head swooned, and his vision became blurry.

Solar backstepped from his fury. "I think you need to calm down."

Zaph remained on the edge of hyperventilating. "My kin have been searching for something like this for over four centuries. How did you create this shield?"

"This is a power granted to me by Terazhan, and only available to his disciples. The power and size of the shield grow with your devotion," replied Solar.

Zaph took a deep breath and stared at the ground. "Can a dragon become a disciple?"

Stifling a laugh, Solar coughed. "Unlikely but not impossible. Many moons ago, a copper dragon followed the teachings of Terazhan for many years."

With a cold stare, Zaph said, "Next time I say climb, don't attack, and climb straight up. Before the old drakes fled this world, they told me this is how to avoid their voice weapon. Trellbac can't incline their heads back that far."

"Fine." Solar mimicked the dragon's earlier statement and tone. "So, where to?"

"This way."

76

Curmudgeon

Lykinnia

The passage of time continued to allude Lykinnia—her best guess, they had just slept for two or three more days—but the functionality of her mind had returned. She no longer believed they were sleeping or the bread to be food. *Maybe our bodies are frozen in time. If I only consider the time I have been awake in this prison, it would only be a few hours. I am never thirsty, and I never have the urge to—*

Lykinnia noticed another prisoner—a dark elf with ebony skin—arrived since her last awakening, filling the last of the empty racks directly across from her. Blood dripped from the unconscious newcomer onto the floor.

Why have they not attempted to heal her many lacerations? At least she fought when they tried to capture her. Lykinnia practiced the hand movement to release her wrists, the new one she had discovered to release her ankles, and finally a gesture she hoped would release the manacle around her neck. Of course, nothing worked at the moment, since the manacles were still in position.

Ronks railed against his restraints. He pulled and twisted one way, then quickly reversed directions. The acrid scent of burnt flesh filled the cavern.

"Easy, Ronks, you are going to hurt yourself," said Lykinnia.

"Shut princess mouth or Ronks eat you when we out of here." He roared like a madman in her direction.

Well, that did not last long. I thought we had a real connection starting. Lykinnia sighed. *His starvation anger is clouding his mind. His big question about riding dragons to escape could be easily solved. I will simply open a portal back to the Peak of Power—if I can open a portal at all—but I have no way to perform a test without being discovered.*

The others stirred, blinking and fighting against the dazed confusion. Only the dark elf remained unmoving.

"Ronks, a little more patience. I am getting close," she said as softly as she could.

"No! No escape—fight." His struggle against his confinement renewed.

Two draconian priests appeared from the alcove with the customary basket of bread, but this time a platter came with it.

The pungent scent of roasted meat hit Lykinnia like a gut punch, and she almost retched. She did not eat the flesh of other animals.

The effect on Ronks was quite different. He became mesmerized, wide-eyed, and unmoving.

A large haunch of meat, including bone, lay on the platter surrounded by several smaller ones.

"Did I hear the word escape again?" asked one of the priests.

Lykinnia could not tell them apart. For all she knew, two different acolytes serviced them every time.

Ronks licked his lips. "No one say that word."

The draconian holding the platter hesitated, then turned slightly, as if to leave.

"Ronks told us how he used to fight wearing *a cape* with a cowl, similar to yours," Lykinnia chimed in.

"I doubt that," replied the priest. "Settle down and you can have the large one."

"Yes, Ronks be good." When his arm released from the manacle, he snatched the large haunch off the tray, almost spilling the others.

"Careful! I don't want to eat mine off the floor," said Leighton.

The priests moved on to Lykinnia.

"Not me. Do not bring that tray over here. I cannot stand the smell."

The priest with the basket of bread approached, locking eyes with her. "*Watch my hand closely. I will show you the final gesture component.*"

"What?" asked Lykinnia.

The draconian priest shot her dagger eyes and resisted a full glance over his shoulder. *"Use that infernal brain of yours! Do not speak aloud. This is how you release the manacle around your neck."* After he performed the movement he said, *"You must wait to escape. You are in no danger until Lorelei is healed, and the last prisoner is delivered."*

"*The last prisoner. There is another?*" asked Lykinnia.

"*Yes. The most important and powerful. You must wait until she arrives!*" replied the priest.

Lykinnia grabbed a second loaf of bread to delay his departure. *"Why are you helping us?"*

However, the priest had already severed the mental link.

Melandri bless me. Is this a trick? Lykinnia bit into the second loaf and it hung from her mouth. She quickly practiced the movement just shared. The neck manacle grew, but only in one direction, zapping the back of her neck. *Terazhan be blessed!* She quickly broke the magic link, and it returned to normal size.

"You eat like a wild boar," groaned the newcomer at Ronks. "I could hear you chewing in the nine hells, you oaf."

In between bites and slobbers, the ogre replied, "You snore—like a—banshee—wails! And you smell funny."

"I smell funny? I knew you were an ogre before I opened my eyes, although I hoped it was just a dead body," countered the new prisoner, Lorelei.

Lykinnia turned to Jenaleya. "The curmudgeon has met his match."

Jenaleya chuckled. "Which one?"

Ronks stared at Lykinnia. "Stay out of this, Princess, with your princess words."

Heat rushed to Lykinnia's cheeks. "I am not a princess." She stuffed the bread in the top of her blouse and swiped her long hair behind her ear with her free hand. "I am a half-breed, like you."

"Check it out, Haskins. She got pointy ears," hooted Ronks.

Haskins stared at her in wonder. "You's pretty."

Lykinnia chewed her bread and retreated into her mind. "*There is another prisoner, more important and powerful than the rest.*" The priest's previous words echoed in her mind, and a pang of jealousy shot through her. *If this person or creature is more powerful than me, maybe they can save us, instead of everything falling on my shoulders.*

"Eat!" yelled one of the draconian acolytes.

Myra would take neither meat nor bread. She whispered to herself in soothing undertones and would not look in anyone's direction.

"Myra, you has to eats," said Haskins.

Lykinnia finished her first loaf of bread. *Where is this last prisoner going to go? There are no more restraining devices.* The large gap between Myra and Leighton drew her attention.

Lykinnia glanced at Jenaleya, who gaped in a different direction. "What are you staring at?"

"It's orange again," replied the princess.

"What?" Lykinnia's face wrinkled, following her gaze. Her eyes went wide, and her mind swirled. "It *is* orange…why did I not see this before?"

77

Charge!

Talo

The warhorses charged, followed closely by Grendella's pony. They rode flank-to-flank, no wider than a man's shoulders apart, a wall of muscle barreling toward the enemy. To pass unharmed between the charging equines was highly unlikely. They were trained for this. They had been bred for this.

Any normal enemy would have faltered under the onslaught as the warhorses bore down on them. However, these were demons and devils, and their number had grown from five to twelve. The enemy rampaged through the forest toward them, hooting and howling.

Jalko and Joharie protected Grendella's pony on both sides in the second line, thunder rumbling in their chests.

Talo's nerves were set ablaze—even the hair on his head reported erratically—and panic raced through his body. *Why am I here instead of home with my wife and family?* he thought for the tenth time since they fled Armak. *Jalko and I could be hunting jackrats. How many bonfire parties have we missed? Cymm's stories made everything seem so romantic and heroic, but this is the reality.* He suddenly felt very sad and sorry for his cousin.

Katara's face had gone ghost white, along with Tanya's, who sat in front of her aunt on Cymm's horse.

"Give the horse more rein!" Talo yelled at Katara. His whistles and clicks were loud enough for all three horses to hear.

In theory, Talo knew what to do. The Knights of Kharad had provided specific training requirements, but this would only take them so far. Horse training at the Reich Farm involved running through and over grass figures. After the Knights of Kharad took ownership, the training in the field advanced to lances and real bodies, typically marauding orcs or gnolls.

Although Brogan's warhorse, the largest of the three, was the youngest and least experienced. Both Talo's and Cymm's horses had some minor experience with riding through and even trampling wolves in the grasslands, but nowhere near as big as their current enemy. Talo tried to trample the demon when he met Joharie, and that had not gone so well.

Before the impact, the warhorses were already blowing hard, and their eyes wide with fright. Talo did everything he could to keep them stalwart—horses and riders—using soothing clicks and a commanding voice to convey confidence he did not have.

The pounding hooves of the horses echoed off the ground and through the dimly lit forest, but the ferocious growls of the enemy drowned out everything else a moment before impact.

Grendella called out, "Lord Terazhan protect this faithful servant of yours!"

A golden sphere of light came blazing to life, engulfing them.

The fiends shielded their eyes but continued to charge.

Talo braced himself and held his breath. The force from the collision sent catastrophic waves through his body.

The demons and devils stood no taller than a human, but they were thicker and denser. One demon bounced off Talo's warhorse, then immediately off Brogan's and folded under the powerful hooves beneath him. Forceful tremors transferred through the horse's flank and the saddle into Talo's body.

Brogan slashed a devil across the face, Talo had forgotten about his bow, and Katara screamed in agony.

The jarring impact had slowed their mounts more than he could have imagined, and the second wave crashed into them.

Another demon went under the hooves of Talo's warhorse with a grunt and a moan, but before they cleared the body, bone cracked, and his mount faltered. With an ear-piercing shriek, his horse attempted to take another step, but its front left leg would bear no weight.

Talo's hands went to his head. "No!" This horse was the closest thing he had to a best friend—next to Cymm—and the pairing occurred when he turned off age.

Tanya and Katara exploded through the enemy line to freedom, as well as Grendella, but Jalko and Joharie pulled even with Talo.

"Was that your horse?" Brogan cried, grimacing, a moment before two devils blind-sided him and hauled him off his mount.

Talo stared in dismay as they pounced upon the big man.

78

The Mantle of the Gods

Azreala

Two days passed after Terazhan put a halt on Lykinnia's rescue mission. Deities reported consecutively to take their turn at the scrying window. Even Azreala became part of the rotation when Jakarrak failed to show. Dilantro then Sehaleah relieved Terazhan at the window, followed by Azreala, and finally Melandri and Vallerielle finished the cycle before Terazhan reappeared to start it all over again.

Melandri arrived to relieve Azreala of her third rotation. "Any news?"

"A new prisoner arrived an hour ago. Now, all the holding devices are full," replied the goddess of death.

"Hmm," replied the goddess of fate, then stared into the window for several moments. "The new prisoner is Lorelei, Marekai's daughter. He will not be happy."

Azreala made a strange face. "He has a daughter?"

"Indeed. One even older than you."

"Interesting. Where's Jakarrak?" asked Azreala.

Melandri shook her head slowly. "He should be here."

"I trust you can handle this."

Melandri nodded.

Azreala walked off the platform. *What in the nine hells is Jakarrak up to? His constant scheming has its benefits but comes at a price.* Other than the last Council Meeting, she had not seen him in almost two years. A strange encounter she could not forget.

ꝏꝏꝏ

Jakarrak had requested an unexpected visit to the Plane of Spirits, which Azreala had approved.

"Good morrow, my sister. How are you today?" greeted Jakarrak.

Azreala slowly returned the tanzanite figurine to the table with the rest of her collection. "It has been a while since we last spoke. I would guess a decade."

Jakarrak cleared his throat. "Yes, well, I have been quite busy. I remember when your father commissioned an artisan to craft that figurine set for your sister. Have you been able to recover all the power words of summoning?"

"Not one of them. My sister kept them well guarded."

"A simple visit to Vallerielle's disciples at Bard Keep would remedy that, assuming you are on good terms with the goddess of time," said Jakarrak.

"You know I'm not. Why are you here?"

"I have traveled far and wide this past decade. In fact, my recent travels took me through the outer planes where I heard an interesting rumor."

"Which was?"

Jakarrak wore a disapproving visage. "Not much of a hostess, are you? May I sit? Can we have a glass of wine?"

With a skeptical glare, Azreala indicated the lounging area. While pouring two goblets of wine, she asked, "Why would you travel into the outer planes? I thought our phylacteries malfunctioned there."

Jakarrak accepted his refreshment and walked past her. He took a seat in a large reclining chair with plush crimson pillows. "That is true, but sometimes it is necessary to get the information I need, and scrying into the future is much more accurate there."

Azreala ran her finger around the rim of the goblet and remained standing. "So, what rumor did you hear?"

"I traveled through the Soul Realm and discovered a tribe of balor. They invited me to join them for feasting." Jakarrak sipped at his wine.

"Why would they invite you?"

Jakarrak quickly transformed into a balor—a necromantic creature of fire and shadow. "More specifically, they invited me."

A cold terror ran through her body, immobilizing her. The day her father and sister died came rushing back.

"Forgive me." He transitioned back to his normal form. "I have discovered why the phylactery did not work for your father at the time of his greatest need. The balor had determined how to create a protective circle of their own, encapsulating the soul of your father's killer, Grumgresh, and negating your father's safeguards and the protection provided by the phylactery. Basically, they created a temporary phylactery, a protective bubble from the Soul Realm, that pushed into your home plane."

"What?" The floor dropped away beneath Azreala. Her stomach rolled and old wounds festered. "No, how can a phylactery fail? My father's death, and my sister's screams were all a manifestation of balor malice?"

"As a member of The Council at that time, I can assure you we did a thorough investigation of the incident and found nothing amiss. It would appear we were wrong, and I feel compelled to share one more detail and implore you not to react hastily."

"What is it?"

Jakarrak shifted uncomfortably. "Grumgresh is still alive. I spoke with your father's and sister's murderer. At least he claims to be the same creature."

Azreala's eyes flamed a dazzling red, temporarily fogging her vision. "Where—where do…" Tears streamed down her face.

"There were at least fifty in this tribe. You do not stand a chance against them." Jakarrak swirled his wine and sniffed the bouquet.

"You will tell me how to find this vile creature—this Grumgresh," Azreala hissed.

"No, not until your power increases significantly. In the meantime, you can visualize and plan your revenge." Jakarrak rose to leave.

Azreala screamed, almost masking the sound of her shattering wine glass against the hearth. "That could take centuries. You better have a plan that involves quicker retribution."

"I do not. Unless you plan to take the mantle from Terazhan." Jakarrak paused. "No? I did not think so."

Crimson skulls materialized above Azreala's outstretched hand. "You've done me no favors. This knowledge will be torturous and cause many sleepless nights."

"Careful, sister. There might be another way, but it will require detailed planning and patience. I have become aware of a young man who is a power magnifier, but only for those he is willing to assist. If you could form a bond or an alliance…"

79

Wyrmling

ZaphMordakai

For three days they searched with very little sleep, flying in the air most of time. ZaphMordakai flew great distances frequently, but each new day forced him to decrease the pace slightly to allow Solar to keep up. Zaph's newfound respect for the winged man had subconsciously brought an end to the demeaning nickname he had created.

Over the past few days, they spotted several more trellbac, and Solar even killed two of them, but Zaph had put an end to the hunt until now. Below, were two adult, red dragons and a wyrmling on a mountain pass trail, trapped between two approaching trellbac hunting parties.

"We have to help them!" cried Zaph, his own childhood experience flooding his emotions.

Solar scanned the vicinity and doubled back. "Come on!" He swooped down into the ravine behind the converging trellbac.

The ravine narrowed, and Zaph struggled to stay aloft. The walls loomed so close he could see the tiny cracks with tufts of moss growing out of them, and when he extended his wings, the tips scraped against both sides. His confidence plummeted. *How am I going to help like this?* He dropped to the ground as a dark elf and immediately transformed into a panther. His head rocked back, gazing up at walls far higher than he expected.

He sprinted ahead, trying to keep up with the winged man. Zaph managed ably until the ravine took a sharp turn to the right, and Solar flew out of sight. He bore down and pressed on, determined to assist in the rescue mission.

Lightning crackled up ahead immediately followed by several caterwauls. The battle had begun.

Zaph shifted into stealth mode and slid to the side of the ravine. Silent and somewhat camouflaged, he continued forward. *Lykinnia's invisibility spell would be very useful right now.*

The winged man came into view, as did the five trellbac, three of which were already dead.

Zaph climbed the rock wall and positioned himself strategically. He had one chance at this.

Solar tucked his wings, and they folded neatly into his back and disappeared. He landed heavily on the ground bearing his shield in front of him. He had hit one of the remaining trellbac with two lightning bolts already and yet it fought on.

His wing lightning must be significantly more powerful, thought Zaph, readying himself to join the fight. *One caterwaul in my direction, and I'm dead.* He continued to crouch.

The two remaining enemies synchronized their next attack, and the sound waves pummeled Solar's shield, pushing him back. His feet dug into the ground and ceased his rearward slide, but he relented to avoid being bent over backward.

Zaph could wait no longer. He backed farther into the shadows and transformed into a drow, then summoned three large balls of lightning. He sent one forth quickly to aid the winged man, now pressed against the rocky mountain wall.

The caterwauls ceased and Solar summoned a massive golden hammer. It struck the wounded trellbac, ending its life. Cautiously, he circled away from the enemy and the incoming ball of electricity.

Unaware of the attacker behind him, the trellbac shifted its gaze above Solar and caterwauled a moment before the blast hit him.

Pebbles, rocks, and boulders rained down on Solar as he stumbled back toward the wall, raising his shield.

The second and third balls of lightning bore down on their target and slammed into the trellbac before it could locate Zaph. He watched the monster's golden skin and feathers scatter. For a heartbeat, pride flared—but it curdled as quickly as it came. They were not safe yet. He searched for any sign of life—chest, hands, toes—any movement on this one or the others. More than one drake had fallen victim to the death throes of a trellbac.

Solar, buried beneath the rubble, had not moved either.

He transformed into a dragon as he leapt toward the last to die. When he landed, one swipe separated the head from the body. He roared defiantly down the ravine, sending a signal to the red dragons.

He scanned the other dead trellbac as he backed his way to Solar. *I should have decapitated them all.* His concern for the winged man surprised him, outweighing his own safety.

The red dragon family roared back.

Zaph ripped through the pile of boulders throwing them in every direction.

Solar had curled up against the rock wall and under his shield. He appeared uninjured, until he fell back into the wall upon standing.

Dragon roars and caterwaul calls became interspersed, and Zaph's head whipped around to inspect the ravine. "They're coming. Can you fly?"

"I am unsteady." Solar rubbed the back of his head.

"Can you cast your wing lightning again?"

Solar stumbled again. "It is still charging."

"Get on my back. We need to get to higher ground," said Zaph.

Solar attempted to climb Zaph's scaley hide twice and failed, even with the numerous spikes protruding from his body.

"Here they come. You need to run with the drakes!" ZaphMordakai lifted off the ground, out of the canyon, and found a lip to hide behind. *How am I going to defeat five of these things?* Across the ravine he discovered another large rock outcropping. *Maybe, I can slow the hunters down.*

The red dragons scampered past the dead trellbac, barely staying ahead of those chasing them. The wyrmling's tongue hung out and the tips of its wings were dragging on the ground.

ZaphMordakai lashed out, releasing his violet lightning at the rock wall across from him. The outcropping cracked and creaked, then gave way and crashed to the ground.

The enemy pulled back to avoid the falling rock at the last moment, except for the lead trellbac, crushed beneath the tumult.

A billowing cloud of dust obscured the remaining hunters, allowing Zaph to back away unnoticed. He ran parallel with the ravine and caught the male red dragon glance at him a moment before he roared. A smile began to creep upon his face then froze. *Where's Solar?*

He had fallen behind, not even able to keep up with the faltering wyrmling.

Glancing back toward the pile of rock, Zaph found the trellbac had only been mildly delayed. Their six legs allowed them to skitter up and over the rocks with minimal effort.

Solar glanced back and tried to fly but landed before hitting the wall again. His golden shield appeared as he continued to stumble forward.

ZaphMordakai, in his dark elf form, sent two more lightning bolts into the far wall, but they were much less effective. A caterwaul chased him away from the edge of the ravine, and out of sight, then he reversed directions. He sprinted back as a jaguar, retracing his path to where he created the rock pile. He popped up well behind the enemy, and he fired a lightning bolt at the one in the rear.

It grazed the side of the trellbac and struck the ground with an explosion of shrapnel, sending the creature sailing to the side. All four dragon hunters turned to find another bolt incoming. They scattered and vacated the impact zone before it hit. Two made eye contact.

Zaph withdrew before they could blast him with their voice weapon. The ravine stretched out of sight.

Solar peaked over his shoulder at the pursuers, as he pulled even with the family of red dragons. The little wyrmling had finally exhausted his energy reserve and slowed to a walk. The winged man appeared emotionally distraught as he passed the wyrmling and stopped, staring at the little one. His wings were held wide, but no energy coursed through them. He hoisted his golden shield and turned to face the enemy.

ZaphMordakai launched one more lightning bolt at the four remaining trellbac, then pulled back from the edge, trembling as his courage faded.

80

Unusual Movement

Talo

A sudden and severe wind picked up and whipped the tree branches about frantically. Chaotic energy permeated the air.

The creaking of the trees returned with a fervor. *How can this be normal?* Talo glanced around nervously before hopping down to relieve the pressure on the horse's broken leg. He took a deep breath and began firing arrows in rapid succession.

The tree branches thrashed the air and thrashed the mound of combatants. A demon flew through the air, its arms flailing, then struck the ground hard. Tree limbs pummeled it to a bloody pulp.

Daylight faded quickly, unable to filter through the branches and blocked by the tree trunks. The trees were…they were…moving.

Talo froze among the chaos with mouth agape, unable to fire any more arrows. *The trees are moving. I don't care what everyone says, this isn't normal. The trees are moving.*

The belt at Talo's waist twisted and wrenched to the side, followed by several aggressive tugs.

Tanya glanced up at him as she slid the short sword out of its scabbard—the sword Cymm had given him from the dragon treasure, the sword Cymm had intended to give Tanya.

Katara materialized a moment later to form a triangle with their backs together.

A branch wrapped around the ankle of the last devil and ripped him off the back of Brogan, revealing many deep gouges across his entire body. His shredded armor hung in tatters from his shoulders. He rose slowly to all fours.

The demons and devils did not relent, nor did the tree abominations. Two demons busied themselves tearing Grendella's backpack apart and sniffing the contents.

Not every tree moved, and no two creatures were exactly the same. Some ambled forward with a side-to-side rocking motion, while others propelled themselves with their roots in one of two manners. Either they formed hundreds of small appendages to crabwalk, or the trunk split allowing the roots to form the feet of a bipedal creature. However, they shared a similarity: a pulsing green orb half the size of a human's head, as well as two smaller plum shaped orbs which seemed to function as eyes.

Grendella tripped and stumbled in her frantic attempt to reach Brogan, leaving her pony behind. "Hold on, I'm coming." Her voice cracked midway through.

A demon lunged for the dwarven cleric as she arrived. A tree limb batted the monster away by with a resounding *crunch*.

Talo, Tanya, and Katara had their own worries and no tree creatures to defend them.

Katara parried the attack of the first devil, relieving it of its clawed hand, while Talo drove an arrow through its eye socket at point blank range.

A golden light blossomed behind Talo, the aftermath of Grendella's healing prayer and lighting the immediate area for several moments.

Two more enemies broke through the ring of defense over the top of a fallen tree.

Tanya released a sob but quickly stifled it. "Oh Terazhan, protect us!"

Beoww! A golden sphere of light exploded into existence.

Talo nodded in gratitude toward a confused Grendella, then took aim and fired, clipping the side of an enemy's head.

The agents of evil hesitated, allowing Katara enough time to step in front of her niece and Talo.

"You can't take them both on!" exclaimed the bowman.

"Then you better not miss again." She raised both swords and stood her ground.

The enemy charged hooting and howling.

A steady knocking of the arrow against the stock of the bow distracted Talo, and he missed.

Twelve feet away the fiends lunged, and Katara braced herself.

Branches coiled around their ankles and violently ripped them back toward the fallen tree creature, where they were pummeled by limbs and thrashed by branches.

Brogan and Grendella rejoined the group in time to observe the final crushing blows.

The forest fell eerily quiet, broken only by the creak of living wood and the ragged breaths of the survivors. A solitary leaf spiraled to the ground amidst the group.

The sphere of golden light dissipated.

"How did you do that?" asked Grendella, staring at Tanya.

"I don't know."

"Shh," hissed Brogan.

Two tree creatures approached.

Brogan stepped forward with sword drawn but lowered. "Thank you. Caretaker is our—"

"You friend." One of the tree creatures pointed at Brogan's left shoulder.

A brilliant, emerald-green marker blazed to life on Brogan's bare skin, resembling a tattoo.

Talo sputtered, then whispered, "This is normal?"

The circumstances were quite serious, but no one could stop laughing.

81

Warm Reception

Cymm

Three days passed, and Cymm could wait no longer. Azreala finished her shift at the altar, watching over Lykinnia, and Melandri arrived to relieve her. When Armak fell, it had a tremendous effect on Terazhan, he had lost the most followers, a devastating impact to him personally. Every deity had lost followers, but not as many.

"Azreala," called Cymm as she stepped off the platform.

She waved and headed his way.

"Have you spoken to Feldarius yet?" he asked.

The goddess's tail snapped like a whip behind her. "No. I have been a little busy."

"We must save Lykinnia. We can't wait any longer," said Cymm.

Azreala put her arm around his shoulders and pulled him in her direction. "Not until Terazhan returns."

"What happened to the urgency you had to rescue her?"

Azreala shrugged. "She is safe for the moment."

Cymm sighed. "When is Terazhan coming back?"

"You may not realize this, but deities do not sleep. Rather, they do not require sleep, unless severely injured, or in this case depleted. We may not see him for several more days."

"Well, you don't look busy now. Let's talk to your brother and put a plan in place for when Terazhan does return," said Cymm.

"Have you been this stubborn your entire life?" asked the goddess.

Cymm returned a deadpan stare. "If Feldarius can portal us to the same location he did last time or closer, I think we can get in and out before they know we are even there."

"Fine!" With a flick of her wrist, a portal appeared. "Don't expect a warm reception."

Ahh, what do you know. Feldarius has always welcomed me. Cymm stepped through the portal with Azreala on his heels.

"What is this place?" Cymm said with pursed lips and a stitched brow. "Where is the River of Tides?" Twilight reigned with no apparent light source, and shadows danced everywhere.

"This is my home," Azreala said producing a second portal. "It is easier this way. My brother will know who has gained entrance to the Plane of Tides if we enter from here."

Suddenly more interested, Cymm glanced about, concentrating on details. A large structure surrounded them, a room with walls but no ceiling. Surrounding him were chairs, a table, an immense horseshoe-shaped couch, a bed, and a nightstand. He could not be certain, but some shadows had a bipedal shape and moved on their own with pools of darkness for eyes.

"Are you coming?" asked the goddess.

"Yes." He began walking toward the portal. "When you said this was your home, I thought you meant the Plane of Spirits, but this is your actual home. Isn't it?"

"It is. Not much, but I don't need much," she replied.

Cymm could appreciate that. He entered the second doorway and found himself standing next to a crystal-clear river, sparkling like a gemstone. The sun gently warmed his face and the tension in his shoulders melted away. He sighed with peaceful content.

Feldarius materialized, pacing with frantic steps. "Are you enjoying my home?"

"Yes, this is a very beautiful…" Cymm trailed off after seeing Feldarius's contorted face.

"Maybe we could build you a little hut right here by the river. Would you like that?" asked Feldarius.

Cymm glanced at Azreala in confusion.

She whispered, "Careful."

Feldarius ceased his pacing and stepped close. "You don't like my idea?"

Cymm cleared his throat. "I was thinking you might—"

"You were thinking? That's where your problem began. I already told you I do the thinking. So, we have the brains," he pointed to himself, "we have the brawn," he pointed at Azreala," "and we have the pawn, you. The Brains, the Brawn, and the Pawn, it sounds like a good title for a book, or maybe, The Pawn for the Princess. It has a good ring to it. Don't you think?"

Cymm wanted to say, "I'm not allowed to think," he held his tongue.

Azreala stepped to intervene with a stern visage. "Feldarius—"

"No! I am tired of playing this game." The god of spirits peered at Cymm. "You are tolerated out of necessity. Your power and influence are not as great as you assume."

Cymm stood transfixed, frozen with indecision on how to proceed.

With a wave of her hand, Azreala demanded her brother's attention. "Enough, Feldarius! You have made your point. You will treat him as a guest. If not your own, then mine."

Feldarius grumbled his acquiescence.

After several heartbeats transpired, Cymm asked, "Would you be able to create the same portal we used to rescue Azreala?"

Feldarius glared at Cymm, then Azreala, and back to Cymm. "That's why you are here? I am your portal agent. Should I block off some time each day to—"

Azreala cleared her throat. "We intend to free Lykinnia and the rest of those imprisoned."

"I just rescued you from there, and now you want to return willingly?" Feldarius shook his head.

"They're getting close, I can feel it. We need a backup plan in case Terazhan comes up with nothing," replied Azreala.

Feldarius hugged his sister, then motioned toward Cymm. "This one thinks I still owe him something, and I'm getting tired of seeing his face." He brooded for several seconds. "I can't lose you. If anything feels off, get out of there."

Azreala squeezed him in return. "We'll get in and out. Our focus will be saving Lykinnia. If time allows, we will consider bringing the others."

Feldarius took a deep breath and sighed while tightly gripping a sword that had materialized in a scabbard on his hip. He turned, took two steps, and dissipated on the wind.

Cymm gulped and half-smiled at Azreala. "I promise to better trust in your judgment in the future."

82

Hatred

ZaphMordakai

Hyperventilating and sweating, ZaphMordakai lay on his back far enough from the edge to be hidden from view. His eyes darted from side to side while he futilely attempted to listen to the battle raging below him. A twitch in his chest grew into an ache, then rapidly morphed into a substantial pain. He tried to control his breathing, fighting through each agonizing breath. His wyrmling days, wrought with terror, flooded his mind. The constant fleeing and hiding from an unseen enemy, and when he finally met his first trellbac, his father had died in front of him. Nightmares haunted Zaph for a decade after that day, but surprisingly his fight against his childhood fears continued.

A whistle transformed into a baritone horn, then built to a crescendo and abruptly ended. The ground shifted and shook beneath the dark elf, followed by a primal roar. A massive black body soared over top of him.

A dragon.

ZaphMordakai rose, shaking off the remnants of his impediment. He stared after the departing form. "Uncle Deton?" He quickly spun and crept toward the ledge to peer over it.

A deep, dark furrow bifurcated the path below, and smoke drifted into the air from the edges of the scorched trough. Trellbac bodies lay broken and strewn to both sides, their feathers still burning.

"DetonKonraber the Devastation. My uncle's breath weapon is powerful," Zaph said in awe as he transformed into his dragon form, then glided down to the trail.

One of the red dragons had also been scorched by the destructive lightning bolt, as evidenced by the blackened scales.

Solar's shield remained in position, guarding the little wyrmling, a strange behavior given the massacre. When Zaph alighted, the winged man's eyes went wide. "Watch out!"

Zaph spun to find an injured trellbac attempting to rise, and he froze.

The trellbac turned to face him with purpose, and its eyes blazed with hatred.

Why do they hate us so much?

They both opened their maws simultaneously, directed at one another. A lightning bolt raced forth, but the trellbac could only muster a cough instead of a caterwaul. It did not get a second attempt; the bolt struck it in its open mouth. Brains, golden skin, and feathers flew in every direction.

Zaph had killed his enemy, and even with the unfair advantage, he felt a sense of pride. *We have a reason to hate them because they hunt us and kill our families and friends, but they have no grievance against the dragons.*

The ground shook from an impact behind him. His uncle had arrived. "If you ever freeze like that again, you won't have to worry about the caterwauls."

Zaph's body flinched, instinct from a thousand childhood terrors. He tried to stand tall, but shame washed through him, and his tail trembled against the rock. "Yes, Uncle Deton. How did you find us?"

"I didn't even know you were here. I was scouting for any dragons, so they could lead me to the final refuge—our dragon stronghold," replied DetonKonraber. "What are *you* doing here?"

"We saw the reds trapped between two hunting parties and—"

"No, what are you doing in this world?" his uncle snapped.

"Fleeing from Ledaedra. She almost killed me," replied Zaph.

"That's why I'm here, I know it. I almost killed that bag of hot air, BrimStrakenstone, and somehow, she sent me back to this world." Deton casually decapitated every trellbac.

"I saw the battle. She placed a portal between the two of you on your final approach."

"We'll discuss this more later. We must get out of this ravine." Deton lumbered over to the red dragons. "You need to keep moving. There are many miles until this ravine ends."

The injured red replied, "My son can't go much farther without rest, and you hit me with your lightning. My pace will be much slower."

Uncle Deton cleared his throat. "That was accidental. I had to be sure to kill them all."

"I know. I'm very grateful for your help and that of your friends. I have no doubt we would all be dead right now," replied the red.

Solar approached with his hands glowing yellow. He appeared recovered.

As he approached, the injured dragon asked nervously, "What are you doing?"

"Just let him touch you," instructed Zaph.

Even DetonKonraber wore a skeptical visage as he moved closer and stared at Solar with his throat ticking.

The golden light blossomed into an extraordinary ball of woven tendrils, then receded as quickly as it came.

The red dragon stared at his body in shock. The red female joined him and coiled her neck around his before caressing his check with hers.

"How is this possible?" asked Uncle Deton.

"We have a lot to talk about, but his god is fighting against Ledaedra, too."

83

Ariata

Lykinnia

Myra glowed green and screamed incoherently, while Haskins tried unsuccessfully to calm her.

Ronks began shimmering in an ice blue aura. "You not powerful enough." His stone-cold eyes locked onto Lykinnia's.

Leighton threw an entire loaf of bread and hit her in the face. His eyes glowed a brilliant orange.

Now, everyone had an orange glow.

You must wait… You must wait… You must wait…

"Lykinnia!" hollered Ronks.

Her eyes blinked open. "Huh?"

"You talking in sleep," Ronks said with a strange tone.

Lykinnia struggled to shake off the residue of her drug-induced sleep, a slumber riddled with inconsistencies. Every acolyte had a different colored aura, and by the end, so did the prisoners. The dream kept resetting, and each captive took their turn telling her, *"The most important and powerful prisoner is not here. You must wait until she arrives!"*

She knew what had precipitated these thoughts. On the first day of Lykinnia's imprisonment, one of the acolytes had cast a spell with an orange aura—tangerine to be exact. The detection of the discrepancy had alluded her, until Jenaleya noticed it on the previous awakening. Disciples of Ledaedra should have a dark brown or hickory colored magic, and the followers of Jakarrak were tangerine.

Her bleary eyes finally cleared and fell upon the unwelcoming stare of a new prisoner. However, this one sat comfortably in a large chair—not held upright in a prison rack—although chains emerged from her sleeves and bound her to the seat.

Lykinnia recalled what the disciple of Jakarrak had told her, *"You must wait to escape. You are in no danger until Lorelei is healed, and the last prisoner is delivered."*

She swallowed hard. The time was nigh.

"Hello Lykinnia," said the stranger, now wearing a look of disgust.

Leighton and Naterion were awake.

"Should I know you?" asked Lykinnia.

"You should. I'm your sister," replied the newcomer.

"I do not have a sister."

"And yet, here I am. Did our father never mention me?"

Lykinnia's face screwed up. "And who are you?"

"She your sister. Haven't you been listening," said Ronks with a chuckle.

"Not now, Ronks," Lykinnia scolded.

"My name is Ariata, and I *am* your sister. Although maybe I should be denying I know you."

Ronks's chest, still rumbling with laughter, went silent. He glanced in disbelief from one woman to the other.

Lorelei, on the other hand, wore an amused expression. Lykinnia had not noticed when she had awakened.

"I am not contradicting your heritage claim, but only recently ZaphMordakai mentioned I had a sister. So, this seems somewhat contrived," said Lykinnia.

"Maybe my *claim* would be more believable if I looked like this." With a quick motion, Ariata took on a new appearance.

Lykinnia gaped as she stared at her own reflection.

"What is going on?" asked Jenaleya groggily.

Lykinnia whispered, "She claims to be my sister."

"What is the mouth saying?" Ariata asked angrily.

An eerie orange glow temporarily filled the acolyte's alcove behind her.

Jenaleya whispered back, "You do share some similarities."

Lykinnia's eyes rolled. "Of course we do! She has stolen my appearance." Pieces of a puzzle snapped together in her mind. "You were the prisoner chained to the column in the Plane of Ashes."

The corners of Ariata's mouth touched her ears.

Liar! You are not my sister. What sort of creature are you? She had no answer, but she had more important questions. *Why has Uncle Jakarrak placed his own draconian acolyte in Ledaedra's stronghold or how did he befriend such a creature? The acolyte must be keeping an eye on me. By his own words, the time to escape is here. Lorelei has been healed, and the final prisoner delivered. We are all in danger.*

Myra and Haskins stirred, and four draconian acolytes entered the room. None of them carried a basket of bread.

A glance from Ronks let Lykinnia know he shared her concern.

Every adamantine rack shifted back toward the roughhewn, cavern wall with a gesture from the acolytes.

Chanting filled the chamber and energy sparked off the acolytes' hands. Smoke collected in the center of the magic-users in the shape of a gigantic egg. Many seconds expired as the smoke thickened and darkened, then many more seconds transpired before something protruded from the swirling smog.

A wooden staff of pure darkness, the harbinger of the creature carrying it, a hulking, stoop-backed beast. It was twelve feet tall, as dark as night, and as broad as a wagon, with dark pools for eyes. The fur on its body was kinky, scraggly, and only slightly lighter than its skin.

The smokey aperture wafted away as the creature turned in a complete circle, scrutinizing those present. With a deep, rich, raspy voice, it asked, "Why have you summoned me?"

A draconian acolyte responded with a reptilian hiss, "The Dragon Queen commands your presence."

With wild eyes the creature screeched, "The Balor have no master! The queen would be wise to remember such." As if on cue, a large patch of fur on its shoulder combusted with a hearty *whoosh.*

Myra gasped.

Lykinnia noticed Naterion for the first time since the monster's appearance. Sweat glistened on his face, and he trembled profusely. These creatures had chased him relentlessly in his dreams. His nightmares were coming to life. Her resolve hardened and she initiated the motion to remove the first manacle.

Her wrist scraped against the cold metal. *No! My one hand needs to be free of the anti-magic restraints for the entire plan to work.* Her eyes darted from side to side searching for an answer, with no bread to be served she needed a miracle.

"Patience." A soothing voice whispered in her ear.

"Remove the chain from the prisoner, and you may be on your way." The acolyte walked behind Ariata and placed his hands on her shoulders.

The balor lunged at the speaker in a howling fury, then collapsed to the floor like a ragdoll after striking an invisible barrier. It staggered back to its feet and examined the surrounding floor and ceiling.

"Remove the chain. Now." The acolyte motioned once again toward Ariata.

With a haunting rasp, the balor said, "There have been others who thought these circles of protection made them indomitable."

"Shall I pass those sentiments on to the queen as well?" hissed the acolyte.

With a growl the balor lumbered over toward Ariata, who sat chained to the chair. The ebony staff lifted, and white runes of power danced across its surface.

With a solitary *clink*, the chains sublimated into the air.

Ariata coughed and wheezed, trying to expel the toxic gas from her lungs. Before her second gasp the balor disappeared. She continued to struggle to breathe while new acolytes flooded the chamber.

A draconian magic-user in the center waved the newcomers on. "Quickly! Get in position. We need to summon the balor again."

An acolyte stood directly behind each of the prisoners, except for Ariata. The multitude remained in the hallway outside the chamber.

The four acolytes in the center resumed their chanting and magical sparks filled the air.

Lykinnia's self-proclaimed sister rose unsteadily and hobbled forward to join in the center ring. When she raised her hands, the power amplified substantially.

Black smoke collected in the center of the room again, but not in one location. The outline of four separate, egg-shaped portals formed.

"Now," a voice whispered in her ear.

The manacle on her left wrist expanded.

84

Earn the Right

ZaphMordakai

Two days after DetonKonraber the Devastation had saved them, the group with Zaph exited the ravine in route to the hidden sanctuary. According to the red dragons, they had already passed through the worst region, but they expected more trellbac encounters.

ZaphMordakai's uncle had pleaded with the red dragon parents from the beginning to "leave the whelp and let's get moving," and with each passing hour he became angrier.

Uncle Deton landed in a huff. "How much farther?"

"Maybe a day. I'm not sure. I've never been there before," said DarkAshenrein, the red father.

Mertensia, the wyrmling's mother, stepped before her son. "Once again, we are grateful for your help. We will mention your support and heroics at the sanctuary."

He couldn't care less about accolades or your gratitude. He stays only in hopes of building an army to battle Ledaedra. Zaph's eyes flitted from dragon to dragon, then settled on the wyrmling, DarkAshenten. *Poor little wyrmling.*

They shared a few things in common: they were first born in their family, neither had been abandoned by their parents when the trellbac came, and both had garnered the ire of Uncle Deton at a very young age.

Solar landed next to them. "We should keep moving. Zaph, we—"

"Do *not* call him that! He has not earned that name," screeched Uncle Deton.

"When will I earn the right, Uncle?" asked ZaphMordakai.

DetonKonraber the Devastation's neck reticulated side to side, then came to rest close to his ear. In a scathing whisper, he said, "When you no longer cower behind the lip of a ravine while your friend and three dragons are massacred. Your father was the biggest, the smartest…the best of us. You will not taint his name."

ZaphMordakai's lower jaw dropped. He had stopped listening to his uncle many seconds ago. *Friend. Did he say friend?* He glanced at Solar and quickly looked away. *My uncle and father were best friends. They would have done anything for each other.*

Only the wind spoke for several seconds.

Solar cleared his throat, "We need to keep moving. It will get dark soon. I will find a cave—"

"No, not a cave. In case we need to make a quick escape. An outcropping could work though." Deton extended his wings.

"Wait. I will have a word. Alone." Zaph surprised himself with his forcefulness.

Within moments only the two remained.

"Are you going to cry on my shoulder and tell me how mean I am?"

"No." Zaph paused. "Deny it all you want, but I will never forgive you for murdering my mother."

Uncle Deton's voice struck like thunder. "I did not kill her! Not intentionally." His eyes wandered in several directions before he continued. "When I entered your childhood lair and found them twisting, I attacked. I towered over him, shredding him, when your mother tried to intervene. It was...an accident."

A large lump formed in Zaph's throat. He finally said, "Why did you let me think otherwise? Hate and despise you for all these years."

Uncle Deton's eyes arched in toward his snout—DetonKonraber the Devastation had returned. "I don't care what you think of me!"

Zaph sighed, "Right now we cannot afford to be enemies. Your assessment of Ledaedra has proven correct."

His uncle's visage never softened. "Why? What happened?"

The younger black dragon replied, "Let's see. Where do I start? She claimed to have taken my mother prisoner and to have chained her up, then promised to release her if I helped her capture Lykinnia. As you might suspect, the prisoner wasn't my mother, and I received a magical blast that nearly killed me as my only reward."

"Why would you think—"

"Let's just say, she can be very deceptive and convincing. However, I think you will find this very interesting. I caught her conversing with a trellbac chieftain on the Plane of Ashes."

Uncle Deton's upper lip quivered. "ZaphMordakai, if you are lying to me..."

"I'm not, and it gets worse. I believe she gave him orders, and when they parted, he casually retreated back through the portal."

DetonKonraber's great bulk shifted. "I should have killed her long ago, when I first came into this world."

Zaph fanned his wings in agitation. "You don't have to fight this battle alone anymore. We must inform everyone of Ledaedra's duplicity, and we can start with the sanctuary."

"Hmm. Much to consider." DetonKonraber took wing without a glance back.

In some ways, it felt the same as when he left Zaph and his mother all those years ago upon arriving in the new world.

85

Guaranteed Success

Cymm

The sun dipped low on the horizon twice more before Terazhan returned. His arrival, sudden and unannounced.

Sehaleah domineered the altar while Cymm and Azreala stood nearby, awaiting the changeover. All three of them deeply involved in a lengthy discussion concerning the captives.

Azreala interrupted Sehaleah mid-sentence. "Terazhan, welcome back."

"Thank you." Terazhan drifted close to the altar. "Sehaleah, how is my daughter?"

Cymm inspected his deity. He seemed livelier and had recovered much of his vigor but not his stature. It made sense from what Azreala had explained. His lord had lost many followers and therefore, significant power. He estimated Lord Terazhan to be a full two hands shorter than before.

"Everything is status quo. They follow the same routine," replied Sehaleah, the goddess of nature.

"Has Jakarrak been here yet?" asked Terazhan.

Azreala replied, "No. I have been filling in."

"I am surprised and disappointed. His bond with Lykinnia is very strong, not to mention four of the captives are his children." Terazhan stepped up to the altar and surveyed the situation within the scrying window.

"Any word from Solar?" asked Cymm.

Terazhan smiled. "Yes. He used a healing spell two days ago, and I traced him. He is on one of the outer planes connected to the Plane of Ashes. I cannot scry out there, but at least I know he is alive."

Azreala's face quirked. "Connected to the Plane of Ashes, what does that mean?"

Good question, Cymm thought.

"Three outer planes are connected to each major plane of existence. So, my home, the Plane of Mists, has three unique outer planes attached to it, as does your home, the Plane of Spirits," replied Terazhan.

"My Lord, Azreala and I are planning to rescue Lykinnia, the same way I saved her." Cymm shot his thumb toward the goddess. "Do you have any concerns?"

Terazhan drummed his fingers on the altar. "You need to wait until Dilantro, Melandri, and Vallerielle arrive. With all of us here, your chances of success will greatly improve."

"There is one way to guarantee success," said Azreala coyly.

Sehaleah sighed. "This again?"

"Enough! We do not have time for this," commanded Terazhan.

Cymm glanced from deity to deity confused. "If there is a way to guarantee Lykinnia's safe return, why wouldn't we use it."

Azreala nodded and smiled in appreciation.

Terazhan shook his head. "Cymm, you do not know what you speak of."

"Can someone explain it to me then?"

Sehaleah snuck a peek at her brother. "Azreala wants us to use the Mantle of the Gods."

Why wouldn't he use it to save his own daughter? Cymm's gaze shifted to Azreala, who stared back at him. *But why do you care?*

"Terazhan!" Sehaleah's voice contained a considerable edge.

The Lord of Healing returned his gaze to the scrying window.

Azreala and Cymm glanced at each other then rushed onto the platform.

Terazhan huffed. "A balor?"

"It is being dismissed." Sehaleah sighed in relief.

"We must act fast. I will summon the others immediately." Terazhan's eyes rolled up in the back of his head.

Cymm turned to find Azreala shaking like a leaf barely clinging to its branch. "What's wrong?"

"I'm fine," she snapped.

Unconvinced Cymm put his hand on her shoulder. "What's going on?"

Sehaleah gasped. "There are four more portals forming."

Terazhan moved by her side in an instant. "This is not good. Both of you need to go now if you intend to help."

Azreala's hand firmly grasped Cymm's arm and pulled him through a portal.

86

Fazekas!

Lykinnia

The acolyte's whispered word still hung in the air. “Now.” Before Lykinnia could react or even formulate her plan, the manacle on her other wrist expanded, allowing her to withdraw her second hand.

Four portals of black smoke continued to take shape, and a nervous energy filled the room. Whispers from those present and more gathering created a low-level din.

Lykinnia slowly withdrew her wrists and set them upon the open rings to give the illusion they were still held in place. With quick, nonchalant movements, the restraint around her neck doubled in size. Her deliberate gestures had gone unnoticed thus far, and her first ankle restraint expanded.

“Now, Fazekas. Uncle Jack says now!” Myra leapt down, already free from her captivity, clutching an enlarging wooden staff.

Hmm, the little one is full of surprises. Lykinnia hastened to catch up and released her remaining ankle. She quickly turned her attention to emancipating Ronks and garnering his strength and magical power.

Before she could free him, the roar of a wild cat filled the chamber.

Ariata yelled above the chaos, "Do not let them leave!"

Myra cried out in pain, then disappeared, only to reappear by Lykinnia's side a moment later.

"And they must be alive," said Ariata.

"How did you do that?" Lykinnia asked the little girl as she finished with Ronks and moved on to Jenaleya.

"Fazekas did it. He moves fast." Myra twirled her staff and confronted the acolytes charging Lykinnia from behind. A solid *thunk* confirmed a successful first swing.

Out of sight, Leighton called out, "What about me?"

What is going on over there? Lykinnia received a glare from Lorelei, apparently in no rush to be freed or to help her fellow prisoners.

When the final shackle opened around Jenaleya's neck, four balor stepped out of the smokey portals. The bottom of their ebony staves cracked down on the rock floor in unison, but any further movement forward ceased.

The acolytes had formed a wall—a living barrier—three rows deep at the edge of the chamber, blocking anyone from leaving.

An enormous black panther leaped at a balor only to be turned aside by an invisible barrier.

Lykinnia recognized the cat as Naterion immediately. The ferociousness of the attack and his subsequent growls told her he had not forgiven them for invading his dreams.

One balor spoke, "Why have you summoned me again?"

"Let go!" Ronks growled and pulled his arms free. A sheet of flame brightened the chamber followed by screams and cries.

Leighton, no longer a captive, asked, "Ronks, why did you do that?"

Only Lorelei and Haskins remained shackled.

Two bodies lay on the floor, their robes still blazing.

The chamber exploded with activity, as the throng of acolytes charged.

Lykinnia's right fist pumped up into the air. "Terazhan, Father, protect me."

A golden sphere of protection detonated around her, throwing bodies away like corn husks. It shimmered a moment later as a form passed through the defensive perimeter.

Myra had returned to her side and glanced up at her. "Fazekas." She waved toward the long-gone apparition.

"Get behind me." Lykinnia turned back toward the smokey portals and discovered Ariata straining, sweat beading on her face. One of the summoners had fallen but struggled to his feet. He gave Lykinnia a baleful glare, then stared down in horror as a balor's staff blade erupted from his chest.

The balor lifted him off his feet at the end of his staff and hissed, "I told you these circles of protection don't last forever."

The other three balor watched with a gleam in their eyes, then slowly stepped forward through the space the barrier had occupied.

"Myra, protect my flank. We need to free Haskins." Lykinnia moved toward the half-orc boy. She had no intention to assist the dark elf captive; her unfriendly smile unnerved her.

Scores of pink balls of energy zipped through the air from the acolytes' outstretched hands. Most of them struck the balor, but two burrowed deep into Lykinnia's flesh.

Cries of pain rang out from everyone, except Myra. She had several balls bearing down on her, but her invisible guardian had intercepted them.

The last of the summoning acolytes fell to his knees, dispatched by the balor. With a deafening roar they spread out to wreak havoc. One seemed hellbent on Ariata, who quickly transformed, taking the appearance of a balor.

It froze momentarily, confused, but as understanding replaced recognition, it charged.

The prison chamber, once a pit of stone and shadow with racks near the outer walls, had become an arena of chaos, and the descendants were scattered throughout it.

An acolyte materialized beside Lykinnia's self-proclaimed sister and interlocked his fingers, then shot them forward. Chains glowing with magical tangerine glyphs sailed forth, wrapping around the balor.

Myra mumbled, "Yes, I heard you," then yelled, "Fazekas, we must go!"

"Haskins, stay with Myra and protect each other," said Lykinnia.

"Like family?" asked Haskins.

Lykinnia rewarded him with a smile. "Go!".

Ronks roared from the far side of the room. He swayed side to side, and large patches of charred skin covered his body. After blinking several times, he steadied himself and smashed a nearby acolyte.

Naterion, still in panther form, fought alongside him.

"Leighton, get over here!" yelled Ronks.

The crowd around the Prince of Bruc parted, and he leapt forward to join them, but the crowd had not separated for him. It had divided for something much larger.

A balor stomped into the open space with its blade almost touching the cavern floor. With one swift motion, the staff surged forward like a spear. It pierced Leighton's chest and stopped him in his tracks. He dropped to his knees, clutching the shaft of the weapon. Red, frothy bubbles formed on his lips.

The balor lifted him off the ground and threw him against the wall.

Leighton crumpled to the floor, unmoving.

With short, ragged gasps, Lykinnia struggled to breathe. Her hand reached out, and she whispered, "Leighton?"

The acolyte standing near Ariata screamed, "No!" Twin swords twirled through the air at his bidding, leaving a trail of orange motes behind. One slashed and the other hacked—not once but twice—and cut the balor down to one knee.

Ronks howled in anger and conjured a large ball of fire, which he cradled in front of him like a baby. Before he could hurl it at the balor, the black panther—Naterion—pounced on the killer's back with raking claws and snapping jaws. His bite sunk deep into the creature's neck and he tore a large section free.

The balor slumped to his side, gurgling in its own blood.

The ogre mage's eyes went wide as the ball of fire grew and became more difficult to control. To find an alternative target, he performed a panoramic scan, unable to throw it in Naterion's direction. He hopped twice to his right then hurled it toward the exit and the swarm of acolytes standing there.

The explosion rocked the chamber, hurling those nearby in every direction. Bodies smacked into the walls and even the ceiling; the acrid scent of burnt flesh hung in the air. White smoke drifted throughout the area, stinging Lykinnia's eyes.

Lorelei screamed in agony, her entire right side scorched from the half-ogre's fireball spell, then produced a laugh of madness. Her depravity continued and she commanded the balor to approach. She railed against her constraints. "Get me out of this!"

She must be Marekai's daughter, the god of pain and suffering, and apparently more comfortable with the monsters than the humanoids. Lykinnia dodged the wild swing from an acolyte's staff and electrocuted him with a bolt of lightning.

A portal appeared—not a smokey one of the balor, but a normal one—on the backside of the room behind Ariata, who had resumed her original appearance. This portal sparkled around the rim with orange light.

The creator—the same acolyte defending her supposed sister—waved them on. "Come on, we must leave!"

Myra entered the gateway first, and not surprisingly, it flickered twice.

Ronks and Naterion made their way over, the half-ogre's belly jiggling as he ran.

"Where is Jenaleya and Haskins?" Lykinnia scoured the skirmish fervently.

Lorelei, now free, approached with a balor flanking her on both sides.

Why am I not surprised? Lykinnia sidestepped toward the portal—looking more like a glissade—still searching for her missing friends.

Naterion bounded ahead of the ogre and leapt through the portal.

"We must go!" The acolyte tried to wrap his arms around Ariata to pull her backward.

She whirled on him with the heels of both palms touching. Her fingers flared, and she hurled him into the back wall with an audible *crunch*. "No! I will stay with Mother, Father."

Ronks bellowed and went down only a dozen steps from the escape doorway. Lorelei's magical bolt still dissipating across his body.

The acolyte transformed as he staggered to his feet, his face contorted in anger.

"Uncle Jakarrak?" Lykinnia gasped in confusion.

Enraged, the deity pointed his finger at Ariata. "You cannot defeat them by yourself. They will kill you!".

"They wouldn't dare, and Mother will be here momentarily." Ariata dodged an incoming projectile.

Lykinnia came to a stop right before the portal and turned back. "Where are they?" She scanned the entire prisoner chamber that had transformed into a slaughterhouse. Bodies were everywhere and the stench of burnt flesh filled her nostrils.

Uncle Jakarrak hit the right flank of the enemy with a torrent of wind, driving many of them back, including the two balor next to Lorelei. He immediately wrapped Ariata in his magical chains and pulled her struggling form toward the portal.

About to give up, Lykinnia called out, "Jenaleya, where are you?"

Straining under the weight of the half-orc boy, the princess replied, "Here. Help me!"

"Oh, thank Melandri!" Lykinnia rushed forward to help, then skidded to a stop.

A balor loomed behind Jenaleya with its staff blade held high.

The Princess of Norfolk followed Lykinnia's eyes to find the blade descending. The downward arc of the weapon cut the two descendants, her friends, in half.

For a moment, silence reigned. Only the incessant drumbeat of her heart in her ears and a cold chill in her body existed. Horrified, Lykinnia stumbled backward, mumbling to herself, "No… no, no, no."

Uncle Jakarrak shoved Ariata into the portal. "Lykinnia, move!"

She turned to comply.

"Lykinnia…," croaked Ronks.

"Ronks?" Lykinnia paused at the gateway.

The half-ogre crawled toward her with one arm on his belly. "Help me."

The Daughter of Twilight's hands shot out, and he levitated toward her.

Dozens of enemies converged upon them, their visages a mixture of hatred and bloodthirst.

Lykinnia's desire for freedom had come at a great cost. She had lost several friends. Never again would she see Leighton or hear stories of his bravado, share a smile with Haskins, or enjoy the camaraderie she had built with Jenaleya. She wanted to cry. The escape portal stared her in the face, but where it emerged, she did not know.

As the enemy bore down on them, she pulled Ronks into the gateway without a moment to spare.

87

Terror

Azreala

The portal closed after Lykinnia and Ronks—horizontal and levitating—passed through it.

Azreala glanced at Cymm to ascertain his reaction.

With minimal emotion, he whispered, "We need to leave."

The goddess of death had seen her fair share of battlefields, but this ranked up there for the number of deaths in such a confined area. She resisted the urge to assign the awaiting souls—so they could continue on their way—and focused her attention on the enemy.

They had managed to go unnoticed thus far, even the three balor had intently charged those fleeing through the portal.

"Yeah," she whispered back, spinning the handle of her red-hot mace in the palm of her hand. *I could take out at least one before we run.*

Her eyes blazed as she stared at the back of a balor, even as a large patch of fur combusted. The putrid musk coming off the creatures dredged up old memories. She had replayed the events leading to her father's and sister's deaths countless times, but never like this. Her heartrate accelerated and a sharp pain shot through her jaw from clenching so hard.

Cymm's firm grasp on her bicep brought her back to the present. "We need to go."

She wanted to punch the wall. *Even if I merged with Cymm, we couldn't take them all.* Sighing in defeat, she let him pull her around.

"Nothing should last forever, little one," said one of the balor—the exact phrase her father's killer had used.

Azreala closed her eyes for a long second, then forcefully pulled free of Cymm's grasp.

DragonSin began to sing.

Cymm closed a tentative hand around her arm. "No—"

"Your sword agrees with me." Ten lavender skulls bounced gleefully in her upturned palm, then flew toward her target.

"That phylactery didn't work so well for your father. Do you think you will have better luck?" The balor took two lurching steps before the wailing skulls struck. He waved his staff blade and severed three tendrils, then groaned in submission.

Everyone turned to observe the battle, but no one moved to intercede—yet.

Cymm had ceased pulling on her arm. "What in the nine hells is that?"

Azreala glanced to the side. "No. Stay out of this Ledaedra!"

The Dragon Queen could not stand erect, but even her stooped form emanated a perverse power.

DragonSin went silent.

With wide eyes, Cymm smashed into the rock wall, the corner of the entrance to the chamber. He reversed direction and ran straight into Azreala. His flailing arms severed a tendril, and he became entangled in a second.

"What are you doing?" Azreala cried.

The drow priestess joined him in her own dash of terror until a balor corralled her and cast a soothing spell.

Azreala demanded one more surge of energy.

With one swipe of her talons, Ledaedra severed the remaining tethers, freeing the balor.

It also released Cymm, who turned and ran straight for the platform and the thousand foot drop.

"Cymm?" Azreala took two steps backward. "Cymm!" With a hesitant glance back at Ledaedra, she sprinted after Cymm.

The Dragon Queen cackled in delight, offering no further resistance.

Azreala reached and stretched to grab the hood of his cloak.

The platform ended and a raucous roar went up when Cymm jumped off the side.

88

Sanctuary

ZaphMordakai

The following day, in the middle of the afternoon, the band of dragons and Solar arrived at Sanctuary. The air reeked of rotting, half consumed carcasses and decaying dragon scales that had lost their luster. Temporary lodges built from boulders and mushroom stalks covered the ground as far as the eye could see, but most had been abandoned.

ZaphMordakai counted fifteen dragons, including two juveniles and an injured one. In a low voice, he asked, "This is The Resistance?"

DetonKonraber stomped toward a lodge and thrashed his tail, demolishing the mushroom stalks. "And what exactly are you resisting here? The urge to scratch yourself or the urge to sleep? A complete waste of time!"

A red dragon approached. "Welcome. All dragon kind is welcome here." He stared at Solar. "And what are you?"

Solar's wings bristled. "An ally. Sorely needed from what I can see."

With an exhale borne of exasperation, the red replied, "We were over three hundred strong a couple days ago before Ledaedra came calling."

"Ledaedra was here—herself—recruiting? Or did she send an emissary?" asked ZaphMordakai.

"The Dragon Queen herself appeared, making promises of free passage to the new world, and almost everyone believed her," replied the red.

"But not you," said Uncle Deton, his tone condescending.

The red dragon glowered at him. "Nothing is free. You had to join her army and prepare for battle."

"If she has three hundred more dragons, then she doesn't need to wait for The Final Conflict. The Dragon Queen's reckoning could begin at any time." Zaph glanced at his uncle for confirmation.

Uncle Deton grumbled his agreement.

Solar appeared quite agitated. "We need to get back immediately. I must warn Lord Terazhan about the dragon horde."

"Is the portal still open?" asked Zaph.

"As far as I know, but it is heavily guarded," replied the red.

Uncle Deton yawned. "We'll pretend to be volunteers for her army—"

"That will not work. The Dragon Queen opened a separate portal. This is how she *guaranteed* safe passage." The red dragon took no caution with his tone, despite Uncle Deton being twice his size.

ZaphMordakai jumped in quickly, hoping to diffuse the situation. "Can we use the new portal?"

"No. It is closed." The red dragon's wing flared to the right as he peered in the same direction.

"The portal was right here?" DetonKonraber's plangent roar echoed off the distant mountains. "You fool! We must leave now!"

Fear crept into the previously calm visage of the red dragon, and he retreated several steps from the black dragon's wrath.

Zaph did not wish to trade positions with the foolish red leader. He had experienced this fury many times before.

A dragon descended rapidly through the clouds and galloped toward the group immediately upon landing. "General, we are under attack. Hundreds of trellbac are coming!"

"How long do we have?" asked the general of The Resistance.

"A few minutes at the most."

Mertensia, the female red who had traveled with them, wailed, "No, my son!"

"Let's go!" DetonKonraber the Devastation took flight.

Solar glanced at the wyrmling with sadness in his eyes and shook his head, then launched himself into the air.

DarkAshenrein moved close to his wife to comfort her.

ZaphMordakai's neck craned from one group to the other—the departing versus the staying—and the flavor of ozone mixed with bile flooded his mouth.

89

The Love Affair

Lykinnia

Lykinnia paced back and forth with her arms flailing, the sounds of slaughter still echoing in her skull. She paused briefly in front of Uncle Jakarrak, but intelligible words escaped her. She stomped off, fuming.

Myra observed her, then turned to the deity. "Uncle Jack, why is Lykinnia so furious with you?"

Uncle Jakarrak knelt beside her. "Not now, Honey." He peered at something off to the side of her. "Solar, can you occupy her while the adults talk?"

"Yes, my Lord," came a voice from thin air. "Come, Myra."

Myra reached up and grabbed something—an invisible hand. "Where are we going, Fazekas?" They walked down the small side street toward a bazaar or marketplace in a large square.

Lykinnia stomped back toward the demi-god. "Let me see if I have this straight. While Ledaedra imprisoned me for two weeks, you and your Solar stood by doing nothing, watching and waiting to save this *thing*—this doppelgänger—instead of me."

"Princess—"

"Do not *princess* me! You told me I had to wait until the most important and powerful prisoner arrived. The only thing she would be good at is a game of polymorph."

Ariata chuckled. "Poor Lykinnia. Both Mother and Father love me best."

Lykinnia's mouth fell open, then she finally responded, "Terazhan is my father."

"Are you certain?" Ariata's smirk infuriated Lykinnia.

With a deft maneuver, her hand slipped into a hidden pocket, and she grasped a pinch of sand. "Obleeka sosan tyfar."

Ariata's head fell forward, in response to the sleep spell.

Lykinnia dusted her hands off on each other. "As Jakarrak said, let the adults talk."

"I do not believe you have ever addressed me without my proper title. You must be angry, but your feelings will have to wait. Ledaedra will be here soon."

The recently healed half-ogre stepped shoulder to shoulder with Lykinnia, like an over-protective father.

"We lost a lot of friends today because of your delayed rescue, Jakarrak." Lykinnia reached up and patted Ronks on his shoulder.

"Only the balor could remove the chain, and do not assume I am not mourning the death of your friends. Two of them were my children—Jenaleya and Leighton, but as I said feelings will have to wait, or everyone in this world will soon be dead." Only the slightest tremor in Jakarrak's voice revealed his true emotion.

Lykinnia shook her head in disapproval.

His shoulders shrugged. "Myra and Naterion are also my children."

"Which is why your solar protects her," said Lykinnia.

"She is innocent and naïve. She kind of reminds me of you in your younger days." Jakarrak leaned against the wall of a building on one side of the alley.

Lykinnia intentionally ignored his comment. "How long have you known that Cymm had the white aura?"

A disingenuous smile bloomed upon her uncle's face. "Remember you asked about the long play. I discovered him first, then set your father's solar on the trail of discovery."

"You also set the dragons on the same path. I assume the spellbook was a bribe or a payment for attacking the village." Lykinnia could taste the bitterness of her words.

His irreproachable demeanor transformed instantly to that of deviousness. His upper lip even curled. "Welcome to the game, Princess. Everything you have ever needed has always been given to you. Why should that change now?"

"Solar has been right about you all along. This is just one big game of altagee to you, and you do not care how many pawns you sacrifice. I am not playing your game. I hate you!"

Two portals appeared behind the deity directly on the building's wall. "Naterion, the one on the left will take you home if you choose to use it. Lykinnia, Ariata *is* your sister. Once I remove the poison with which Ledaedra has filled her mind and soul, maybe you two can be friends. In time, you may even forgive me."

Lykinnia scoffed. "I would not count on it. Are you claiming to be my father?"

"No, I am not. Do not think poorly of your mother. We loved each other for a while. In fact, I am still in love with her." Her uncle stepped through the other portal with Ariata in tow and disappeared.

Lykinnia sighed feeling very small and tired, and she finally let the building tears flow.

"Does anyone know where we are?" Naterion nodded at a women staring at them through a window on the opposite side of the street.

"Armak," replied Ronks. "You stayin'?"

Naterion thought about it for several seconds. "I have been gone from my homeland for too long. It is time for my farewells. I wish I could have killed more balor."

"If you stay, you will get your chance," replied Lykinnia. "What about you, Ronks?"

"I not leavin' till you conjure food n ale," said Ronks with a belly laugh.

Lykinnia giggled. "Hey Naterion, if you go home, Ledaedra will come for you. The only safe place right now is the Peak of Power."

Naterion sighed heavily. "It would be a shame to waste this portal. It will take me weeks to travel home from here."

"Terazhan or Solar will be able to recreate the portal," said Lykinnia.

A large crowd of onlookers entered the side street from the bazaar.

With a circular motion of her arm, Lykinnia conjured a new portal. "We should be going."

"What about the other portal?" asked Naterion.

Ronks grabbed a handful of pebbles and tossed them in, causing them and it to disappear.

Lykinnia grinned. "Come on. Food and ale this way, through the portal."

Naterion glanced around. "What about Myra?"

Lykinnia's heart pounded. Myra—who had survived so much—could not simply vanish. "I do not think she is coming back. Jakarrak's Solar, Fazekas, will protect her as he always does."

After searching the street in both directions, they entered the portal.

Lykinnia had great confidence in Fazekas to protect her from physical harm, but this world had a way of swallowing even the most innocent—especially the innocent.

90

Trust

ZaphMordakai

ZaphMordakai did not want to leave DarkAshenten, the wyrmling, behind. Zaph asked his parents, "Do you trust me?"

"Yes," the mother answered immediately.

"My friend will heal your son." He strode over and sunk his talons from one paw into the wyrmling, then lifted off the ground with minimal effort.

The wyrmling howled and whimpered in obvious pain, he even tried to reach back and bite him.

Zaph had no other ideas, so he pushed the pace to catch up with Solar.

They flew opposite the direction from which they had come, to avoid the approaching enemy's army, but only after they had climbed high above the clouds.

ZaphMordakai cringed at the sounds of battle below, but he knew nothing could be done and had no intention of dying needlessly.

The weight of the young dragon caused the puncture holes to extend into claw tracks.

Mertensia caught up to him. The glare in her eyes warned him of an imminent attack. "What do you think you are doing? We trusted you. You're killing my wyrmling."

"I am saving your child. The trellbac were going to kill him. Tell him to stay strong." Zaph picked the pace up yet again and left her behind.

With every swoosh of Zaph's wings, Solar drew closer. He must have sensed Zaph's presence and glanced back, then pulled up short, hovering. "What in the nine hells are you doing?"

"Saving his life! You are going to heal him as soon as we land," replied Zaph. "Do you know where we are going?"

"Your uncle mentioned the portal, but I am not sure how that is going to work." Solar quirked his face.

Zaph checked on the wyrmling briefly, then his vision drifted back to find the parents close behind. To his astonishment, a line of dragons dragged out through the sky behind them. He chortled. "It looks like my uncle is the new leader of The Resistance."

They slowly made-up ground on DetonKonraber the Devastation.

"Solar, you told me you could polymorph into any creature. Does that include a trellbac?"

Solar cocked his head with a half-smile. "Yes. Indeed, it does."

91

Freefall

Azreala

Azreala's heart jumped into her throat a split second before she jumped off the platform after Cymm. She had no idea if her half-developed plan would work, but her call upon the necromantic arts had already begun.

"Cymm! You fool, snap out of it," Azreala screamed above the wind raging in her ears. Her attempt to connect with his sword proved equally fruitless.

A thousand feet seemed so far when peering down from the ledge, but the ground rushed up fast.

She gained on him but not as rapidly as she would have liked. Her rough estimate put them together when they hit the side of the mountain.

Vallerielle flew next to her in ethereal form. "I am going to stop time from Cymm down to the mountain, but I can only do it for a few seconds. Do not fly past him!" She raced ahead.

Azreala took a deep breath and prepared herself, trying to keep in line with Cymm. Red and blue eyes were gathering, escorting her forward past the halfway point.

With a wave of her hand, Vallerielle froze time and Cymm mid-flail.

His body rushed toward Azreala at blazing speed. With fear flooding her mind, she braced for impact. Their bodies collided, but not as forcefully as expected.

She hugged him close and commanded the spirits all around her from the battle above to slow their descent, then sighed in relief, knowing two hundred feet still existed between her and the ground. She hoped Cymm would not notice the presence of Princess Jenaleya's spirit.

He turned to gaze at her with wild eyes instead and punched her square in the face. The sudden attack startled her and drove them apart.

A platform formed beneath Azreala and slowed her fall. She lunged for Cymm but missed by quite a stretch. Her heart leaped into her throat as the ground raced toward them. One hundred feet. Fifty. She urged the spirits to go faster.

Dilantro appeared out of nowhere and blasted Cymm with a torrent of wind, driving him into her body.

Azreala mentally pulled up hard on the spirit platform almost like riding her hellsteed and careened off the side of the mountain. Transparent hands gripped her ankles, and they narrowly missed the decaying carcass of a blue dragon.

It stared at her blankly, beckoning her to join him.

Terazhan materialized ahead of her and so did a portal.

They raced through the doorway still riding the platform.

92

Psychological Damage

Lykinnia

The wind at the Pool of Age blew sharp and cold, the water whispering against the rocks. Lykinnia shivered, remembering the last time she stood here—before she knew about Ariata, before her opinion of her uncle had changed so drastically. She greeted Cymm upon exiting the portal. Her entourage had not yet dispersed, given they had only arrived ten minutes ago. The goddess of death held him in her firm grasp. Lykinnia rushed over and began peeling Azreala's fingers off him.

"Stop!" cried Azreala.

Lykinnia persisted until neither of them had hold of Cymm and he lurched for freedom, bowling them both over.

Aunt Sehaleah's vine-like arms corralled Cymm, then locked him in place.

His frantic eyes flitted from side to side.

"Azreala, cast your resist fear spell!" insisted Vallerielle.

"It's too late. Should I try to bind with him?" asked the temptress. "Maybe I can reach him from inside."

Lykinnia seethed down deep, but her concern for Cymm held her jealousy in check. She grabbed his hand. "Cymm, my sweet Cymm, come back to me."

"Maybe *you* should bind with him," said the temptress.

Lykinnia wrinkled her nose. "Is this some sort of trick?"

"I can show you how," offered the goddess.

"Azreala!" cautioned several of the deities simultaneously.

Her father added, "I do not believe that is a good idea."

"I already know how." Lykinnia lied.

Without hesitation, Azreala launched herself and two darts entered Cymm's eyes.

"Aunt Sehaleah, you are choking him!" cried Lykinnia.

Her aunt released some of the pressure created by the vines, and Cymm grew a full two feet.

A struggle appeared on Cymm's face. It contorted, then relaxed, only to twist in an unusual way again.

A strong temptation to reach out telepathically to Cymm and eavesdrop persisted, but Lykinnia feared her presence in his mind could do more harm than good. She rubbed her temples and forehead vigorously, and her thoughts drifted to her mother. *For four hundred years, while I tried to prove you were alive, you were raising another daughter. How could you do that to me? Let me think you were dead. How could you leave and not look back? What did I do to upset you? And then you have the audacity to reappear in my life four hundred years later, anticipating my millennial lifeday and trying to reconnect, so you could take advantage of my power. One way or the other.*

The avatar's eyes fluttered open to reveal blood-red orbs. "I have him. She preyed on his greatest weakness—his cousin Talo and the little girl. He is convinced the entire party has been killed."

Aunt Sehaleah recalled the vines into her body.

Azreala separated and took her own form. "I told him these are the lies of the Dragon Queen. She intentionally misled him to intensify his madness. It is the path evil chooses."

"Do we have any idea where his friends and family might be?" Lykinnia addressed everyone except for the temptress.

"They were headed to Bard Keep," replied Azreala.

Vallerielle nodded. "I will tell the monks to watch for them."

Azreala locked eyes with Terazhan. "Grendella's with them."

The micro-expression passing over her father's face told Lykinnia something had happened.

Cymm stumbled forward, breathing heavily. "Azreala, we must find them."

Lykinnia rushed forward to stabilize him. "I will begin searching immediately."

The distant look in his eyes unsettled her, but after a moment, it slowly shifted to recognition. "Thank you, Lykinnia."

"Of course. While I am searching for them, would you like something to eat or drink?"

"No, I just need to sit down for a minute," replied Cymm.

She helped him past the platform and over to the nearest tree, then returned to the altar. "Father, I saw the look on your face. What is going on?"

In a whisper, he replied, "A battle occurred and several were injured, including his cousin, and one of them died. The rest would have been slain if not for the help of your tree revenants."

"Strange. They are not known for getting involved. Where should I begin looking for Cymm's friends?" asked Lykinnia.

Terazhan included others as he turned and walked toward the altar. "The last time Grendella prayed, she said they were headed back to Armak, chasing Dego. He is free again."

"A plague upon Erogoth," said Aunt Sehaleah.

"We will need to deal with him again," added Uncle Dilantro.

Melcorac shouldered his massive warhammer. “I was always well loved by the people of Armak. I shall be there to greet this Dego and to protect them.”

ooooo

Two hours passed and Cymm stood by Lykinnia's side at the altar, resilient as always. She finally found the band of travelers and dropped in close to eavesdrop on their conversation.

Tanya rode on Cymm’s warhorse behind Katara. She asked the dwarven cleric, “When you pray to Terazhan, does he ever answer you?”

“Sometimes, he is very busy. Don’t lose heart, he has already taken favor in you. That was no small feat you performed during the battle in the forest,” replied Grendella.

“What exactly did I do?” asked the young girl.

The dwarf chuckled. “Your prayer was answered with a shield spell. It protects all your allies within it, and it works against your enemies. It blinds them, makes them slower to react, or can force them to lose faith in their cause.”

Tanya beamed.

Even Katara found her smile. “How is this possible?”

“If I had to guess, Cymm has already discussed his plans for her with Lord Terazhan,” replied Grendella.

Tanya winced. “Should I be calling him Lord as well?”

“Yes. We’ll continue your formal training this afternoon. The demons and devils don’t appear to be interested in us anymore. They must be chasing the shard.”

Cymm turned to face Lykinnia. “Zecarius is missing.”

Lykinnia grabbed his hands in hers, inadvertently closing the scrying window. “I am sorry, Cymm. He must have been injured in the battle.”

“He would never leave his daughter. I fear the worst—”

Terazhan placed his hand on the paladin's shoulder. "Cymm, a demon killed him. Somehow, the enemy can track the dark shard, which is no more. Dego has escaped and is searching for you again."

"He was a good man. His daughter has lost both parents." The young man shook his head. "What does Dego want?"

"I have been searching for an answer to that question for many weeks, since we defeated him the first time. More than likely, it is your unique power, your aura." Terazhan pushed forward up to the altar.

"*Father, tell him where his cousin is heading.*" Lykinnia said with an edge.

After a long hesitation, Terazhan said, "Grendella, Talo, and the others are currently chasing Dego through the plains, back toward Armak."

Cymm growled. "Haven't they learned their lesson yet?"

Lykinnia clasped her hands in front of her. "That is not all. Jakarrak claims Ledaedra will arrive at Armak imminently to retrieve the surviving Descendants of Twilight."

93

Assumptions

Talo

Talo called upon his average tracking ability to determine Dego's obvious destination. So, for the past four days, they backtracked through the plains toward Armak to recover the ebony shard, leaving the forest and the tree creatures behind and the security they provided.

Katara had resisted the plan, but Tanya emphatically told her she would sneak away in the middle of the night to follow the group, ending the conversation.

Talo glanced at the two of them riding double on Cymm's warhorse. The sword he had given her dangled in its scabbard attached to her belt. The girl hugged the horse's neck passionately, then continued to braid his mane. Her extreme fondness for the equine grew daily. She had told him a story about Cymm charging her with the horse's care, but she had failed, and when he returned from the gnoll cages, Cymm had had to save them both.

Talo said a quiet prayer to Terazhan to protect his cousin and wondered if he survived the battle.

Another war dog village appeared in the distance above the sea of grass. They had intentionally avoided the last three.

"We are going through the village," said Brogan. "We need supplies and any information we can gather about Dego or Armak."

Grendella rode next to Brogan and wrinkled her nose. "Dego probably went around the villages, but it's worth a shot."

"Heads up," Talo whispered, followed by a click and a whistle.

Several hackles and their war dogs approached.

Jalko and Talo's warhorse slowly came to a stop.

The others followed suit, except for Brogan and Joharie. The war dog seemed confused by the sudden contact with his recent past.

Joharie, standing next to Brogan, glanced back at Talo.

I guess I should start training him, too, if he is going to stick around, he thought.

"Good morning," called Brogan. "We were hoping to enter your village for trade, then continue on our way."

The hackles gave no indication of their thoughts for several seconds, then one replied, "Strange creatures are roaming the grasslands, and our village is on high alert. On better days I would offer you entrance, but I must insist that you move on."

"I understand. We'll move along." Brogan pulled his mount around with a dour expression darkening his face.

Joharie remained.

"Joharie to me!" called Talo, then dismounted to collect him. *Definitely needs training.*

Grendella said in a low voice, "Maybe he wants to stay."

Talo gave the war dog's rump a hearty pat, then moved up to scratch behind his ears. "You comin' boy?"

Joharie replied with a quick lick to the face.

The hackles whispered amongst themselves.

Talo felt awkward and tried once again. "Are you comin' with us, or do you want to stay?"

Jalko pushed up next to Talo to collect some of the attention being dispensed.

After wrapping his arm around the dire wolf's neck and hugging him, he turned and pulled Jalko with him. "Come on."

"You may enter our village," replied the spokesman. The hackles parted, creating a pathway between them.

Brogan and Grendella stared at one another for several seconds, then shrugged.

"What changed your mind?" Brogan asked the speaker.

The hackle raised his arm toward the village. "Come. We will discuss with the village elders."

Grendella shook her head. "Brogan, let's keep moving."

When the big man motioned to leave, the lead hackle stepped closer and whispered, "Is that Cymm Reich?"

Brogan peered at Talo. "Yes, it is, but we are traveling undercover."

The hackle winked back in confidence. "I knew it."

Brogan, apparently changing his mind, followed several hackles toward the village. Their escort numbered twelve friendly but silent warriors.

Talo caught Brogan and Grendella whispering back and forth in a heated exchange, but they ignored his inquiring look.

The party dismounted before entering the village, and shortly after they were met by several others. Each one took the opportunity to stare.

"Welcome to Mongrel Rise. My name is Elyria and I'm one of the village elders. Please follow me." She stared at Talo, flanked on each side by Jalko and Joharie as he led his warhorse. "It is true. Never has dog, wolf, and horse followed one man. You're the Guardian."

Talo broke into nervous laughter. "No, I'm just a simple horse farmer." He glanced at his companions for support as they wound through the grassland huts, similar to his home but smaller.

The elder smiled. Her weathered face and white hair indicated she had earned her title through wisdom. "I have heard several say that Cymm Reich is a humble man. I would expect you to answer thus."

"You think I'm Cymm?" Talo asked incredulously.

Brogan cleared his throat. "Cymm, they already know."

"They're not going to tell anyone. Let's just trade and be on our way," added Grendella.

The procession came to a halt outside a large building, equivalent in size to Talo's barn before the dragon had destroyed it.

Elyria motioned to the villagers. "If it's provisions you need, we can assist you. Where are you headed?"

Talo glimpsed Brogan's nod. "Back to Armak. Do you know whether the dragons have departed?"

"We have heard they're gone. The battle occurred ten days ago, and repairs on the outer wall have already begun," replied Elyria.

A man standing next to the elder said, "No one blames you, Cymm. You can't fight hundreds of dragons alone."

Another hackle added, "I heard he killed a lot of the scum and even made them fight each other."

"Is it true you flew away on a dragon, bent it to your will?" shouted a voice from the gathering crowd.

Cymm survived? Could it be? A lump formed in Talo's throat, and his eyes were misting. It took every fiber in him just to nod.

94

Deceptions

ZaphMordakai

They had spent the night in DetonKonraber's former lair. Zaph's uncle had taken on a role and demeanor he had never seen before—a steadfast leader—one that would be accepted even admired. He had sent two dragons on a reconnaissance mission to the portal and had ordered two others to patrol the area. By the morning, their rebel band had grown to more than twenty-five.

Solar approached ZaphMordakai from the labyrinth of caverns and tunnels. "You did a good thing yesterday."

"What's that?" Zaph stood at the precipice to the entrance, daydreaming.

Solar's face twisted. "Oh, do not play games. You saved the child's life, and in doing so, that of his parents."

"We don't call them children. They are wyrmlings." Zaph eventually conceded a smile.

"And what do they call you?" asked Solar.

"An adult. I am still a couple centuries away from my uncle's status of ancient one. He is an enigma, a freak of nature. Most ancient ones can no longer fly with their tattered wings, and rarely do they leave their lairs due to the difficulty of moving their enormous bulk around. I attribute it to our shared ability to regenerate." Zaph stood at the entrance to the massive network of caverns, gazing out at the break of dawn, and in the distance, the returning scouts.

Solar placed his hands on his hips and joined him noiselessly for several seconds. "I spoke with the wyrmling's parents after I healed him, and the mother had something very interesting to say."

"The *wyrmling* has a name—DarkAshenten." Zaph stared back stoically. "And what did the mother say?"

"The mother also has a name, Mertensia," replied Solar.

They both started laughing.

"After Mertensia praised you for saving her son, she asked how long we have been friends." Solar paused. "She said you called me your friend."

Zaph no longer gazed at the horizon and suddenly shot the winged man a glare. "Does that vex you?"

Solar frowned. "Of course not. Lykinnia would be quite proud of you."

Zaph harrumphed. "Maybe. She is the one who taught me the value of friendship."

The scouts landed—one almost hitting the entryway wall and the other stumbling upon touchdown—and hurried over to the assembled dragons.

"General!"

"Yes?" answered the red dragon and DetonKonraber simultaneously.

Uncle Deton glared intently at the former general, causing him to slowly retreat. Zaph's uncle nodded to the scout. "Continue."

"The portal has been abandoned. There are no sentries," said the scout.

The second scout's head bobbed in affirmation.

"It must be a trap," replied Deton.

The former general cleared his throat. "It has been guarded night and day for four hundred years. Why would they abandon it now?"

"Who cares?" spouted a blue dragon in the gathering. "I say we soar for it."

"We could send groups of two or three in the beginning to see if it is a trap," added a green dragon.

Zaph stepped forward. "Hold on. Before anyone volunteers for a suicide mission, my friend," he lingered on the word and gave Solar a sideways glance, "can change his shape into a trellbac. If he is willing to search the area, this would be the best plan."

All necks craned toward Solar.

The winged man considered this for a moment, as if weighing the risks. "I will do it."

∞∞∞

After transforming into a trellbac in a large mushroom grove close to the crater housing the portal, Solar received some basic pointers from the three dragons escorting him on how to carry himself. From a distance, ZaphMordakai followed him out of the grove using his drow form, while the other two hung back.

At the edge of the crater, Solar disappeared from view.

Zaph crept forward and dropped down low, scanning in every direction. Sitting out in the open had his nerves on edge. The tightening of muscles along his back distracted and confused him, and accelerated as Solar descended toward the barren, sandy floor. By the time he reached the bottom, a rigid posture made it difficult for Zaph to move.

He glanced over his shoulder toward the mushroom grove and found the other two dragons anxiously awaiting any news.

A resounding drop of water echoed off the walls of the crater concurrently with Solar's third footfall. He froze in place, searching for the source.

Zaph examined the dry, barren bowl. He swallowed hard, realizing too late that his miniscule experience on this planet could be detrimental.

Small waves rippled through the sand, then stopped abruptly. Another water drop resonated off the walls.

Zaph could not breathe, only short, shallow breaths. *He is in danger.*

A tidal wave of sand formed suddenly, bearing down on Solar, ten feet high, quadruple in width, and at its apex, rode a trellbac.

"Get out of there!" Zaph transformed back to his natural state a moment before Solar and rocketed down the slope with his eyes fixed on the enemy. This species had killed his father, tormented his childhood, and scared him even four hundred years later, and yet, he charged into danger before he even realized it.

The trellbac focused on Solar, oblivious to Zaph's approach, but before he could get close enough to rip off a lightning bolt, the wave crashed over the winged man. The enemy went soaring through the air to land in a crumpled heap. Tentacles erupted from the ground all around the trellbac and sucked it back into the sand.

"What in the seven heavens…?" Zaph trailed off, unable to comprehend what happened.

Solar exploded up out of the ground momentarily, only to be encircled by flailing tentacles. Blue lightning traced along his wings before scorching several appendages in a radiant burst of energy.

Zaph added his lavender lightning closer to the intersection with the ground and the tentacles slowly withdrew back into the sand.

A minor earthquake sent cracks running in three directions before a colossal spider-crab-scorpion thing burst forth. Bigger than ten DetonKonrabers and furious.

The other two dragons from the mushroom grove arrived.

"Stop! You're angering it," yelled the white dragon.

"We're not trying to upset it. We're trying to kill it!" Zaph inhaled deep.

The other dragon scout flew in front of him. "No! They kill trellbac."

"Do you have any better ideas?" asked Solar.

"Yes. Get out of my way," replied the white dragon. A cone of frosty air billowed out of its maw from a carefully calculated distance beyond the tentacles reach. After the third blast, the sand creature began burrowing back into the ground.

ZaphMordakai ruffled his neck spikes, impressed. *He has done this before.* "What was that thing?"

"A krell, the only predator of the trellbac, and it is immune to their sound wave attack," replied the white dragon.

A drop of water echoed through the area.

"They regenerate quickly. Let's gather everyone and get through the portal while we can," said the second scout.

∞∞∞

The sun drifted past its zenith by the time the last dragon circled back to the grove. All around him, dragons spoke in low, tense voices. Their ranks had swollen by a dozen more, primarily due to DetonKonraber's simple philosophy. He did not ask for any commitment to join him and in return he promised them nothing.

Deton addressed those gathered. "The ice dragons will remain by the portal until everyone is through. If the sand creature emerges again, they will attempt to immobilize it. To minimize the risk, we will fly high above the portal and come down on it. Do not slow down going into or coming out of it, or you will collide with the dragon behind you."

Mertensia whispered to Zaph, "Will your friend be able to heal him again?"

That word made Zaph smile. "Yes. Are you going to carry him?"

She swallowed hard. "I want to try."

The little wyrmling shot Zaph a glare.

Zaph sniffled. *If you only knew what I did for you.*

Dragons were already taking off and forming phalanxes in the sky. Solar gathered among them, eager to report back to Terazhan.

The migration occurred rapidly, and the first dragon zipped through the portal, as well as the next four.

Two water drops echoed in the bowl back-to-back, and the sand rippled.

Tentacles shot out of the ground, and the next two dragons maneuvered around them, but not the third. The spikes on the krell's tentacles tore at the dragon's wings until they were tattered and broken, then sunk deep into its torso.

Zaph sighed, most of his kind could be so self-centered and uncaring. He prepared to dive and help.

One simple word from his uncle froze him in place. "No!" With a commanding voice he continued, "We will sacrifice him so the others may escape."

Zaph replied, "But—"

"Then maybe the wyrmling, because that is who would have been snatched." Uncle Deton snapped his neck and head aggressively toward the portal. "Let's go."

The ice dragons dove and coated the appendages in frost, allowing the remaining dragons to plow through the portal without incident.

With relief and excitement, Zaph emerged on the other side of the portal almost hitting the dragon who entered immediately before him. Before he could berate him for not following orders, he discovered their band amidst a horde of other dragons—Ledaedra's Army.

95

War Council

Lykinnia

Solar popped into view near the platform in a disorderly fashion, unlike his typical method of unzipping a window and casually stepping through. His eyes were wide, and he scanned those assembled before settling on his liege in front of the altar.

"Lord Terazhan, Ledaedra recruited three hundred more dragons from their home world a few days ago, and now they are amassing at Fire Island. A major offensive is about to occur, but I do not know where."

"It must be City of the Mystics or Kharad," said Uncle Dilantro, in both of which he had a strong following.

Aunt Sehaleah shrugged. "It might not be a human city. It could be the elven city of Breezeport."

Lykinnia's father pondered this for a moment. "Those are the three largest cities on this continent, but we are missing something. Even with a thousand dragons, the City of the Mystics would be difficult to conquer. There are over four thousand mages there, and Kazkackarus could destroy two score on his own."

"Jakarrak said she was coming to Armak. I assumed he meant to capture the escaped prisoners, but maybe he knows something we do not," said Lykinnia.

"He usually does," added Solar.

"Where is Jakarrak?" Uncle Dilantro stepped onto the platform.

Lykinnia glanced apprehensively at her father, not knowing what, if anything he knew about Ariata. "He has what he wanted. I doubt we will see him again for a while."

Cymm threw his arms in the air. "You don't need a thousand dragons to take Armak. They routed us before with less than a hundred. I need to get Talo out of there."

"And a few hundred demons, but there could be thousands this time and more powerful ones," said Azreala.

"Why do you say this?" asked Aunt Melandri.

A circle had formed on the platform, and all heads turned toward Azreala.

She beamed from the attention. "A fortnight ago, I caught the two knuckleheads combining shadow and spirit essence to create a devikin."

Terazhan gritted his teeth. "And you did not think to share this before now?"

"I didn't know it mattered." Azreala sucked in her lower lip and stared at the ground.

Aunt Melandri wrapped her arm around her sister's shoulder. "Everything matters; the balance is already tenuous at best."

Two silver dragons circled overhead.

Azreala patted her sister's hand. "Then what about the balor in the prisoner chamber?"

"I saw them too, which means Feldarius is working against us," said Lykinnia.

Azreala's eyes blazed red. "If you knew what they did to my family you would never say such a thing!"

Lykinnia withdrew slightly. "Forgive me."

"It would appear our list of enemies is growing. But why attack now? What is she hoping to gain?" asked Uncle Dilantro.

"Power?" asked Aunt Melandri tentatively with her back against the altar.

Aunt Sehaleah nodded in confirmation, brushing a stray curl behind her ear. "If Ledaedra and Sendaria are in fact the same person, then she only cares about power. As a young girl, she worshipped me and prayed to me constantly, but her prayers always revolved around enabling and helping her to gain more power."

"If she attacks Armak again, all of us will lose more power, but she will not *gain* any. This does not make sense." Vallerielle absently froze a butterfly midflight, then released it. It landed on the stone column at the back of the altar, fluttering its wings.

With a glance at Terazhan, Aunt Melandri said, "Some of us will be hurt more than others. Is it possible this is merely a personal vendetta?"

"No!" exclaimed Solar. "Whatever monster she has become, let us not build false narratives."

Lykinnia scanned the group. Not everyone agreed, but no one argued the matter. *Apparently Solar is unaware of Ariata and her lineage also.*

"Maybe she has found a way to combine phylacteries," said Azreala.

Terazhan shook his head vigorously. "No, I already tested that hypothesis, and I do not believe the location, Armak, is significant. We are missing something."

Lykinnia, standing on her father's right side, said, "She could be trying to remove the banishment penalty when the phylactery encases your soul and saves your life."

"My dear daughter, what are you talking about?" asked her father. "She must be killed before she is banished."

Lykinnia had let her mouth override her brain once again. "Well, the creature chained up next to her altar is a doppelgänger or changeling, which is why we all saw someone different. Maybe she is masquerading on—"

"No. When Lord Terazhan performed the trace spell she appeared on the Material Plane." Solar fixed her with a knowing stare and shook his head slowly.

Lykinnia continued, undaunted. "That only tracks the phylact—"

"I fear more bad news has arrived." Her father gestured toward DyFarastine and MynDartain as they transitioned from silver dragons to elves.

The crowd parted to allow entrance to the platform, except for Melcorac. "More dragons who can take the human form. What madness is this?"

Terazhan sighed. "Melcorac, please step aside, they are our guests."

He begrudgingly gave ground.

"The Council welcomes and recognizes the Order of the Silver Dragons. What news?" asked her father formally.

Lykinnia noticed they scanned the group a second time. *Hmm, clearly, they thought Jakarrak would be here.*

With some hesitation, DyFarastine began, "There are disturbing rumors from the plains, claiming the Guardian has arrived. Entire villages are emptying and crusading to Armak to see him with their own eyes and do his bidding."

"We had the same problem a millennium ago when everyone believed Melcorac was the Guardian. Do you remember?" Uncle Dilantro directed his question to his brother, Terazhan.

MynDartain quickly added, "But this is different. This young man actually travels with a horse, a wolf, and a dog, not to mention a priestess of Terazhan, giving him even more credence."

Cymm glanced over at Azreala, and mouthed the words, "Is that Talo?"

She shrugged.

A pang of jealousy coursed through Lykinnia. "Of course, it is Talo and Grendella."

Terazhan waved his hands wildly to gain everyone's attention. "Assume for a second the Guardian *has* arrived. Why would Ledaedra care?"

"She would not care," replied Uncle Dilantro.

Aunt Sehaleah yawned. "It is just a story."

The god of healing pshawed. "It is *not* just a story. What can the Guardian do that no one else can?"

No one answered for several seconds.

Cymm drew shapes on the stone platform with his right foot. "He can summon the One True God."

"Exactly! And if Ledaedra drained the power from The Descendants of Twilight, she could open the ancient portal and bind The Evil One to her will. She would no longer require a phylactery and increase her power substantially." Terazhan paused and gauged the impact his words were having.

Cymm's face screwed up in perplexion. "I thought *you* were the One True God."

Lykinnia wrapped her arm around her boyfriend's shoulders and whispered, "So did I until recently."

Terazhan glanced at his brothers and sisters uncomfortably. "A common misconception. Think of me as an ambassador for His Lordship."

"A legendary battle between good and evil," said Solar in awe.

DyFarastine's excitement boiled over. "Yes! Yes—yes. Ledaedra is always spouting off to her generals and captains about The Final Conflict."

"And how would you know this?" asked Uncle Dilantro.

MynDartain smirked. "We have spies everywhere, even in her army, which has proven to be very beneficial. Who do you think provides DetonKonraber with their attack plans."

Uncle Dilantro spun himself into a mini tornado before simmering down. "Brother, you are speaking of The Rending, an event millennium into the future. How can it be upon us?"

"Has anyone seen any indication of this event in their scrying activities?" asked Terazhan.

Every deity glanced around in turn, shrugging.

Melandri gulped. "None of us really spends as much time scrying as you do."

Lykinnia snorted.

Solar glared at her with a slight head shake. "Except for Jakarrak. Where is he?"

Tears trickled down Vallerielle's cheek. "She is manipulating time. This is why our scrying into the future is failing."

"So, potentially we have the Guardian about to arrive in Armak followed by an army of plainsmen, to confront a deity none of us could challenge. In addition, she is supported by a thousand dragons and an army of demons and devils. Did I miss anything?" Aunt Sehaleah summed it up nicely, the most pragmatic of them all.

Azreala shifted nervously. "The balor…"

"Ah, yes—the balor. Add a hundred balor. *Now*, we have a problem," replied Aunt Sehaleah sarcastically.

Lykinnia, with her arm still around Cymm's shoulders, felt him begin to shake. She pulled him toward her. "Do not worry. We will get Talo out of there."

96

Homesick

Talo

Brogan, Grendella, and the rest of the party arrived at the eastern gates of Armak; the same gates from which they fled. A long line of people and animals waited to enter. Loud voices and arguments assailed their party, and they grew irritable as well. With the western entrance under repair along with several other breaches in the outer wall, everyone converged on the eastern option. Wizards from City of the Mystics had offered their services to the conclave in Armak and had large sections of stone wall levitating around the city to the delight of a few that waited.

For the past two days, their horses and pony had carried them back to this point, while Jalko and Joharie patrolled from the far left to the far-right flank. Their agitation grew with each weaving pass but so too did the magnitude of the caravan following them.

Sitting atop a small rise, offering decent visibility across the plains, Talo scanned the horizon behind him. A knot formed in his gut. "There are so many. What are they doing?"

"They have come at the call of the Guardian," replied Brogan, who had intercepted most of the well-wishers the past couple of days.

"First you tell me to stop trying to be Cymm, then you tell everyone I am Cymm. Which is it?" asked Talo in dismay.

Grendella pushed in close. "Shh! Keep it down. That has nothing to do with this."

"Talo, Cymm does not have a war dog." Brogan shrugged. "They are here because they believe *you* are the Guardian."

Talo Reich heaved a deep breath and his shoulders slumped. "I didn't ask for this, and I didn't ask for them to come. We are supposed to be searching for Dego."

Katara walked up next to him, leading Cymm's warhorse while Tanya rode. "The Guardian is not only a prophesy in the plains. Although there are slight variations, the mountain people share a similar belief. For countless generations it has been ingrained in us to answer the call of the Guardian. Your existence alone is the call."

After passing through the gateway and between whispering, pointing guards—of which, not one asked a question—they made their way to the Broken Horse Inn.

Talo stumbled along in a daze with random thoughts flitting in and out of his mind. *How can this be? I'm not the Guardian. Why did I force myself to be a part of this stupid journey? Cymm warned me and tried to keep me home. I wish he were here. I was always so jealous of his adventures, his fame, and his exploits. I just wanted a little piece for myself, and I foolishly believed he prevented me from growing, experiencing the same things.*

The young man sighed. *Maybe I can slip through the back gate tonight, push my warhorse hard until we reach Stallion Rise, then grab my wife Vena and kiss her.* He actually felt better about himself until his father's words from the past came back to him. *"Talo may prove to be more confident, less fearful, and someone we can trust to lead this family."* He withdrew further inside himself.

This bothered him immensely, but he could not figure out why. He did not care who carried the head of household title and had no strong desire to be one. *But I want to make my father and mother proud. I wouldn't be able to handle a look of disappointment. What would Cymm do? He would try to find Dego. He might even use the small army of plainsmen to root him out.*

He nodded to himself. *That's what I'm going to do, then head home. I've had enough. I'm not the Guardian and this adventure is over.* To Brogan he said, "How are we going to find Dego?"

Brogan glanced at Grendella, who shrugged back at him. "Let's get to the inn and we can discuss our plan there."

As they passed through the main square, a high-ranking guard took an interest and approached. "I am Lord Barrister, First Sword to the King. I hear you just entered the city from a pilgrimage through the plains."

"That's correct. Have we done something wrong?" asked Brogan.

Lord Barrister never took his eyes off Talo, and he sidestepped the big man. "I am curious. What's your name?"

Talo cringed under the powerful gaze of Lord Barrister, and he faltered.

"Did you forget your own name?" asked the city guard.

Grendella bristled, but Brogan cut her off. "You already know who this is. Everyone knows this is the Guardian."

"What is your name?" Lord Barrister persisted.

Thoughts swirled through Talo's mind. *I have wanted to be Cymm or like him most of my life. Just tell him you're Cymm.* His father's words returned. *"Talo may prove to be more confident, less fearful, and someone we can trust to lead this family."* Talo's mouth went dry. Under the city's watchful eyes, he wanted to slip away, unseen and unremarkable. He clenched his fists and breathed deep.

The big man jumped in again. "This is Cy—"

"I am Talo Reich from Stallion Rise."

Lord Barrister scratched his chin. "Then why are you telling people you are Cymm?"

"They're assuming I'm Cymm, just like they assume I'm the Guardian," replied Talo.

"You have a war dog, a dire wolf, and a warhorse, it doesn't get much clearer than that. Let's take this conversation inside." Lord Barrister motioned toward the guard barracks.

"Are we under arrest?" asked Brogan.

"No, not yet. I would have a revolution on my hands," replied Lord Barrister. "Have you seen how many plainsmen are out there?"

The muscles in Talo's neck tightened. "Yes."

"You should see it from the battlements, and more are arriving by the hour. By the way, I consider your cousin to be a friend, he even saved my life, and I would know him anywhere. It is a good thing you didn't lie to me."

Talo scowled at Brogan then Grendella, who both looked away.

Tanya pointed to the sky directly above them. "What is that?"

Overhead, clouds as black as ink coiled in on themselves. The air crackled, and a large black vortex had formed above the city.

Every hair on Talo's arms stood upright.

97

The Great Red Dragon

Cymm

Cymm continued to berate himself for allowing his cousin to come with them. He might not have had an option when ZaphMordakai initially arrived at the Reich Farm, but after the black dragon had left, he could have recanted his consent.

"Cymm, come on!" Lykinnia pulled him toward the altar. "Things could be worse. We will find Talo, I promise."

"Thank you, Kinni."

"Kinni?" she said, rolling the name around like tasting wine for the first time, and wore an inquisitive expression.

Cymm realized his mistake. "I'm sorry. I didn't mean…"

"No, I like it." She smiled warmly.

"Lord Terazhan," Solar began formally, "ZaphMordakai and DetonKonraber are currently surrounded by Ledaedra's entire dragon army. They are either dead or fighting for their lives. We need to decide if we are going to help them."

"What would you have us do?" asked the deity.

Solar sputtered, at a loss for words. "I do not know. We could…what if we—"

"We could provide them an escape portal. At least they will have the option to fight another day," offered Azreala.

Lykinnia's fingers danced across the altar's cold stone, conjuring a scrying window.

Cymm turned his back on the conversation, his boots scrapping against the smooth stone of the platform.

The sun had reached its zenith an hour ago and had begun its descent in the sky.

"Where do we start?" asked Lykinnia.

"The east side of Armak. They fled in that direction the last time we saw them," replied Cymm.

DyFarastine had filled the gap behind them and between their shoulders. "My sources told me they should be arriving today, maybe even a few hours ago."

Cymm smiled in gratitude for the assistance. "If they are in the city, we should start with the Broken Horse Inn."

When Lykinnia began zooming in on the city, a specter appeared above it, floating in front of a black vortex. Although it appeared to be unmoving, it descended at a slow purposeful pace.

Ledaedra.

As more citizens became aware of her presence, the city filled with moaning and wailing.

The Dragon Queen dispensed with any formalities. "You will deliver the Guardian to me. If you are listening, Guardian, do not fret, I do not require too much from you, only your soul."

"Things just got worse," said Cymm.

Ledaedra conjured an immense portal and pointed toward it. "You have until sundown; at which time my dragon horde will raze this city."

Dilantro shook a clenched fist at the Dragon Queen.

Cymm glanced around. Everyone on the platform had formed a semicircle behind him, captivated by the scene unfolding before them.

"She will do it," said Azreala.

The city below, already trembling, seemed to hold its breath.

Lord Terazhan placed his own palms upon the altar, and called out in a commanding voice, "It would appear the great red dragon is missing a head and a couple of horns."

Ledaedra's head snapped up, and she locked eyes with her nemesis. "That title is reserved for one who comes after me." She issued a death scream and raced toward the window.

Terażhan removed his palms and pulled his daughter's hands off the surface in one quick motion, ending the scrying session.

"Wait! We never found Talo," cried Cymm.

"He is in the city, and our time is limited. We must act now," replied Lord Terazhan. "The Great Red Dragon is coming."

98

Dark Council Reconvenes

BrimStrakenstone

BrimStrakenstone stood near the altar on the Plane of Ashes next to his liege lord. Neither spoke as they waited for the others to arrive. He could taste brimstone on the back of his tongue.

Harendread arrived first. At well over nine feet, approaching ten, the gruff giant stood the tallest of their allies. He had agreed to shelter the ice dragons in the early days and teach them the ways of the wilds. The extreme climate in the north land made its denizens vicious. In some cases, the creatures there engaged in daily battle for survival.

Brim smiled inside and peered at the only deity he could relate to.

Malekai and Hymnoch appeared next, through different portals, and took their assigned positions.

An outer plane portal appeared in the distance, and Grumgresh emerged. The balor agitation grew quickly as he made his way over toward the altar.

The Dragon Queen continued to hum in a droning fashion, and her eyes rolled up in the back of her head.

When the balor finally took his place, Ledaedra's eyes rotated back into place. "Thank you for joining me."

Brim exhaled sharply. *As if any of us had a choice.*

Malekai's brow wrinkled. "We should wait for my brother, Marekai."

"He is unable to join us. As is Bardonril and Feldarius for obvious reasons," replied Ledaedra.

"Where is he?" asked Malekai. "I haven't seen him in a week."

"Nor have I." The Dragon Queen peered at Brim. "Have you seen or heard from him?"

BrimStrakenstone cleared his throat. "I have not seen him in the past week. Not since I delivered the monthly sacrifice."

Malekai growled, then mumbled, "Him and that damn sacrifice."

Ledaedra's needlelike teeth glistened in the light. "There is a need to accelerate our plan. Recent events have changed the timeline. The Rending is upon us. I will open the gateway shortly and welcome the Dark Lord to join me."

Harendread had a thin layer of perspiration all over his body. He could not tolerate the heat for long. "Are you still confident in your ability to control him?"

"No one controls the Dark Lord!" hissed Grumgresh. His eyes were insanely wide, and he slammed the bottom of his ebony staff into the ground.

The volcano in the background belched almost like it agreed with the balor.

Brim tsked inside his mind. *Even I know not to insult the balor's deity.*

Several draconian acolytes entered from the portal to Fire Mountain, escorting the adamantine racks holding both prisoners and corpses.

"What in the seven heavens is this?" asked Hymnoch, turning away from the ebony altar.

"We had an incident." Ledaedra gave her hand a wave toward the racks.

"More like a debacle," said Grumgresh. "We no longer have the energy required to release my Lord."

"Careful…the balor were responsible for the attack," replied the Dragon Queen.

The balor's head sunk into his massive shoulders. "A mere misunderstanding."

Lorelei, the only living descendant, hung limp in her rack. In a gruesome display, the Dragon Queen ordered the acolytes to return the bodies of the dead to the racks and parade them in front of the council members.

Brim grew tired of the games and had no idea how she planned to recover from this setback.

Malekai cried out in alarm as an adamantine rack slammed into his back. While the procession had continued in front of them, a sole rack had circled behind them and ensnared the Prince of Demons.

"Sure, we do. Malekai has volunteered to help return your lord to greatness," cooed Ledaedra.

"No!" Malekai flailed against his bondage.

Harendread and Hymnoch immediately gazed behind themselves, then created portals and fled without a word.

"We could have used their help in the war," said Brim.

"We do not need them. Prepare the army for battle," replied the Dragon Queen.

Grumgresh had already begun to chant, over Malekai's yelling and cursing.

"Yes, My Queen." Brim proceeded to drag his feet in no hurry to leave. He wanted to see what happened, an odd mix of satisfaction and fear knotting in his gut.

Malekai's yelling turned to wailing, causing Lorelai to stir.

The dark elf priestess attempted to hide her fear and pain, but she succumbed.

You deserve everything you get for killing my warriors. Brim paused, halfway to the portal.

Grumgresh hesitated. "You know what this means?"

"Yes," replied Ledaedra.

"Say it!" screamed the balor.

"The Dark Lord will have overall dominion," she replied.

The balor seemed satisfied with this and returned to the incantation.

The prisoners had ceased their screaming; they had ceased to live. An explosion of violet hues came from Malekai before instantly being sucked back into a vortex, leaving a mangled and partially melted adamantine rack. The dried husk of Lorelei's body screamed in silent agony, even the corpses shriveled to half their original size, the mystical energy sapped from them.

A doorway opened, much smaller than Brim expected, but it began to grow and stretch like a living organism. A clawed, reptilian hand grasped the threshold, then another, and pulled itself into the aperture. A head with two horns.

Ledaedra's green arm shot forward discretely, transforming into the head of a dragon. It grew until it struck Grumgresh's left forearm and bit clean through it. The Dragon Queen extended her black arm, and the staff flew into her clawed hand. She ripped the severed appendage off the shaft and tossed it aside.

While the balor gaped at the remains of his arm, an altered adamantine rack slammed into him from behind, locking him into place.

Brim did not even pretend to be leaving anymore. He stared in horror and fascination at his liege lord's audacity once again.

With a wave of the staff, the aperture constricted. "Not too big. I won't be able to control you."

The hideous face of the Dark Lord contorted into a grimace of pain.

Ledaedra cackled. "Fool. Did you really think I would let you back into this world to rule it. To rule over me!" She swirled the ebony staff and stretched his lower extremities until they were as thin as a little finger, then stuffed him into a hollowed-out dragon spike.

Two draconian acolytes approached the prostrate Dragon Queen and slammed the spike into her back between her shoulder blades.

At last, Brim decided to leave and entered the portal.

99

Snakes

BrimStrakenstone

Ledaedra's entire dragon army had assembled at Fire Island, at least those within two and a half days flight. The rest would join them outside the human city of Armak, including the white dragons in the far north.

BrimStrakenstone had received clear instructions from the Dragon Queen. Although, the change in plans were drastic and sudden, he awaited her summons via portal to bring their host through.

They had discussed The Final Conflict many times and had agreed even recently that they were at least fifty years away.

What had changed, and why Armak? Brim wondered. This city had already been destroyed. He only required five dragons to crush them again, not the entire dragon army. The demons and devils were already marching on the city, and he could only assume the balor would be joining them as well. Their enemy was unknown, or Ledaedra had refused to share. He had secretly hoped to avoid this battle by wearing the humanoid races down with smaller skirmishes and through attrition.

Marekai had not presented a problem as Ledaedra had promised, and the balor numbers had swollen with each successive summoning sequence, requiring them to move to the lower levels for temporary housing.

The island had never been this crowded before, making it difficult to inspect the soldiers and organize the phalanxes properly.

A commotion on the far side of the island drew BrimStrakenstone's ire. He had already broken up enough fights and lost soldiers as a result. A shimmering portal indicated that infighting may not be the issue.

A circle of observers had formed and continued to grow.

"I do not ask you to fight with me, but I will not hesitate to kill you if you fight against me!"

Brim could not see the speaker. He extended his neck up as high as he could, and his tail slammed to the ground. "Deton, you snake! Stealing my army will not be that easy."

The two archenemies lunged toward each other, but the throng blocked their way.

"Your army? This is Ledaedra's army! You and the rest are slaves to her bidding," replied DetonKonraber.

"Move!" Brim bellowed to anyone in his path. *He's not wrong, but his fearless bravado will finally get him killed, and I will be rid of this menace.*

Deton went airborne with his neck craned back along his body and a massive lightning bolt screaming from his maw.

The four or five dragons brave enough to assault him fell back writhing in agony.

Brim's back reflexively twinged with sympathy pain. He did not want to repeat the experience. The whining of a wyrmling red dragon caught his attention as it scrambled away from the melee. "What is he doing here?"

He lurched forward to shield the wyrmling with an outstretched wing, even though he did not believe it was his bloodline. He wanted to be sure.

A black dragon raced through Brim's field of vision. *ZaphMordakai?* He bounded forward and pounced upon Zaph. Brim could not help but feel pride; he had caught his enemy completely unaware.

While trying to defend himself, Zaph had inadvertently rolled to his back and now lay pinned under the massive girth of BrimStrakenstone.

Zaph groaned as the air escaped his lungs.

Brim chortled. "You thought you and your uncle could take on my entire army? You fool! You always were a crazy drake."

Through huffing and puffing, Zaph replied, "Better to die a fool than a slave. Did you know Ledaedra is working with the trellbac?"

Brim could not conjure a response.

"You are a disgrace to our kind." Zaph could not breath in to release a lightning bolt.

Anger welled from deep inside Brim. His head rocked back, and he took a deep breath.

Zaph continued to struggle futilely, but he could not escape the inevitable gout of flames that would surely end his life.

100

Welcome to the Game

Lykinnia

A mass of confusion and chaos swarmed through those crowded onto the platform. Dozens of suggestions were offered, but everyone spoke, and no one listened.

"Quiet!" shouted Terazhan, reinforced with a bit of magic.

Only Uncle Dilantro did not obey. "They might be able to fight the demons and devils, and even stave off the balor, but we must deal with the dragons."

"Even the lot of us cannot defeat that many dragons," said Aunt Sehaleah.

Azreala spun her mace in her palm. "Cymm and I can raise ten to fifteen zombie dragons to fight."

"That is only a drop in the bucket," said Solar.

"Do you have a better idea?" Azreala demanded with stitched eyebrows.

"Where is Jakarrak?" asked Aunt Melandri. "He would probably have some kind of devious plan."

Lykinnia felt a tickle in the back of her mind, which usually led to some greater revelation. *Why does everyone put so much stock in Jakarrak? He failed me. To think I would so easily forgive him. "Welcome to the game, Princess. Everything you have ever needed has always been given to you. Why should that change now? In time, you may even forgive me."*

"Bring them through the portal one at a time. I'm good for a couple hundred of the beasts," boasted Melcorac.

Terazhan finally shared his thoughts. "All of these ideas are good, but it is not enough to turn the tide."

"So, we give up?" asked Uncle Dilantro.

Lykinnia's thoughts slipped away. *There is nothing Jakarrak could do to make me forgive him. Nothing! Unless he helped us win this war.*

"Of course not. We will create a portal and run skirmishes through it. When the resistance grows to be too much, we will retreat, close the portal, then open a new one," said her father.

"Everything you have ever needed has been given to you. Why should that change?" Everything has been given to me? What has been given to me? Lykinnia's brain churned like a raging river. *Jakarrak has given me nothing. Or has he. Could he possibly have orchestrated even that?*

Terazhan proceeded to conjure a portal.

"Father, I think I have figured it out. Wait for me!" Lykinnia did a quick pirouette, then took off running for her abode. "Cymm, Azreala, with me!"

Azreala grinned. "This is a pleasant surprise."

Once they created some distance, Lykinnia asked, "Are you still willing to show me how to bind with Cymm as an avatar?"

101

Prone

ZaphMordakai

ZaphMordakai recommended a political approach, far less confrontational than his uncle's. He told many of the dragons coming with them from his home world to ask anyone who would listen, "Did you know Ledaedra is working with the trellbac?"

Almost two score had followed them through the portal, substantially smaller than the army surrounding them. His Uncle Deton already fought for his life, and Zaph lay on his back about to die in the shadow of the volcano.

The little red wyrmling crawled up his neck and unto his chest, facing Brim. "Leave him alone!"

Brim's exhale caught in his throat. He coughed fire and singed his own lips. "I am not the villain!" he yelled at the wyrmling.

DarkAshenrein and Mertensia, the wyrmling's parents, darted in, but they did not talk, they attacked.

BrimStrakenstone fell back off Zaph from the onslaught, even though he could have slain them both with a swipe of his mighty paw.

The red dragon parents gathered their son and fled, knowing they were no match for the behemoth.

ZaphMordakai took a quick peek at the dragon general and did the same.

The audible *pop* of a portal materializing cut Brim's roar of frustration short.

Small skirmishes were everywhere, but intense fighting erupted toward the mountain. Zaph knew he would find his uncle there, making his final stand. *Do I even care? He tormented me as a wyrmling, and he killed my mother.* Zaph drifted in that direction anyway, to witness the death of a monster.

Halfway there, a third portal materialized.

"What is going on?" he asked no one in particular, then wanted to repeat himself when he realized a group of dragons had joined with his uncle to renew The Resistance.

A colossal red tail whipped out of nowhere, delivering a crushing blow to Zaph's midsection. Scales cracked against each other when he hit the rocky ground, and he tasted blood as he coughed the acrid dust from his lungs. The big, red bulk made it impossible to breathe—suffocation—a favorite game of his childhood tormentor.

The face snaked around. It had three long scars running the length of it—not Brim, KorEmberstrike. An evil grin bloomed across his enemy's visage. "If nothing else, I am patient. It was only a matter of time."

Talons dug deep into Zaph's chest, limiting his ability to squirm. In halting breaths, he said, "Ledaedra lied to us all. She sent the trellbac to kill us."

KorEmberstrike chortled. "Who cares. I have waited a long time for my vengeance, and it will be mine. If only your uncle could be here to witness this."

The red dragon was larger than Zaph, but nowhere close to the size of Brim or the other generals. Kor's throat turned brilliantly red with a sharp intake of air.

Electrical energy surged through Zaph's body like never before. His teeth chattered and his own scales smoked. KorEmberstrike danced with jolting jerks before biting deeply into his own forearm. Zaph pulled his legs in tight between them and gouged the red dragon's belly. Then he launched his own savage attack, biting, tearing, clawing at his adversary. They rolled and roared and raked, but the lightning had turned the tide, and KorEmberstrike lay still.

Zaph reveled in the lightning power he had just unleashed until the form of Solar hovered over the shoulder of his combatant.

"You can thank me later. Get up! We need to get out of the middle of the battlefield." The winged man's head darted from side to side.

Zaph attempted to rise. "I can't fly. I can barely move."

Solar shook his head in disbelief. "I do not understand your ability to feel no pain."

Golden light blasted Zaph's flank, drawing more attention from nearby foes, but rejuvenating him, nevertheless.

They raced toward the main battle to find dozens more had rallied to his uncle's side.

DetonKonraber currently fought a monstrous blue dragon, the sergeant-at-arms, XanChilxakxus. A blue dragon's breath weapon required the presence of water, but unfortunately for his uncle, the nearby ocean of water swelled with the tide.

Solar pointed to the far right. "That portal is ours and leads to safety. Tell your uncle to stay away from the third portal. We will center our attack there." Solar bent his trajectory toward the right gateway.

"We?" Zaph yelled after him, but he knew the answer an instant later and his breath caught.

Lykinnia had come through the portal.

102

The King of Armak

Talo

Two hours after the demon in the sky departed, the ominous vortex and the huge portal remained. Lord Barrister and the rest of the King's Guard had expeditiously ushered Talo to a holding cell, or so he thought, until the King of Armak entered the room.

"Your…Your Majesty," sputtered Talo.

"I am told you claim to be the Guardian," said the king, unimpressed.

"I claim no such thing. Others claim this," replied Talo.

"You have a wolf and a dog, where is your horse?" The king pointed at each in turn.

"Your Majesty, we secured our horses in the stalls," replied Brogan.

The king shrugged. "Can't be the Guardian without a horse."

Grendella huffed and puffed. "The animals don't make him the Guardian. They are an indicator of who he is." Then under her breath she muttered, "Idiot."

Clearly the king did not hear her remark. He made a gesture toward a banquet table being set by royal servants. "Well, you might as well get comfortable. There's no telling how long we will be here this time?"

Brogan wrinkled his brow. "This time?"

"Yes. The first assault on the city lasted for only a day, but not to worry, these walls could withstand the fire from an ancient red dragon. Even if they did breach this chamber, we have tunnels our dwarven friends dug deep underground." The King of Armak seemed very pleased with himself.

Talo blinked twice. "If I *am* the Guardian, how will I summon the One True God from here?"

"How will you summon him out there?" asked the king. "You're not a prisoner, but you must make up your mind. Stay or go."

Talo turned to his travel companions. "Well?"

"They came to see you, not the city walls being repaired," said Grendella.

"A hero would not hide in here," said Katara, then apprehensively regarded the king, but he had already lost interest. "However, my first priority is to keep my niece safe. So, we will be staying in here."

"Ahh…why?" asked Tanya.

Talo peered at a distracted Brogan for his input.

Lord Barrister rushed back into the small-banquet-sized room, straight to his lord with urgent whispers.

"What is going on?" asked Brogan.

"What is it?" asked Talo.

Sentries blocked their way forward on both sides of the bountiful table while the two conferred.

The First Sword to the King eventually came over. "A legion of fiends approaches from the western plains. Scouts are reporting small pockets of fighting have already begun."

Katara's face blanched. "How many?"

Lord Barrister shook his head slowly. "Thousands. Early estimates are over ten thousand strong."

"We need to pull the clans together. Talo, call them to you! Bring them in the city, even broken walls are better than no walls," said Brogan.

Grendella hefted her warhammer. "Lord Terazhan protect us."

Talo's confusion and indecisiveness continued until his eyes met Tanya's. Her fourteenth lifeyear in the middle of Rhomerian approached quickly. Her fearless demeanor bolstered him. In the past year, gnolls killed her mother and her father died at the claws of a demon, but a glimmer of hope blossomed upon her innocent face.

"Very well." Talo drew in a deep breath and tousled Tanya's hair. "Let's go. Spread the word. I want to speak with all the leaders at the western barbican."

"Lord Barrister, arrest this man. I will not have anyone stirring up trouble and pretending to be someone they are not," ordered the king.

The smile disappeared from the honor guard's face. "My Lord?"

"You heard me. Arrest him and his trouble-making friends, then send word to all the leaders to go home." The king switched to grumbling, "Only I shall address the people. They are *my* people."

Brogan brandished his sword within a second. "No disrespect intended, but that is an asinine idea. The demons and devils will slaughter your citizens, then roll through the countryside killing villages one by one. The only chance—"

"Silence! Get them out of—" The king froze mid-sentence.

A dagger appeared across his throat and another poked into the front of his ribs before the voice of a shorter Katara boomed, "You will be quiet if you want to live."

"I am the king!" blustered the royal man.

Katara applied more pressure to both daggers. "You're not *my* king!"

For a heartbeat, stillness reigned.

The king's face went white, and Katara's knives were gleaming.

A shudder ran through Talo's body.

No one moved.

Brogan let out an audible breath, and everything rushed forward again. "We will be leaving now. Let's go!"

Lord Barrister slid his sword back into its sheath. "Talo, I would have a word with you."

Talo, Brogan, and Grendella exchanged skeptical glances.

The First Sword to the King raised his empty hands, then took several steps off to the side. "On my honor."

Against his party's wishes, Talo joined the guard. "What?"

In a barely audible whisper, Barrister said, "We will be coming for you. The king will not tolerate this insult. I will help if I can but surround yourself immediately with those you trust."

Talo's mouth hung open. "Why?"

"I don't know. Your cousin has had a bad influence on me."

"I wish he were here right now." Talo sighed.

"Speaking of…several villagers from Stallion Rise have arrived asking to see Cymm Reich. One of them claims to be his uncle," replied Barrister.

"No." Talo turned and fled with the others right behind him.

ꝏꝏꝏ

An hour later, they found themselves at the western gate, the same gate Talo had planned to meet with the leaders of the different tribes, but the throng of plainsmen made it impossible to leave. The gate appeared to be repaired and open. Most were traveling into the city, and

Talo found himself turning sideways as he pulled his horse along behind him.

"There is only one place they could be waiting," Talo said to Brogan, with three people between them.

"What?" asked Brogan loudly.

"My family—they must be at the three dragon skulls. We just need to get through this gate." Talo's cloak flapped in the wind, and he cinched it tighter.

"It's the Guardian!" someone yelled.

A shared whisper rushed through the crowd. "It's the Guardian."

No one moved. No one spoke.

Talo glanced around trying to find him, but he knew who they meant. *I need to find my family. There's an army of fiends coming.* He sighed and removed his hood. "There is no time for a speech! We need to get everyone in the city and fortify the walls. I will speak with the leaders under the barbican in thirty minutes. Spread the word. Now go!"

Brogan and Grendella cast shocked looks at each other.

"What?" asked Talo.

"Nothing, and besides there's no time for speeches." Brogan guffawed.

Everyone in his party joined in.

"Great. Now I'm the butt of the jokes." Talo waved them on. "Come on. Let's go!"

"Yes, your Guardianship." Grendella bowed.

Talo groaned. "How long have you been waiting to use that one?"

They passed under the barbican at a trot and urged the horses into a canter. The skulls were closer to the gate than Talo remembered, and he almost passed them. Fragments of dragon skulls lay scattered about, destroyed in the last dragon siege.

"Talo!" his sister called out.

"Mare? What in the nine hells are you doing here?" asked Talo sternly.

"Nice to see you, too. I came to see the Guardian. Have you seen him yet?" Mare hugged him. "There's a rumor the Guardian is Cymm."

"Talo, my son!" Daro, his father, called out, rushing over.

He embraced his father briefly. "It looks like you brought half the village. Please tell me you didn't bring Mom or Vena or any of the little ones."

"Talo!" his father said firmly. "What's gotten in to you?"

"There are thousands of hellions coming this way as we speak! This was not a good time for a visit to Armak!" Talo answered furiously.

His father clenched his jaw and his eyes grew large. "We answered the call of the Guardian. Don't you remember your duty? I would sooner die than fail the Guardian."

A distant howl set Talo's nerves further on edge.

"We need to get everyone in the city. Now!" commanded Talo.

"Our warhorses will be of little use behind the walls, big brother." Toma patted him on the back.

Talo bordered on the verge of tears. He could not breathe. *So, this is how Cymm feels every time. This is why he leaves me at home. I sure could use his help right now.*

His family began to squabble with others about how to arrange the horses.

"Quiet!" he shouted like he had never shouted before. "If you are not moving toward the city in the next ten seconds, I will—I…"

Joharie and Jalko pushed up on each flank. Jalko nuzzled his head into Talo's chest, probably trying to determine if he should whimper in support or growl in defense.

Mare's face went white, and her jaw dropped. "You—ya—ya—you…"

"You look like you've seen a ghost. What's the matter, Mare?" asked Toma.

"Talo is…the Guardian," Mare stumbled through her words.

A brief laughter ensued until everyone saw what she had seen—a war dog, a warhorse, and a dire wolf.

"Son, how is this possible?" asked Daro.

"There's no time for this. Get everyone in the city and I will address the leaders under the barbican shortly," replied Talo.

Brogan stepped forward. "He's not kidding. Move it!"

Daro stared at his son in admiration.

ꝏꝏꝏ

Talo had never given a speech before, never stood in front of a crowd, not even at the bonfire parties, except when he received his dirk from Old Man Semper.

Where are you Cymm? We could use one of your "and who will answer the call" speeches. He loved that memory, and he prayed once again for his cousin's safety and future memories.

They drew within sight of the western gate. A mass of people surged at the base of the wall, pressed tight to get a look. Guards in battered mail held the line with locked shields, their faces smudged with ash and fear. The hum of panic, prayers, and rumors of the Guardian filled the air.

"Father, Mare, take everyone to the eastern gate. I will have our village patrolling the bailey for now," instructed Talo.

As they approached, Lord Barrister stepped forward and proclaimed, "Talo Reich, by order of the king, you are under arrest for sedition against the king and the empire."

"You can't arrest the Guardian!" yelled a plainsman.

Several others shouted their agreement.

A hush fell over the crowd.

An old woman chanted the Prophesy of the Guardian, her voice cracked but clear. "The war dog will run at the Guardian's heel while the dire wolf patrols in front of him, and never will his faithful steed—"

"Enough!" Lord Barrister banged his sword into his shield.

Others had joined in the recitation.

Talo's heart pounded, and for a moment, he almost believed it himself.

"Furthermore, everyone traveling with Talo is under arrest for the attempted assassination of the king." Lord Barrister motioned his guards forward.

Thirty plainsmen blocked the path of the ten guards with weapons drawn. Impossible to swing a sword or wield a mace in the confined space, so the two groups resorted to shoving each other.

"Stop!" yelled Talo, and to his surprise, everyone listened. "We will not fight against each other. The enemy is coming."

No one moved.

"Make way!" Talo said to the men protecting him. "Lord Barrister, do you and your men forget the Prophesy of the Guardian?"

"You insult me and my men," replied the leader of the King's Guard.

"That is not my intention. Would anyone like to verify that I have a war dog, a warhorse, and a dire wolf?" Talo pointed at the guards. "Would any of you like to challenge me, the Guardian, to single combat?"

A few guards shifted uncomfortably.

"I didn't think so. The Guardian does not answer to kings, or dragons, or demons. My duty is to protect all of you by summoning the One True God. I do not want this burden, nor do the thousands of plainsmen who have answered the call. So, my question to the King's Guard is, will you answer the call of our heritage—a call for the people—or will you answer the call of the king?"

Barrister stepped close. "Please come with me to avoid bloodshed."

"What happened to helping me?"

"I've done what I could. I put you in a position to convince most of my men not to arrest you, but they are honor-bound and have a duty to the king. Many of them will self-inflict their punishment."

Talo glanced about and hung his head. "Fine, but Brogan stays here to help the commander with defensive preparations."

Joharie rubbed his head against Talo's chest, then nudged him.

"What's the matter, buddy?" Talo glanced about. "Where is Jalko?" Talo turned to leave.

Grendella barred his path. "He'll be back."

Lord Barrister escorted Talo back to Heroes Square—not as a prisoner but to discuss a reasonable solution with the king.

"How should I approach the king?" asked Talo.

In a low voice, Barrister replied, "The king is a proud man, excessively proud. I would assume his concern revolves around the Guardian usurping his throne."

Talo's mouth fell open. "I would never do that!"

Barrister's eyebrows lifted. "I genuinely believe you, but the king won't. You need to make him believe your intentions."

Talo nodded and walked along in silence, trying to determine how he would even start the conversation.

A dozen horse lengths before they entered the square, he heard a disturbance brewing. Gasping turned to groaning and moaning, as those in the courtyard gazed skyward.

From his current position, the two-story buildings with peaked roofs on either side of him, blocked his line of sight, and he could not determine the cause of this latest commotion. Talo and Grendella pushed ahead of the King's Guard and discovered the demonic creature had returned through the black vortex in the sky. Its arms and legs each ended with the head of a dragon and now there were two heads bursting from its back. In addition to the seven heads, it also had ten horns, another indication the prophesy was at hand.

The monstrosity called out in a booming voice, “Sunset draws nigh. You shall deliver the Guardian to me now.”

103

The Holy One

Captain Beckwith

From above the barbican, the Captain Beckwith could see several miles across the plains, as he and his soldiers diligently watched for the approaching army.

"What is going on down there?" asked one soldier. "Is the Guardian going to help us or not?"

"I don't know. The King's Guard tried to arrest him," replied another.

"Quiet! Attend to your duties," commanded Captain Beckwith.

Stomping on the stairs alerted them that several people were about to arrive.

Captain Beckwith performed a quick visual inspection of his troops. Satisfied, he moved closer to the doorway to receive them.

Commander Strongbow came through first, his curled mustache leading the way. "Captain Beckwith, report."

"No visual contact yet, Commander, but we have heard several howls from their lead scouts and there have been a few reported skirmishes. Everything is to the west," replied Beckwith.

"Very good. This is Brogan Cragstrike of the mountain tribes. He will be assisting us in our defensive preparations," said the Commander.

Brogan partially ducked to enter the room.

Some of the men grumbled. "What do mountain men know of battles on the plains?" one asked.

Before Captain Beckwith could reprimand him, Brogan said, "And what do city folk know of war? I have traversed this entire continent and even Hagarth in more campaigns than I can count. Now, we don't have time for speeches." He smiled at some personal or inside joke. "I want the warhorses in the outer bailey; the long and narrow corridor will provide a perfect kill zone and minimize the risk to the riders. The plainsmen riding coursers will be assigned to platoons and will stay outside the walls. They will lead the enemy away from the city on pointless pursuits, splitting the army and relieving the pressure on the walls. Everyone else will congregate in the inner bailey, defending the mostly intact inner wall. Send runners and riders, and let's move."

The Commander's stone face could not be read, but he did not contradict anything the giant man said.

Beckwith extended his hand, "It is nice to meet you. We will make ready."

Brogan shook his hand. "My friend, Cymm Reich, speaks highly of you."

"You know Cymm and the Guardian?" Beckwith withdrew his hand slowly, awestruck.

The mountain man cleared his throat. "Quickly! The assault will hit without much warning."

Captain Beckwith began barking orders and sending messengers.

ꝏꝏꝏ

The standards above the outer wall indicated a stiff westerly breeze as the sun continued to descend, well past its zenith.

"Movement on the plains!" cried a sentry.

Beckwith's neck stiffened up and seized. He had only sent runners half an hour ago. "How far out?"

"Half a league, but they're moving fast."

Brogan intervened. "Send two platoons of coursers to each flank and split the army. Only engage with bow then ride hard to the north and south to draw them away."

Beckwith glanced at Commander Strongbow, who returned a brief nod. "Reinforce the bastions, bring the war dog forces from the east to the west, and ready the trebuchets and catapults."

"Yes, Commander, and the ballistae?"

"No, save those for the dragons."

Soldiers lined the battlements, bows in hand, while runners from the barbican hastened down the stairs, heading in every direction.

The enemy drew closer. In the late afternoon sun, the violet hides on the demons and the indigo skin of the devils swallowed the tan and green grasses of the plains like a plague—an end to the torturous wait.

"Fire the siege weapons at will!" called the Commander.

The troops immediately complied. Dozens of devices engaged in a symphony of *hum, whoosh, zing* before repeating the cycle.

Payload after payload pounded the plains, yet the enemy remained undaunted. They had lives to spare, or maybe they had no regard for life at all, even their own. The stain spreading across the field had been underestimated at ten thousand. This force equated to twenty thousand at the very least.

Uninvited guests ran rampant through Beckwith's mind. He would never admit to his fear, but he would politely ask these intruders to leave, and if they did not, he would be forced to take more stringent measures.

The payloads from the siege engines continued to crash down upon the ground, and the enemy's screams of agony followed.

This is a good thing, Beckwith thought. Many of the trespassers in his mind took notice. He scanned the battlefield and counted the dead bodies. *The enemy can be killed…this is a great thing!*

"Archers—release!" demanded Commander Strongbow.

For every fiend they killed, Beckwith swore two took its place.

The horsemen astride coursers tried valiantly to harass the flanks and pull the enemy force with them when they ran, but dozens instead of hundreds gave chase. They dispatched them quickly, then camped on each flank and sent barrage after barrage of arrows into their lines.

"Commander!" the urgent call of a soldier drew everyone's attention inside the barbican.

A giant indigo demon at least fifteen feet tall appeared amongst the enemy ranks. Its horns curled around the side of its head and its pointy ears, which matched its pointy chin. Spikes erupted in several places from the creature's wings, and its back seemed to nurture an eternal flame. The muscle bulged on its chest, arms, and thighs—the envy of every warrior.

"It's headed for the breach!" Beckwith shouted.

It began to pick up speed and the fiends in front of it scrambled to avoid being trampled.

"Archers!" The Commander pointed at the enormous demon, but most of the arrows glanced off its rugged hide.

The impact with the outer wall shook the entire barbican, and Beckwith grabbed the stone window frame to stabilize himself.

The monster extended its long arms and hooked its clawed talons in adjacent battlements.

"Stand your ground!" yelled the Commander furiously, then turned to Beckwith. "They're fleeing!"

Soldiers on the north side of the breach had lost hope and were falling back, pushing each other to get away.

Captain Beckwith's face blazed with heat. Everyone feels fear—he should know—but cowardice was unacceptable. His anger climbed steadily until he noticed the south side—the side closest to the barbican—held their ground behind a fearless leader. "No, look!"

The restoration of Beckwith's faith and hope continued until the unidentified leader threw himself off the wall.

"What's going on down there?" An answer came back that only Beckwith heard. "Are you mad?"

"What is it?" asked the commander and Brogan simultaneously.

"The men are saying Melcorac has come to fight with us," replied Beckwith. The captain hurried from the side to the front windows, hoping to get a better view.

The warrior had not thrown himself from the battlements but had jumped onto the back of the demon. The presumed Holy One—Melcorac—currently bashed the head of the demon into the rock wall with his hands, his mighty hammer slung across his back.

"Brogan, where are you going?" Commander Strongbow asked with a clenched jaw.

The giant man's eyes were lit with excitement. "To fight with Melcorac!" He raced out of the room and down the stairs.

"Could it really be the Holy One after a millennium?" asked Beckwith.

The commander shrugged. "He had always promised to return during our greatest need."

As if on cue, the insane warrior's hammer discharged a yellowish orange starburst. "Warsong, heed me!" He grabbed the haft with one hand and struck the demon a mighty blow to the head.

Every soldier watched in awe, and no one fought. The hellions were already climbing the wall and bashing the front gate.

"To arms!" boomed the Commander.

Captain Beckwith ran from window to window around the room. "Archers, the approach!" *Where are the wizards? Will they fail us again?*

Oil and pitch rained down on the enemy from the top of the barbican, and the fire arrows immediately followed. The burning stench of devil flesh made the defenders recoil from the windows as the black smoke drifted upward.

Melcorac had fallen to the ground outside the wall when the giant demon's grip on the battlements had failed. The ancient hero fought valiantly to protect the breach with his back pressed against the wall. He swung the massive hammer effortlessly, back and forth in a blur of motion, creating a sparkling amber aura amid a sea of violet and indigo, but the swarm overpowered him. First one enemy, then another, penetrated his defenses causing him to bleed and stagger.

Brogan had managed to push through the warriors on the walkway until he stood above Melcorac. With his belly on a crenel, he hollered down, "It's time to go! Grab on."

"Where in the nine hells did he get the rope?" Beckwith asked no one in particular, still hanging out the side window.

Ten soldiers were heaving to expedite the extraction of the Holy One, and he almost made it to the top before his grip failed, and he fell.

Brogan lunged between the merlons and grabbed Melcorac's wrist. He would have gone over the wall if two others had not grabbed him by the belt. Huffing and puffing he hoisted Melcorac up. "How can you be so heavy?"

The Holy One smacked him on the shoulder in gratitude. "I'm not, Warsong is." He extended his hammer.

"Incoming!" A nearby soldier ducked low behind a merlon, causing everyone nearby to mimic his action an instant before a fireball collided with the wall.

Beckwith examined the field of battle and refined his assessment when he saw the enemy wrapping around the corners of the outer wall in both directions. *There must be thirty thousand.*

Large, hairy creatures with black staves stepped forward to summon their dark, arcane magic. Two more fireballs hit the wall in the same location, and the pre-existing breach became much larger. Now, instead of one or two slipping through, the enemy poured in by the dozens.

The defenders on the wall were growing tired and sparser; they would not be able to hold the outer wall much longer. Already the warhorse platoons were working hard to keep the outer bailey clear.

Beckwith glanced at his superior and knew they thought the same thing. "Commander?"

Strongbow nodded. "Sound the retreat. Back to the inner wall."

Within seconds, an orderly retreat commenced down the stairs. One flight down, soldiers from the top of the wall merged with those from the barbican.

By happenstance, Beckwith descended next to Brogan, who wore the expression of a man who had just met his idol. They emerged from the gatehouse and into the bailey, becoming part of a mass exodus toward the next gatehouse a hundred horse lengths away. A deafening war cry drew their attention.

Sword in hand, Captain Beckwith turned to his left and found demons and devils flooding the bailey through the breach.

Melcorac landed amongst them like the payload of a catapult—his hammer intentionally striking the ground—and the detonation hurled two score of the enemy in every direction. He rose quickly and sprinted toward the fleeing soldiers, guarding their backs.

Two tall, hairy creatures as wide as an ancient tree, stepped through the breach and raised their black staves. The hair on their bodies combusted with a *whoosh*, one after the other. Mystical runes blazed bright before smokey scourges shot forth to strike at Melcorac.

The ancient warrior appeared amused by their bravado. His voice penetrated the din of battle, booming forth, "I kill balor as easily as hellspawn. Come and see!"

Beckwith and Brogan paused, side by side.

Melcorac's hammer passed right through the smokey scourges, but they solidified in time to flay his exposed flesh.

The scraggly-haired magic users spread out, placing distance between each other, and a third walked through the breach comfortably carrying a polearm.

Melcorac charged.

Dozens of indigo skinned creatures with black horns and a barbed tail scaled the outer wall and launched themselves into the bailey. They ran like apes, but were as fast as a horse, and they were quickly gaining on the retreating soldiers. Their proficiency at killing astonished the onlookers as they moved from one victim to the next.

With a howling screech, a tremendous bolt of lightning ripped through the bailey, scorching horses and riders attempting to assist the retreating soldiers.

Beckwith gazed up at the portal in the sky to find more dragons coming through and more of the hairy creatures with staves slowly descending. "Oh, by the nine hells!" He sprinted for the inner gateway.

104

Rage

Lykinnia

Lykinnia had her feet on solid ground and stared into the sky. She had never seen so many dragons before in her life, nor had she ever seen most of these species. Cymm stepped out of the portal and stood shoulder to shoulder, waiting.

A distant Solar glanced her way a moment before ZaphMordakai did the same. She turned away, aloof, and observed two monstrous dragons battling. So primal and savage, she almost shielded her eyes. Blood rained down upon the ground below them, and chunks of flesh splattered against the rocks as they hit.

While Solar raced through the air back toward her, she mentally rehearsed the procedure to bind with Cymm and create an avatar. It did not seem too difficult, but she had always assumed the deity's individual phylactery awarded the ability. Upon deeper reflection, the process nearly replicated a teleportation spell.

The dragon battle raged on. Ice javelins hurtled from the sea toward the enormous black dragon that could only be DetonKonraber.

ZaphMordakai unknowingly flew right into their path and took one to the chest, while several others ripped through the soft membranes of his wings.

At least two dozen other dragon clashes were occurring all around them. Some were similar one on one battles, while others were all out melees.

"Ready?" asked Cymm.

"I will be. Here comes Solar," replied Lykinnia.

Her childhood caregiver landed in a huff and pointed. "The far portal—I am not sure if something is coming out or going in—but it is the target."

"I understand. Keep everyone on our side away from that area," Lykinnia instructed.

"I gave that assignment to Zaph," said Solar.

Lykinnia wrinkled her brow. "Zaph? You mean ZaphMordakai."

Solar crossed his arms over his chest. "Do not be so hard on him. He regrets what he did and wishes to make amends. He even told me to thank you for teaching him what true friendship is and what it means."

With a final screech, the enormous blue dragon fell to the rocky ground below. Its final death cry, a message to all.

DetonKonraber trumpeted his own roar of victory, but he did not look well. There were several puncture holes from ice lances, flayed scales from steam blasts, and deep slashes across his chest. He appeared to be having difficulty staying aloft.

"I must go," said Solar. "Deton needs to be healed; they just keep coming for him." He zipped away.

"Zaph…Deton…I guess I am not the only one with a poor taste for friends." Lykinnia addressed Cymm, but he did not respond. "Alright. Are you ready?"

"I've done this with several others, but the result is different every time." He smiled briefly, then his gaze went over her shoulder.

The priestess of Terazhan spun in confusion, prepared to defend herself, but she was not under attack. Seven red dragons swarmed the behemoth, black dragon like angry hornets.

ZaphMordakai frantically fired off a lightning bolt to defend his uncle, and DetonKonraber flailed and slashed, causing three of the red dragons to detach and tumble away.

Lykinnia's head tilted toward the right in confusion. One by one, the three dragons became insubstantial and disappeared, never hitting the side of the mountain.

With Solar's arrival imminent, DetonKonraber had gone berserk. He flailed, with furious and deranged motions, he killed two more as he rolled over and faced upward.

An eighth red dragon plummeted from the sky like a fireball, a torrent of flame hitting red and black dragons indiscriminately.

It was the largest dragon Lykinnia had ever seen, even bigger than Talon, the golden dragon who had attended her Millennial Lifeday celebration.

A massive lightning bolt erupted from the flame, splitting the conflagration and striking the newcomer in the chest. The deep violet lightning framed on both sides by molten lava flames created a beautiful sight. The short-lived display sputtered, then disappeared.

The black dragon began to lose altitude. It happened slowly at first and accelerated with each passing second. His wings flapped weakly—a wasted effort, the webbing had mostly disintegrated—but his legs seemed froze in place. He slammed into a rocky surface, then slid down the side of the volcano to rest next to the two blue dragon corpses.

A mountain of black scales, motionless and broken. His wings had folded over, and steam rose from his open wounds. For a moment, nothing moved on the battlefield.

DetonKonraber the Devastation was dead.

The massive red dragon bellowed a triumphant roar, immediately answered by a dozen others around the island. He arced his flight path straight for the injured ZaphMordakai, whose arial acrobatics were quite impressive to avoid the gout of flames.

Solar's hands were still raised to heal Deton—frozen in shock—when the enormous red flew past him. The buffeting of its wings driving him into action.

ZaphMordakai released his lavender lightning after a feint to the left and successfully scored a hit, infuriating the opponent twice his size.

A huge golden hammer materialized above the red dragon and pummeled him three times, but the red was more agile than he appeared. He rolled to his back, flying upside down for several seconds, while he slashed and destroyed the hammer with his front talons.

Lykinnia stood mesmerized, unwilling to glance away. "Solar, get out of there," she mumbled, but golden light shot forth to heal the black dragon. She caught them glancing at each other and sharing a smile.

A strange noise drifted through the air, growing in volume. It vaguely sounded like a horse stampede.

Invigorated, ZaphMordakai swooped around and blasted the red dragon with another forked bolt.

Solar added his deadly wing blast. Two super-charged, blue bolts snapped in the air and pounded into the red dragon with speed and force.

The immense dragon howled in pain and fury, then lost altitude before recovering. Brim's health was fading. In an instant, seven more red dragons appeared surrounding Solar and ZaphMordakai.

Lykinnia knew these creatures were phantasms of the creator. Barely real in substance, they could only inflict minor wounds, but she could not determine which one created them.

The stampeding horses—or whatever made the noise—grew louder, calling to her, trying to distract her, but her attention remained on her best friend.

Solar and ZaphMordakai each picked one and attacked. They each picked wrong. The two phantasm-dragon bodies fell, spinning toward the ground. Racing up from the bottom, passed the falling illusions, stormed the real red dragon. His inhale sharp and terrifying.

The inferno that killed DetonKonraber did not compare in size or intensity to this firestorm. Before the flames engulfed them, ZaphMordakai reached out, grabbed and pulled Solar close, then wrapped him with his wings.

"No!" Lykinnia reached her hand toward them.

With her other hand, she grabbed Cymm's, and they held their breath.

As soon as ZaphMordakai dropped below the orange plume, Lykinnia averted her eyes.

Terazhan's voice cried out through the heavens, echoing off the volcano. "Solar! No!"

With a cracked voice, she said, "Cymm, ready." Her command preceded her body falling to the floor by only a second. In its place, the ghostly form of a unicorn galloped toward the young man. At the last second it leaped, splitting into two equines before entering his eyes.

Cymm reached out to her. "*Lykinnia, calm down! I can feel your anger.*"

She heard the words with a numb mind. "*Is Solar dead? Is he? Cymm! Is he?*"

"*I don't know. I can't see anything. My—my eyes are filling with red,*" he replied.

The stampeding creatures finally burst forth from the mountain. Hundreds of balor poured out of the tunnels and down the steep slope toward the targeted portal, while the dragons congregated into phalanxes as they flew in the same direction.

Lykinnia lifted off the ground near the portal she entered from with ease.

"*Lykinnia, I still can't see. Are we flying?*" asked Cymm.

She raced half the distance to the portal, then hovered above the shifting mosaic of dragon bodies. The priestess took one more tentative glance around, hoping to find Solar flying in her direction. Her eyes came across the charred remains of her once friend, ZaphMordakai, and she croaked. She arrived hyperventilating. "Solar! Solar!"

Solar's shingled, skirt armor survived the inferno, but the feathers on his wings, incinerated, and his flesh charred. This unrecognizable mass had once been her guardian, her mentor, her friend.

"Lykinnia…" came a raspy, broken voice. It belonged to ZaphMordakai. A mangled heap of cracked scales and smoking flesh.

Sobbing, she replied, "How can you be alive?"

"Lykinnia—I'm sorry—please…," ZaphMordakai's voice cracked with emotion and pain. "Please…forgive—"

"Zaph? Zaph?" The priestess's hands shot out and amber beams with red strands zipped toward the black dragon, but nothing happened.

A light breeze brought the stench of scorched flesh to her nostrils. She screamed while removing a scroll from the avatar's belt. She had transcribed her mother's spell on the scroll before she had traded the book for Zaph's life. The words rolled off her tongue as she read it. The wind picked up, whipping her hair—the avatar's hair—from side to side, and the misty clouds surrounding the top of the mountain scattered. She lifted back off the ground.

"*Lykinnia, I'm so sorry,*" Cymm said.

With an audible report, a black window appeared above the targeted portal.

The avatar's body began to shake, and Lykinnia commanded its arms to rise and its hands to fall like rain, completing the physical component of the spell.

Some of the balor drifted closer in route to the portal and took notice of her actions, but Lykinnia's reinforcements had arrived.

Ronks and Naterion arrived, flanking her with primal growls. She could not determine which sounded more ferocious.

The sky tore open with a crack louder than the peel of thunder, immediately followed by an ear-piercing whistle. A large boulder of molten lava howled through the clouds and smashed into the dragon ranks near the gateway, vaporizing everything it hit—dragons, trees, rocks, dirt, and even the ocean water. Two more hit close by, initiating a symphony of whistles as different sized meteors crashed upon the enemy army.

The ground shuddered from the pounding onslaught.

She spotted the enormous red dragon, the murderer, and tried to control the location of impact. *You will pay for Solar's death.*

"*Lykinnia, I am sorry about Solar. He was a good man.*" Cymm tried again to reach her, his voice full of melancholy.

She grunted in response and renewed her focus. His sentiment had only fanned the flames inside her.

The imprecise targeting of each falling star deteriorated further with every passing second, but she kept it to the far side of the island to avoid Kamac and Camak who had joined the fray.

After the first minute, Lykinnia began to lose track of how many fireballs had crashed down. Each impact cratered the rocky slopes, boiled the surf, and sent plumes of dust or scalding steam skyward. They came fast and furious as the enemy attempted to flee through the open portal. Dozens of balor had already made it to safety, but very few dragons. Now the ground beneath the portal cracked and fell into the ocean, much of the twenty-foot-deep cavity had previously been ionized. This made it impossible for any to enter the gateway unless they could fly.

The putrid scent of burnt dragon and balor flesh did not mix well with everything else on fire, not to mention the hot steam coursing through the area.

The red general of the dragon army stared in her direction, seething, before barking out orders.

Lykinnia's anger flamed anew, and her rage intensified. As she drew more power from Cymm, her scream turned into a cackle.

Crimson skulls rocketed past the priestess and smacked into the lead balor bearing down on her.

Spikes flew from the end of the sphinx's flailing tails.

Ronks growled and released a giant fireball in the same direction, and the sleek black fur of Naterion in his panther form, bounded off to engage the approaching enemy.

Lykinnia barely hovered above the ground; she expended most of the energy on the attack. She could feel the power flow lessening further as her anger abated.

Azreala grabbed and pulled back on the collar of the avatar's mithril armor.

"*Don't stop!*" Cymm's attempt at a commanding voice sounded weak.

Naterion transformed back to his human form as he returned, bloodied and beaten. "There—are too—many," he said between gasps.

Ronks conjured another ball of fire and delivered the payload, then turned to run.

Aunt Sehaleah replaced him and drove her hands into the rocky soil. Thick vines erupted from the ground like tentacles, winding around anything and everything nearby.

The balor were bound and held fast, but the next wave hurtled over their brethren, intent on getting to their target.

Another tug on the avatar's collar kept them in constant retreat.

"*You do not sound very good, Cymm. Are you alright?*" Lykinnia's concern replaced her focus, and the bombardment slowed to a trickle.

"*Please don't stop if there are any dragons left. Remember I asked you to help me destroy them all.*" Cymm was growing weaker.

"*Yes, a mass extinction, but I am killing you,*" Lykinnia replied on the verge of tears.

"I am stronger than you think!" His powerful voice returned. *"Think about what they did to Solar and my family. One more wave, just one more surge."*

Death and desertion had devastated the dragon army, but pockets of survivors persisted and those that had recently exited the mountain caverns.

A white feather, no longer pristine, fell upon Lykinnia's hand, slightly singed and discolored. It had belonged to Solar. A memory flew into her mind. "*One of these days I am going to pluck a feather from your wings.*" How many times had she vowed to do this. She tucked it into the avatar's belt.

Lykinnia and the avatar screamed in primal rage and the onslaught resumed. She could feel the resurgence of pain within her boyfriend as hellfire rained down around them. *"Hold on, Cymm."*

"I love you, Lykinnia." His voice had resumed its weakened state. *"DragonSin."*

"This is highly unorthodox, but yes, Cymm?" replied the sword.

"Attack!"

"With pleasure, sir." DragonSin began to sing.

Uncle Dilantro stood next to her with his arms up and braced as if pushing against an invisible barrier. Gusts of wind were spouting off his hands and keeping the approaching balor at bay.

The ground began to shake, and tremors rippled through the bedrock, and still Lykinnia screamed. The island rocked and shifted away from the mainland.

Each iteration of the spell stole more from her soul—grief, love, memories—all burning within the cauldron that scorched her enemies. She wondered, dimly, if there would be anything left of her when the fires ended.

Portals were appearing everywhere and the balor were jumping through them.

A more forceful tug on the collar came from Azreala. "We must leave!"

The avatar's arms came down, and she allowed Azreala to lead her away after she dropped to the ground. Up ahead of her, Naterion leaned heavily on Ronks and her material body still lay in a heap before the home portal, guarded by a semicircle of taviian warriors. With their arms up near their faces, she wondered if they were praying for her safe return.

Although the ground continued to shake, meteors no longer fell from the sky. The cataclysm spell had ended.

Aunt Vallerielle appeared by her side, hands out, arms extended. An eerie hush fell over the island. Nothing moved, nothing shook, the wind had ceased to exist.

"Move it!" Uncle Dilantro stormed past them.

Lykinnia hooked her arm under Azreala's and flew her toward the portal.

The sphinx brothers led the way through the gateway, followed closely by the taviian warriors, Ronks, and Naterion. The deities piled through, last leaving only Lykinnia. She turned for one last glance, and her shoulders slumped—no Solar. The balor were gone and the remaining dragon army, fragmented and decimated.

With a creak and a groan, the island shifted farther away from the mainland, and the wind picked back up quickly, racing up toward the black window above the targeted portal.

"*Cymm, we did it!*" Lykinnia exclaimed with tired excitement. She dipped to retrieve her body and magical mace, then hesitated in front of the portal. *"Cymm?"*

105

The Altar of the One

Azreala

Azreala gave and received accolades on a battle well fought, and smiles and camaraderie were in abundance.

Vallerielle leaned down to embrace her. "I have heard you would like to recover the power words for your sister's tanzanite figurines. I will see what my monks can do when I return to the Keep."

Returning the hug fiercely, Azreala said, "Thank you!"

Only Terazhan did not participate in the celebration, which occurred all around him, the Altar of the One, and the stone platform. A slight breeze ruffled his cowl. He remained at the altar gazing into one of his scrying windows, deliberating with himself. "No, no, no."

Lykinnia stepped through the portal in a panic and collapsed to the ground near the platform. "Cymm!"

Azreala rushed over. "What's the matter?"

"Cymm is not here," replied the daughter of Terazhan.

"What do you mean? You're still in his body," replied Azreala.

"He will not reply. He is…gone." Lykinnia placed her forehead on the ground.

Azreala blinked twice. *Jakarrak said this might happen.* "Do you want me to try?"

"No! Lykinnia, what have you done?" Terazhan demanded.

Her response barely audible above the whipping wind. "He told me to keep going. He begged me."

"No!" he screamed again. "How will I fix this?"

Melandri stood by his side, rubbing his shoulder. An intense cobalt blue aura surrounded her, and tendrils of the same color snaked toward Terazhan.

"He said he was strong enough," Lykinnia whimpered.

Azreala moved next to Lykinnia in her avatar form but stared toward the altar. *Terazhan has no clue what is going on over here. He can't even hear what we're talking about.*

Dilantro and Sehaleah rushed over to the scrying window above the altar and gasped.

Vallerielle and Azreala locked eyes then hurried to join them.

The Mantle of the Gods appeared around Terazhan's neck with one quick motion. "Get off the platform! I want everyone out."

Eyes flitted back and forth. No one moved until the next gust of wind pushed against them.

A gemstone popped off the usekh near the top of the shoulder of its own accord and burst into shimmering dust, followed by two ingots of differing hues. Soon, an entire kaleidoscope of colors swirled around him.

Although the wind pushed toward the northeast, the dust never veered off its path, as if it had a mission.

The altar began to resonate with a baritone hum when the hunter green emeralds and the dark cobalt sapphires exploded.

"It is time to go," said Dilantro.

"Where?" asked Sehaleah.

Melandri walked over to collect Lykinnia. "We should head to Armak. The war is not over."

Azreala could not take her eyes off the mantle. *What are you doing? Why are you wasting its power?*

Over two dozen ingots, beads, and gems had disintegrated into dust and infused with both Terazhan and the altar, which no longer had a pure white cast. Touches of orange were spreading like wildfire through the entire base. It pulsed in size, then began to whine at a high pitch.

Dilantro summoned a portal. "Come on!" He stepped through it.

Sehaleah quickly followed, as well as Ronks and Naterion.

"There is no time to transition back. Azreala, can you carry Lykinnia's body?" Melandri had a firm grasp on the avatar, and she escorted her toward the portal.

Terazhan lifted off the ground with his head rocking back. He hovered over the altar with a maelstrom of power orbiting him. The wind began to slow, but the altar continued to blaze—now red hot. A resounding *crack* drew the attention of everyone remaining.

The altar fractured. Large, angry fissures riddled both the surface and supporting legs.

The taviian warriors skittered into the portal, followed closely by the sphinx brothers.

Terazhan gazed at his daughter with love and compassion for a fleeting second, then anger erupted. "Run!"

The altar burned with every color of the gods, then turned white hot and exploded.

"No!" Azreala screamed. *This wasn't supposed to happen.* Her mind reeled. *Will the mantle survive?*

Vallerielle wove her magic into the fabric of time centered around the platform. "You have three seconds to get out!" She quickly stepped through the gateway.

Azreala, carrying Lykinnia's body, paused at the portal next to Melandri, as she escorted the avatar. She glanced over at Terazhan.

Halos of every color spawned off the altar before creating vertical sheets of light that radiated high above The Lord of Healing. He wore a mask of concentration, beaded in sweat, and straining from the channeling of massive power to maintain the structural integrity of the already compromised altar. Anyone in the path of the shrapnel…

The avatar continued to be guided into the portal by Melandri.

Father and daughter peered at each other simultaneously.

Azreala's heart ached for her own father and for the intense bond they once shared.

At the last moment, Lykinnia's arms extended slowly, reaching for him. "Father!"

A concussive blast threw all three of them into the portal.

106

By Melcorac's Hammer

Captain Beckwith

Smoke swirled through the bailey, as dragons and a couple of plasma darts sailed by overhead. Captain Beckwith sprinted for the next gatehouse but could not help viewing the battle over his shoulder. Melcorac's hammer flashed, and a staff creature went airborne to land fifty feet away. One of the skin-flailing scourges disappeared. The enemy—the newcomer with the polearm—pounced on him before he could complete his backswing.

At least a dozen dragons had come through the portal already and scores of hairy creatures with the black staves were descending from the sky.

Brogan pushed him to the side. "Watch out!"

One of the sprinting devils lunged for Beckwith, its snapping jaws just missing.

Brogan slashed it and assumed a defensive position while the captain regained his feet.

A dozen arrows from the wall above ended its life.

Beckwith could no longer see Melcorac as he ran for the gate and up the stairs to the wall with Brogan on his tail. By the time they gained access to a merlon, a sea of violet and indigo once again surrounded the Holy One. However, he remained engaged in single combat. The enemy's polearm danced in and out of his defenses, but Melcorac's dexterous swings could not make contact.

Brogan leaned forward; eyes glued on the battle. "What are these creatures?"

The Commander had appeared soundlessly on Brogan's other side. "They are called balor, the terrors of the night. The blazing fur makes me quite certain."

Brogan's fist pounded the stone wall as the balor's blade erupted from Melcorac's back. "No!"

The Holy One fell to his knees, holding the shaft of the polearm in one hand and his hammer in the other.

Raucous hooting and hollering rang out across the bailey when the balor extracted his blade and Melcorac fell to the dirt.

The balor briefly paused over his body, then struggled to lift the fallen man's hammer. He dropped the weapon and turned to leave.

The fiends' celebration turned to mute horror as Melcorac—bleeding and staggering—rose.

Beckwith pulled excitedly on Brogan's arm. "Look!"

Before the victorious balor with the polearm could not determine the source of their discontent, a hammer struck him from behind driving him to his knees. A second swing ended his life.

Brogan's jaw dropped.

"By all that is unholy, what in the nine hells is he?" asked the Commander.

On the walls, a war cry, raw and joyous rang out.

Two full, warhorse brigades stampeded through the bailey, spearing and trampling a swath through the enemy, then continued south and around the corner with many of the swift devils chasing after them.

A gentle breeze whipped up out of nowhere, hitting Beckwith in the face.

Melcorac swung his hammer as he ran toward them.

The hellions running with him gave him wide birth as if sensing the power running through him.

Two more brigades of warhorses came thundering through the bailey, crushing any resistance, and opening an easier path for Melcorac.

Death descended from above, devastating the galloping warriors with fire and lightning. The red and black dragons banked away after demolishing half the riders.

"By Melcorac's hammer! Where are those wizards?" asked Commander Strongbow in frustration.

Beckwith gave a sideways glance, wondering if anyone else realized that expression finally made sense.

The enemy had made it to the wall, past the horses and the arrows, and they were climbing. Ten feet higher than the outer, the inner curtain wall did not seem to slow the enemy's progress.

"Beckwith, go to the east gate and monitor the horse brigades. I don't want them trapped in the bailey for the dragons to pick off. Open the outer gate so they can come and go as they please. I only trust your decision," said the Commander.

He paused to watch Melcorac finish climbing the wall on a demon's back. When he crested the battlement, Beckwith sighed in relief. He took off running and felt a stiffer wind pushing him toward the palace on his way to the far gate. Before he entered Heroes Square, a commotion assailed his ears and within moments wizards were rushing past him. The square opened in front of him, and he found magic users pouring out of the tower and running toward the four corners of the city.

The King of Armak came running out of the town hall where he typically held court with his hands flailing. "Lord Dilantro is in the temple!"

The First Sword to the King, Lord Barrister, sprinted ahead to intercept his lord, immediately followed by his retinue. He pointed toward the sky, then glanced back at the temple.

The king pushed him away and entered the holy place.

Barrister glanced at the Guardian and a female dwarf accompanying him, then all three ran after the king.

107

Dilantro's Temple

Azreala

Melandri dusted herself off after being launched through the portal. "What in the nine hells just happened?"

"Where are we?" asked Vallerielle.

Dilantro finished speaking with several priests and approached. "I created a portal to Armak as suggested. We are inside a temple dedicated to me."

Sehaleah sighed. "Lykinnia channeled more power than the atmosphere and the conjuring window could sustain." She motioned toward Dilantro. "We saw what happened. The conjuring window collapsed and began sucking the atmosphere into a giant vortex."

"Terazhan saved the atmosphere by shutting the vortex down." Dilantro gazed at Lykinnia with sorrow in his eyes. "Your father sacrificed his life to save us all."

True, but... Azreala's eyes rolled. *What about the mantle?*

Lykinnia remained in the avatar form, her material body and heavy mace still lying where they had landed after being thrown by the explosion through the portal and into this room.

"He cannot be dead!" said Sehaleah emphatically.

"He is banished but not lost. When he is ready, you will hear from him," said Dilantro.

Melandri hugged Lykinnia.

"What is the plan?" asked Azreala.

A look of concern washed over Sehaleah's face. "I sense a great evil presence. Ledaedra is near."

"I sense it as well," said Dilantro.

Lykinnia shrugged off Melandri's arm and approached her material body.

A man dressed in regal attire hastened into the grand hall and prostrated himself on one knee before Dilantro.

The deity's bright yellow cape wrapped around his massive deltoids and back, shimmering with magic. "This is the King of Armak."

"Only by your good graces," said the king humbly.

"What can I do for you?" asked Dilantro.

The king rose timidly. "There is a man in the city who claims to be the Guardian. I need your help and guidance. Could this really be the one to fulfill the prophecy?"

"As hard as it was for all of us to believe, yes, the Guardian has arrived. You will help him in his mission."

The king groaned, then groaned again when Talo and Grendella entered the room.

Lykinnia returned to her own body. She cradled Cymm's head in her lap.

An officer rushed into the sanctuary. "My King, the assault has begun. We need to get you to safety."

"Look around you, Lord Barrister. How could I be any safer than here?" asked the king.

Talo appeared to be awestruck. Besides the ten-foot tall Dilantro, there were four women all over eight foot tall, and many of them had powerful auras, or orbs orbiting their heads, or partial and full halos.

Barrister eyed the group suspiciously. "Nevertheless, it is time to go. Is that Cymm?"

"Soldier, what is going on out there?" asked Dilantro.

"There is a full-blown assault underway, primarily from the west, comprised of demons and devils ten to fifteen thousand strong, plus hulking beasts with magical powers. The dragons seem to be holding back as well as the main demon in the sky," he replied.

"The demon in the sky with six heads is the Dragon Queen, Ledaedra," said Melandri.

"Seven heads now. She returned with an additional one." Lord Barrister could not take his eyes off Cymm.

The room went silent.

A white aura burst forth from Cymm's prone body, drawing the attention of everyone gathered, and when the light faded a white dragonfly with gossamer wings remained.

"Talo!" Grendella grabbed his arm urgently, her eyes teary.

"Oh, blessed Melandri. Cymm!—No!" cried Lykinnia. "I cannot lose you too."

The insect flew a lazy loop around the immediate area. The ivory bands outlining and running through its wings sparkled when it traveled through the natural sunbeams descending from the ceiling. Up and down, it fluttered in random directions, trying to stay aloft. Finally, it seemed to give up as if the effort had taken its toll, and it drifted down toward the floor.

The dragonfly landed on Talo's shoulder.

108

The Rending

BrimStrakenstone

After a harrowing experience on Fire Island, BrimStrakenstone exited the portal Ledaedra provided, elated. He had barely swerved in time to avoid two falling meteors but the third struck him when he swooped instead of dove. Fortunately, his scales were highly resistant to fire, and he shook it off quickly. Nevertheless, the large black circle on his rump resembled the center of a target.

He approached his liege lord carefully. "That's it. The rest are dead or dying." He could not tell her hundreds of dragons had fled.

"How many?" she hissed.

Brim considered his answer momentarily. "Fifty-two."

Ledaedra hissed up at him. She no longer had her eighteen-foot stature—closer to fourteen. "I no longer need you to win this war now that the Dark Lord is under my control."

"Will you be joining us, My Queen?" asked Brim.

"No, you imbecile. I need to reserve my strength for the coming battle."

Brim clenched his jaw. "We'll be fine. Last time we demolished this city with only—"

"Go!" Ledaedra screamed. "I need to conserve my energy. Every moment you waste costs us all. Bring me the Guardian. I will not be denied."

The new creature attached to her back, the Dark Lord, exuded happiness.

Brim quickly removed himself from the area and gathered his remaining forces. *If I deploy them strategically, I should lose very few of my warriors. Some of them are already destroying the horse riders.*

Brim scanned the battlefield. The weakest of the demons and devils—the calendri and the doveki—were already scaling the inner walls, and many were inside the city. He held back the more powerful fiends—the towering ashara and the quick devikin—to be used once the defenses had fallen. He believed Ledaedra provided them with direction given Malekai and Marekai were banished and Ariata unavailable to impersonate them. They currently were overrunning the remaining fortifications.

The balor were uncontrollable and unmanaged, but fortunately, they had chosen to destroy the walls and siege engines with their mystical magic, creating a safer battlefield for the dragons.

It is time to end this conflict. Brim planned to kill everything living down there before the sun set.

Let the killing begin. He sent one phalanx to each compass point with the intention of sending a second wave soon after to cover their retreat. He tried to observe the death and destruction in all four quadrants of the city. Walls and buildings exploded under the powerful lightning bolts of the black dragons, while the green dragons blanketed an area with a cloak of poisonous fog. The red dragons disintegrated flesh and fabric, melted rock and stone, and incinerated the very air the humanoids were breathing.

This will be over even quicker than I imagined. With a slight chuckle he sent the second wave. They dove in perfect formation, roaring their challenge as they went. His pride in their commitment and the power they wielded made him confident he would prevail.

Orange darts of plasma zipped through the air. At first only a few, then like lightning bugs at dusk they multiplied quickly. Dragons were falling from the sky with wings of stone and crashing into the bailey or the stone walls. A few of the dragons hardened into a solid statue after being hit by many darts, then exploded into hundreds of stone shards upon impact.

Brim watched in horror as his entire second wave, four phalanxes of warriors, crashed to the ground to be slaughtered by impact, sword, or ballistae. The sky fell silent. He could feel the eyes of those who remained upon him, seeking a leader to provide direction.

BrimStrakenstone dove, never intending to show the remaining dragons his maneuvers and never intending to join the battle. He leveled off quickly and fixated on his southern destination, the burning sands of Ashara.

109

Inconsequential Being

Azreala

An emptiness filled Azreala as she stared at Cymm's lifeless body and the dragonfly perched on Talo's shoulder. This had always been the expected outcome, but she could not deny her kinship with Cymm.

"No! You can't pick me. You belong with Cymm." Talo hurried over to Lykinnia's side, while she stroked Cymm's hair. The dragonfly fluttered its wings, but its tarsi remained attached to Talo's shoulder. "What happened?"

"We attacked the dragon army," Lykinnia sobbed, as if that said it all.

A sentry rushed into the sanctuary. "Lord Barrister, the enemy is flooding the inner bailey. There isn't much time."

Deities and mortals rushed outside for their own reasons, except for Lykinnia and Talo.

The wind had ceased and on the far side of the city, a yellowish green gas hung thickly in the air.

"I will take care of the gas." Dilantro spun himself into a twister and flew off on his mission.

The royal guards ushered the king toward the town hall while he pleaded with them. "But the wizards are in the turrets. I demanded the City of the Mystics send them and they did!"

The King's Guard continued to corral him anyway and led him away.

Melcorac raced into the square followed closely by Brogan. Once they made eye contact with Azreala, they headed straight for her.

Brogan, slightly out of breath, said, "They broke through the final defenses. They're coming. Where's Talo?"

Azreala pointed to the temple.

"Talo, get out here!" Brogan ran toward the temple, repeating himself several times.

Talo emerged with rounded shoulders and dragging his feet as Brogan reached the steps. "What do you want?"

Joharie rose from the step closest to the entryway and flanked Talo.

"You need to summon the One True God." Brogan stammered, "What in the nine hells is on your shoulder?"

Talo waved him off. "I have no idea how to summon him."

A young man with black hair, Dirk Darkmane, ran past Azreala toward Talo. "I could smell you when you entered the city."

Grendella, standing next to the goddess of death, hefted her warhammer. "Dego, stop!"

Dego kicked Dirk's body off like an old shoe and emerged in his full glory. A two-headed monstrosity as dark as night with haunting eyes that blazed an eerie red. He gave Grendella a quick glance, then lurched toward the Guardian.

Melcorac blindsided Dego, tackling him to the stone pavers a few feet from his target. They rolled around for a few seconds before

Melcorac gained the advantage. Sitting on his chest, The Holy One brought his hammer to bear.

Crack! Warsong smacked the ground between the heads.

Dego's hips thrashed like an unbroken horse, and Melcorac flew off to the side.

The dragonfly must have sensed the eminent danger and took wing a moment before Dego stretched for it. His leap brought him within inches of success.

"You are a creature of vile darkness, and you will not touch my aura!" Melcorac spun his holy hammer in his meaty fists.

Dego squared off with him. "I will not return to a prison. No one will have it! All this power should not be wasted on fools and weaklings."

Fiends were collecting at two of the entrances to the square awaiting some unknown signal. While the balor traded magical barrages with the wizards from rooftop to rooftop.

Sehaleah sprung forward followed by the others to form a protective barrier between the enemy and the Guardian.

"What are you smiling about?" Azreala asked Sehaleah.

"The elves have arrived. Led by little Miss Myra."

Lightning snapped and crackled above as Ledaedra descended.

"Talo, do something!" Brogan yelled.

The young man's palms went up with his shoulders and stayed there.

"Pray to Lord Terazhan for guidance," yelled Grendella.

Dirk Darkmane hobbled over to them with pallid cheeks. "Accept the white aura, then call the One True God to appear before you."

Brogan's glare bore into Dirk. "How do you know this?" The big man frantically lunged for Talo. "Wait!"

The dragonfly, seeking protection, attempted to cross the open space, and Talo met it halfway.

Melcorac and Dego lurched forward to grab the dragonfly, but Talo, a step ahead, arrived first and melded with the insect. The white aura consumed him in a bright glow. Both Melcorac and Dego grabbed a different arm and pulled him until the light's intensity caused them to shield their eyes, but Dego persisted, and ripped the dragonfly out of Talo's body.

With a voice of thunder, Talo yelled, "I call upon the One True God to appear before me. We need your help!"

Dego exploded.

A shock wave pulsed through the square both deafening and blinding. The mortals—soldiers, wizards, even demons—paused in their violence, breathless. For a heartbeat, all of Erogoth waited.

When Azreala's senses returned, she found a being floating in the space above the point of genesis. His pure white wings did not flutter, and the tips almost touched the ground, even though the bottom of his feet were above Azreala's head. His eye sockets were filled with white, sparkling energy and he carried a staff twice his height that radiated a brilliant true silver. There appeared to be a sun behind his head, and a halo that arced vertically from shoulder to shoulder with intricate patterns woven inside.

His magnanimous presence gave Azreala a comfort of familiarity, and she knew instantly he was the father. Not her father, but the father to all and of all—The Creator. She knelt before him.

The One True God gazed at Talo. "You have summoned me. The time of deliverance is at hand."

Ledaedra's voice boomed like the crack of thunder. "The One has graced us with his presence. You should say your greetings and farewells all at the same time."

With a hearty laugh, The One replied, "Bold words. You brought Abaddon back in a weakened condition, and even at full strength he was never my equal."

Ledaedra puffed her chest out. "That was before—"

"You are inconsequential!" Without hesitation, he rocketed into the sky, his massive staff leading the way with a blinding light.

All of Ledaedra's heads recoiled except for the Dark Lord. "You were never my better then or now."

A shimmering prism popped into view encapsulating the One True God. Celestial bonds materialized, pulling his arms and legs in four different directions, and a fifth band wrapped tightly around his neck. He choked out the words, "How is this possible?"

Talo's heart twisted in his chest. "I must do something to help, but what?"

Brogan's hand clutched his shoulder. "Pray."

Ledaedra cackled. "Apparently, I am not so inconsequential. I figured out how to replicate the ability of your white dragonfly to magnify power, and now that I control the Dark Lord, I am unstoppable."

"No one controls the Dark Lord!" A voice wailed from the empty sky a moment before a balor appeared. He held a black staff in his remaining hand. The other, recently amputated, still dripped blood from a raw stump.

More balor appeared on every rooftop in mass numbers, chanting.

The magical prison shrank and with it, the One True God. The celestial bonds minimized his struggling and choked off his ability to speak.

"Grumgresh, I am not sure how you escaped your confinement, but I will deal with you next," Ledaedra's excitement could not be contained.

Azreala's eyes blazed hot with anger. "If I could fly, I would drain your miserable life right now!"

"No one will control the Dark Lord, especially not you!" The one-handed balor raised his ebony staff and the runes upon its shaft blazed to life. Smokey energy collected at its tip, then shot forth, striking the Dark Lord. And he began to grow.

The balors' chanting from the rooftops continued with vigor and the power transfer surged.

Grumgresh—no longer twelve feet tall nor as wide as a tree—shriveled and shrank. He finally faded from existence with an audible *snap*.

The Dark Lord roared like a wild beast, then sunk his fangs into Ledaedra's neck.

The shadow dragon attached to Ledaedra's back retaliated, breathing its shadow magic.

The One True God curled into a ball then sprawled rapidly. The cosmic box containing him exploded into a million shards. He flew toward the seven-headed monstrosity, wielding his lengthy staff. It came down hard on the shadow dragon's head, cleaving it in half.

Arms grew on the Dark Lord's body, and he wrapped one under the red dragon's chin and cranked it while continuing to suck.

"No!" cried Ledaedra. "Nooo!"

The holy staff came back horizontally and severed the Dragon Queen's lower body, right through the prismatic swirl on her belly. It crashed upon the city below.

The Dark Lord had finished feeding and shed Ledaedra's shriveled torso. "You owe me!" he hissed.

"I am listening," replied the One True God.

"The Plane of Ashes and its three outer planes are mine to rule."

"You will have to contend with Ledaedra and her phylactery to take ownership. I will not help," replied The One.

"Her phylactery was blocked. She is dead!" hissed Abaddon.

"It is done." The One True God waved his staff, and a bright flash of light blinded those present.

The Dark Lord and all his balor minions had vanished.

110

Reunited

Talo

Talo stared out at the city from the steps of the temple, it stank of ash and blood and the wailing of the wounded and dying formed the background din. Any remaining dragons had long since departed. It took several hours to rout the demons and devils, but with the help of the elves and the wizards from the City of the Mystics, they were successful. Only at this point did they share Cymm's fate with Brogan.

Bloodied and disheveled, the big man rushed into the temple and continued straight to the sanctuary. Grendella and Talo followed close behind.

"Where is Cymm's body?" asked Talo, spinning in a circle.

Grendella pulled a priest around by the elbow. "Where is the woman who mourned her dead friend?"

The priest shrugged, as did the other three she asked.

Azreala entered with an ogre by her side and scanned the entire room.

"She's gone, and she took Cymm's body with her," said Talo.

Azreala's eyes went wide. "This is not good!" She left with an urgency in her step.

"You don't know that for a fact, Talo," said Grendella.

Brogan ran his hand through his hair. "It is the most likely scenario. Where you going?"

Talo half-turned, glancing over his shoulder. "I need to find my family and fellow villagers, then I'm heading home. How about you?"

"We are heading north." Brogan poked his thumb toward Grendella.

"An escort home for Katara and Tanya, plus I am not done with her training," added the dwarf.

"Safe travels." Talo walked out into the square, his mind in a fog. The absence of Cymm had created a hole in his soul.

Brogan caught up with him and grabbed his arm. "Hey, we all miss him. You don't have to suffer these feelings alone."

Talo shook his hand heartily. "You're a good man. I can see why Cymm admired you so much."

Orts entered the city square on the far side—the entrance closest to the Broken Horse Inn—scanning the crowd. His gaze briefly passed over Talo.

"Captain Beckwith! Post sentries at every entrance to the square, then work on the perimeter. Grom and Bostak will be bringing the king out of the saferoom," ordered Lord Barrister.

Talo gave a subdued smile and a wave, then headed for the east gate. Before he reached the exit, his sister entered the square and ran toward him. She had tears in her eyes, and Toma, Katara, and Tanya followed behind her.

"Mare, what's the matter?" asked Talo.

She crashed into him and sobbed into his chest. "Father's dead."

He hugged her back fiercely. "What! How?"

"He saved my life, and Toma's. They pulled him off his horse and…and…"

"It's ok. You don't have to say it." Talo paused, then blurted, "Cymm's dead too."

Toma joined them with red eyes. "No, not Cymm too."

A childish scream blared behind Talo. "No!"

He rotated his head to find Orts staggering backward and balling, then turned and fled.

With tears in her eyes, Tanya chased after him.

Joharie tried to push into the middle with a whimper.

Talo tousled his brother's hair. "I know. I already—miss him. Let's round everyone up. We have a long ride home."

111

Council of Harmony

Azreala

The following morning, The One summoned Azreala to a place she had never been before. She did not answer the call but could not resist it. She glanced around the gathered circle, and found every other deity present, including Terazhan and her brother, even the Dark Lord. Everything was—white.

"Where are we?" asked Azreala.

Sehaleah shushed her.

The Mantle of the Gods sparkled in the supernatural light as it adorned Terazhan's torso.

The air in the center of the circle shimmered slightly. *Welcome to the Plane of Light*, The One spoke telepathically. *Through Terazhan's quick actions he saved the world of Erogoth, but much needs to be done to restore the equilibrium. An Ice Age is coming.*

Harendread smiled broadly.

"What happened to Melcorac?" asked Terazhan.

He is back where he belongs, answered The One.

The outline of a body deionized in the middle of the circle, then solidified into the familiar form they had witnessed in yesterday's battle. He waved his hand across his chest from shoulder to shoulder and the Mantle of the Gods relocated to its new owner.

Azreala shot ice cold daggers with her eyes at Jakarrak, who returned the look with a shrug.

For too long, you have bickered and broken faith with each other and your own creations. I have watched all of you quarrel and sabotage each other for the past millennium. The world must heal, and we must let it. Once a moon cycle you will come to speak for all to witness. Do not squander this opportunity. The One shimmered into nothingness.

The deities began to fade.

Quickly, Azreala said, "Terazhan! I need to find Lykinnia. It is most important."

"There is a plateau in the Lower Darken Wood she favors. She said she would live there one day." Terazhan faded away.

Vallerielle hung back. "Sister, come visit me at Bard keep when you are finished. My disciplines have already found one of the power words for your sister's figurines."

"Really! Which one?" Azreala asked.

"Apparently, the most used statue was the griffin. They said they found that power word over and over again."

Azreala squealed in delight.

112

Alone

Lykinnia

Three days had passed since Cymm had died and Lykinnia had tried a new variation of her resurrection spell each morning. Cymm had told her it would not work, but she had persisted anyway.

She sat on the ground, knees up, and her head hung low between them. Tears had washed trails down her cheeks in the dirt and blood. She had no idea what the customary burial rites were for a horseman. After digging a grave, she had built a pyre but still could not bring herself to use either one.

"Maybe I should freeze him in a block of ice or turn him into a stone statue. At least I could see him every day." Lykinnia began to cry again.

Kamac paced an endless circle around her position and had worn a path already these past few days. Camak's empathy had drawn him closer, and he laid down next to her, unmoving.

The taviian warriors, led by Gillygahpadima, patrolled the forest around them since the day they arrived.

Sitting next to Cymm, she closed her eyes for a mere second, but Kamac's growl alerted her.

"Lykinnia, it's Azreala." The goddess of death walked cautiously toward her.

"No! You cannot have him." Lykinnia rose with clenched fists.

Azreala raised her hands. "I tried to find you immediately after the battle."

"Go away!"

"I harbor no interest in Cymm. I wish only to speak with you."

Lykinnia wrinkled her nose and scoffed.

Azreala cleared her throat. "It's true. My plan always revolved around you, and Cymm a mere tool to get to you."

"Do not speak of him that way!" Lykinnia waggled her finger.

"Cymm was my friend. I would never disparage him. Given your current state of grieving, I hoped you might understand my reason for planning to extort you and your father into a trade of two very valuable items. The balor, specifically Grumgresh, killed my father and sister. The only way for me to be powerful enough to get my revenge—and kill the murderous worm—involved me acquiring the Mantle of the Gods," Azreala continued.

"Pfft. Good luck. My father will never give it up, no matter what you offer." Lykinnia's face quirked. "What do you have to trade?"

Azreala rolled her eyes. "It doesn't really matter anymore. The One took the mantle from your father, but I planned to trade you."

"Me? What are you talking about?" Lykinnia asked.

"I would have forced you into an indentureship—to worship me and serve me as my solar—with a deal you couldn't refuse. Then—"

Lykinnia broke into hysterical laughter.

Azreala's eyes flared a brilliant red. "Then, I would have traded your contract, your promise to me, to your father for the mantle. It would have worked!"

"No, it would not have. There is nothing you could do to force me into such an agreement to leave my father's faith," Lykinnia chuckled. "You are an—"

"I have Cymm's soul." Azreala locked eyes in a battle of wills.

What? Lykinnia's eyes shifted side to side, and she came across Cymm's ruined body. *How could she have his soul?* Her mind caught fire, a wild, raging fire beyond control. The goddess of death's words cut like knives. *I could bring Cymm back. We could be together. The war is over, my confinement to the Peak of Power has ended. We could be together like we always wanted.*

Lykinnia approached Cymm's corpse and stared down at him. His skin had taken on a green hue since yesterday and now he started to bloat. With his face swollen, he no longer looked like her precious, sweet Cymm. *What would he do for me? What would he do for others? My father will understand. I will still visit him, and we can speak telepathically.*

Azreala had taken a seat, watching her intently.

"For how long?" Lykinnia asked.

"One thousand years."

Lykinnia clasped her hands and placed them on top of her head. "On my next millennial lifeday, my servitude will be complete."

"Close enough. Do we have a deal?" Azreala rose with a smile.

Tears streaked down Lykinnia's face, and she nodded once. "Yes."

Azreala walked over to Cymm's body and removed the necklace he wore. It was his sister's and contained a message from Bria after she had died. Cymm considered it a priceless treasure. "Are you ready?"

"Now? I—ah—right now?" Lykinnia stammered.

Azreala spun the ring around the leather thong, slowly at first, then with increasing speed until a turquoise image materialized. Cymm. "Quickly, cast your spell."

Lykinnia lurched to comply, removing an effigy from her pocket made from braided unicorn hair. "Dominimus arathi basin restarni lockwar ebo zegvara!" She traced the outline of his frame with the doll, then lay it on his forehead.

Instantly, the turquoise apparition rushed forward and slammed into Cymm's chest. Frost crawled across the earth and up the stone block on which he lay. Convulsive spasms rocked his body, and the air filled with the scent of burnt sage and grave rot.

Lykinnia's heart pounded as if she were the recipient of the spell.

Cymm's back arched, a silent scream escaping his lips. Color slowly returned to his skin. The spasms finally subsided into small twitches and eventually a chest heaving breath. His eyes popped open and rolled around in circles for several seconds before he finally sat up.

"Where am I?" Cymm's voice sounded dry and husky.

Lykinnia rushed into his arms. "Our new home."

ꝏꝏꝏ

Two months had passed since Cymm's resurrection. He and Lykinnia were sitting together staring into a scrying window.

"Why don't you search for your sister?" asked Cymm.

Lykinnia removed his arm from around her shoulders. "Please, I cannot have this conversation again. How about you tell your family you are still alive?"

Jalko the dire wolf, pushed between them, his head panning back and forth as each one spoke.

"It's better this way. Now I don't have to explain why I am not growing old, and everyone dies but me," replied Cymm.

"That is a lame excuse. You are missing your cousin's wedding." Lykinnia pointed toward the scrying window. "Look how happy she is."

Cymm did stare for a long moment. A smile blossomed on his own face. "I love you, Lykinnia. I want to make each other a promise. No more lies, no more half-truths, and we answer each other's questions."

Lykinnia sighed extravagantly. "What? What do you want to know?"

"Do we have a deal?"

"I asked my father last week why he was not upset with Sendaria or Jakarrak, and you know what he told me? You have to love a person for who they are, not for who you want them to be, and you will never be disappointed. How about we just love each other unconditionally?"

"I agree. Do you agree with my proposal?"

"Yes, Cymm. Now ask your question."

He smiled and caressed her hand. "Why has your aura changed from gold to red?"

Lykinnia's face blanched. "Sometimes you have to make sacrifices to get what you want."

"That is a half-truth, Lykinnia!"

She growled. "Remember when you told me you could never love a Red Priestess of the Phoenix? Surprise! Now, you do."

Cymm lower jaw dropped. "That is not possible. How?"

"I made a deal with Azreala to get you back, and you will abide by my wishes and not speak with her about this. I mean it, Cymm."

He put his hands up in submission. "Ok, ok."

"What are you smiling about?" Lykinnia asked.

"It is nice to know how much you love me. I will never be able to repay you this debt." Cymm gazed at the ground shaking his head.

Lykinnia smiled deviously. "Hmm. Your cousin, Talo—now Head of Household—used your money to castle and keep Mare on the farm, and her wedding is taking place as we speak."

"So?"

"So, I feel like dancing." Lykinnia waved her arm, and a portal appeared. Her hips were already swaying and her arms swinging.

Cymm groaned. "I don't have anything to wear, and I'm dirty."

With another wave of her hand, she cast a polymorph spell and a princely Cymm appeared.

"Maybe a little less noble. See how the men are dressed," Cymm said exasperated.

Lykinnia made another attempt. "Yes, or no?"

"Let's go!" Cymm grabbed her hand and spun her.

Lykinnia squealed and clapped her hands vigorously, then they walked through the portal holding hands, Jalko leading the way.

"Cymm!"

Epilogue

The citizens of Armak worked diligently to restore their city with the help of several cities. Many had died, and even more displaced from their homes. Two beggars huddled together in a vacate alley, facing each other.

"Where did you find this ring?" asked the beggar with the walking staff.

"I told you. I took it off the shriveled body of the arch demon," replied the other.

The beggar with the staff examined it closely. "Name your price. I will be taking the ring. I had Feldarius cast an important spell on this." The hand behind his back began to glow with a faint orange aura.

ooooo

A year had passed, and Fire Island drifted to its final resting spot over eighty leagues off the western coast of Eragath, forming a huge collection of water called Cataclysm Bay. The entire island had been abandoned and nothing moved but the wind. Many decaying corpses and skeletal remains blanketed the island. Only one portal remained open—the portal back to the dragon's homeland—the other two long since closed. Slow and deliberate, a head peaked out, golden and feathery. The world would forever change. A trellbac gazed from side to side and stepped through.

www.ingramcontent.com/pod-product-compliance
Lightning Source LLC
Chambersburg PA
CBHW020616310726
48979CB00008B/1510/J

9798985962284